TRIBE OF LEOPARDS
Legends of the Shifters

by

Jason McCammon

2.0

Written and created by
Jason McCammon

Brown-Eyed Dreams LLC.

Published by Brown-Eyed Dreams LLC.
Oak Park IL 60302

Copyright © 2015 Jason McCammon
Version 2.0
Inside artwork by Shawn Alleyene
Ancient Lands logo by Splash @ Shrapnel Studios
Logo copyright © 2009
Other cover art by Jason McCammon
Front cover copyright © 2013
Back cover copyright © 2013
Back cover design by Jason McCammon
Edited by Barb Bartel
ISBN 978-0-9843120-4-7

For ordering information of current and future books please visit:
www.theancientlands.com

www.twitter.com/theancientlands

Find us on Facebook

For my Grandmothers:

-Gwendolyn McCammon-
-Vennie Madison-

You are missed.

LEOPARD

Greek
leon - lion
pardos - panther

PROLOGUE

-26 YEARS BEFORE THE BIRTH OF PRINCE BOMANI-

"You killed him!" The sound of the villagers' voices cut through every inch of Tau's body in the brief moments of his awakening. His mind rekindled the looks of disgust on their faces.

These were not just any people; they were the only people he had ever known in the small Makazi village, population 92. His friends, his teachers, the girls he was always too afraid to talk to, everyone he knew was in this village except Chad. Chad was his best friend, and Chad was the one that he had killed.

Awakening more thoroughly, he noticed that it was no longer day. The only light around him came from the flicker of amber fire. Everything else was covered by the darkness of the night. The loud, violent temperament of the crowd that he remembered was replaced with the simple sounds of nocturnal animals and insects in the distance; it was quiet.

Tau focused on the vertical slabs of wood in front of him and quickly realized that they were all around him. He sat up, or tried to, only to hit his head on something hard above him. With a look at the ceiling, he had the disturbing sensation of being trapped. They had put him in a cage. Not one for a man either, but a small cage built for the holding and transport of an animal like a boar or a goat.

Then he vaguely remembered the people throwing a net on him. He touched his head and the side of his ribs to comfort the pain of someone hitting him. That memory came back clearly. Someone had hit him and then thrown him in this cage.

Tau was sixteen, yet not nearly as big as most kids his age. He looked more like a twelve or thirteen year old. Even his small body felt cramped inside this wooden cage.

"Hey!" he shouted. "Let me out!" He grabbed the planks of

wood and shook at them as hard as he could until he felt the pain of something smack against his fingers that were on the outside of the planks.

"Break out of that cage and I will let the people kill you. I might just do it myself!" he heard a voice tell him. It was one of the guards whose job it was to protect the people of the Makazi village. So why was the man keeping him caged?

"But let me out of here!" Tau screamed.

The guard stuck a sword inside the cage until the tip of it just barely touched him. Tau jumped back and the sword followed him until it had him pinned to the other side.

"The people are sleeping, and if you know what is good for you, whatever you are, you will keep it that way."

Another guard stepped forward. "We are not here to guard you, boy. We are here to keep everyone else from killing you."

Tau quickly yielded. "How long do I have to stay in here?" he asked quietly.

"They've sent someone out to Ufalme with word of the...incident. We will know what to do with you upon their return."

Ufalme was a very large kingdom to the south of Makazi. Makazi was generally under their protection; still part of the Ufalme kingdom. Along with their own guards, Ufalme usually kept a handful of guards in the Makazi village as well. The men keeping watch over him were not from his village. They were from Ufalme.

Tau's small cage sat in the middle of the village on the *spectacle*, a large rock two and a half feet high, with a flat surface five by seven feet at the top. Items of great interest were placed there and more often, people stood on top of it to speak to crowds about anything important or interesting. The two guards stood near him, keeping the fires lit through the night, and keeping watch just inside four wooden four-foot high posts in the ground that surrounded the spectacle.

"It's too small in here," Tau told them. "Why am I in here? Why did you put me in a cage built for the animals?"

One of the guards took a torch from the post and walked closer to Tau's cage, bringing the light of the fire closer.

"Maybe you ARE an animal, maybe you are a demon. Until we find out, you're staying in that little cage."

Tau looked at the man and then looked at his own skin, more adequately lit by the fire of the torch. His skin was not brown like it should be. It was dark grey.

He looked at his hands, his arms, and bent down to look at his legs. "No! Why is it staying like this? It's never done this before." He rolled over to his knees and looked down at his hands; this specific point of view brought yet another memory to the forefront of his mind. He remembered having paws, and fur on his arms.

"Animal? Am I an animal?" he whispered to himself.

Suddenly one of the torches went out, snapping him back into the present situation. A hissing sound of fire into water resonated from the extinguished torch. The guard close to him quickly turned and raised the torch he was holding toward the diminished fire when another flame went out behind them, then another, and another, until the only light came from one torch held in the guard's hand. Everything else faded to blackness.

"Pull your sword out," said the guard to the other as he continued to wave his torch through the dark. "Someone is here. Come close to me."

"For this boy? This thing?" the second guard responded. "If someone wants him, let them…"

His voice was silenced, followed by a grunt and then the sound of his body hitting the ground. Tau fearfully looked through the bars of the cage, aware of his own heartbeat. His ears focused on every sound around him.

"What the...?" the guard murmured as his torch also went out.

"What's going on?" Tau asked, voice trembling. "Is someone coming to kill me?"

The guard shushed him. He was standing there with his sword in one hand, his other hand stretched out, searching the air as if he were a blind man trying to feel for something in front of him.

Tau's eyes began to focus in the dark. The separation between object, moving person, and nothingness slowly became more apparent.

The guard quickly turned to his right, then to his left, and then he began to walk around the spectacle. Tau could hear the sound of the guard's heavy breathing, which meant he was scared. And if the guard was scared then there had to be some real danger around.

"Right there!" Tau told him as he saw a shadow come toward the guard.

He heard another grunt, and then the guard hit the ground. Suddenly, Tau could no longer see anyone. He panicked, breathing rapidly, and fear raced through his body, making his hands tremble and sweat.

He lay on his back and began kicking at the top of the cage. He could feel the wood start to give. He began to shout, "Help! Help me!" Then he felt someone cover his mouth and grab at his body through the bars.

He shrieked and tried to yell louder, only to be muffled by the hand pressed firmly against his lips. He reached up, and tried to pry it off.

"Tau," a familiar voice said, "Tau, stop it, be quiet!"

Tau stopped moving. He mumbled something under the man's hand and then the man lifted it off.

"Uncle?" Tau asked.

"Yes, it's me," he whispered.

"Uncle! What's happening? I thought you were someone coming to kill me."

"No, I've come to get you out. Come on, quickly." He unlatched the gate, opened the cage, and then helped Tau out of it.

Tau's foot hit something. It was the guard lying on the ground.

"Was that you? Did you do that?" he asked Uncle. "What happened to me? Was I...was I an animal?"

Uncle paused for a moment. "I wish I could tell you different, but lies don't solve problems."

"Then..."

"A leopard, Tau. You changed into a leopard."

"A leopard? But..."

"Listen to me, Tau. We don't have time. You have to go, and you have to go now."

"Go where? What happened to me? This is crazy!"

"Away from here. Don't come back."

"Don't come back? You mean ever?"

"At least not until this is all sorted."

"But I..."

"They are looking for you. They are almost here."

"Who?"

"The Brood."

"The Brood Army? But why?"

"I've brought you your weapons, some food and some water. You remember where the Whispering Pond is?"

"I don't think so. It's been a long time."

"You must. That's where you need to go. Take this vial. Fill it with water from the Whispering Pond. If you hear the voices again, take one drop and one drop only."

"The voices that I hear, what do they mean?"

"Listen. You must not drink too much or you will go crazy. Take one drop and one drop only. Do you understand?"

"Yes, but this is..."

"I know, boy. But out there somewhere, somewhere in the

world, somewhere in Madunia, are the answers that you seek. I don't have all of them, but I have been preparing for this."

"What do I do after the pond?"

"Expect a friend of mine named Hagga. She will meet you there."

"And this Hagga…"

"We can't talk any more. You have to go. The Brood Army is almost here. I fear for what they will do to you if they catch you."

"Now?"

"Now."

"Right now?"

"Tau."

Uncle grabbed him and held him for a moment. "I love you, son. Remember everything I've taught you. Now go."

Tau started to walk away from him, and then he turned back.

"Uncle, I didn't do what they think I did. I mean, about Chad."

"I know."

That was the only comforting sensation that Tau felt in all of this mess. Everything else about the world felt empty; as if his life was a big hole filled with unanswered questions. The only thing that he knew was that he trusted Uncle, and if Uncle said that he must leave his village and go to the Whispering Pond, then that's what he had to do. He had the terrible feeling that something big was happening to him.

I THE MESSENGER

Three days of walking. Staggering, his feet caught the weight of his body with painful steps as if, at any moment, he would collapse to the ground. But he kept moving. He had to get to the pond.

Suddenly a terrible pain from inside his head screeched into his ears with the most awful high-pitched noise. It was so loud that his whole body froze and he lost control of himself, collapsing to the ground as his body jerked and rolled in the dirt.

He began to hear whispering voices that spoke to him. A thousand whispers came to him, loud and jumbled so that he could not distinguish the words. He shut his eyes, but inside his head he could see vague images of whiteness, like a landscape through blinding snow.

"What is it?" he yelled. "What do you want from me? I can't hear you!"

He could not tell how long this episode lasted. The pain made it seem like forever, but after a while, the voices stopped and the vision disappeared. He did not move. Tau was already exhausted, and this episode felt physically demanding and draining.

He found himself laying on his back, looking at the blue sky above him. The sky reminded him of water. For a while, he envisioned himself swimming in the lake near his village, something he could do for hours, swimming for miles, sometimes diving underneath for several minutes at a time. Finally, he imagined himself simply floating on top of the water. He could feel the motion of the waves; there was nothing as soothing. When Tau was in water, he was usually at peace.

Tau considered himself to be a master of water. There was only one person in the village that even came close to being as good a swimmer as he was, only one person that could and would compete, and that was his best friend, Chad.

"I'm so sorry, Chad. I'm sorry that I couldn't save you."

After he rested for a while, dreaming of the pleasantness of water, he realized that he did not have any left. He had not had anything to drink all day. The very real sensation of thirst swept over him. He realized that he could not stay there; he had to move.

He rolled over to his stomach, using as little strength as possible, dragging his face into the dirt. He lifted his head up, barely noticing dirt on his lips or the small grains in one of his eyes, forcing him to keep it shut. The one open eye focused on a cloud of dust straight ahead of him. He kept looking at it, noticing that it was quickly coming closer to him. The only thing that could move that fast was a messenger.

Finally the messenger reached Tau, kicking up even more dust as he plunged his bare feet into the ground to slow himself. He was breathing heavily. "Tau, you look terrible."

"Dwanh?"

"Forgive me. I just meant..." Dwanh stood still for a while, as if he was not sure what to do.

"How is the village?" Tau asked, moving to a sitting position and wiping the dirt from his eye.

"Here, I have water for you. Thirsty?"

"More than anything!" Tau grabbed the water and began drinking.

"I left the village two days ago looking for you."

"Two days? To get here? But you're a messenger. Why did it take you so long to find me?"

"Young man, you are far off track. I've already been to the Whispering Pond yesterday morning."

"Off track? I'm lost, aren't I?"

"Very much so."

Tau put his hand up to his head in disgust. "I thought you

were coming to tell me to come home."

"Sorry," Dwanh said as he looked at Tau's skin. "So, you're skin, is it staying like that now? Is it going to stay grey? Or are you still sick?"

Tau suddenly became embarrassed. "No, not sick. Hungry, thirsty, tired, hurt, but not sick. I wonder if it is going to stay this way too. I don't know."

Dwanh paused for a moment. "I've got food for you too, here." Dwanh pulled some meat, smashed beans, and flat bread he had wrapped inside a cloth out of his sack.

From the way Dwanh handed it to him, Tau got the feeling that he was afraid to touch him. "Thank you," he said, with his head toward the ground.

"Yesterday I found two of the Brood guards in pretty bad condition. Like an animal had gotten to them." He looked confused for a second. "Was that you?"

Tau stopped chewing for moment. He was afraid to speak; embarrassed. "Yes. It happened again. Are they dead?"

"No. But they probably wish they were. I did what I could for them, and continued to look for you. It felt strange, helping them, Brood Soldiers, but I had to do something."

"I'm so sorry! They caught up with me. I tried to fight them off, but I couldn't. I ran as fast as I could to get away, I just wanted to get away, and then…"

"Tau, I have known you your whole life, but this *thing* that is happening with you has us all confused. I don't think it would be safe for you to come back until you figure out what's happening. I think that if you look hard enough you will find what you are looking for. Out there in the world, there are stories about you."

"About me? What stories?"

"I can't be sure. But as messenger, I go many places. I know that I have heard something about people like you. People that change into leopards. I've never much paid attention. Sorry I can't be more helpful."

"I bet everyone back home hates me."

"They don't hate you. They're just afraid. Why didn't you take the water from the guards back there? The ones you..."

"I don't know; I just ran. Didn't even know what was happening." Tau paused for a second. "Are you afraid of me?"

"I'm concerned. And I must tell your uncle about those Brood guards; what you did to them. But I will tell no one else."

"Thank you," said Tau.

"Where will you go? I mean after you find the pond?"

"Uncle said a friend would meet me there. A shaman, named Hagga."

"And this Hagga will know what to do?"

"I hope she will. I had another one of those episodes. I heard voices, but I couldn't understand them. It hurt so bad, I couldn't move. The same thing happened when Chad died. You have to believe me Dwanh! You have to tell the others! I didn't do it on purpose. It was an accident! And now, I can't believe he's gone."

Dwanh stood there, shaking his head slowly, appearing to be in deep thought.

"Can you come with me to the Pond?" Tau asked.

"I cannot. I must return to Makazi. I must at least go back to tell your uncle that you are okay. A bit lost, but okay. He will be worrying."

"Just like I worry about him, and everyone else. Are they okay?"

"Some of the soldiers left, some of them stayed, but they are still trying to find you; the, 'grey-skinned' one. Maybe, by now, they are gone."

"Then they are still after me."

"I did take the liberty of covering your tracks, so they won't find you easily."

Tau nodded and continued eating. It was quiet for a short while. Tau looked out across the savanna and the hills in the distance, just where they met up with the sky.

Dwanh pointed. "That's the way you ought to be headed. Just to the right of those hills. You'll see the green. There are many more green plants near there." Dwanh began drawing star points in the sand and connecting them. "At night, follow this line of stars. You should be there by early tomorrow."

"Thank you. Uncle didn't have much time to explain to me how to get there. He just expected that I would remember. It is good that you came."

"That's why he was wise enough to send me after you. Am I going to have to come out tomorrow again to make sure you didn't lose your way?"

"Would it be so bad if you did?"

"I'll see what I can do. I can't make any promises though. It all depends on what is happening back at the village." Dwanh stood up. "I should be heading back now. I've been gone for quite some time."

Tau stood up as well. He threw himself at Dwanh and hugged him tightly. "Thank you. I might have died if you hadn't found me."

Dwanh paused for a moment.

Tau felt his hesitance, like he wanted to pull away.

Finally Dwanh wrapped his arms around the Tau. "No problem, kid."

They broke from each other, and Dwanh turned away.

"When I saw you approaching me, I couldn't help but to wonder."

"Wonder what, Tau?"

"How fast can you run?"

"Not even a cheetah could catch me."

"What is it like to be able to run so fast?"

Dwanh grinned, "Like flying!" Then, he winked and took off running. A trail of dust kicked up behind him.

Tau stood there watching until Dwanh had run far into the horizon, which only took seconds.

"Here's a thought, Tau. Have the super-fast guy go to the Whispering Pond for you."

Tau shrugged at the image of Chad, his best friend, standing beside him. "You might have said something BEFORE he left."

"I couldn't. I just thought of it now," said Chad.

"Well, there is no way to catch up with a guy like that," Tau said, disappointed. "I'm sick of walking."

"Standing here isn't going to get you there any quicker. Get moving," said Chad.

Tau shrugged. "I'm going. Don't be so pushy. And why am I talking to you anyway?"

"Hey, I'm just trying to give you some motivation. You don't have to get mad. If anyone should be mad, it should be me. You killed me, remember?"

"Honestly Chad, I don't think I will ever forget it."

II ALONG CAME A SPIDER

Tau approached the Whispering Pond with apprehension. A towering wall of dark grey rock met the far end of the water. He looked at his own skin, noticing that the color of the rock was not too much darker than he was. Just before the wall met the water, the rock began to recede as if there was an underwater opening behind it. Perhaps this pond led to a cave of some sort.

He walked closer and noticed some markings partially covered up by the moss on a large rock sitting in front of the pond. Trembling as if the words were going to jump out and bite him, Tau carefully removed the moss. Any doubt he had about this place was resolved by what was etched into the stone. It read, "Beware! The Whispering Pond. Do not drink!"

"I guess I'm in the right place," he said to himself, loud enough for the stranger behind him to hear.

"That depends on what place you are looking for," the stranger said. This old man was simply dressed with one brown sheet draped over his shoulder and wrapped around his thin, frail, brown body. He did not have shoes. His ugly feet, covered in dust, looked rough and battered. His face was scruffy with patches of an unmanaged short, black and grey, curly beard. The man looked so thin and scrawny that it seemed as if the smallest wind could knock him over. He carried nothing but a branch that he used to lean on. Tau started to reach for his blades, but it was obvious that this man was harmless.

"It isn't many that come here that know why they have come," the old man said. "Even less, are those that come who should be here at all."

"You sound like my uncle."

"How is that, friend?"

"I don't know who you are, and you're already trying to teach me something."

"Life is a lesson, boy; every day, every second. I wonder what lesson you'll learn today, my friend." The peculiar man smiled at him, showing that he had many missing teeth.

"The Whispering Pond; is this it?"

"Hmm, you not satisfied with the writing, friend?"

"I want to be sure, that's all. I have come a long way."

The man sat down on a rock and pointed his walking stick toward the pond. "My boy, if you are looking for the Whispering Pond, you have found it." He smiled as if he owned the place.

"I'm supposed to drink from it."

"Oh my, that could be quite dangerous. It says right here," the man said while pointing his stick to the writing. "'Do not drink!' This pond is a lot more dangerous than it looks." He walked over to the pond and knelt beside it, looking at his reflection. "Come, look at it," he said, gesturing with his hand, displaying a happy grin.

Tau followed and knelt beside him by the edge of the pond.

"Look at the water," said the man. "Looks calm, harmless, doesn't it?"

"It looks like a pond," Tau agreed.

"Ah, but an undertow is there. Not normal for a pond. Anyone who decides to take a pleasant swim is at the pond's mercy. They will be swept into the underground cave at the other end. Drowned."

"Uncle didn't have time to tell me all of that. But I wasn't planning on swimming in it anyway."

"Your uncle, the wise one, eh? He sent you here?"

"I trust in him, if that is what you mean."

"Must have sent you here for answers. Answers about that grey skin of yours. Not too many people have grey skin."

Tau suddenly felt a wave of embarrassment because of his skin color. "Um... yes. How did you know?"

"I've been around a long time, my friend, longer than you can imagine. I know many things. I can tell when someone is lost and I don't mean lost as in where you are; more so, who you are. Why else would you come to the pond?"

"What do you mean? Do you know who I am?"

"Your skin tells me who you are. Easy for someone who knows, but confusing for those who don't. Would you like to know who you are boy? Would you like to know why you have that grey skin?"

"Yes! Yes, I would."

"Then in the pond you go!"

Before Tau could react, the man took his walking stick and thrust it against the back of his neck, tossing him into the pond. He hit the water, and submerged at least five or six feet. A terrible fear shot through his entire body. He thrashed around. All he saw were bubbles and streams of sunlight that penetrated the surface into the dark water. Tau made his way to the top and took a deep breath. He was a least 10 feet from the land. The man was still kneeling close to the edge, still smiling.

"Why?" Tau shouted. "Why did you do that?" He started swimming back, intending to rough up the stranger as soon as he could get his hands on him.

The man shrugged. "Seemed like a fun thing to do at the time. And it was! Hehe. But now is not the time to be asking questions. Now is the time to swim!"

As Tau swam toward the edge of the water, a current began to drag him back. He swam faster, but the current became stronger; soon Tau was swimming as fast and as hard as he could. The water pulled him back even harder until he was going nowhere, swimming in place. "What's going on?" Tau shouted in between desperate gasps for air.

"I told you," said the man. "This pond is dangerous! But you wouldn't listen!"

"But you pushed me in!"

"Oh, if the pond could talk, it would tell you that I'm dangerous too! You can't go blaming your problems on other people, boy. Now swim! Swim like your life depended on it!"

The current became stronger until Tau was moving backwards. Then he felt the undertow pulling at him from underneath, not only dragging him backwards toward the underwater cave, but down as well. He sank below the surface again as the pond pulled him down. Behind him, he could see the black void of the cave. He struggled harder under the water until he managed to surface again.

"My, you are a strong swimmer," said the man, sounding surprised. "But still, the pond won't give up, and even a nice, young, strong, boy like you has his limits."

"Help!" Tau shouted. "Help me, the water is too strong. I can't get out!"

"I could help you out, but you put on a good show. I'd like to see how much stamina you have."

The man watched for a couple more minutes as Tau struggled in the water, screaming and shouting for his help. "All right, all right!" he finally said. "Here, take this rope." Seemingly out of nowhere the man pulled a long silky rope from under his cloth. He kept pulling as more of it came out. "Here boy!" he shouted. "Take this!" He threw it out into the water.

Tau fumbled around until finally he had a good hold. This rope was strange, thick, soft, and sticky. "Wrap it around your hands and wrists and I'll pull you out."

Tau was still fighting the current, bobbing up and down, dipping beneath the surface and then up again. In the midst of all the chaos, he noticed the man had changed. Tau thought that he was going crazy. The pond must have been messing with his mind. There must have been some sort of drug or magic spell making him see things. The man was not a man at all, but a huge spider with a leg span of at least six feet! It was the ugliest, most terrible thing Tau had ever seen, especially with all those thick hairs that covered it.

The rope must have been its web! Tau tried to pull it from

around his hands, but it was too sticky, and he could not pull it off. Who was this man/spider? Was he helping him? Why had he pushed him in the first place?

The spider reeled in its web and Tau along with it. Four of its legs stayed put on the ground, while the front four, one by one, pulled at the web, until Tau was pulled entirely out of the water, too tired to move. He was well beyond exhausted, in no condition to go to battle with a giant spider. Tau was not too fond of little spiders, not to mention a giant man sized one!

He coughed water out of his tired lungs, holding his stomach with each painful clenching of his muscles. All he could do was focus on breathing. The giant spider dragged him to a tree and moved quickly to tie him up against it. Before Tau knew it, he was totally bound to the trunk.

"What are you doing? Don't hurt me! Don't eat me!"

"I'm not going to eat you, Amotekun. You'll be a nice prize for the Brood. There is a bounty on your head. Then again, I don't care much for riches."

As the spider spoke to him, Tau saw the oddest flash of purple light coming from behind it. About 6 feet off of the ground a thin watery purple substance appeared. It was flat, shimmering in the light, and rippled like water as it hung in the air.

"Why? Why do they want me?" he asked.

"Oh, that's their business, I'm afraid," said the spider, with the same voice it had when it was a man.

A short old woman came falling out of the purple, watery light. She hit the ground with a thud, accompanied by the sound anyone would make when suddenly being whacked in the chest. She wasted no time. Without even getting up, she raised a crude wooden staff with small bits of bone and bead on it. "Be gone Anansi, before you have me to deal with!"

"Hagga!" the spider turned and shouted. Then he hissed. "Spying all the time, are you? Is this boy one of your pets?"

"I said be gone! Or do you want to find out what new tricks

of the Shaman trade I have been studying?" She glared at him with one eye. The other one she seemed to keep closed the entire time. Then she shook her staff at him again as she made her way to her feet.

"Eh, perhaps another time boy," the spider said. Then he cut himself loose from his web and ran off.

Tau was glad to see this woman. He sat there bound to the tree, still breathing heavily. His fear slowly gave way to relief. "Thank you, thank you! I thought that ugly thing was going to eat me. I don't think I will ever sleep again! I've never seen anything like that."

"Anansi is not the type to eat a human. But you can bet, whatever he wanted, it wouldn't be good for you."

"What was that thing?"

The old lady then began searching up into the air for something; still only having one eye open and the other squinted shut. "My name is Hagga. I am a Shaman. I'm the one who told your uncle about this place, and for you to come here. We have been talking about you for some time now."

"Ah, you're the friend that he spoke of."

She still looked up in the air for something. It seemed odd; she looked to the air, with her arm stretched upward, twisting her hand around and around. "Yes indeed, that would be me. Ah, I think it's over here somewhere."

"What's over there? What are you looking for?"

Then she stood on her toes and reached her hand higher into the air above her. Her hand disappeared as if she had slipped it into some invisible pocket in midair. She grunted a bit, making a face as she felt around for something.

"What are you doing?"

"Left something. It's here somewhere, no doubt. Just have to…ah here it is." She pulled her hand out of that invisible pocket and showed him an eyeball. "Been keeping an eye on things here for a while. I had to know when you arrived." Then she shoved the eye into her eye socket and blinked several times, apparently trying to get the focus back. "Much better. I've been walking around for a week without my eye."

"You're a strange woman."

"Humph, that's your perspective. To me, I'm perfectly normal. You're the strange one, tied to a tree in the web of a giant spider. I can't say that happens too often."

"Yeah, can you get me out of here, please?"

"Oh no, I can't do that. At least not yet."

"Why not? I thought you came here to help me."

"Oh, I did. No doubt about that."

Tau struggled against the web. He was not strong enough to move. "Then help me out of here."

"I will, deary, when it is time."

"What's wrong with now? Look, put my blade in my hand. I'll do the rest."

"Look boy, I know what I'm doing. I am here to help you." She looked at the sun. "It's almost sundown. You don't know it yet, but you're in for a terrible night. You'll thank me in the morning, trust me."

"Thank you for what? Leaving me tied up against a tree in a spider web all night?"

"My eye was watching. I saw Anansi haul you out of that pond. No doubt you swallowed lots and lots of that water. You can't drink that much of the Whispering Pond; it will drive you mad. My guess is, in a minute or so, you'll start hearing the voices. Ten minutes after that starts, you'll be screaming. And another ten after that, you'll be ready to tear your ears right out of your head! No, for your own good, I'm going to leave you tied up the way you are!"

Tau had no idea what she was talking about, but she was right. It was not long before the whole thing started. At first it was a faint whisper. He heard it coming from inside his head. He could not make out what it said or if it was man or woman, or if he was sure he had heard it at all. Then it got louder. He winced a bit, trying to decipher the words.

Hagga said, "Oh boy, here we go. Did you hear something?"

"Yes," he said. "I'm not sure what, though."

The whispers became louder and louder. Soon there were many of them, but not soft delicate whispers. It was as if people were right inside his head whispering as loud as they could with strong, sharp emphases on the s's p's and k's. He still had no idea what they were saying but it was annoying and getting downright painful.

Hagga watched him closely.

"This is the part that I really hate," she said to him. "But I'm afraid you're going to hate it even more! Don't mind me; I'm going to leave you here for a while. I won't go far, but I would rather not sit here and watch.

"Where are you going? Make it stop! All these voices in my head! I can't understand what they are saying!"

"You drank too much of the water boy. There is nothing I can do but wait and keep you from trying to kill yourself."

"Wait!" Tau cried out. "Don't go, don't leave me here!"

But Hagga walked out of sight.

As the night came and lingered hour after hour, Tau spent the entire time yelling and screaming. "What are you saying? I can't hear you! Hagga come back. Come back and help me please, Hagga!" He wanted the voices to stop. He needed them to stop! He would have done anything to get them to stop!

It was not until after midnight that Hagga came around to check on him. He was sweating and crying. His whole body was shaking. He pleaded with her to find some way to make the voices stop. He begged her to cut him loose from the tree.

"I can only think of one way to make it stop, boy."

"Whatever it is, I don't care. Make it stop and cut me loose!"

"I've got this stick here. I can shove it in one of your ears, through your head, and out the other side. That ought to make it stop."

"Do it! Go ahead, I don't care!"

"Right, and kill you right along with it! No, surely you're not thinking straight. You're in no condition to be cut loose!"

Again, Hagga left him there, and he spent another hour yelling and screaming before he passed out altogether.

III TWELVE YEARS OLD

"I don't want to practice anymore!" Tau exclaimed to Uncle, while standing blindfolded, holding a wooden stick in his hand. He stood in the middle of six wooden pillars that were six inches thick and six feet tall. From the center, where he stood, they were each about six feet from his position.

The idea was for Uncle to call out a color, and for Tau to immediately know where that pillar was, and then strike it with form, skill, and without hesitation. Tau was failing.

"Red," said Uncle.

Tau paused for a moment, trying to remember where the red pillar was, and then reached his stick out to the left, barely touching it.

"Tau, you wouldn't hurt a chicken striking your weapon like that, let alone a man. Black!"

Tau did not hesitate this time. He quickly spun 180 degrees to the right and swung his stick as hard as he could; hearing the swooshing sound the stick made through the air as it completely missed everything. Tau shrugged.

"I wasn't any good at doing this with the blindfold off. Now that I have it on, there is no way I can."

"You must, Tau, I have told you this time and time again."

"I've been learning to fight for a year now. How much more do I need to know?"

"And for a year you have resisted? Apparently, the first thing you need to learn is acceptance."

"But Uncle, we have guards here. We even have guards from the Kingdom of Ufalme. We are under their protection. Why should I learn to fight if they are here to guard us?"

"Because the dangers of life do not present themselves at your convenience, Tau. You must always be prepared for what may come. You never know where your destiny will take you. It could be far away from here."

"My destiny is here in the village with you. I don't want to fight; I'm no good at it. I like the sea, the water. I'm the best swimmer here and I can hold my breath longer than anyone in the village. I want to be a fisherman, not a warrior."

"If you recall, young Tau, you didn't used to like the water either. You were afraid of it. You hated to swim."

"That was different. That was back then. I swim great now."

"And back then, who was it that told you that you would appreciate the water in time, that it would be useful to you?" Uncle asked in a condescending voice.

Tau put his head down. "You did, Uncle."

"And when you were no good at climbing trees, who told you that you would develop a natural ability for it?"

"You did, Uncle."

"And when you had so much trouble starting a fire, who told you that it would get easier the more you do it?"

"You did, Uncle."

"And when you..."

"All right, all right! I get it!"

"Sooooooo..."

"So you're probably right about this too."

"Remember, son, your elders aren't here simply to make your life harder."

"Sure seems that way sometimes," Tau muttered under his breath.

"We make you do and learn all these skills because we know that someday you will need them. We have what you call, 'life experience.' And when you grow older, as I did, you will come to understand that this is true. Until then, know we are doing what is best for you. We are preparing you for your future. It doesn't matter if you want to do it or not, I'm your Uncle, I said do it, so DO IT!"

"I can't know where the pillars are AND hit them AND hit them the way you want me to with a blindfold on," Tau said.

Uncle came up behind him, and grabbed him by the shoulders. "That is because you assume that you are doing this alone."

"No, I know you are trying to help me."

"That is not what I mean. It is not me that is trying to help you, it is the universe."

"Oh yeah, Uncle, tell me again how the universe is helping me," he said with as much sarcasm as he could muster.

"Tau, everything in the universe has a conscious energy, or Orisha. You, and everyone else, are connected to it. Feel the wind blowing against your skin? We call that Oya. Feel the ground beneath your feet, and the sounds and presence of the forest nearby. We call that Osain. You are already a great swimmer. That is because you have accepted the Orisha of the ocean, Yemoja. When you swim, you are one with the water, you are aware of all of it and that awareness empowers you. Even from here, can't you smell the lake?"

"Yes."

"Can you see it in your head, hear its waters?"

"Yes, I can see it."

"Don't stop there. Picture the sky and the sun above it; feel its rays upon your skin." Uncle began to move back from inside the pillars. "See our village, and our people; now see us. See me standing by you. See yourself, holding the stick. Feel your inner peace. That is Obatala. It will keep you calm and clear. Now feel the war inside you, the Orisha of Sango; it will give you strength. It will let you see your enemies and strike them with thunder. The Pillars, they are the enemy. You know where they are. Now don't hesitate; strike them, because they are the enemy. Green!"

Without hesitating, Tau lunged to his front left toward the green pillar. He swung his stick horizontally, as if to hit a man in the mid-section, connecting with strength and accuracy, and then stepped back to his original position.

"Yellow!"

Tau turned, took one step and chopped downward with the stick, once again connecting with his opponent.

"Black! Red! Green! Blue! Black! White! Yellow!"

Each one was called out, and each time, Tau swung his stick and hit the pillar. When it was over, he was surprised at himself. He looked at the pillars and the nicks made from his weapon landing against them. He looked over at his uncle standing there with a smirk upon his face.

"Now it's time for a real weapon," Uncle said with pride.

Together, they made the short walk to the metal smith's workshop. They walked on the ground of the floorless shack. It was only about twenty feet wide, with a low ceiling. The walls were made of several thin branches neatly placed right up against each other and driven a foot into the ground.

Zuberi, the smith, was at work when they arrived, shaping and twisting a metal clasp. His apprentice was arranging different weapons in the corner by the entrance as they stepped inside. It was dark, other than the small fire burning in the corner of the room where the walls were coated with hardened clay. Zuberi sang as he worked.

"'…And even for a man that likes to dance, there's nothing stronger than his hands, and a blade for weapon by his siiiiiiiiide.' Oh hello friends. I bet that you've come for that sword."

"Yes brother Zuberi, we have, and how are you?" asked Uncle.

"Boy, grab the sword that I made young Tau, will you?" Zuberi yelled to his apprentice, and then turned back to his customers. "As long as Shango continues to bless me with the gift of making weapons, you will see a smile on my face."

The apprentice found the sword and began to hand it to Uncle.

"No, no," said the metal smith. "Give it to me, and I'll give it to them; that's the way it should go. Next you'll be taking credit for making the thing, won't you?"

The apprentice stopped in his tracks and turned to Zuberi to hand him the sword. Zuberi held it horizontally and presented it with pride to Tau. "Here you go! Great sword for a beginner. I bet in no time you'll be slaying wolves, hyenas, and hippo-whales; or even protecting the village from the terrible Brood. I hear they are growing in territory these days. I fear one day they will come here. From that point, our lives will be a lot different if we don't find a way to fight back. We will probably need young, strong men like you."

The idea of fighting soldiers did not appeal to Tau. He grabbed the sword from him and studied it for a moment, frowning.

"Aren't you going to thank the man for the sword, Tau?" Uncle asked.

"Oh yes, um, thank you. Thank you very much."

"Excuse me for saying so," said Zuberi, "but you don't sound very convincing. I put good work into that sword."

"Oh, it's a wonderful sword sir, it's.... well...."

"Well, what?" asked Uncle.

"Well, it's kind of long and it's really straight."

"You barely know how to swing a stick. And now you are already dictating the shape of your sword?"

"I had something different in mind."

"Different, like what?" Uncle asked.

"One of the warriors was telling a story, a story about a

lion." Tau became excited. He raised his arms up, mimicking a lion attacking with an angry face. "He was saying how the lion attacked with its paws pointing out to slice its victims. I want something like that." He dropped to the ground and began drawing the shape of a lion's claw with his finger in the dirt. "I want some like this!"

"Hmm," said Zuberi, stroking his chin. "I have seen something like that before in one of the kingdoms to the North. I've never made one like that myself. But I suppose that it would be a task worth trying."

"You could make one?" Tau asked, excited.

"Hold on there, Tau," said Uncle. "I've already paid for that sword. You don't even want to be a warrior; what difference is it to you what sword you have?"

"I don't know. It's the one I have in my head. If I had something like that, I promise to practice extra hard on my fighting. The way you like."

"I don't know, Tau. With a weapon like that, you would have to change your entire way of fighting."

"I'll tell you what," said Zuberi. "Since the boy wants it so bad, I'll do it for half price."

"Uncle, can it be two of them!" Tau asked.

"Let's see how you do with the one, for now."

IV THE HOP

Tau awoke in the early morning with the glare of the sun coming up over the horizon in his eyes and the cool briskness of the morning air upon his skin. Hagga sat on a rock not far from him, softly humming a happy tune while knitting. When he stretched his arms to push the tiredness from his body and wipe the cold from his eyes, he realized that he was no longer tied to the tree. He suddenly felt aches and pains all over from struggling against the web through the course of the night.

"How did you sleep?" Hagga asked without even looking his way.

Tau winced at every movement of his joints. "Okay, I guess."

"Okay? Surely a lie. More like the deepened sleep of my drunken Uncle, I'd say. How's your head? Still ringing?"

Tau paid attention to his head, the only part of him that did not hurt. "No, but I remember the pain. You wouldn't believe how much it hurt."

"Oh, I believe it. That's why I kept you tied up; to keep you from stabbing yourself in the head. You'll be okay now, as long as you keep a vial of that water with you. I took the privilege of filling it. Next time you hear those noises again, take a couple of drops. But don't take too much; a drop or two will do fine. Or do I need to remind you of what effect an overdose of the Whispering Pond will cause?"

Tau looked around for a moment, keeping his eyes sharp for anything that may lie hidden in the tall golden grass. He stood up, searching even more.

"He won't be coming back," Hagga assured him, still knitting.

"Who?"

"Who are you looking for?"

"The spider."

"Like I said, he won't be coming back. I don't see him in your future any time soon."

"You can tell the future?"

"Maybe. Or maybe that is the sort of thing you tell someone to calm their nerves."

"I am calm."

"Young boy, you got attacked by a giant spider and then spent the night screaming, yelling, and hallucinating. Don't bother telling me that you are calm." She finally put down her knitting tools. "A nice walk will do you good. Are you ready to go?"

"Where are we going?"

"You, my friend, need a ride to the Red Barrier City. Come, help an old lady up."

"You're not so old," he said.

"Perhaps not in this time, but in others, I am very, very old. Do be polite."

He helped her up.

"Here, eat this," she said.

She handed him a thick bar that looked like a bunch of beans mashed together. It looked awful, but when he bit into it, it was quite good. Then she handed him a jar of melon juice.

As they started walking, Hagga began knitting again. She kept a shaggy cloak over her head, which hid most of her face. The rest of it dragged down over the ground, picking up plenty of dirt around the bottom edges. Her other coverings, or decorations, were the worst collection of beads and bone that Tau had ever seen. Bones from what, he did not know, but nothing about this woman seemed fashionable.

She was a little more than 4 feet in height. Tau kept peering down at her every minute or so as they walked. She only looked about forty in age and yet her voice sounded as if she was at least eighty. Perhaps she was much older than he thought. The way she wobbled from side to side when she walked was even more reason for Tau's eyes to continue to drift down to her. She was odd.

"So what did you see?" asked Hagga.

"When?"

"During your little screaming episode. Don't tell me you went through all of that and you don't even remember what you saw."

"Oh," he thought for a moment. "I saw mountains; mountains with snow on them. They were far in the distance, across some sort of leafy green marsh."

"And what did you hear?"

"A voice. Actually, it was a bunch of voices at once. 'Find the White Forest,' they said."

"Yes, you were screaming that through the night. That make any sense to you?"

"No. You?"

"Eh."

"What does that mean? Eh."

"It means that if I had something to tell you, I would."

"Can you tell me why I must go to the Red Barrier City?"

"Have you heard of it?"

"Of course. A city built around a big red dome. Though, I'm not quite sure what the dome is."

"No one knows, son, and that is what makes them so interesting. As far as why you are going, they'll be able to help you get to where you need to go."

"Where is that?"

"Weren't we just discussing white mountains?"

"The one's in my dream?"

"Yes boy, what other mountains?"

"Will someone there help the ringing stop?"

"In a way, yes. But then again, that is what the vial of water is for. I say again, one drop is all you need."

They walked for about five more hours. Tau had absolutely

no idea where they were going. To make matters worse, Hagga did not seem to want to answer any of his questions directly about what he was supposed to do, yet he had the distinct feeling that she had all of the answers. He found that intensely frustrating.

The whole time, she knitted. At first, Tau found the clickety, clack clickety clack noise of the needles pounding against each other annoying, but soon the sound faded to the background. She was knitting so fast, he could barely see her hands moving. The ball of yarn feeding into her creation was tucked into one of the pockets of her raggedy cloak. At least Tau was beginning to see that she was making a brown cloak. The threads were very tightly woven together to have been done by hand so fast.

"All done," she said. "And we are finally here. Funny how things work out exactly when they need to."

Tau looked around. There was nothing important in sight. They were still in a very open landscape of the savanna.

"What do you mean here? There is nothing here."

"Not yet," she said. "But there will be. You, wait. As for me, I've got another place to be." She began fumbling around in her pockets.

"You're leaving? So now I wait here by myself?"

"That's the plan. Oh, here it is." She pulled a carved rock from out of her pocket and showed it to him. It was about half the size of her hand with strange markings on it.

"What kind of writing is that?"

"First tongue."

"You can read the first tongue?"

"Of course."

"What's the rock?"

"*Space rune*. It gets you from where you are to where you want to go."

"Like magic?"

"Yes boy, like magic."

Tau reached his hand out, "Wow. How do I use it?"

"Oh, I didn't mean YOU specifically. It's for me."

"Well, couldn't I use it to get to the White Forest?"

"It's not designed that way. You have to at least know where a place is for it to work. Besides, do you have any idea how hard it is to conjure up a rune? Especially a *space rune*. I only have the one with me. Now an earth rune, those are much easier. Don't have any of those on me either. I'm actually close to learning how to make a Water Rune. After that, the Fire Rune! Remember, you're never too old to learn something new!" Hagga sounded excited and surely proud of herself.

"So then, I don't get one?"

"Sorry boy. But if it matters to you, in the future, I will look into making enough to give away. Have to practice my craft first, getting better all the time."

"How long do I stay here?"

"Until your ride comes. Shouldn't be long. Don't worry boy, there is nothing around here that will eat you and I doubt that the Thread will be coming around here anytime soon."

"The Thread? What do I do if it DOES come?"

"I just said it wouldn't."

"Then why bring it up? Besides, no one knows when or where the Thread will show up, so you can't actually say that it won't come here."

"If it makes you feel better, I suppose you are right."

"No, it doesn't make me feel better. First a giant spider and now the Thread. Do you even know what it is?"

"I know this much, boy; the Thread is a storm fueled by pure evil. If I'm right, it will grow as the Brood takes over more territory. If people don't find some way to stop the Brood, one day, the Thread will destroy us all."

"You are not any good at making people feel safe, are you?"

"You asked." Hagga gripped the space rune tight with both hands and closed her eyes. Then she tossed it into the air and, before it hit the ground, a strange purple, watery, disc was created. It had waves in it, like the puddle of water that had appeared in mid-air that Hagga fell out of when she saved him from the spider.

"And there is the rift," she said. "So long, boy. I wish you well on your journey. I'd stay longer, but there is a particular matter concerning frogs dropping from the sky that needs my attention."

"Frogs? From the sky?" Tau asked.

Hagga turned towards the purple rift and then stopped for a moment. "Oh yes, this is for you. It is probably a good idea to stay hidden, especially in the city. I hate to make a big deal about your skin color, but it is the way things are. Remember, even if that is the way the world is, doesn't mean it is the way it *should* be." She tossed him the cloak that she had knitted, jumped into the rift, and disappeared.

Tau put the cloak on, sat down, and waited in a patch of tall brown grass for hours. Over and over again he practiced jumping up and snatching his blades out to engage any danger that might appear. Hagga had told him not to worry, that nothing out here would bother him while he waited. But it was the savanna: there could be nothing for days, or there could be a pack of hyenas waiting to prey upon him. There were also plenty of humans to be wary of. One solemn boy would be easy picking for a thief or a murderer. Then, of course there was the threat of the Brood, an entire army that was already looking for him. It was dangers like these that made him wish he never had to leave the Makazi village in the first place; especially alone.

He checked the time, positioning his hand straight above him with his palm out toward the sky. "12," he said, and then placed his other hand, also with the palm facing the sky, toward the East. The sun aligned, about midway with his palm. 11:30.

An hour later, a large pack of elephants migrated near him. This pack of about forty elephants had several small calves with them. The adults studied him as they passed. Tau made it a point to back away, and to let the adults know he was yielding. Even elephants could become fierce if they thought that their young might be in danger. The biggest of the males stopped, looking directly in Tau's direction while the rest of the herd slowly walked by. He made Tau nervous.

"Relax, back away," again, he was hearing the voice of his dead friend.

"That's what I'm doing, Chad," Tau assured him. "I don't want the big guy to think that I want to challenge him to a fight."

"That's a fight I don't think that we can win. We could climb up one of those trees if need be."

"And he'll knock it right over…"

"Yes, Tau, yes he will."

Another large elephant joined the first. Then they both stood up on their hind legs and spread out the large wings that were folded on their backs. Their wings spanned the length of about 20 feet each. Despite the size of their wings, these winged elephants could not fly, not even a little. The wings were mostly used to protect each other from the sun and the rain. When Tau was younger, he had seen elephants in a huddle with their wings spread out to protect one another; especially the calves.

The wings served another purpose; intimidation. At that moment, the two winged elephants were doing an excellent job. The underside of their wings were colored bright red; a warning to anyone. They stood as tall as they could with their wings spread outward and let out a deep roaring sound which Tau took as a definite warning not to come near. Tau had no intention of coming near.

He hoped that was all it was, a warning. He stood there motionless, scared to move, scared to do anything that might make them attack.

Having Chad there helped him keep calm. During the hardest times of his life, Chad was always there with him. They fed off of each other's strengths, though Tau always felt like he needed Chad more than Chad needed him. Chad was the strong one, both mentally and physically. The exception was whenever they took to the water, Tau excelled every time. When it came down to brute strength or any type of fight on land, Chad was the better, but the water was Tau's domain.

The last time Tau was in a situation like this, it had been just Chad and him. The older hunters had taken a bunch of the boys on what they called a ten-day hunt. The purpose was part of the process of turning boys into men. They left the village for ten days, with the adults teaching the boys to hunt and to starve. For anyone in the wilderness, learning to go without food was as important as learning to catch it. During the first two days, the boys had gorged on the meat caught by the men. Then the men purposely kept the boys' bellies empty while they showed them various ways of obtaining food and water from the earth. The purpose was to insure the boys could survive, should they ever be out on their own in any sort of unexpected situation such as this one.

Through simple young boys' idiotic behavior, Chad and Tau became separated from the rest of the group on the sixth day, and for the rest of the time they had to fend for themselves. At least they were together. Together, they had analyzed their situation and had worked out solutions.

The herd passed. The large elephants that seemed to be serving as guards soon joined the rest of the pack. An hour after the elephants had gone, Tau began practicing again. He chopped away at the air, at the grass, and at his shadow. He imagined Uncle there with him, shouting out commands and even getting angry at the lack of Tau's skill and effort.

"Okay Chad, if the Brood comes, I'll hit the first one like this, then I'll duck the next guy, then hit him like this." His two blades swooshed through the air as he pretended to take down a whole patrol of the Brood army. He was so wrapped up in his fictional battle that at first he did not see the large caravan of animals coming his way.

These were the biggest elephants he had ever seen. They were three times as wide as normal, and they were covered in long fur. They were probably only a hundred yards from him when he realized that they were not elephants at all. He was not sure what they were, but there were about fifty of them. He wondered if the heat was somehow tricking his vision.

Then, he noticed the structures on their backs. They looked like square pens with wooden posts at the corners that held up some sort of cloth tarp coverings. And there were people in these structures, sitting and walking around. People, he thought to himself, and, as quick as possible, he ducked down behind some grass.

Tau began to panic. He crouched on the ground with one of his hands on his weapon. The caravan stopped and soon one man walked his way.

Tau stood up as the man approached. He looked at Tau and then beyond him, as if he was being careful to study the subtleties of the grass and who may be hidden within.

"Are you alone?" the man asked.

"Um, no. There are lots of us out here hiding," Tau lied.

The man did not carry a weapon. He did have a small wooden flute stuck into the belt at his waistline. The man took his flute out and played a short soothing melody. A light wind rustled the grass and the man studied it.

"No," the man said. "You're alone, all right. No need to worry boy, I'm not here to hurt you. Tau, is it?"

"Yes, how did you…"

"Hagga sent us a message, but didn't say what you wanted or where to find you exactly. Only that we would run across you in our travels sometime today. She's never too specific about anything."

"Yes, Hagga. She left me here, and said to wait for my ride."

"Well then, c'mon, boy. We are it."

Tau stood there confused for a moment.

"C'mon, boy. There is a whole caravan of people out there waiting on you."

Tau started walking. For some reason, he liked this guy. There did not seem to be anything sly or slick about him. He seemed like a confident, trustworthy man. And yet while Tau followed, he kept his guard up. The last man he met that seemed utterly harmless ended up being a giant spider, and he still was not over that experience.

"I came out alone to make sure you were you. Better that than to put the whole caravan in danger; although, there is not much danger that we cannot handle. How old are you?"

"Sixteen," Tau answered.

"Sixteen? I would have guessed about thirteen or fourteen. My son, Chega, is fourteen. I'll introduce you. Now, don't get our names mixed up: I'm Chaga, he's Chega. He wanted to come out instead of me. It's not his time yet. Young boys are anxious to grow up. Where are you headed?"

"I guess wherever you guys are going."

"That's no answer, son. We go to a lot of places. Pretty much all we do is go places. Now, where specifically are you headed?"

"The Red Barrier City, sir."

"Ah yes, you're in luck. We *are* going that way. Of course, I'm sure Hagga knew that, so it isn't much luck at all now, is it?"

They approached the others. Tau stared at the huge animals before him. He used to think elephants were big. The last ones he saw were bigger than any elephants he had ever seen before; but these things were two or three times as tall as those. Their fur ranged from black to brown to grey to white. And they had eight legs instead of four. It seemed odd, but then again, with an animal this size, four legs would not do. They did not have trunks like elephants, but they did have long thin snouts, mouth and nose included. Their tails were like beavers, wide and thin, with no fur on them, and long enough to hover about a foot off the ground.

Wow, eteboons, Tau thought to himself. He vaguely remembered hearing about animals such as these but not in true stories, only in tales.

He soon realized that *he* was the star attraction, not these beasts. Everyone was looking at him from on top of the animals, watching as he approached. He swallowed a lump in his throat as if he was about to perform in front of the eyes of a thousand people.

"Can you climb?" asked Chaga.

"Yes," he said while tilting his head back to look up the side of the animal. "No problem."

"Then up you go. You'll be staying on our eteboon for now, in our plot. Chega's up there. Don't let him talk your ear off."

The eteboons had ropes crossed like a grid around their whole bodies. They made for an easy ladder. Tau made his way up, still feeling the eyes of everyone around him, especially those of the people right above him, whom he was about to join.

"Hello friend, I'm Chega." He was the first to greet him – hand out and eager. "My dad is the one that walked you here."

Tau looked at the ten other people standing and sitting around, shyly reaching out his hand. Chega startled him, jumping into the plot behind him. The plot looked very inviting with an area was about 15 feet wide by 25 feet long.

There were blankets and pillows everywhere of various designs, making the place look very comfortable. There were also small tables in the center that one would have to kneel to eat at. He saw small wooden boxes about a foot wide in a few places along the sides and in the corner, and one near the front that was about three feet wide. The entire outer edge of the rectangular plot had a railing about 3 feet high around it. Much of the railing was covered in fabric.

"Hi. I'm Tau. I guess you are giving me a ride."

"Yes. We rarely ever take others into the caravan. I'm not sure why, but the adults usually choose not to. Here, you want to sit?" Chega led him over to the back of the plot where there was linen stacked into a pile. "It's pretty comfortable. You hungry or thirsty?"

"Actually, both." Tau had forgotten how hungry he was.

"Hey, dad," Chega yelled toward the front. "He's hungry and thirsty. What do we have?"

There was a lot of movement of the people on board and then someone handed Chega a clay jar, some bread, and some fruit.

"Here ya go. You like twilka berry juice?"

Tau laughed. "Who doesn't?"

"Haha, yeah, haven't met anyone yet that doesn't."

A man at the front of the eteboon, standing next to Chega's dad lifted a flute and played one long note. He stopped for a moment, then played the same note again. This time other flutes from other eteboons could be heard joining in, playing the same note. Suddenly, all of the eteboons began moving forward, wonderful soft music began to play from the entire caravan.

"So where are you guys going?" Tau asked, shoving bread into his mouth.

"Where we going, dad?" Chega shouted.

"Red Barrier City, son." Chaga yelled back.

"Red Barrier City," Chega told Tau.

"Yeah. That's where you guys are dropping me off. I mean where are you going after that?"

"Oh, I don't know. Who cares? Let the adults worry about that."

"Oh. Well, how long have you been gone?"

"Gone? What do you mean? Gone from where?"

Tau indulged himself for a second in a large gulp of twilka berry juice. His eyes rolled back into his head. He wiped his mouth with his arm. "I mean gone from home."

"This is home," Chega replied, taking a swig of twilka berry juice from his own clay jar.

"You mean riding on these eteboons?"

"Yes, this is where I live."

"All the time?"

"All the time. We keep it moving. 'If you can't carry all your stuff with you, then you've got too much stuff,' my mother always says."

"Hey, Chega! Who is the boy?" The voice of a teenager from another eteboon shouted from across the way.

Chega stood up and yelled back. "His name's Tau. We're giving him a ride!"

"Ask him if he wants to play the Hop?" the boy asked.

"Are we playing now?"

"Yes."

"Set it up, I'll ask him."

Chega gazed down at Tau. "Hey, you're not full, are you?"

"No, not full. Satisfied though. Thanks."

"Good, because it's no fun playing the hop on a full stomach. It will give you cramps."

"What's the hop?"

"The 'eteboon hop.' I'll show you."

Chega and Tau stood up. The eteboons were moving into a straight alignment side-by-side, yet still moving in a phalanx formation.

"See, if you look, the plots don't take up the whole back of the eteboons. There is a bit of room in front and in back to walk on the backside of the eteboon and on their shoulders. So, we jump from one eteboon to another in a big circle. Whoever makes it back to their original position first, wins.

"That sounds pretty tough."

"It is. You could fall easily. Happens all the time. That's what makes it so fun! You see that eteboon three down from us?"

"Yeah."

"You see that girl climbing out of her plot onto its back, in red and black?"

"Uh, I think so."

"Someday, I'm going to marry that girl."

"You guys have arranged marriages?"

"Ha ha, no. I can feel it. See look, she's waving."

The young girl was looking back at them, waving her hand with a coy smile on her face. "Hey, Chega. Try not to fall off this time! Ha ha."

"I got you this time, Nyah!" he shouted, and then turned back to Tau. "See, I told you. She is definitely into me. If you fall, I can't help you. I've got to beat her."

"How many times have you beaten her?"

"Never. Come on, climb out of the plot, onto his back." He then turned into the plot to speak to a young woman who was talking to his father. "Mrs. Efua, will you be our whistler?"

"Sure, Chega, I can do that," she responded. "Are you sure that your new friend is up to such a game."

"I can do it madam, it's okay."

"All right," she replied.

"What's a whistler?" Tau asked, climbing out of the plot and onto the eteboon's backside.

"Oh, that's how we can tell who wins," Chega responded. "It's easier than trying to look at who got back to their eteboon first. When one of us gets back to here, Mrs. Efua will sound her whistle."

"Oh, I get it. Well, how do we know when to start?"

"Wait for the sound of the horn, Tau. Wait for the horn. But get ready, it will be soon."

Tau stood next to Chega and matched his pose, ready to start the race. He balanced himself on the hind part of the giant animal, feeling it shift below him as it walked. He watched the ground move slowly past, hoping that he did not fall.

A horn sounded.

"Now," Tau asked anxiously.

"No. That one means get ready. The next one starts the game."

"Will they keep moving during the race?"

"Of course! That's what makes it so fun!"

"But couldn't we fall and get hurt?"

"Are you going to play or not?"

Toooooooooot. The horn sounded.

"Go!" Chega yelled, taking two steps before jumping to the next eteboon. "C'mon Tau, I won't wait for you!"

Tau hesitated. He looked up to see the others jumping from eteboon to eteboon. Then, someone from behind him jumped right next to him. "Hey new kid, are you playing or what?" he said as he rushed by.

Tau looked to see others coming up behind him as well. In one swift moment, he went for it and jumped to the eteboon in front of him. His balance shifted as he landed, and he rocked sideways, placing his hand to the animal's back so that he did not fall. That wasn't so bad, he thought as yet another player passed him up. He put his head into the game and jumped from eteboon to eteboon as the others were doing. He was actually quite good at it. He had a natural sense of balance, his feet and body shifted easily to accommodate for the moving animals.

He came to the eteboon at the end of the line, not quite sure what to do next. Again he hesitated.

"Through the plot. Through the plot!" the people inside the plot instructed him, gesturing with their hands. They sat on either side of it, making room for those in the game to run through.

He did. Then he was on the huge animal's shoulder, right behind its head. Its body seemed to move more vigorously than it did on the back end. Its shoulder blades made large movements up and down as the eteboon walked.

He kept going, on to the next and to the next. He was having fun. He noticed one boy from the ground climbing back up the laddered nets around one of the animals. He must have fallen down, Tau thought. He wanted to be sure that would not be him. He continued on; once again made it to the end of the line and passed through that plot as well.

"Go Tau, Go Tau!" he heard someone shout. Great, he just met these people and was famous already. Maybe that was a good thing.

Once he moved to the backside of the animals again, Tau heard a whistle. Someone had won. He stopped for a moment.

"Keep going!" the people on the plot shouted. "You don't want to be last!"

He noticed that more and more whistles were going off as the other contestants returned to their plots. He started going again, as fast as he could. He only had five more backs to hop. When he came close to his plot, Chega was there cheering him in. He jumped into the plot. Mrs. Efua blew the whistle again, and in a few moments, he heard two more whistles going off.

"Good!" Chega said. "You weren't last. Three cheers for the new kid. Woot! Woot!" he screamed as he danced back and forth.

"Did you win?" Tau asked.

"Nope, I came in third."

"Did you beat Nyah?"

"Nope, she came in second. But there is always next time."

"You seem in good spirits. I thought you wanted to win."

"Oh, I do, I do. But you see, it doesn't matter if I came in ahead of her, or one step behind her. Either way, I'm on her mind. And that's a good thing." He snapped his fingers then pointed two of them at Tau, confidently winking his eye. He leaned out of his plot. "Next time, Nyah!"

"You can try, Chega!" she yelled back.

V SEEDS

During the rest of the day, Tau acquainted himself with the daily activities of the caravan, which seemed to mostly consist of games. They taught Tau to play Mancala, a kind of board game where the players move their rocks around an elongated wooden board. Tau found it to be a lot like the Eteboon Hop.

What a delightful people, he thought. They were probably the nicest people he had ever met. Not one of them mentioned a thing about his grey skin.

The children played with him as if they had known him all his life. The adults too took great effort to make sure he was comfortable. They kept asking was he hungry; was he thirsty; was he too hot or too cold; did he require anything, anything at all? And while they traveled, someone was always playing the loveliest music.

They took him to the various eteboon plots where different activities were being held. In one plot they were making food, while another held school for children. The schools took up four different plots for children of different ages, and all of them took at least a couple hours to teach the children to play instruments. They learned to play, to dance, and to sing. This was school for these people? Playing music, singing and dancing?

Tau had never learned to play an instrument. At home, he enjoyed the music from the village musicians. But to learn to play, one had to show specific interest in the subject. Here, it was mandatory. He also had never seen so many different kinds of instruments. There were drums, flutes, horns, sticks, thumb pianos, and more, all different shapes and sizes.

After a while the caravan stopped. They were close to a small-forested area in a low valley. He wondered why they stopped since these people seemed to constantly move all the time. From what Tau understood, that's all they did. So why stop here? He sat in a plot playing the Mancala game with Chega and three of his other friends.

"Why are we stopping?" he asked.

"Not sure," said Kai. He was a bit older than Chega, a tall lean fellow. He was in mid-thought, and made a move in the game before he continued his answer. "Ask the grown-ups."

"Hey, dad!" Chega stood up and yelled four plots down. "Why are we stopping?"

"Planting seeds!" he said.

"Oh, yea," said Kai, "I forgot all about that. We were supposed to do that today."

"I didn't even know about it, but whatever. I'll go down and help," said Chega.

"Me too. I'll be down after this game. You should take Tau. Let him see how we do things."

"What's seed planting?" Tau asked.

"You know," Chega answered. "Putting seeds in the ground so things can grow. C'mon, I'll show you."

Tau felt terribly stupid. He knew how to plant seeds, but he assumed there was more to it than that. He followed Chega to the back of the plot and hopped over the wooden rail. Chega smacked the eteboon far back on its butt, "Tahta Tail!" he yelled. The tail of the animal rose up and stiffened. "Now we can slide down."

Tau slid down the tail after Chega. He looked around and many people were doing the same, climbing down from the eteboons. Some took the tail, while others climbed down the rope ladders. Chega took Tau over to a man carrying a couple of large sacks. "Do you have one for us?"

"Of course I do," the man said, smiling.

"What do you have?"

"You two can do the eggplants. Take that area over there, right by where those bushes end."

"Will do, sir." Chega stood at attention with a playful salute.

"Um, yeah, thank you, sir," said Tau.

"Sometimes we go to small farms like this," Chega began as they started walking. "We plant the seeds and help them grow. It's not for us, it's for other people. So we'll plant these for the people here, and then move on."

"What do you get in return?"

"I don't know. Sometimes some of the crop, sometimes some cloth, sometimes nothing at all. It depends on what they need and what we need, if anything."

They walked into position with their sacks. Tau took notice of others tossing seeds onto the ground.

"Toss them out like this Tau. Spread them around."

Tau watched questionably as Chega tossed the seeds on the ground. "It's never going to grow like that, Chega."

"Sure it is, Tau."

"Don't you have to till the soil first or something?"

"I suppose you could if you wanted to Tau, my friend. But you'd be here all day if you did. I'd rather not waste my day tilling."

"Okay," Tau said as he tossed his seeds onto the ground. "But don't say I didn't warn you when a month goes by and nothing happens."

"Haha. A month! You've got much to learn about us Tau. You'll see. It would be easier to show you than to tell you. We'll know if something is going to grow right after we are done planting. You'll see!"

They spread seeds out all over the area for about an hour and a half; until Chega's bag was almost empty.

"Hey Tau, why don't you finish up your sack. I'm going to go to Nyah's plot. See if they have more seeds to plant."

"Sure, I bet you are, Chega."

"What?"

"You are so obvious. Why don't you let me go for you?"

"And why would I do that?"

"I'd be doing you a favor. Think of it as surveillance. I could figure out what she thinks about you."

"Hmmmm. You do have a good point. But don't be obvious about it."

"You mean, more obvious than you?"

"I don't want her to know that I like her."

"I think everyone knows that you like her."

"Yes, but I don't want her to know that I know she knows I like her."

"Do you want me to go or not?"

"Okay, okay. Give me your bag. I'll finish the seeds up."

Tau left him and went over to find Nyah's eteboon. He suddenly realized that he was not actually sure which one it was. They all looked so similar. But then, he saw her standing up in her plot in her wonderful red and black clothing. He found himself feeling nervous. He did not know why he volunteered to talk to her. He was not the one interested in her, although she was pretty.

"Hey, Nyah!" he shouted up to her.

"Hi, Tau."

"Um... Can I come up?"

"Sure!"

Tau climbed up the rope ladders on the side and hopped into the plot. "Uh...hi, how are you?"

Nyah mocked him a bit. "Uh.... hi, I am fine. I thought you were planting."

"Yes, I was. But I was wondering..., um Chega wanted to know, if you had any seeds. We ran out."

"If you ran out, then why is Chega still down there tossing seeds around?"

"No, we almost ran out."

Nyah looked down to the ground, over to where Chega was planting. He was actually barely working at all. He was much more concerned with looking up at them. And as soon as she looked over at him, he looked away. She smiled and playfully moved over closer to Tau. "He didn't send you up here for seeds at all, did he, Tau?"

"What do you mean?"

"Oh C'mon, out of all the plots to come to, you came to mine."

"Uh...coincidence?"

"Give me the message." She leaned all the way into him, face to face, smiling with anxiety.

Tau was confused. Message? What message? He did not have any message. He looked around at the others in the plot. Nyah's mother was still there. She had not gone planting either. She looked to be sewing; yet she obviously was listening in on this conversation.

"I don't have any message, Nyah." Tau tried to assure her.

"Sure you do!" she said with an anxious grin.

"Uh, no really, Nyah, I don't have any message."

Her smile dropped, leaving her with a more serious expression. She began poking him and pushed him all the way to the edge of the plot as if she was going to push him over. "Look, new kid, I've been nice to you. We've all been nice to you. I could be not nice. I would hate for something unfortunate to happen to you."

Tau's back was leaning over the plot; he took a gander over the side and to the ground. Nyah's mother looked up at them out of the top of her eye while she continued sewing.

"Nyah, let's not threaten or kill our new guest. Let's get him to his destination as we promised."

Nyah grunted and turned around. "Well, does the boy even like me?"

"Yes!" Tau blurted, happy to deliver good news. Then he remembered that he was not supposed to do that either. He quickly covered his mouth, but it was too late. She already heard it. She turned back around and replaced the smile on her face.

"Really? Are you sure?"

"Yes, he told me."

"But no message?"

"Nope, no message."

"I guess that is good enough! Come here! I want to show you something." She grabbed him by the arm and pulled him to the floor. Tau caught a glimpse of Chega looking up at him as he was suddenly pulled down, out of sight.

Nyah fumbled through a small wooden box in the corner and pulled out a roped necklace with a very large crystal on it. "His birthday is coming. I'm giving him this. What do you think?"

"Sure, it's nice," Tau said.

"But wait," she said. "Watch." She held up the crystal and gently whistled to it. A high-pitched noise suddenly came from the crystal, and it soon became accompanied by a voice. It was probably the most pleasant voice Tau ever heard. Aaaaahhhhhhhhh, aaaaaaaaahhhhhhh it sang in melody. The voice was so clear, so crisp, so perfect, and pure enough to send a tingling sensation through his body. Tau could hardly believe his ears. He would have thought that a voice that high would have been irritating, but not this one; it was definitely pleasant and soothing.

"Well, what do you think?" she anxiously asked him. "It's an echo gem."

"I think it sounds beautiful. Really, it sounds great."

"It's me!"

"That's you singing?"

"Yes."

"Chega said you have a wonderful voice. He was right."

"Thank you."

"Nyah," her mother chimed in once again. "Why don't you show the boy the other qualities of the crystal? You know; the other thing."

"Oh, yes, mother." Nyah went back into the basket and found another crystal. "This crystal is not nearly as pure as the echo gem, but dad says that only one voice in a thousand is as pure as the purest crystal. When that happens, the gems can also harness and amplify some of the power of the voice. Watch."

She raised the echo-gem once again, and then whistled. Again the voice and sound from the gem grew stronger and stronger until the gem was glowing. Then she brought the other crystal over to it, holding them right next to each other. The second crystal, not the echo gem, shattered.

"That's pretty cool," said Tau.

She held the echo-gem tightly in her hand and the singing stopped.

"Even better is you could do it too. Anyone can. I've trapped the power of my voice inside. Try." She handed him the echo-gem.

Tau tried whistling at the thing, but his tone was totally off.

"No, no!" she exclaimed. "You have to match my tone, like this, whhrrrrr." She whistled again. And once again it turned on. "It has to be the right tone." Then she held it tightly in her hand again and it stopped.

Tau tried a few more times, whistling at different pitches, trying to match hers until, eventually, he got the echo-gem to work for him. He smiled at it. It was as if he had the power to make it happen.

"Yes, I think he will like this."

"Good. Don't tell him though; it's a secret," she told him while coupling her hands around the echo-gem. Slowly the sound got quieter until it was silent.

"But how does it work?"

"We are Music Wielders," her mother said. "We are masters of sound. The power of sound is a great one. It can create and it can destroy."

"What are you guys doing?" Chega suddenly appeared on the outside of the plot.

They were startled. Nyah quickly threw the echo-gem under

some blankets, and she and Tau both stood up. Tau felt guilty, even though he knew they had not been doing anything to feel guilty about.

"Nothing, Tau," said to Chega. "They were telling me about the power of sound,"

Chega stood there with a questioning look on his face. "Okay, well, the planting is done. I figured that Tau would like to see them grow." He took one look at Nyah, but said nothing to her, only made his way back down the eteboon.

Nyah slapped Tau on the shoulder. "See what you did!"

"What?"

"Now he's mad at me. Go fix it. Go, go." She pushed him toward the edge of the plot.

"Okay, okay, I'm going."

"And don't forget, it's a secret."

Tau made his way down to the dusty ground. He hurried after Chega, yelling to him to "wait up" as Chega walked slowly back to the planting grounds.

Then it hit him, that awful noise. The same one that almost drowned him back in his village, that same terrible noise that led to Chad's death. The piercing, paralyzing sound brought him to his knees. He grabbed his head in pain, unable to keep himself from falling to the ground.

He remembered what Hagga said to him, "… one drop of the water from the Whispering Pond." He struggled to grab hold of the vial and open it. He put it to his mouth, tasting the water on his tongue. It only took seconds to work.

The harsh sound faded away, replaced by soft whispers. "Find The White Forest," the voices said over and over again. Soon he began to see the vision as well. He saw the marsh, like a field of green leaves with hundreds of small canals of water twisting and turning through it that stretched far and wide. In the distance beyond, he saw the same snow-capped mountains.

The visions and voices lasted for about 30 seconds. As they

faded, he could hear Chega yelling to him and shaking him. "Hey, are you okay? What's wrong? Tau!"

"Yes, I'm fine. I think. I had a vision. It's why I'm here. There is a place that I have to find. I get these attacks that haunt me, giving me visions of where I need to be."

"A vision? Of what?"

"Snowcapped mountains; I think that is where I have to go."

"Snowcapped mountains? There are plenty of those."

Tau struggled up to his feet.

"Is he okay?" a voice yelled from behind.

"He's all right!" Chega yelled back.

"But I also heard voices. They kept saying, 'The White Forest," over and over again."

"I've been a lot of places, Tau. But I have never seen a White Forest."

VI FESTIVAL DAY

"Watch," Chega said to Tau. They sat among many of the others near the planted fields. Fifteen men and women sat in a line next to the fields with instruments, while the rest looked on. In front of the line, facing the rest, was one man they called *the conductor*. He began moving his hands elegantly while the musicians followed in tune and soon a sweet, slow song emerged as pleasant to the ears as a mother's lullaby.

The conductor closed his eyes, moving his body as if hypnotized by the tranquil melody. Chega nudged Tau with his elbow, then pointed to the fields for him to take notice of the plants sprouting right there before them. The leafy greens curved upward as if weeks of growing were happening with every second. Tau watched in awe as each of the plants became fully-grown ripened vegetables. The eggplants he had planted were already plump with vibrant color that made him hungry. Where there had been nothing but unnourished soil and scattered seeds moments before, there were suddenly carrots, tomatoes, onions, kidney beans, lentils, cabbage, and wheat, all ready to harvest.

"Nice," Tau said, completely amazed.

"See," said Chega. "I told you. And you wanted to wait months."

"Yes. You could feed a lot of people like this."

"And we do. It is part of why we travel so much."

Everyone clapped at the success of the crops. They had done their job. An entire village could eat because of them, and they were proud of it. The Wielders began to walk back to their eteboons in gleeful satisfaction.

"Well, that's it," said Chega standing up and walking back toward the eteboon.

"What now?" asked Tau as he followed Chega.

"Now we move on."

"Time to go?"

"Yes, it is almost sundown. We've got to start getting ready for the festival."

"What Festival?"

"I'm not sure, hold on." Chega yelled up to his dad standing in the plot, "Hey dad, what is today's festival?"

"I'm not sure son. Ask, Jengo. It's his turn to choose."

Chega and Tau walked along the ground to a different eteboon and Chega yelled up again. "Hey Kai! Is Jengo up there?"

"Yes, he is."

"Ask him what today's festival is."

Jengo stood up in his plot and leaned over the side. "Today's festival?"

"Yes," said Chega. "What is it called?"

"What's your friend's name?"

"Tau!"

"All right then, since he is new here, we will call it The Celebration of Tau!" Then Jengo yelled out again, shouting to everyone that could hear. "Today's festival will be The Celebration of Tau!"

Tau heard someone else yell the same thing, then another person even further away. Soon people were yelling from each eteboon so that all could hear. "Today is The Celebration of Tau!"

"What is he doing?" he asked, honored, confused, and embarrassed at the same time. "How can he name the festival after me? Doesn't it already have a name?"

"Jengo always forgets. He always waits until the last minute to name the festival. But he can name it whatever he wants to; it's his day." Chega replied.

"His day? How often do you have a celebration?"

"Everyday. Well, every night really."

"You celebrate every night? You mean like a party?"

"Yes, we do."

"That's crazy!"

"You don't have parties where you come from?"

They were at the back of their eteboon. Chega smacked the animal on his leg and yelled out, "Tahta tail!" The eteboon's tail became stiff and lowered to a height of easy access. Chega hopped on and gestured for Tau to follow. Tau was unsure, but he followed anyway. The tail rose up and both of them were able to easily walk to their plot.

"Yes, we have parties, but not every day. We have them on special occasions. You know, when there is actually a reason to celebrate."

"Every day is a reason to celebrate, Tau." He raised his hands into the air. "Being alive is a reason to celebrate. Tonight we are celebrating your visit. I think that's good enough. '

"What did you celebrate yesterday?"

"Last night was the Celebration of the 'lovely wind.' It was very hot at first, and later in the day, we experienced the most perfect soothing wind. So, there you go, The Celebration of the Lovely Wind. Jonna named it."

"Strange. Have you ever named a Festival?"

"Of course, everyone gets their turn. A couple weeks back we crossed a very wide river. The eteboons hated it, but after much struggling, we made it. So I named it, The Celebration of Crossing the River."

"I guess I do get it. I never heard of such a thing. What do you guys do at the parties?"

"You'll soon find out my friend. Tonight is the Celebration of Tau!"

* * * * *

People were talking, laughing, and having a good time throughout the caravan. All the kids got to drink as much twilka berry juice as they wanted, while the adults drank their *adult* drinks. Chega told Tau that it made the adults talk a whole lot and act more child-like than most of the children. There was plenty of delicious food for everyone to gorge on while games were played for hours. Eventually, most of the games were put away and people began picking up instruments. Some people climbed down to the ground and walked beside the eteboons. Others climbed into the plots on the backs of the younger calf eteboons. These were small and usually only two people at a time sat in these plots that were lined with plenty of comfortable blankets and pillows. Chega told Tau that those people were on dates. For a short while, all the music stopped, and so did the talking. Everyone was quiet.

"What's going on?" Tau asked.

"Shhh," Chega responded as he pointed into the darkness. "Watch."

The music started again, this time louder and more prominent than before. In the night, it was not only lovely to hear, but also a pleasure to see. The air became filled with colorful waves of energy created by the instruments that flowed in sync with the sound.

Then Tau noticed colorful lights coming from the below. He leaned over and saw the light coming from the people on the ground dancing. As they stretched and moved their bodies to the music, they painted the night with beautiful colors of wispy light.

It was magnificent. The entire caravan was encompassed in a show of light and music. Tau had never seen anything like it.

The music started off slow for the first forty minutes, but as time went on, the pace became faster and more aggressive. The drums beat with a fearsome rhythm; splashing beautiful colors of light into the air each time drummers hit the stretched skin, as if the tops were covered with vibrant paints. The dancers followed the music precisely, hoping, jumping, twisting, turning, and spreading their arms toward the sky with the upbeat music.

Numerous acrobatics were a part of their dance, tumbling and flipping their bodies above the ground higher than Tau had ever seen before. Their routines were in perfect unison with each other. At times, many of the dancers walked as their brightly lit bodies faded to darkness to let the attention of the crowd focus on one illuminated dancer performing a solo act. After each performance, the featured dancer slowed to a walk, his or her light faded, allowing another to have a turn.

The musicians did the same. Sometimes they performed all in unison; at other times most of the musicians played a quieter melody, their light dimming to a soft glow, while a solo act was played loud enough to be heard above the others, and that performer's color became so bright it could be seen by everyone. The soloist played along with the melody, yet still was masterful enough to make up his or her own notes as the music moved along. These people truly had the power of sound at their fingertips. They were, indeed, the Music Wielders.

The party went on for hours, taking up much of the night. By the end, the music slowed again to a drifting melody. Some of the people retired and went to sleep, one by one, as the night went on. Others continued to play blissful music for as long as they could. It was obvious that they loved it.

Tau spent the evening happy. For a short time he forgot about being banished from home. He felt calm and at peace, like he felt when he was floating in water. He even forgot about Chad. The melodies began to carry him to sleep, and as he closed his eyes, he could still see the wonderful colors in the blackness of his eyelids until they were replaced by his dreams.

VII THE SOUND OF WEAPONS

"Tau wake up, wake up!" Chega was shaking him vigorously.

Panic struck Tau's heart as he looked all around them for the cause of the alarm. Tau stood quickly and reached for his blade. "What is it?"

"Look! Montok warriors!"

"The Brood?"

It was daylight. Tau looked over the edge of the plot, discovering the army for himself. Montok warriors stood at the top of a large hill in front of them.

The two boys spoke in unison.

Tau: "They found me."

Chega: "They found us."

"You mean they're looking for you too?" Tau asked curiously.

"They're always looking for us."

"They have been following us," said Chega's father."

"Why?" Tau asked.

"We are a powerful people," said Chaga. The Brood's intention is to either control us, or kill us. Since we have made it clear that they cannot control us, they will try to attack."

"But if they were following you, then why did they not attack already?"

"It is very rare that they are able to find us. The men you see here were probably waiting for more reinforcements before they tried to attack. We have purposely waited here bellow this hill to engage them. They did not know that we were waiting until they reached the top. And now it is too late, they must engage."

"Reinforcements? There have to be at least 300 soldiers there!"

"Heh, yes. A good number for us to fight."

"With what? You said you don't have much for weapons."

"I said not like weapons that you would know," said Chega. "We have our music."

"Music?" Tau asked, a little ticked at Chega's absurdity. He must be toying with me, Tau thought. "Hey, I can fight too. I've got my blades. At least it's a real weapon."

Chega smirked. "Hey dad!" he shouted. "Tau here doesn't think we have any weapons. He wants to know if we need him to fight the Brood off with his blades."

"Keep calm, Tau. I don't think we will need you for this fight. Keep that blade sharp for another day," his dad responded.

"You heard him." Chega shrugged. "Don't feel bad. I'll be lucky if I even get a piece of the action."

The conductor swiftly jumped down from his eteboon. He faced the approaching army, waving his arms one way, then another.

Others with their various instruments jumped down, swift and agile. The eteboon commanders moved animals into a line with their tails facing the enemies.

Both men and women with bongos lined up behind the conductor, still in front of the eteboons' tails that were fully unrolled, stiff, and lowered. Others with their harps, flutes, and finger pianos arranged themselves in groups of five, spaced out along the line.

Chega and the other young boys and girls looked on in excitement, all leaning over the edge of their plots. The people were still; quiet, none of them made a sound. They waited as if eager to watch a spectacular show.

Tau, however, was still confused. "I still don't get it," he whispered.

He was thoroughly entertained by these wonderful people so far. He had seen the magic of their music, the way it brought the plants to life, the way Nyah's echo gem cracked the crystal, and the wonderful colors they could make in the night. But how all of that was supposed to help them against a Brood army, he was not sure.

"Sssshh," Chega said, trying to quiet Tau. "Watch. You'll see."

The Brood army stopped their approach for a moment while one man, riding on the back of a giant lizard, moved forward from the others. "We all know why we are here," he said. "Bow to the will of the Children of Montok or perish!"

"We choose to perish!" the Conductor yelled back. "We will not relinquish our power to the Brood. The Children of Montok will never control us. You may as well kill us now."

"Kill us now?" Tau whispered in concern.

"Here we go." said Chega.

The Brood General pointed a sword toward the caravan. A second later, arrows flew into the sky from the Brood army.

Tau watched, tilting his head back to follow the course of the arrows, which were obviously headed straight for them. He glanced at the cloth that covered the canopy of the plot he was in, and then the canopy of all the other plots on the rest of the eteboons. There was no way any of them were strong enough to stop the arrows. He was no longer feeling curious. He felt frightened, winced, and jerked in a direction as if to take cover.

The Conductor raised his arms to the sky. Every musician on the ground focused intently on him. He moved his hands back and forth then up again, and all the flute players pointed their flutes to the sky and blew in unison.

Their melody was perfectly in sync. The tones were high-pitched yet harmonious, pleasant to the ears. The sound was accompanied by a fast moving green rippling effect emanating from the tips of the flutes into the air. This green ripple quickly scattered across the sky, shattering the arrows into pieces that fell to the ground before reaching the caravan.

Tau opened his eyes wide.

Balls of fire came next, flung from slingshots. The ivory

horns were brought up for the task. Their long low sounds rippled through the air, changing the fireballs' trajectories to many different directions. None of them hit the caravan.

As soon as they hit the ground the fire spread through the tall dry grasses. The Dancers intervened. Twenty of them jumped, twisted and turned as if they were of one mind. They moved toward the fires with white light radiating from their bodies, swiping with their arms and kicking their feet. In no time, the fires died.

The conductor commanded the drums to begin. They started with a low steady rumble. Tau felt sure that his heart was moving as fast as the beats. Chega handed him some water. When he looked up from his drink, he saw the army begin its charge.

The conductor had his arms spread out, his head pointed down, but his eyes looked forward. His hands shook vigorously in sync with the sound of the drums, their rhythm pounded faster and faster, while with every moment, the army came closer. Tau could feel the rumbling through his feet.

Then the conductor stepped one foot forward and lunged out. With both hands, he drew a sweeping motion forward; the drummers, all at once, thrust their hands forward across the skins of the drum. The ground before them lifted and rippled. A huge wave of dirt and rock two feet high and as wide as the army itself rolled away from the musicians toward the attackers. The wave hit, smashing into their formation, tossing the soldiers to the ground.

Next the thumb pianos played. Plucking away, the musicians sang a song to the tall grass. As commanded, the grass twisted and locked itself around the soldiers' arms, legs, and bodies, confining them to the ground. That quickly, the battle was over.

"Hurray!" the Music Wielders all cheered, congratulating each other and patting one another on the back.

"I told you," Chega said to Tau, grabbing him at the shoulders and shaking him.

"Is that it?" Tau asked. "Is it over?"

"That, my friend, is how Music Wielders fight," another man said to Tau as he then turned to give someone else a congratulatory hug.

"If you knew you would win, then why did you look so panicked when you woke me?"

"Oh, that," Chega thought for a second. "I didn't want you to miss it."

"What now"?" Tau asked.

"Now," said Chega. "We leave them there and move on. We will play music to ground behind us to cover our tracks."

With the battle over, the people proceeded back to their eteboons, climbing up the sides and the tails. There was still a great deal of gleeful cheering going on, and they included Tau in the celebration of laughter and smiles.

What everyone failed to notice was the general; shifting and struggling in the grass that held him to the ground. He managed to grab a knife from his hip and cut himself free. In seconds he was up and rushing toward the musicians.

"He's up!" Chega shouted. He quickly hopped out of his plot; his small harp in hand, onto the back of Tahta. "Tail jump Tahta!" he yelled as he smacked him on the backside. Chega slid down the tail and when he got to the end, Tahta flicked his strong tail upward. At the same time, Chega jumped and went flying through the air. He positioned his harp and started strumming as he went through the sky. A blue wind emanated from his harp. It hit the general, slowing him down. Chega sent three more of the blue winds at the general before he landed, but he did not stop there. He kept plucking the harp strings and the general clearly found it harder and harder to move.

Two more harp players joined him in playing, strumming their instruments and emitting the same blue energy to paralyze the general. He fell to his knees while Chega continued to strum away, walking closer and closer to the general who struggled even to crawl. Finally the general fell flat on the ground, unable to move at all. Once again the thumb pianos played and the grass bound the general to the ground much tighter this time than before.

Chega walked up to the general. Before he could do more, his father Chaga walked up, grabbing the general's knife from the ground.

He gave Chega a glare as he picked it up. "You know that you are too young to engage in the battles, don't you?"

Chega dropped his head. "Yes sir, I do."

Chaga looked at the knife, flipped it around in his hand, and smiled, as if to be proud. Chega smiled back at him.

That night's festival: THE CELEBRATION OF ONCE AGAIN STICKING IT TO THE BROOD!

VIII RED BARRIER CITY

"Why did the caravan stop so far away?" Tau asked as he and Chega walked toward the Red Barrier City. The red dome seemed small, barely visible in the distance.

"We don't like people to see us coming," Chega replied. "We are technically fugitives of the Brood. Dad says that it's best if people don't know that we're here."

"With all of that music, who could miss you? I'd bet people could hear it for miles."

"Do you remember how loud the music was when we first approached you?"

"Actually, I don't remember hearing it at all."

"That's because you didn't. No one outside the caravan can hear the music unless we want them to."

"Wow," said Tau as he thought for a moment. "You Music Wielders have a lot of power."

"Yes. It is why the Brood wants to control us. But it is also why we cannot let them."

"With all of that power, you could probably take over this land. Or maybe all of them."

"Why would we want to do that?"

"Because then YOU could be in control."

"We have no desire to be in control, Tau. We don't want to take over anything. We must use our power wisely. Once someone with a lot of power starts having thoughts of conquering and taking over lands, then it isn't long before they end up like the Brood and take over everything."

"But you would not have to be evil."

"Then again, if we are so powerful, and we start taking over everything for *good* reasons, then there wouldn't be much to stop us from becoming evil. For now, we stay hidden, we keep on the move, and we help out when we can because that is what we do.

We have been here many times, so we should not have any problems."

"You've been here before?"

"We come often, every couple of months or so to get our seeds. As payment, we use our music to help the seeds grow in soils that are parched of nutrients throughout the land, where nothing of value will grow. If the Brood found out that the general gave us seeds, they would probably do away with him in some terrible way, so please don't tell anyone about it."

"What general?"

"General Jelani. He runs the city."

"I can keep a secret," Tau responded, then looked at his grey hands. "It looks like right now, I am the secret."

"I know. So stay hidden under your cloak."

They soon came closer to the city. Tau was able to make out the guards standing outside the gate. "They look like Brood Guards!" he said.

"They are. Don't worry; these guards have more of an allegiance to General Jelani than they do to the Children of Montok. The guards here know me, so I'll do all the talking. Don't worry my friend. It will be okay."

Once they came to the wooden gate that surrounded the city Tau took a moment to be completely astonished by how huge the red dome was. He figured it would probably take a couple hours just to walk around it. Exactly what it was, he was not sure.

"How big is that dome?"

"I don't know. I've never measured it. I don't think I've ever been concerned with it."

The dark wooden fence that surrounded it stood twenty feet tall. It was made out of large black logs that stuck up out of the ground, tied together. There must have been thousands of them if they did in fact encircle the whole thing. Two guards were posted on each side of the gated entrance. They stood with their long body-length spears gripped in their right hands; their five foot elongated wooden shields in their left.

Each guard wore a wooden black and red mask on his face that gave an intimidating impression of power. The red designs on their masks and bodies were definitely trademarks of the Brood. They wore no sandals on their feet. Their calves and biceps were covered by black straw-like materiel. Tau felt a bit unsteady; he was being hunted by the Brood, but here he was walking right into a city that was run by them.

From inside the fence he heard strange noises: pounding, sawing, banging, whistling, and animals, along with many voices. He tilted his head back as far as he could to see the top of the red dome. From his angle, the top was out of view.

Chega nudged him. "Hey, don't do that. Keep your head down. You're supposed to stay hidden, remember?"

Tau dropped his head. He was so in awe at the size of the dome that he had forgotten.

"Chega," said one of the guards. "We have been expecting you.

"Gentlemen," Chega nodded respectfully.

"Who is your friend?"

The other guard whispered something into the ear of the one talking.

"Oh, it seems that we have been expecting your friend as well."

Tau lifted his head barely enough to peek at who was speaking, his face still shadowed by the hood.

"Normally we would demand to see who you are, stranger, but we were told of your arrival and to make an exception. Come, I will take you to General Jelani."

"Thank you," Tau said in a raspy voice as if to disguise himself as the guard escorted them inside.

They walked past the gate, into what seemed to be a large village. The gate was a good forty yards from the boundary of the red dome. Between it and the gate there were numerous houses, huts, tents, cabins, shops, stores, and booths. They all were of a different design and material. Some were made out of adobe; some were wooden with rows of horizontal logs, some were made from brick, while others were made out of stacked rocks with clay filling in the cracks. Others were topped with hay, or long thick grass, or even huge leaves. They all were built on either side of a dirt walkway that appeared to circle the dome.

There were hundreds of people moving in and out of the shops, stores, houses, and along the walkway. Seeing all of those people reminded Tau of the times he had accompanied Uncle to the Kingdom of Ufalme. Of course in Ufalme, everything was much more organized, as if every structure was carefully planned before being erected. The whole kingdom of Ufalme had its own theme and style. It was a place that had its own culture; unlike this place which did not have any sort of theme to it at all. It was not one culture, but obviously many.

In general, Ufalme was a much cleaner place. The people were always decently dressed. He always was impressed by the sweet smell of flowers and the delightful scents carried by the breeze. In this city, the smells changed with every step. He could smell delicious meats cooking one moment, and then rotting food the next. He could smell the odor of people who had not bathed in weeks, then the wonderful scented oil of a woman passing by him.

Tau quickly darted out of the way of a large domesticated elephant. The man on top was naked except for his loincloth. His skin was so black that it shone like onyx in the sun. He had white stripes painted on his body widthwise from head to toe and the man peered down with an intimidating glare as if Tau was in the way of his very large elephant. Tau peeked from under his hood. He shivered as the man stared back while the slow motion of the elephant's body rocked the man on top rhythmically from side to side.

There were animals everywhere; goats being walked by

people holding the reins, oxen, over-sized ostriches, and an assortment of foul hopping around them. One man traveled with an enormous Gila monster big enough for him to ride on. Tau had never actually seen a Gila monster before and certainly never even heard of one so large. This man's pet was decorated with red, yellow, and white paint. It was trimmed with thin gold ropes that were fastened at different parts along its body. It seemed to Tau like a lot of work for a pet lizard. But the man walked with his head high. He was obviously very proud of it.

One woman passed them whose entire body was painted purple. She draped herself in different species of bone; with one large bone through her nose. In her hands were animal skins that draped almost to the ground. Tied to them were several different items.

"Jewelry, candles, seeds, I've got anything you need," the woman said to Tau as he went by.

"No thank you," Tau responded keeping his head down. It was the same response he gave to all of the merchants and vendors offering their goods when he passed.

He soon began to notice a number of wooden machines, carts, and wheelbarrows with people wheeling around wood, food, metals, weapons, rocks, dirt, animal carcasses; more things in one place than he had ever seen. Some of the people tried to peek under Tau's hood to get a glimpse of him, but he was careful to keep dipping his head down when he needed to.

Tau's eyes suddenly caught the swift motion of a cart hovering off of the ground as it moved. It was made of wood with four big crystals on each corner, then smaller ones across the side. Four men in cloaks were on top of it while one woman stood at the front end, moving her arms in sync with the movement.

"What is it?" Tau asked Chega.

"Those are Movers. You've never heard of Movers?"

"They can fly?"

"Well, they are Movers. They can move things. All of them

on the moving cart are using their power as Movers to lift it, but that lady in front is the one controlling it."

"Wow," Tau said. The cart moved past him. The lady driving caught his eye and smiled before moving on.

"I've never seen so many things in my life," Tau added.

They passed three men in dashikis with staffs in their hands. Their crystals glowed at the top of the staffs as their hands were raised against the red dome. The dome itself seemed to pulsate with a glow in the area surrounding the men while they chanted something unrecognizable and strange. Into the center of the glow, six large ogres rammed a huge log with a metal tip over and over again. These things that were nothing but stories were here right in front of his eyes. The ogres were big, robust, hairy looking creatures and they all made vigorous grunts every time the big log hit the red dome.

This was all too strange for Tau. He kept an eye on the dome as they continued to walk. He could not quite see inside it, but there was light coming through from the inside.

"General Jelani," the guard said, pulling Tau's attention from the dome to the man standing before them. "Chega is here, and the young boy."

Tau was even more astonished than before. He raised his head to get an adequate look at the man who was dark skinned, lean, and muscular. The perfection of this man's body did not seem real, almost as if some artist had drawn him. He wore leather tassels above his biceps, which helped define them. His skin was well oiled, giving it a shiny luster. Atop his head was a perfectly round Afro at least a foot long. It too was conditioned with oils that gave it a wondrous sheen in the sunlight, as if the sun came out for the specific purpose of shining upon this man. He wore a goatee that was perfectly cut against his smooth skin with a face that looked as if it was chiseled from stone.

A beautiful maiden stood next to him, holding a tray of fruit, cheese and bread. On his other side a second maiden was ready with a pick to fix the slightest hair on his head that dared move out of place. He was the most masculine man Tau had ever seen, and still the man stood there with the most fantastic charming grin on his face. This man was General Jelani.

"Hello, General," Chega said in a stern voice, as if trying to sound as mature as possible.

"How is the music these days?" asked the General, never letting his grin leave his face.

"Always well, sir. I've come for two bags of seeds."

"And you shall have it." The General leaned down with a widened grin on his face. "Tell your father that I have been continually pleased with the harvest that you have been able to maintain."

"Our pleasure."

"And you, young man, who is trying so hard not to be seen. You must be Tau."

"Yes, pleased to meet you, Inkosi," Tau answered, figuring that he should address him as a King. General Jelani took the compliment and nodded. "Lift your head a bit, Tau, I would like to see your face."

"But sir, I am supposed to remain hidden."

"Haha! It is okay. I am in control here."

Tau timidly raised his head a bit as the General helped him along by pushing his chin upward with his hand. "A handsome young man you are Tau. Perhaps you need only to stay hidden from the young maidens we have here so that they can stay focused on their work." His charming words were followed by an even more charming smile. One of his maidens went to work picking his already perfect hair and straightening his garments.

Chega laughed a bit at the General's remark. Tau however, felt more uncomfortable with all the focus being on him.

"Don't look so grim, young Tau," said the general. "We will stick with Hagga's request to keep you hidden and perhaps we can provide you with what you have come for." He pulled on Tau's hood to fully cover his face, pulling his head down. "Let us move to more private surroundings." He turned around and began walking, giving a slight glance and a nod to the maiden on his left. She quickly grabbed a grape and placed it into his mouth.

Tau and Chega followed.

"You know of Hagga?" asked Tau.

"Yes, very well and for quite some time. If she hadn't aided me in helping Lord Onoc, I might not be ruling this place." He stopped talking to eat some cheese.

"Onoc is one of the Children of Montok. Part of the Brood, said Tau."

"Oh, yes, and the Brood is in control of this city."

"What is this place?" Tau asked. "I mean what is inside the dome?"

"Would you like to have a look?" The General changed direction to bring them closer to the dome. "To answer your question, no one really knows what is inside. That is what we are trying to figure out."

"What are all these people doing around it?"

"Trying to get in. We use any means that we can think of to try and penetrate the dome: magic, sorcery, brute force, machines, weapons, and fire. I even have people on the other side trying to dig their way under it."

"So why are all the people here?"

"Well, once you get enough people here and they need to stay for some time, sooner or later someone is going to build a house, then the people are going to need food, so more people come to provide that. Then they need new clothes or their weapons fixed or something of the sort, and more people come to provide that. So then, all these people need places to live and they build themselves homes or other people build them for them. Then, people come to provide materials to build things, and of course, they need somewhere to live too, and something to eat. Soon, you have so many people that they need to be governed and you have got yourself a city!"

"It seems so complicated," said Tau.

"No," The General explained. "See once a certain number of people come..."

"No, I mean.... well never mind," he said as he carefully placed his hand against the dome. It was soft, very unlike what he thought it would be. His fingertips easily made dents in the smooth exterior, almost like pushing against someone's skin.

"Feels a bit weird, doesn't it?" asked Chega.

"Yes, it does," said Tau as he ran his hand across the surface. "And nothing can penetrate it?"

"Nope, not a thing," said the General with a smile on his face as if he actually held some sort of admiration for the dome. "It's an impenetrable barrier. That's why it is called the Barrier City. There are of course more of them across Madunia, with different colors, all of them inaccessible."

"How did they get here?" Tau asked.

"No one knows that either. Forty years ago, they simply were not here; then all of a sudden, they were."

"You should see it at night," said Chega. "It glows."

"Really?" said Tau, and then he was startled and jumped back at some type of movement inside. "There's.... there's... something in there! I saw something moving!"

"Haha," the General chuckled. "Yes there is. It's pretty common to see something moving in there. Don't bother asking what it is because no one knows that either. Perhaps, as we are trying to get in, someone is trying to get out."

"Or something," Tau squinted, trying to get a better look inside the barrier. He could almost make out the shapes, but his mind could not lock on to any specific form; only vague shadows.

"Come now, let us continue on." The general started walking; his cape flapped heroically behind him, his maiden shifted the top of it by his shoulder to make it lie perfectly.

"So, that is your job here? To get inside the barrier?"

"My job is to continue the efforts, but mainly to maintain order and law amongst the people."

"You sure do ask a lot of questions," said Chega.

"Only about stuff I don't know."

"Heh, I guess that makes sense."

They approached a large bricked structure; actually the largest Tau had seen so far in the Red Barrier City. It had only one floor, but at the top had four tall pillars on each corner and a large tower at the center. Four flags connected to the pillars barely moved in the light wind. They were Brood flags. Two guards were posted at the door and gave a respectful nod to the General as he entered, followed by his maidens. Tau paused at the doorway, puzzled.

"So, you DO work for the Brood."

General Jelani stopped and turned around with his grin. Somehow, even out of the sunlight, this man carried an elegant glow. "Does that trouble you?"

"No, sir, "Chega butted in and gave Tau a poke with his elbow. "It doesn't bother him at all." He leaned in closer to Tau and whispered, "Don't asked stupid questions."

"Hmmm." The General nodded, then spoke to the nearest guard as he continued inside. "Bring me Goddy, the Animan."

"Yes sir," the guard nodded before proceeding out.

The interior was nicely decorated. Torches that sat atop carved wooden pillars gave a warm inviting feeling. Patches of kente cloth were hung along the dark grey-bricked walls. In between the kente cloths were the skins and heads of different animals. The floor was also blanketed with animal skins right up to the large chair sitting far to the back of the room. There were sets of rectangular tables seating ten and on top of those were baskets with beautifully colored flowers. On one of the tables sat two woolen sacks, which the General immediately gestured to.

"I believe those are for you, Chega."

"Thank you, General. We are grateful."

"No, it is I who am grateful. Your music beckons the seeds to sprout in places where nothing else will. Many will eat because of you and your people's good will. I have an orchestra of music here you know. But nothing can compare to the sound of a Music Wielder. I have to be sure to keep the Brood off of your back. You people are as much fugitives as your grey friend."

Chega went to inspect the sacks of seeds.

Tau however was a bit disturbed. He did not like the way that word, "fugitive," fell upon his ears. It had never occurred to him that he was a fugitive. Still part of him was not inclined to accept it.

"I'm not a fugitive, sir."

The General sat in the large chair and sighed. "It is safe here, boy. You may take off the hood if you wish. Secondly, it is important for you to understand that the House of Montok has nothing good in store for any of us. They have gone to great lengths to control many lands throughout Madunia, this one included. The Brood is the law; if you must be hidden from them, then by definition, that makes you a fugitive." His grin never left his face.

Tau slowly pulled his hood down. "I'm sorry...."

"I should probably be leaving." Chega butted in again, holding his seed sacks in each hand.

"Leaving? You're leaving already? We just got here."

"I'm sorry, Tau, but I can't stay long. The caravan is waiting."

"Being a wanted clan, the music wielders like to keep on the move," the General explained.

"Yes, we never stay in one place too long. It's our way. I wish you luck, Tau. I hope I see you again."

"You too! Maybe I'll try to find you after all this is over. Or you can come find me back at my village."

"I don't know about finding me, but finding you, that I can probably do." Chega said with a smile, and held out his hand.

Tau accepted the gesture with a firm vigorous shake.

"Good luck with Nyah."

"And good luck to you, Tau, in finding what you need. I'd come with you, but I'm destined to live my life aboard an eteboon." Then Chega walked past the guards and was out the door.

The room fell uncomfortably silent. The guards at the door and the general's two maidens seemed as if they did not even exist; only Tau and the General were real. Tau felt uneasy about it, because he was currently at a life low, and the General emanated nothing but greatness.

"So, tell me about this place. Where is it that you need to go?" the General asked while one of his maidens gently patted parts of his Afro into place.

"I've only had visions of it. I see mountains, but I hear the words, White Forest."

"From what I understand, it is all the way across the world. That would take some time even if you could ride upon the back of the fastest cheetah or the swiftest twilka bird. Not that we have any around here anyway."

"Yes, and Hagga said you would be able to show me another way. A faster way."

Then a guard entered, followed by a man, a boy, and two wolves. The man and boy wore similar styled, yet different colored clothing. The odd thing about them was not the cloaks that covered them, draped over their bodies, or their faces concealed in darkness under their hoods; but the wolves that walked with them. The man's cloak was olive green. He wore a warrior's skirt, showing the strength of his legs. He walked with a long wooden staff with a light green gem hovering at the top. The wolf walking next to him was big enough for the man to ride on. And as the man's cloak and clothing was olive green; the color of the wolf's fur was the same.

The boy that walked in after him followed the same pattern

of clothing. His cloak was a fiery red; his clothing, mostly the same color with black trim. His wolf was much smaller than the other one, but then again, he was much smaller than the man. And of course, his wolf's fur was the same red color as the boy's cloak. At the top of this boy's staff was a red crystal.

After entering, both of them took their hoods off and smiled.

"Ah, just in time," said General Jelani. "I'd like you two to meet Tau. You'll be taking him to the forest. Tau, meet Goddy and Juran."

After greetings were exchanged, four women came in with trays and bowls of food, placing them on one of the tables.

"We will eat while we talk," said the General, making a welcoming gesture to the table. He joined them, sitting at the head.

"Now Tau," he continued, "Hagga was right; we do know of a way of shortening your trip. Goddy and Juran are Animen, great sorcerers from the south. They will take you where you need to go."

"The White Forest, huh?" asked young Juran, stuffing some nicely spiced meat into his mouth.

"Yes," Tau replied, "Have you been?"

"No, don't know anyone that has. Not even sure where it is. I only know that it's far from here."

"Then how can you help me get there?"

"It's not us exactly," said Goddy. "However, we can find you someone that will know. Have you ever heard of a tree imp?"

"No."

"If all goes well, you will. They have a knack of getting from place to place. There is nowhere that they have not been, or cannot get to."

"But you are not sure that they know?"

"Simply put, a man once happened upon a white forest and it was through dealings with an imp. He was lost and didn't know exactly where the forest was, but we are pretty sure that the imps do."

"So, tell us about yourself, Tau," suggested General Jelani.

"I'm a swimmer and a fisherman."

"A noble profession."

"My Uncle wants me to be a warrior."

"Do you not like to fight?" asked Goddy.

"Not as much as I like to fish."

"Take heed of your Uncle's teaching, young man. Being able to fight is never a wasted skill in the world that we live in. Juran here wants to be a metal smith."

"Well, actually," Juran corrected, "I want to be an artist; you know, make things out of metal. But my dad here makes me learn all sorts of metal crafting."

"Son, that's my job, to make sure you learn a skill. Make all the art you want, but you will live better if you are able to fashion a good weapon for payment and get yourself some good high-grade crystals."

"Like we're living the same life, Tau," said Juran.

Tau nodded. "So do you guys live here?"

"Juran and his father are two of several sorcerers that we have here, using their skills to try to break into the dome. Also, they are the only two Animen in the city," said the General.

"Yes," said Juran." We've been here for eight months. We were due to stay for a year, so we have four months left."

"Yet, I have known the great General most of my life," said Goddy.

"I wouldn't have you in the hands of anyone that I didn't trust, Tau," the General assured him.

Right then, one of the guards came in anxiously and whispered into General Jelani's ear. Even though the General looked concerned, the grin never left his face. The General whispered something back, nodded, and the guard left.

"Young Tau, please put on your hood, we have company," the General said as he stood up and walked back to his throne.

Tau obeyed and two guards brought in a man to the center of the floor, forcing him to kneel.

"Ladies and gentlemen," said General Jelani, "it seems that we have a thief among us. What is your name? Or does your mother simply call you, 'thief?'"

"No, sir, she does not." The man trembled in fear, fighting against the way the guards were forcing his arms awkwardly behind his back. "She calls me Banto."

"Banto, I do have law in this city, and by breaking the law you are trying to make a fool of me."

"No, my lord! You are not a fool, you are a great man!"

The General increased his grin, "Using flattery to get the upper hand. Are you a diplomat?"

"No, my lord!" The man began to mumble under his breath. "A thief."

The General leaned closer. "I'm sorry, what was that?"

The man spoke louder, "A thief. I am a thief."

"I am getting old, my ears don't work as they should. I still can't hear you."

"A thief!" the man shouted.

"Good, and to my knowledge there are two of you. Where is the other?"

"I don't know."

The General looked doubtful. He glanced at Goddy, who nodded his head. With a simple thought, Goddy commanded his large wolf to intervene. The olive colored wolf walked forward and snarled as he approached the man until they were face to face.

The man cringed visibly. "He has gone to the Nagotti village to the West. We were to trade the items for some low-grade gems!"

"Low-grade? I figure that you could get at least some mid-grade gems for the items that you stole." The General was silent in thought for a second, and then he gave Goddy the hand motion to call off his wolf.

"Do you have family here, Banto?"

"Yes, sire," the man said, whimpering. "A wife, and an eight year old boy."

"How long do you think they could go without food?"

"What?"

"By stealing, you are taking food from the mouths of others, so perhaps if your family went without food for a while, you would understand what that is like."

"But, sir...."

"Quiet! Unless you want the wolves to know what it is like to feed on human flesh. Your child will go two days without food, your wife, three days, and you will go five days. Your child will go one day without drink, and you and your wife will go two days without drink. You will also spend three days in a hot shack, under the burning rays of the sun. Then you will be jailed for two months. Now take him away from here."

The guards nodded and carried the man out. Tau was trying to fathom the cruelty of this man before him. Having a child go without food or water, having the man sit in the sun for three days without food or water, this seemed inhumane.

The General came back to the table and sat down.

"That certainly is not a happy face," said the General, as he looked a t Tau. "Something troubling you, Tau? You do not like my methods?"

"Well, no sir, it seems.... well.... cruel. I don't see how you can do the work of the Brood, right down to their punishments." Tau thought this, but he could not believe he had said it out loud.

Everyone at the table stopped eating, and their faces went blank. Even the maidens made an effort to act as if his words had not reached their ears.

The General leaned forward, putting his elbows on the table. The wooden planks of the table made a creaking sound under his weight. "Young man, what you don't know is that it is the Brood I am protecting him from. If I don't keep order in this place, they will send someone that will; and as far as they are concerned, stealing is punishable by death!"

Tau put his head down and said nothing. He did not want his mouth to get him in any more trouble.

The General sat back in his chair. "Now, unfortunately, this little incident has altered our plan. These Animen and a couple of guards were to take you to find a good imp in the morning. But now, I need Goddy and the keen sense of smell of his wolf to go and track down this other thief. The Nagotti village is at least a day away from here. I'm afraid it will be several days before they get back. You'll have to stay here."

"But sir," Juran chimed in, "I can take him. I'm ready. Besides, no one is better at finding imps than my wolf, Ekko."

The General looked at Goddy, looking for his opinion on the matter. It seemed that Goddy was looking at The General for the same reason. Then they both looked back at Juran.

"Do you think you are up for it?" Juran's father asked him.

"Yes, sir, I've gone many times with you. I think I'm ready to handle myself. And I'm sure the General will be sending guards with us anyway, won't you General?"

"Well, the boy knows my ways," said the General to Goddy.

Goddy let out a deep sigh and nodded his head. "Perhaps it is time then. I will leave tonight to find this thief. In the morning, you will take Tau to the forest."

IX SCENT OF AN IMP

Juran and Tau entered The Quiet Forest, leaving behind the dry, arid dust of the savanna. The plants and trees quickly became numerous. Tau noticed the dampness of the air beginning to stick to him while the shadows of the moving leaves from the tree canopy above danced along the ground. They walked along a trail of dirt much darker than what surrounded the Red Barrier City. Ekko led the way, nose to the ground, meandering from side to side searching for a scent. Juran and Tau walked behind Ekko while four guards followed in pairs behind them.

"You've been in here before?" Tau asked, turning his head slowly in all directions, taking in the sights of this unfamiliar place.

"This forest?" Juran asked.

"Yes."

"Plenty of times. Sometimes I need a change from the City. And Ekko here, like I said before, is a master when it comes to finding imps."

"And why do I need an imp?"

"Oh, you'll see, if you're lucky."

"Lucky?"

"Yeah. Lucky enough to have it take you where you want to go. If the imp doesn't want to take you anywhere, there is nothing we can do."

"Maybe we can make him take me."

Juran turned around to the guards behind them. "Gentlemen, this guy thinks we can make the imp take him. Haha."

The guards chuckled. Gasat, the lead guard, yelled out, "Apparently this kid knows nothing about tree imps. There is rarely a chance of making one do anything it doesn't want to do."

Ekko darted off the trail. "Wow, that was quicker than ever

before," Juran yelled.

"What? What's happened?" Tau excitedly asked.

"Ekko's got something," said Juran and went off the trail after Ekko.

"An imp?"

"Come," Juran yelled.

Tau went after them, pulling out both of his blades. One of the guards called to Tau, "No! Put those away."

Juran joined in, "You can't threaten a tree imp, or you'll get nothing."

Tau did not quite understand, but he put his weapons away anyway, feeling a bit out of the loop.

The group tiptoed their way through the thick of the forest, wading through long untamed grass and bushes that scrapped against their legs and ankles. Ekko came to a stop beside a hollow log and scratched at it; something was there.

Juran raised his fist in the air. In Tau's village, people used similar signals to communicate on a hunt. Methods like these allow them to communicate without the noise of talking. This signal meant stop.

Juran leaned in intently, focusing on Ekko's movements, until his shoulders dropped and he sighed. He leaned against his staff, shaking his head. "Ekko," he said under his breath, "we are supposed to be looking for tree imps, not squirrels."

"Squirrels?" Tau asked. "How do you know? Do you see it?"

"No, I don't see it, but Ekko knows it's a squirrel and I can sense what he knows."

"You mean you know what he is thinking?"

"Almost. Sometimes. Not exactly. First of all, wolves don't think like we do, so it's not like mind-reading, but I can understand some of the thoughts that go through his head. Come on everybody; let's go back to the trail. Ekko, leave that squirrel alone."

The group made their way back to the trail, this time without carefully pushing the braches out of their way. The guards slashed and hacked at them with their swords, while Juran whacked at them with his staff until they were in the clear.

They spent hours searching, moving on and off the trail, following Ekko who was still trying to get a good scent of an imp. Juran tried to answer as many questions that Tau asked about this new forest and its inhabitants.

"You never want to be too quiet in the forest if you don't have to," Juran explained. "It's good to let some of these creatures know that you are here. Best to scare them off rather than to startle them. There are a few breeds of poisonous snakes..."

"Snakes?" Tau asked, making an effort to search the ground more intently as they walked.

"If they feel you coming, they'll most likely move out of the way. Sneaking around will probably end up with you stepping on one accidentally, and that's something that you DON'T want. They're almost certain to strike."

Tau took the hint. He knew that snakes could not hear. He pounded his foot into the ground twice as hard with every step. If there were any around, he wanted them to feel the vibrations of his feet so they would know that he was coming and get out of the way. He wondered if this technique would work for giant spiders, or any spiders for that matter.

Then it hit happened again, that piercing noise. He fell to his knees, covering his ears and letting out a shriek.

"Hey kid, you all right?" one of the guards asked. "Did something get you?" He looked to the ground for a snake or a pesky rodent or something.

Another guard attended to Tau's legs, looking for bite marks. His cloak was wrapping awkwardly around Tau's legs as he was rolling around on the ground kicking and screaming. "Nothing, I don't see anything. What's wrong, kid?"

Tau did not respond. He tried his best to deal with the pain until he could get to his crystal vial. He struggled, shaking as he pulled the top open, taking his one-drop.

In a few seconds, the piercing noise subsided and he began to hear calm and pleasant whispers to his ears. He lay on the ground, panting as the whispers became clearer and his view of the trees above him was replaced by the vision of snow-covered mountains.

"The White Forest," the same message repeated over and over again. When it stopped he was once again looking at the trees and branches above him. Five excitedly curious and concerned faces peered over him.

"What happened? Are you all right?" Juran asked in an uneasy voice.

"The voices," Tau replied. "The visions, the whispers. They came back again." He slowly made his way to his feet as everyone helped, brushing the dirt and leaves off of him and his cloak. "It's so painful at first, but if I take a sip of water from this vial from the Whispering Pond, it calms the pain, and I can hear the voices clearly."

"And what happens when your vial runs out?" asked one of the guards.

"I hope to make it there before it does."

"What did they say?" asked Juran. "The voices, I mean."

"They always say the same thing. 'The White Forest. Find The White Forest.' What I don't understand is that the vision that I have is of mountains. Why does it tell me to find the forest and then show me mountains?"

"I don't know, Tau. But that's what the imps are for. They've been all over the world. If anyone can get you there, they can."

Tau thought for a second. "Maybe behind the mountain, I don't know."

"So when you get to the forest, the whispers will stop?"

"I don't know. I hope so. Then maybe I can go back home."

For a moment a deep sadness overwhelmed him as he thought of how much he missed his home and of the fate of his friend Chad.

"That's a sad face if I ever saw one," said Juran. A second later he spoke again with a spark of excitement. "Tau, have you ever heard of a mimicking flower?"

"Mimicking flower? No"

"Then I've got something to cheer you up. Look!" He pointed over into the forest where Tau could barely make out a few flowers. "C'mon, I'll show you."

They started in, and what at first seemed like a few flowers turned out to be a whole patch of them in different vibrant colors. They stood about 2 1/2 feet tall. The petals were shaped in a circular-like tube, each flower pointing in different directions. They all had two long leaves curving downward off to the side of the stem. The patch was filled with a hundreds of these lovely plants.

"Watch." Juran crouched down in front of one of them and held his arms out, looking directly at the flower. After about ten seconds, the flower moved. At first, its long leaves were curved downward, the tube shaped petals were pointed off to the side and slightly up. When it moved, the petals changed position as if the flower was looking at Juran, as he was looking back at it. The leaves rose up to match the position of Juran's arms.

Then, Juran waved his arms up and down rhythmically, moving one up while the other was down and then switching back and forth. At the same time, he moved his head from side to side. It was not long before the flower moved exactly as he did. Then Juran stopped, but the flower kept moving. Not only that, but soon, one after another, all the flowers in the patch moved as the first one did.

Juran was right.

Tau was amazed; another new thing for him to see. He completely forgot about his home for the moment. The sadness left him altogether. A smile of astonishment swept across his face. He found himself mimicking the flowers and dancing with them.

"See, I told you," Juran said.

"Yeah, very cool," Tau agreed.

Juran joined in with the dancing. The guards however did not. After about five minutes, the flowers stopped moving. They were back to their still state as normal flowers should be.

"Can I try it?" Tau asked.

"Sure," Juran answered. "Get close and stare at one until you get its attention. Then you have about fifteen seconds to get some movements together before it will follow. Once you get one going, the others will join in. It's fun."

Tau followed the directions that Juran told him. Soon, once again, they were gleefully dancing with the patch of flowers. Once they stopped, Tau started one more dance session before Gasat intervened to ruin their fun.

"Hey kids, are we going to look for imps, or are we going to dance with flowers all day?"

"We?" asked Juran. "Gasat, you haven't danced one time. Come on, it's fun!"

"I doubt it. Let's get a move on, boys."

"Fine then," Juran said, sounding disappointed. "I guess we're back on the trail."

*   *   *   *   *

In a few more hours, Ekko caught yet another scent and began scampering off the trail.

"Should we follow him?" asked Tau.

"No," said Juran. "I don't know what I was thinking before. It hasn't been that long since Ekko's and my *sacred union*. I still get a little mixed up between his thoughts and mine. Before, he wanted to go after a squirrel and for a while my instinct was to go after it too. But I'll tell you what; you'll never get an imp by chasing after it. You have to let it come to you. Wait…" He paused for a second. "The good news is…. he's definitely caught a good imp scent this time. More than one of them, too. Let's camp here, guys."

"Good thing, too. It will be dark soon," responded one of the guards. "Let's make camp a bit further in, so our fire won't be seen from the trail."

"Now we'll try to find a small clearing to camp in," Juran explained as they made their way off the trail. "If we can't find one, we'll make one."

They soon came to a small patch that was more dirt than green. "This is good," said Gasat, putting his sack down and going through it.

Everyone seemed to know what to do except Tau. Everyone put their sacs down and pulled blankets out of them. Back in his village, they never brought blankets. They slept wherever they could find space. Tau was disgusted at himself for never paying much attention to what the other hunters had tried to teach him about the forest.

"C'mon, Tau," instructed Juran. "We've got to get some wood and kindling for a fire. You know how to build a fire?"

"Yes," he said, glad to be of use.

"I figured as much. Why don't you and I get the small stuff?" Juran started by grabbing the smallest twigs lying around, and as much of the dry grass as he could find. "Ekko is busy with a rabbit right now, so he should have something for us to eat by the time we've got the fire started."

Tau joined in on the work. "Where is he? I don't see him."

"He's not far. I don't actually see him either. But I can sort of feel where he is. And if I focus on him for a second, I catch a glimpse of him digging into that rabbit hole."

"That's really cool."

"Yeah, it works for us. In time our bond will be stronger."

"What does *sacred union* mean?"

"You guys done with that kindling yet?" One of the guards yelled out as all four of them came over with bundles of wood in their arms.

"Hey, there are four of you," Juran responded.

"No excuses, young man. Let's get this fire started."

Juran and Tau returned to the camp clearing with their dry grass and twigs. Then Tau struck two fire rocks together until a spark started the dry grass smoldering. Once they blew it to a flame, the rest was easy. By the time they were ready for the larger logs of wood, Ekko returned with three rabbits in his mouth.

"Good boy, Ekko," said Juran, stroking his fur and rubbing the top of his head between his ears.

"Wow, I guess you were right," said Tau, grabbing one of the rabbits on the ground. "I'll do this one." He grabbed his blade and started at his rabbit, slicing into it and ripping off its skin.

Gasat went to work on another one of the rabbits. "Always nice to have a wolf around that will do all the hunting for you." He paused for a moment and pointed his knife toward Ekko. "Of course, there are six of us. That's only a half a rabbit each."

Ekko turned his head oddly toward him.

"All right everyone," said Juran. "Let's put on our shiny stuff." While the others put their skewers of rabbit over the fire, Juran leaned the opening to his bag toward the campfire to catch the light as he looked through it.

"Ekko, come." He pulled out a shiny chain with both gold and silver metal intertwined with a few jewels. Ekko came to him and he placed the chain over the wolf's neck.

"What's that for?" asked Tau as he turned his rabbit around over the fire. He was anxious to cook his meat and eat it, but he knew all too well that sticking it into the flame would leave the inside raw, and the outside burned to a crisp. So he backed the skewer away from the flame a bit, cooking it more evenly.

He was crouched down over the fire. To the right of him he watched Juran slip the metal onto Ekko's red coat where it reflected the light of the fire in star-like twinkles.

"That would be imp bait," stated one of the guards in a whisper, while he too turned his roasting rabbit.

"Sure is," added Juran, whispering as the guard did. "We'll all be wearing as many trinkets and jewelry as possible. Tree imps love things that sparkle, almost like they can smell it. With any luck they'll smell out the stuff that we have and come on over."

Another guard leaned into the whispering conversation. He went into his bag pulling out a net, tossing it to Tau. "We'll each have a net too. If you can, nab the little bugger when he tries to steal your stuff. They're good for stealing things in the night."

"Right," added Juran. "But still, don't be too rough. You don't want to make the little guys angry. Remember, we need to ask these guys politely to take us where we want to go. If you make one angry, he may play like he likes you, then he'll lead you into the trees and off to...well, anywhere. Hey Gasat, what was that guy's name?"

Gasat was busy picking meat off of his stick, testing it to see if it was done, which it was. "Which guy?" he mumbled in between bites. He grabbed as much as he could with his hand and then leaned the skewer over toward Juran.

"You know, the guy who got lost in the imp tunnels."

"Oh, yes," Gasat suddenly remembered. "His name was Tibor, I believe. One of those little buggers must have not liked his attitude or something. They lead Tibor off somewhere, and we didn't see him for four years. Must have been on the other side of the world somewhere."

"That's terrible," whispered Tau.

"Sure is! He was lost for some time. The good thing is that he is the guy who has seen the White Forest. So it's a good thing for you that he didn't get along with the imp. The problem is even if you capture one, and try to keep it in some sort of cage so you can make it take you places, it will soon die in any sort of captivity. They'd rather be dead than be forced into showing anyone the secret of moving through the trees. And only they can do it."

By this time everyone was eating. They split the rabbit meat amongst them all, eating the tender, cooked muscle. Ekko was happy eating the combined giblets of all three rabbits.

A question roamed through Tau's head. "Hey, why are we whispering?"

"Because one of those little buggers could be watching us right now," said Gasat. "We don't want to let him in on our plans to capture him, do we?"

"I guess not," said Tau, feeling stupid once again. He shoved more food into his mouth and kept quiet for a moment.

"So Tau, you want to tell us what's up with your skin? I mean, why is it that color?"

"It's who I am, I guess," he said in a condescending way.

"Hey, I'm not trying to be rude or anything. You look different, that's all. I've heard stories of people with grey skin like yours."

"What kind of stories?"

"Oh, nothing special. Only that they...er you, exist. Supposed to be magical or something. I guess that's why you have the cloak? So no one will see you?"

Tau felt terribly uncomfortable. He looked at his dark grey skin, and then looked at the mahogany colored skin of the others. He knew that somebody somewhere was after him, for something as simple as his skin color. He did not like it.

"If someone reports my skin color to the Montok Army, they'll come for me. They did before; that's when I was forced to leave home."

X THE BOAR

ONE MONTH BEFORE TAU'S SIXTEENTH BIRHTDAY

Small villages have problems with local wild life from time to time. A straggling elephant, a curious hyena, or a hungry wolf sometimes made their way into the human habitat. Usually these mangy animals were scared off or killed. Very rarely, but occasionally, there was a human casualty.

One night a certain boar came into the Makazi Village and was quickly scared off. The second time it came, it managed to grab one of the chickens before again being chased away. By the fifth time of stealing chickens, the villagers decided that it was time to hunt the thing down and kill it.

A party of five was selected, with Tau being nominated by Uncle. It was not that Tau did not like hunting; he was afraid of it, especially at night. However, he did seem to have better natural ability for it than everyone else. He always seemed to be able to hear, smell, and see in the dark better than anyone else. While the rest of the hunters could detect nothing, Tau could hear the slightest footstep or make out the shapes of animals and plant life on a moonless night. His reflexes may have been only milliseconds faster than the average man, but when it came time, it made all the difference.

The hunting party slept in the same small hut for three nights. On the forth, someone sounded the horn calling all to arms for an emergency. The hunting party quickly got out of bed, sheathed their weapons, and followed the sound to the chicken coup, where a young man stood, breathing heavily. The guards from Ufalme readied themselves at the coup as well, but since this was a village matter of a wild boar and dead chickens, not some attack from an outlander, the villagers insisted that it should not concern the guards.

"There, I saw him, the boar! He ran off in that direction!" said the young man with the horn hanging by a rope around his neck. He leaned his torch close to the ground. "I can see his tracks in the dirt!"

Tau and the rest of the hunting party followed the tracks into the forest. The darkness beyond the village swallowed them up as if it was alive. Tau could feel it envelope him like a fog.

Tau hated the forest at night, and therefore he never aspired to be a hunter. He walked with the men though, everyone being as quiet as possible. For a while, Tau kept his attention on the men in the party, making sure to step where they stepped, and move how they moved. He also wanted to make sure he was as close to them as possible for fear of meeting the boar, or anything else, alone.

Soon, Tau began to focus on the search as well. He listened closely to the quiet of the forest, being sure to identify every sound that came to his ears. Then, he thought he heard something; a rustle in the distance. It could have been the boar, but he was not sure. He focused his eyes on one spot in the darkness until he was sure he could see movement. Often he saw things in the night before anyone else, so he turned to tell the others, only to realize that they were gone. He was alone. His breathing became heavy and his palms began to sweat.

Then he heard a terrible high-pitched noise of whispers that paralyzed him. It was, in fact, the first time that he had heard the noise and seen the visions. He dropped to the ground until, after a long time, he returned back to normal again.

He lay on the ground in the night, afraid. He was alone, and something very strange had just happened to him. He sat there for a few minutes trying to figure it out and as he looked up, he saw the boar, no more than ten feet in front of him.

Perhaps, if he remained still, the boar would move away. So he sat there as the boar's gaze remained locked on his with neither one of them moving. Soon the boar grunted. Tau got the feeling that the boar was ready to end the stalemate.

Without thinking, Tau turned and ran. He ran as fast as his legs would carry him. He could hear the boar behind him, but every ounce of his being was focused on getting away. With everything he had, he ran until another strange feeling started to come over him.

The next thing he knew, someone was calling his name.

"Tau! Tau!"

He opened his eyes, and it was daylight. Tau lay on his stomach along a thick branch with his arms and legs straddling the sides.

"Uncle!" Tau shouted back from the tree. He felt extremely disoriented.

His body began sliding off the side of the branch before he quickly righted himself.

The sudden fear sharpened his awareness; he was finally fully awake. He looked down to see five men. Among them were Uncle and Chad and guards from Ufalme.

"How did I get up here? It was just nighttime. What's going on?"

His uncle looked around at the rest of the party, a bit perplexed. "We were hoping that you could tell us, son. There, in front of you, is that the boar?"

Not more than a foot from him, on the same branch, laid the remains of an animal, dead and mangled as if a wolf had been tearing it apart with its teeth and claws. Tau looked at the corpse of bloodied flesh and fur. "The boar? I don't know. How did I..."

He looked at the animal. It had been ripped open. Only when he looked at the head could he tell what it was. "Yes, it is a boar," he said.

"Send it down boy. And then you come down yourself."

Tau pushed the animal over the side and it went crashing down to the ground.

Then a strange black owl flew in, landing on the branch right in front of Tau. It stared at him. The odd way the owl moved its head back and forth made Tau even more nervous. There was no doubt, the owl's eyes were fixed on him, as if to say, "I'm watching you."

"Do you guys see this owl? It's staring at me!"

"Never mind the owl, Tau. Come down!" said Uncle.

Tau dug the blades of his curved daggers into the trunk, and hoisted himself down. The looks on the faces of the party were anything but inviting. They stood there, not saying a word, gazing at him and all the blood that covered him. It was not until he looked down at himself that he understood the strange looks on their faces.

"Um, Tau," said Chad. "You have blood all over you."

"Blood?" Tau asked.

"It's all over your face."

"What has happened to you, boy? Surely you didn't drag that boar all the way up the tree yourself. It has to weigh half as much as you do!" said Uncle.

"I don't know, Uncle. I remember setting off into the forest with a hunting party last night. We were tracking the boar for about an hour, and I got lost. I heard this terrible noise."

"What kind of noise?" asked Uncle.

"I'm not sure. It was so loud, so sharp, I couldn't move. It was like it was coming from in my head. And there were voices."

"Voices?" said Chad as he glanced at Uncle, not sounding at all as if he believed what Tau was saying. "Did they say anything?"

"I couldn't understand them. There were so many, and it was so loud, and I had visions of…of…something white."

"We will have to look into this," said Uncle. "Why did you go up into the tree?"

"I don't know. I remember hearing the boar. It was coming after me. I started to run. I ran as fast as I could, then…then… you were calling me and I woke up in that tree. How is it daytime already?"

"Tau," said Chad, sounding concerned. "Did you do that to the boar?"

Tau looked at the mangled animal on the ground. "I don't think so. I couldn't have."

The Ufalme guard had questions as well. "It is past daybreak, boy. We have been searching the entire night for you. Who has done this to the boar? Was it you? The last time I saw a man with that much blood on him, his own wounds lead him to death within an hour. You don't seem to be wounded at all?"

"Hey," Chad jumped in to defend him. "He said he didn't do it."

"Humph, his story doesn't match what we see."

"Are you calling him a liar?"

"Let us get back to the village and sort this all out there," Uncle intervened. "We will sound the horn to let everyone know that all is okay. But first, let's clean you up in the waters of the pond."

"We must bring him back as is and show them what he has done," said the guard.

"And what has he done? No one saw anything, and he doesn't remember. At most, he has killed a boar, the very boar he set out to kill in the first place. You act as if he has done some sort of crime. I see no need to walk into the village and scare the youngsters with this young boy covered in blood. No, we take him to the pond first to clean him up, and we leave the boar."

"He's right," said another one of the Ufalme guards as he studied the mangled body of the boar. "An animal has done this. Look at the gashes, made by the claws of...perhaps a panther. Let us clean him up, and move on."

Regardless of Uncle's efforts and the guards testimony of a panther's involvement, news of Tau being found asleep up in the tree and having god awful amounts of blood on him spread all over the village. Tau overheard some women talking of the boy that ate a boar raw, served himself on the guts of an animal while the warm blood still cycled through its veins. The story became twisted as it passed from person to person. The man that tended to the oxen told Uncle that he knew that when Tau was supposed to be "sick," he was actually living in the forest, biting the heads off of birds and mice.

Tau became very disturbed by all the rumors. Uncle assured him that with time, everything would return to normal again, the rumors would stop, and so would the odd glances of the villagers. He was right. In another week, all of the rumors had subsided. Things returned back to normal. They probably would have stayed that way if it were not for the next thing.

XI SIXTEEN

"Tau!"

He awoke suddenly, his body jumping to the sound of several loud voices calling his name. Full of fear, he screamed at the sight of several people wearing masks and standing over his cloth bed that lay on the ground. They were not Brood masks, but to see them in that way, huddled over him like a mob of mysterious kidnappers, sent warnings of danger to his mind.

"It's your birthday!" the people in the masks shouted. "Joyous day, it's your birthday, joyous day, it's your birthday!"

The crowd picked him up and carried him out of his hut where more people awaited him. By this time, his fears from his abrupt awakening were pushed aside by relief and laughter. He had known that this was coming. The people in the Makazi village took birthdays very seriously.

The large crowd picked him up over their heads and began to carry him around the village, cheering as they carried him past each and every hut. People that were not part of the traveling crowd stopped what they were doing when the celebration came by. They roared, throwing their hands into the air, or shaking fists with vigorous merriment, or clapping and shouting, "Joyous day, Tau, it's your birthday!"

Tau laughed and waved at everyone as they traveled. He could feel several hands on his back and legs holding him up in the air. He caught many of the flowers that were thrown at him, throwing them back once he had enough to fill his hands.

Soon they came back to the center of the village and placed him on the spectacle. There he stood, looking at everyone as their gleeful faces filled him with joy. More flowers flew through the air and began to gather at his feet. He bent down to grab more of them and threw them back to the crowd as they cheered. Then he felt a hand on his shoulder as Chad stood next to him to address the crowd.

Chad raised his other hand into the air, gesturing for everyone to quiet down. "Quiet, quiet everyone!"

The noisy crowd leveled off into a slow murmur.

"Today is an important day for my friend, umm.... I'm sorry, can you please tell the people your name?"

"My name is Tau," Tau said to the crowd.

They again began to cheer, calling his name until Chad quieted them again.

"Tau," Chad continued, "today is a special day for you. Let me ask you, how old are you?"

"I'm sixteen."

"How old?" Chad asked in a louder voice.

"Sixteen!" Tau shouted louder.

The crowd roared again, "Sixteen, sixteen, sixteen!"

Chad continued to address everyone. "Sixteen. Yesterday, he was a boy, but not today. Today, he is a man! Tau is one of the smartest and the kindest of us, and probably the greatest swimmer that ever lived. Today, your Uncle, your friends, and the rest of us don't honor you Tau; today, you honor us, by being one of us. Today we bring you gifts of food and flowers."

Several people began placing cakes and pastries at their feet on the spectacle. "Today we sing, we eat, and we dance. And tonight, we sing, and we eat, and we dance. And one of you lucky young ladies will have the honor of being the first one to dance with Tau as a man. Shall we choose now?"

The crowd roared and screamed. Many people were pointing out girls who wore bashful looks on their faces. Chad shook Tau by the shoulder as Tau looked out across the crowd, into the faces of the young ladies that attended.

"No," Chad continued. "We will save that for tonight. Until then, no one dances with Tau. Not until he chooses someone after the sun has sunk below the last day-palm. For now, let us all celebrate and be happy, for today is a great day!"

There was more cheering. Chad jumped down from the spectacle while Tau spent a few more moments waving to people before he sat on the edge of the spectacle, greeting those that approached him. He began to taste some of the food that was next to him as several people greeted him, wishing him a "joyous day," and asking his approval for various dishes.

"Do you like the honey cake I made, Tau?" A young girl asked him.

"Yes, it's really good," he said.

"Now, don't eat too much food yet, Tau," said Chad.

"And why shouldn't I?"

"Because you and I have something very important to do today."

"And what's that?" Tau asked while shoving pudding into his mouth.

"Today, you and I are going to the *line.*"

The *line* was a new goal to swim to, marked by something on the shore that he and Chad used to measure their strength and endurance. They set this goal to challenge themselves because no one else could swim nearly as well, or as long as they could. Every time they reached the invisible *line*, they chose a new goal further out from their starting point, and it became their new challenge for the next time.

They only went to the *line* a hand full of times a year. The rest of the time, they strengthened their swimming by diving as deep as they could, pushing the limits on how long they could hold their breath, spending several hours swimming continuous laps, all the while competing with each other for speed and endurance. Chad was gifted with size and strength on land, but in the water, Tau was usually the one that came out ahead.

This competition and love for the water was what bonded them. It was something that no one else in the village could come even close to. Swimming was their thing. Though most of the boys in his village wanted to be warriors, and even though Chad was well fit to be a fighter, a warrior's life was not what either of them wanted. Tau and Chad were seamen. And Tau was very much looking forward to reaching the new *line*.

A few hours later, they took the short, twenty-minute trek through the woods to the lake. From there, they looked at each other and then out to the lake. It was wide. The vast open field of water gave Tau a feeling of freedom; much different than living in a village completely surrounded by trees.

Tau could see land on the other side. His eyes followed the curve of the shore until it led out to more open water filled with nothing but a few fishing boats with men throwing nets into the lake. From where he and Chad stood, they could not see the marker on the shore, which indicated their destination, their *line*. They would have to go out much further into the lake to see it. They dove in.

After a half hour of swimming in the water, finally they spotted the marker and knew they had reached their *line*. This time it was an old fallen tree, one of the largest in sight. A very long time ago it had been stricken with rot, weakened and then broke and fell over about ten feet up its trunk. It had been there so long that no one actually remembered when it fell. From where they were in the water, the tree on the shore seemed small, almost a spec.

They free styled, with their breaths in perfect sync with their bodies as efficiently as any great swimmer. They were experts. They knew that along with a good amount of stamina, it was all in the technique that would keep them going.

Then it happened again, for the second time, violently, and all of a sudden; that same piercing noise that Tau had heard in the forest. He grabbed his head, stopped swimming and in no time at all, he was under the water thrashing around.

After much struggling under water, Tau could feel Chad

grabbing and pulling him to the surface. Tau was still thrashing wildly; Chad was using all his strength to keep them both from drowning. Soon, both of them again began sinking below the surface.

By the time the ringing in Tau's ears stopped and he was once again in control of his body, he was overwhelmingly exhausted. He started to make his way toward the surface again, with every stroke becoming more of an effort to fight his way through this water. He was aware of Chad, slightly behind and below him, also swimming toward the surface. Tau's arms lacked strength so that the water seemed too heavy against his muscles. When he finally reached the surface, he realized that he could not see Chad.

Tau quickly dipped back under the water and, through rays of sun-light, could see Chad struggling about ten feet from the surface. Tau rushed to him. Somehow, Chad had become tangled in seaweed stemming up from the lake's floor. He struggled to get loose, but all the while, the seaweed seemed to entangle itself around him even more.

The more Tau tried to untangle him, the more bound Chad became. Neither of them had a knife to cut with, so Tau began ripping weed with his hands. Still more and more strands continued engulfing Chad. Soon Tau had no choice. Tired and exhausted, he had to surface for air.

He did not have the energy to go back down again, and yet, he did, to no avail. Chad was no longer moving. His body swayed with the current of the water, trapped in the seaweed. The next time Tau surfaced, a fishing boat had arrived. As the four fishermen pulled him out of the water, he screamed in the most terribly exhausted voice. "Chad, he's down there, tangled. You have to cut him out!"

Three of the men jumped from the boat and into the water. None of them was as good at diving or holding their breath as Chad or Tau, and it was not long before they came up empty handed. They tried over and over again. Even though Tau was tired, he wanted desperately to dive back into the water for another chance to save his friend, but the fisherman on the boat would not let him. Tau did not have the strength to struggle against them.

Soon, the rescue was over; they could not even find the body. They did not know if Chad had sunk even further down, tangled in the sea grass, or if they had drifted from his location. He was not found. Poor Tau sat on the side of the boat, wet and shivering in panic, but not from the cold water. The fisherman looked at him as if it was his fault.

"We saw you," he said. "We saw you pushing him under the water. We saw you trying to drown him!"

Chad's death was Tau's fault. That was the consensus of the village. Especially after the fisherman had told them what they saw. "Chad was trying to save Tau, but Tau fought him; he fought him all the way until Chad got tired, then he pushed him under!"

"It's not true." Tau argued against the man. "He did save me, but something was wrong, something was very wrong. I heard the sound again and..."

"Then it WAS your fault!" screamed the mob. "He admitted it!"

"No!" Tau pleaded, "Chad got tangled in sea grass! There were voices in my head again! I couldn't move!"

"What were you doing out so far?" someone in the mob yelled.

"It was Chad's idea. We were going to the *line!*"

Uncle grabbed him by the shoulders. "What sound Tau? The same one you heard before?"

"Yes Uncle! It was so loud, I couldn't move. There were many voices, just like before. I couldn't hear what they were saying."

"Wait!" Uncle pleaded with the crowd. "There is something wrong with my son. Something terrible. We must find out what..."

The villagers had heard enough. They rushed them, and Uncle fell to the ground. Someone grabbed Tau. He struggled, managing to get free.

Tau feared for his life. The people came toward him with angry faces as if they wanted to harm him, to make him pay for what he had done to Chad. He wanted to get away, he had to; there was this terrible fear in the pit of his stomach that made him want to run, and that is when it happened.

He felt the weirdest tingling sensation in his gut and his heart, then the sensation of his skin crawling, or stretching or doing something very, very odd.

He changed into a leopard. He would have run, but he was just as confused as the crowd was scared. There was a net thrown over him, and a man hit him with a stick until he was knocked out. It was later that day that he awoke in a cage.

XII SILENT RAIN

Tau inhaled deeply through his nose, taking in the scents of leaves and trees around him. The forest was calm, filled with the pulsating hum of millions of insects making various calls to attract their mates. The campfire burned in front of them, cracking and popping as it consumed the wood; its orange light flickered and danced amongst the six travelers that sat around it hoping that sometime in the night, they would catch a tree imp. Beyond the reach of the fire's light, the forest quickly faded under a shroud of complete darkness.

Captain Sec was already asleep, laying his head backward against a log, giving a slight snore every time he inhaled. It was his shift to sleep. Throughout the night, someone would be awake at all times.

"What's that you're doing?" Tau whispered to Juran as he watched him cut into a thin piece of gold.

"I'm making a medallion. Basically it's for my dad and me. Our people often have family crests, something that represents their family. The last one my family possessed was lost some time ago, so I'm making a new one."

Tau looked closer at the metal, trying to figure out the outcome of the shape. "Well what and who decides who gets to make it?"

"No one really; someone just does it, and then it's done. I've only recently started going off on my own. I know my dad worries, so from now on, whenever one of us leaves, I'll give him one, and I'll keep one. Only problem is I'm not sure exactly what I am going to make."

"Hmmm, what do you want it to say?" Tau asked.

"Say?"

"You know, mean?"

"I'm not sure. Something about us and something about our

people."

"What exactly are your people? I mean, yes, I have heard of you, but I still don't know much about you."

"We are sorcerers, Tau. Our powers are strengthened by the power of the moon. We don't all have the same powers though. They are as different as we are, but the one thing that we all have in common is our connection with our wolves."

"One wolf each?"

"Yes, a lifelong companion."

Tau twisted up his face for a moment. "So, your wolf…"

"Ekko."

"Yeah, Ekko, he will live as long as you?"

"Nah, I wish," he said as he hugged Ekko and rubbed his head. "He is the best friend I will ever have. I'll never be connected to anyone like I am with him."

"So, what happens when he…" Tau paused for a second. He did not want to actually say DIE in front of Ekko. "You know…"

"Well, to be honest Tau, I don't think about it much, but it will be a terrible time for me. Those that lose their wolves are often lost for a long time. But if I'm lucky, Ekko will be reborn."

"You mean come back to life?"

"Not like that, but as long as I am alive, our souls will be tethered together. We keep new pups in a certain area of the village. His soul will be reborn into one of the new pups. It doesn't happen immediately though. It can take years. I've seen it happen many times. Animen do nothing but sulk without their wolves. They don't leave the village. They rarely leave their house."

"That sounds pretty sad," said Tau.

"I suppose so."

"How do you know when they come back?"

"Oh, I'll know. And only I will know."

"At least you know you will have him back."

"Yup."

"So, your wolves are obviously important."

"Yup."

"So then for the medallion, you could put wolves on it. Oh, and then you could have the moon too, since you get power from it."

"Yeah, I was thinking of something like that; couldn't quite put it together."

Tau started drawing shapes in the dirt with his finger. He started with a crescent moon, and then began drawing images of wolves howling at it. "See, maybe something like this."

Juran took a look at it. "I think you are on to something, Tau. It could use a little tweaking, but it's a pretty good idea. Hey Captain Ko, what do you think of…"

"Shhh," Captain Ko quieted them for a moment, sniffing the air and looking up to the trees. "Do you smell that?"

Juran leaned closer to Tau. "So why do we have to be quiet for a smell?"

"Seriously," said Captain Ko, then he tapped Captain Sec. "Wake up."

Gasat was sniffing too while he got to his feet. "He's right. The smell is strong now, and sudden. It's going to rain. Juran, with all your chit chat, did you tell your friend about the rain here?"

Tau felt a drop.

"Oh, right. We call it silent rain. It's as wet and annoying as any other rain with, well, one big difference."

"What is that?" Tau asked. "And why do you call it silent rain?"

Juran, looked at a couple of drops on his sleeve and said, "You're right Gasat, it is going to come in fast." He turned his attention back to Tau and spoke quickly. "We call it that because not only is the rain silent, but when it comes down you won't be able to hear anything; absolutely nothing at all. But don't worry; as soon as the rain stops, you'll be able to hear everything again."

The rain began to come down a little harder, and Tau could already see that Juran was right. All the noise around him seemed to get lower and lower by the second.

Captain Sec stood up and grabbed his sword, as did the other three guards. He walked over to Tau and Juran; his voice already becoming low enough that he shouted just to be heard. "No! I wasn't talking about the rain specifically. I was talking about what comes along with it!"

Juran's eyes widened as he stood up too, grabbing a firm grip on his staff. Even though he shouted as loud as he could, Tau could barely make out the words. By this time, he could almost hear nothing around him at all. Faintly he could make out what Juran was saying. "Crap! I forgot to tell you! When the rain comes so do the…" The rest of his words fell to silence.

Tau yelled back to him, "What?" He was more than amazed that he could not even hear the sound of his own voice. The rain was pouring upon them in full force, and Tau could not hear any of it. It was like no other rain he experienced before. Usually when the rain fell, he could hear it pounding on everything around him: a billion drops a second splattering down on everything below. Wherever he looked, everything around him was cloaked with an eerie silence that he had never….not-heard before.

There was no splashing sound of the rain hitting the leaves, no sounds made by animals nearby or in the distance, no sound of the hiss the rain made sizzling on the campfire. The only sound he could hear was the sound of the breath inside his lungs and his heartbeat. A few seconds later, he could not even hear that. And not hearing anything at all scared him.

Tau watched everyone around him begin to move defensively. He looked at Juran who was screaming something to him he could not hear. Juran was pointing at Tau's weapons intently with an imperative look on his face. He got the hint and armed himself.

Juran made a gesture that seemed to say, "Come stand next to me. Tau complied. What he wanted to do was ask what was wrong. Why was everyone panicking? But he understood that speaking was pointless. He looked into the eyes of the men and the rain pounding against their faces.

As the rain continued to drop upon them, the fire flickered out, leaving only darkness. Tau took a step closer to Juran, touching him, to make sure he was still there. Then, to Tau's surprise, a red light began to glow from Juran's staff. He could see the red crystal hovering a few inches from the staff. At least it provided *some* light.

Juran directed his light toward the ground all around them. He swept it from right to left, and then over to the bushes behind them.

When the lightning came, Tau got a second to see what was in the darkness, and then the lasting effects of the light blinded him for a few more seconds, more so than the darkness.

Juran kept sweeping the area with the light from his staff. Captain Ko moved around to the other side of Tau and grabbed his arm with one hand.

Then Juran's light swept to the right and Tau's eyes followed it. There, in the beam, he saw Captain Sec on the ground. Half of his leg was engulfed in some sort of huge worm. It was about 6 feet long and fat! It was round, with a thousand thick hairs all over it. The back of it was digging its way back into the ground, trying to pull Captain Sec along with it.

Sec was swinging his sword at the thing, chopping into it. His sword was covered with some slime-like goo coming from the monster. The other guards joined in, chopping at the back of the worm until it stopped moving. They pulled at Captain Sec, freeing his leg from it. He took only a second to recuperate before he jumped to his feet and the defensive line was formed again.

Tau was even more frightened than before. As the rain continued, he could still hear nothing. He anxiously looked all around him for something else that might come. He moved right and then left, swinging his weapons at nothing.

Then Juran's light went off, and Tau could feel him being torn from his side. There was complete darkness again. Tau moved to the ground to look for Juran, but only found his staff on the wet soil. He grabbed it and continued searching for Juran, fearing that he was being eaten by one of the monsters.

A flash of lightning lit the scene. For a quick second, Tau could see Juran, and he was right; both of Juran's legs were inside one of the things. Ekko was busy aiding him, tearing into the outside of the big worm with his teeth and claws. Tau saw another worm heading for Juran, and then everything went black again.

Tau stood up to run to Juran's aid. He moved quickly and tripped over something, tumbled to the ground, and lost all sense of direction. He suddenly could not tell where anyone or anything was. He called out to Juran, momentarily forgetting about the effects of the silent rain; the deafening of his own voice reminded him.

The rain was cold. He could feel it pounding against him. That, and his hands digging into the soaked soil were his only sensations; quickly both of those were trumped by fear. His eyes adjusted and he began to see faint edges of movement, but what was it? Was it Juran, was it Gasat, was it Captain Ko, or was it a monster? Should he swing at it and try to kill it? Was it coming to kill him? The uncertainty made him pause for a moment.

He started to crawl forward when another flash of lightning hit, and he was startled by a face only an inch from his. Ekko stood before him, looking a lot meaner than Tau remembered. His face was far more menacing, and his teeth, longer. Tau jumped backward. Then, in the darkness he could feel Ekko pulling at Juran's staff. Tau let go. He hoped to follow Ekko over to Juran, but Ekko moved away too swiftly and, again, Tau found himself alone and desperate to find his way.

Another flash of lightning allowed Tau to see Juran and Captain Ko chopping at a monster. But in that moment, he also saw more of the monsters surrounding them. Tau wanted to help, he wanted to save Juran, but his fear would not allow him to move.

Then, it hit him, like a switch suddenly went on inside of his head. It felt like he was back in his village, with his uncle, blindfolded, and swinging at wooden posts. He stood up. The next flash of lighting gave him enough information for this recollection to take its course.

He stepped to the right and swung his blade, slicing through the front end of one of the worms. Then he quickly stepped back to his original position and darted behind him to swing at another. In the darkness, he could feel his blade slicing through the flesh of the beast. Then again he moved back to his original position, before darting forward to attack a third worm.

He jumped forward with both of his blades while he landed in a crouched position, bringing his swords down in front of him, tearing right into the mouth of a monster. Leaving one blade in the thing, he raised the other one and tore into the beast three more times before he stopped slashing, and pulled both his blades back from the worm.

Tau jumped as Gasat grabbed him from behind and pulled him up to his feet. He frantically jumped up and down as he pointed in Juran's direction. He yelled out, "They've got Juran, they're eating him." But of course no sound came out of his mouth, and it was far too dark for Gasat to see where he was pointing.

Suddenly he saw a red spark flash in Juran's direction. He and the guard moved toward it. Another red spark flashed, and he saw Juran lying on the ground, hitting one of the monsters with his staff. With each contact, another bright red spark emitted from the crystal.

Tau did not have to tell the guard anything after that. They both rushed over to Juran's position, as did the other guards. They hacked away at the giant worm with their swords until Juran was able to get free. He stood up and saluted the guards. Then he once again let the beam of light flow from his staff. This time, it shone in all directions.

Tau saw movement in the ground, and Gasat began violently poking his sword into the dirt. The other guards joined in. Again, more movement in the ground seemed to warn Captain Sec that something was there, and he began stabbing into the soaking wet soil. The head of the monster poked out of the ground, and Captain Sec sliced its mouth off leaving the rest of its body flailing around in an uncontrolled fashion.

More of the monsters were coming from every direction. The guards lunged at the beasts, slashing and hacking away with their swords.

All of a sudden Tau felt himself being yanked by his leg. One of the things had him. He realized that the others did not see; they were too busy killing their own giant worms. The inside of the worm was soft and slimy, yet he could also feel that there were probably another thousand hairs inside of the monster's mouth, pulling him deeper into it.

The worm began burrowing back into the ground with its back end, and soon it had swallowed Tau all the way up to his chest. He screamed out as loud as he could. The pouring rain silenced him.

It was swallowing him up fast. The creature's mouth was soon covering him until even his head was inside. The horror of this thought, this feeling of being eaten alive, overpowered him. Tau reached out, so that only his hand emerged from the beast's mouth. He was enveloped in silence and blackness. He could not breathe. The inside of the creature smothered him. It was a good thing that Tau had plenty of practice at holding his breath. He felt the sliminess of wet hairs and tight muscles pulling him in further and further. It was disgusting.

Someone's hand gripped his tightly. Then another hand gripped his wrist. They were trying to save him. Perhaps he would not die in the mouth of this beast after all. He felt something thump against the side of the monster from the outside, then he remembered how they were stabbing and slicing at the other giant worms with their swords. He wanted to yell out, "Stop you fools, you'll end up chopping me up!"

They continued pulling at him. It felt like the more they tried to pull him out, the more the worm tightened its grip on him to pull him in. He feared that they would pull his shoulder right out of the socket.

He continued to feel the thumping from the outside, when he suddenly realized that his weapon was still in his hand. The creature's body was tight all around him. He could barely move. Still, he managed to jam his dagger upward and to move it from side to side from inside the monster. The more he dug his dagger into the beast, the looser the beast's grip became on him until his body was free enough to make huge slices in the thing. He cut the worm from the inside in all directions, any way that he could, until the beast stopped moving altogether. The next thing that he knew, he was sliding back out of the creature's mouth, pulled by two of the guards.

He took a huge deep breath, subsequently drawing fluids into his mouth. He hoped it was the rainwater and not the nasty slime-goo from the inside of the worm. Oddly enough, he was not as afraid anymore. He realized that he had saved himself from being eaten alive.

He looked over to see Ekko killing another one of the things. Not far from him, Juran was sacking another one with his staff. Soon, Tau was killing the monsters like the rest of the team. He hacked and slashed with his blades, aiding whoever looked as if they were in trouble. After a few more minutes the team stood in a circle with their backs to each other, poised and ready to kill any more monsters that came their way.

Tau stood there with a blade in each hand, Ko on his right, and Juran on his left. Juran's staff lit the scene while they waited for more attacks. Tau stood there in the silent pounding rain, breathing heavily until he noticed that once again he could hear his own heart beating and the faint sound of his breath moving in and out of his lungs. He looked at Juran in the dim red light who gave him a confident nod and a smile. He felt the rain slowing up more and more with each passing second. One of the guards moved across the ground and Tau could hear his footsteps.

Soon, the rain stopped completely. Tau could not only hear his breath clearly, but also everyone else's.

"They're gone," Gasat announced.

"You want to tell me what those things were now?" Tau said to Juran.

"Those? Yea, those are the marasuu. I probably should have told you about them before," he said, still panting.

"Anything else I need to know about this forest?"

"I'm pretty sure that's it."

"Okay..."

"But look at you, Tau; you sure can handle yourself in a battle!"

Tau took a moment to think about this. He HAD handled himself in battle, quite well actually. Without his even realizing it, his training all came back to him. He could hear the echo of Uncle's voice in his head saying, "I told you so."

"Will they be coming back?" Tau asked. Sure, he had handled himself well; that did not stop him from being scared of the things.

"They only come with the rain," said Gasat. "Let's hope that will be the only rain of the night. The clouds have already begun to roll away. The moon is shining through again. We should be fine. Of course, we'll be wet for the night."

"And our fire," Tau noticed, "There is no way we will get that started again."

Juran gave him a grin of self-pride. "Under normal circumstances, yes. But I can get it going again." Juran walked over to the doused logs that used to be their campfire. He turned his staff upside down and placed the head of it into them and closed his eyes. The red crystal, submerged down in between the wet wood, began to glow brighter, then dimmer, then brighter again. He squinted and frowned as if he were lifting something heavy.

Anticipating something wondrous and cool, Tau leaned in closer as the red glow lit Juran from below. A few sparks popped, but Juran's light soon dimmed to nothing.

"Don't worry," said Juran in between panted breaths, "I can do this." He looked up at the sky and trees above them. He looked for the moon and positioned himself under a clear beam of moonlight that made its way past the high leaves and branches above. "Give me a second."

He closed his eyes again, held on to his upside down staff with both hands, and shifted his feet. He looked up again to take one more look at the moon. The red crystal once again began to glow, getting brighter, then dimmer; the light pulsated under the wood, making sizzling and popping noises. Orange and red sparks flew off to the side until finally the wood burst into flames; the warm light shone on Tau's face, bringing about a smile of admiration. Juran pulled his staff from the fire, still breathing heavily. "See, no sweat."

"Wow," Tau said. "I didn't know you could do that."

"Not all of us can."

"Then why didn't you do that in the first place, when we started the fire before?"

"Because my father insists on me doing things the hard way sometimes." He stuck out is chest and imitated his father. "Trust me," he started in a deep voice, pointing his finger at Tau. "It's for your own good. Even though you can make fire, you should learn to build one like everyone else. You might not understand it now, but you will when you get older."

This all sounded terribly familiar to Tau. He figured that he would join in. "Ha, does he start into you with the..." Tau put both his fists on his hips, puffed out his chest and started in with a deep voice as well, "I've got life experience."

"Haha," Juran laughed. "Yeah, you've got it! LIFE EXPERIENCE, whatever that is. Adults are all the same: overly ridiculous." Juran took notice of the adult guards that were staring at him. "Except you guys; you guys are great!"

Gasat shook his head.

"Careful though Tau," Juran continued. "You don't want to get on Captain Ko or Captain Gasat's bad side. They are elite secret warriors."

"Is that true?" Tau asked.

"No," Gasat assured him.

"Oh, he has to say that, because it's a secret. They never admitted it, but I know. That's why the General keeps them so close."

"Never mind what he says," said Captain Ko. He is a delusional boy. Then again, I think all boys are delusional."

"You see Tau," said Juran. "To fight the Brood, a secret organization was founded with the best warriors. They are spies and they have secret skills. And when it is time, they are going to rise up and smash the Children of Montok!"

"Like Ko said, the boy is delusional," said Gasat. "Forget about this nonsense and let's focus on why we came."

*　　*　　*　　*　　*

They all lay in a circle around the camp. Two guards slept, while the other two lay pretending, ready to grab one of the little imps should they come their way. Ekko also lay not too far from his master, still, but alert. His attention was directed to the darkness beyond them with his keen senses on alert to all movements, sounds, and smells.

Everyone was decorated in trinkets and jewels, perfect bait for any imp thief that may come into the area during the night. Juran was fast asleep, not more than two feet from Tau, who could not sleep at all. He thought of home. He missed Uncle. He missed his friends too, even if they thought he was strange from time to time. This had been the most eventful few days of his life. It almost did not seem real. Back home, he could relieve stress with a good swim. He liked to dive as deep as he could. The tranquility of the water surrounding him always made him feel better. Here, in the forest, there was no way that was going to happen anytime soon.

He looked at Juran, sleeping quietly. How could he sleep, on this wet ground, with who knows how many giant worms living under it? He was amazed at how cool Juran was. He wished he were like him. Juran was not afraid to fight. But why should he be? He was a sorcerer, with great power. He had a pet wolf whose thoughts he could understand and a cool staff that he made fire with.

Tau nudged Juran lightly with his hand. "Hey, Juran, you awake?"

Juran said nothing.

Tau nudged him even harder, whispering even louder, "Hey, Juran."

"Huh?" Juran mumbled, coming out of his sleep.

"Are you awake?"

"No." Then Juran started as if an idea suddenly made him more alert. "Do you see an Imp?"

"No," Tau responded.

"Oh, then go back to sleep. They won't come if we're talking. Ekko will let me know if one comes around."

"Oh, okay." Tau was only silent for a few seconds before he started whispering again. "Hey, Juran."

"Yes?"

"I think your staff is pretty cool."

Juran let out a yawn as he said, "Thanks. All of my people have one," he said. "Different kinds and colors though."

"I think it's cool that you can start a fire."

"I'm still new at it so I couldn't get it the first time." He yawned again. "The moon's light helped."

"So you couldn't always do that?"

"No, only after our Sacred Union."

"What's that?"

"Well it is sort of when our minds start to become joined with our wolves." Juran spoke with his eyes still closed. "It is also around when our powers come. On the day of our Sacred Union, we get to see the full potential of our powers. But then after that we have to continue to train and practice to reach that potential."

"I get it."

"Good. Now go back to sleep."

Tau waited only a few moments before he spoke again, "Can I tell you a secret?"

"Sure."

"I can change into a leopard."

"Really?" Juran asked, suddenly paying more attention, with his eyes open.

"Yes."

"You mean like a shape shifter."

"Sure, if that's what you want to call it."

"Well, what do your people call it?"

"I don't know; I never met anyone else that can do it. Maybe I'm the only one."

"No, you're wrong about that. I have heard of them before."

"Are you sure?" Tau asked, both puzzled and excited. Then a terrible thought entered his head. "What if they are all dead and I AM the only one."

"Don't think that way Tau. It's pointless unless you have

facts on something like that."

"But I have never seen one and neither have you."

"Yes, but the absence of evidence is not the evidence of absence."

It took Tau a second to understand that one, but he got it. "You're right."

"Does it help you in a fight?"

"I think so, but I barely remember the last time."

"Why didn't you change while we were fighting the worms?"

"I've only done it three times, and I wasn't even trying to. I don't know how to control it. I probably need a Sacred Union or something like you have."

"Maybe you need someone that knows how to teach you. They are probably out there Tau, somewhere."

A wonderful calm swept over Tau. He rolled over to his back and closed his eyes. As he was falling asleep, he heard Juran, once again calling his name in a whisper.

"Hey, Tau."

"Yeah?"

"I think that being able to change into a leopard is pretty cool."

"Thanks."

"You're the first shape shifter that I have met. I would love to be able to do that."

Tau closed his eyes, smiled, and went to sleep.

XIII PORTALS

The imp did not come in the cover of the night, but in the early light, just as day broke. Only the two guards on duty were still awake. Even Ekko was already asleep. The imp slowly came down out of the tree and took a sniff of all that precious metal. He seemed unable to resist it. It sparkled ever so elegantly in the new-day's sunlight.

He was a small creature, less than two feet in height. He was thin and furry, resembling a small monkey the way he shifted from walking on two feet, then leaning down to all fours, whichever was more suitable at the time. His ears were long and pointy, like a fox, and both of them were pierced with several hooped earrings. He wore a shirt that was too small for him with four different brooches pinned upon it, two of them gold, and the other two silver.

On his long tail were a few gold bracelets that were incrusted with colorful crystals, as was a silver bracelet around one of his ankles. He tiptoed quietly through the camp, but Captain Ko saw him out squint eyes.

"There he is! Get him!" Ko shouted. With one quick movement he grabbed his net, lunged at the imp, and threw it over him. Everyone woke up. The imp struggled frantically and almost managed to get himself out of the net before another one was thrown over him. They held the net down at the ends, keeping the imp from escaping. Ekko darted towards the little thing, all the while growling.

"No, Ekko," Juran yelled. "Get back, no growling, get back." He held his arms out and told everyone to get back as well. "Hey little guy, we don't want to hurt you. Sorry if we scared you."

"No hurt, huh?" responded the imp sarcastically. "Wolf gonna eat me and why the net? Don't wanna hurt? Humph!"

"No, really, we don't want to hurt you."

"Then move net."

"If we move the net, then are you going to run away?"

The imp thought for a moment. "Hmmmmm, yes, probably. Better than be food for wolf."

"He won't eat you, I promise." Juran gestured with his hand. "Ekko, get back."

Ekko backed up a bit more.

"Me no people food either," the imp explained.

"We don't eat imp." Tau jumped in. "We only want to talk. We have our own food. Are you hungry, do you want some fruit?"

"Hmmm," said the imp. "Move net, give food."

"Okay," said Juran as he slowly went to pull the net off of the imp. "But don't run away, okay." He moved the net, and then reached his hand out behind him to the guards. "One of you guys have some fruit?"

Gasat put a half of a mango in his hand. Juran gave it to the imp who quickly snatched it away and backed himself up against a tree. Hey ate eagerly while frantically shifting his eyes from one person to the next.

"Now, talk," he said.

"We need you to take us somewhere," said Juran.

The imp sighed. "Should have known. Humans always want to go. That all humans ever want. Go here, go there. Where you want to go?"

Everyone looked at Tau. "Tell him." said Juran.

Tau timidly stepped forward. "Well, I get visions."

"Maybe you crazy," said the imp.

"It's strange. I see mountains in the distance across a marsh field. There are large patches of green everywhere sitting on top of water. The mountains are topped with snow, but I hear the words, White Forest."

"Come closer," the imp looked at Tau, seeming a bit intrigued as he gazed upon his skin.

Tau stepped up. "Ah, Amotekun," the imp said, enlightened. "White Forest, been before?"

"No," Tau replied. "And what's an Amo...?"

"Then where do you get vision?"

"I don't know."

"And what do I get?"

Tau began taking off his trinkets and placing them on the ground. "Look at all this that we have. You can have all of it. C'mon guys."

Everyone placed their gold, silver, and jewels on the ground. The imp watched them, until he noticed a certain sparkle in the sunlight. It was the small crystal vial that Tau wore around his neck with the water from the Whispering Pond.

"That," the imp pointed. "Want that."

"This?" Tau asked grabbing hold of the vial, pulling it to his chest. "I need this, you can't have this."

"That what me want."

"We've got all this stuff to give you," Juran reasoned. "Why do you want that?"

"Things you WANT to give, not so valuable. Things you no want to give, VERY valuable. I want it or no take to vision."

"But I need it," said Tau.

"Fine, keep it, stay here then. You give, you go."

Tau looked at Juran who hunched up his shoulders and shook his head. "Like I told you, always on their terms. Not a good idea to argue with them."

"Fine then," Tau took the vial and handed it to the imp. "So you will take us then?"

"I take you." The imp took a second to look at the jewelry on the ground. He pulled up a ring with two small purple jewels on top. "Me want this too. Look good on tail." He brought his tail around to the front of him and slid the ring on. "See! Okay, let's go. Make sure keep up, must run fast, will not wait.

They all started to follow him. "No, not taking all, only

taking him. Only Amotekun."

"What is Amotekun?" asked Tau.

"What?" exclaimed Juran, "We can't go with?"

"Nope, only one. Only him. Grey-skinned one."

"We meant for all of us to go!"

"Follow if you wish, will make sure you lost in trees. Many, many years to find way home."

"Sorry Tau, I guess you're on your own. But if the guy says no, then we can't come. Like he said, we could end up lost on the other side of the world."

"No time for goodbye. Time to go!" The little imp started to hurry off. Tau stood there for a second, confused. He looked at Juran.

"Go! Go! Go!" Juran shouted to him, gesturing forward. "Keep up with him! Don't lose him, whatever you do."

Tau darted off to follow the imp. "Bye!" he yelled out.

"We'll see each other again!" Juran shouted back.

Tau hurried to catch up with the imp. As he closed in, the imp ran to a tree with a trunk about two and a half feet wide. The imp looked back at Tau for a moment and winked before he suddenly disappeared into the tree. Tau was astonished. He ran up to the tree and noticed that the surface shimmered slightly like sunlight upon water. He gently placed his hand on it, and it went right through. He closed his eyes, held his breath, and went in.

The imp was not too far ahead. Tau could see him bouncing about on his two legs. Every once in a while, he scooted on all fours, and his long hairy thin body reminded Tau of a chimpanzee.

Tau kept his eye on the imp, so he did not lose him, while at the same time he did his best to check out this strange environment inside this tunnel. The tunnel was about six feet wide, easy to maneuver through. The walls consisted of mostly dark compacted dirt. There were vines here and there stretched across the walls, giving off a faint glow that lit up the tunnel. He could see branches weaving in and out of the walls all over the place. Or were they roots from trees? Were they underground? Tau could not figure it out. Of course he did not have time to stop and really think about it either. This little guy was moving fast!

They came to a fork were the tunnel split off in five different directions. The tree imp quickly took a turn and sped up. Tau started to fall behind.

"Must keep up, boy, if want to see White Mountains," the imp said.

Tau turned up his face and went faster.

They came to another fork in the road with four tunnels filled with eight or nine other little imps cheering them on. "Run, run, go, go," they yelled.

This was all a game to them, Tau thought to himself.

Suddenly the wall shimmered at a place that was shaped like an arched doorway. He could see light coming through it, and the landscape outside, a grassy plain. The imp went through the doorway and Tau followed. They were out doors, running across a field.

The imp turned back to Tau and teased him, smiling along the way as he bounced across the dry grass. "Keep up, keep up, must keep up!"

He ran straight toward a tree. It shimmered and then he ran inside it. Tau followed. They were inside again, with the same kind of tunnels as before, yet the dirt was a much lighter brown. They passed by more little imps along the way, cheering them on. "Go, go, run, run!"

The wall shimmered again and the imp once again went outside. This time they exited from a tree in the middle of a shallow pond. Tau fell trying to run through the water, but he did not waste time lying there. He got up and followed the imp to wherever they were headed.

It seemed like the imp was taking him on a scenic route around the world. Tau tried his best to keep up. The imp toyed with him, keeping him at a distance, again going back into the tunnels and then out once more. They ended up in a desert. There looked to be nothing around for miles. The sun was hot, blistering even. The imp laughed as he trotted up a sandy hill. Tau was having a hard time getting his footing in the loose sand. He tumbled before righting himself once again, continuing his pursuit.

Soon the imp disappeared over the top of the hill. Tau slipped in the sand after him and fell flat on his face, eating a mouth full of yellow hot granules. But he kept going. When he got to the top, he looked down to see the imp heading for another tree sitting solitary in the sand. The doorway started shimmering as usual and the imp entered, but by the time Tau got there the shimmering stopped. The portal was gone. Tau ran head first into the hard tree, which knocked him backward into the sand again.

"Aw!" he screamed in disgust with himself. "I missed it." He looked around at the open desert lying before him; nothing but him, the tree, the sand, and the sun. "Now I'm stuck out here. I could be thousands of miles from home."

The tree shimmered again. The imp stuck his head partially out and glared down at Tau. "Not going to get to where you going that way. Too slow, too slow. I leave you here in the Never Ending Sands maybe."

Tau looked up to see Chad standing next to him. "C'mon Tau," he said, pointing at the tree. "You going to let this little guy get the best of you? He's toying with you. Get up. Get up Tau and show this little guy what you've got."

Tau nodded. He got up, tossed his cloak to the ground, and ran fast toward the imp. "Here we go," the imp said ducking back into the tree. The imp took him across a snowy ravine, grassland, and a swamp. At one point he even saw another man chasing another imp down a tunnel coming from the opposite way. Tau did not have time to try to figure out where he was going.

Tau exited another portal. They were in a rain forest, high in a tree, seventy or eighty feet up. Tau came out on a large wide branch, totally disoriented from the height. He slipped and barely managed to grab on to the thick branch with his hands. As he dangled, he looked down to see the imp looking up at him from a branch below. He pulled himself up and rested for a second, breathing heavily, crouched on all fours.

"Haha," the imp chuckled, smiling with a pompous attitude. "Me better than you. You no got what it takes to see the White Forest. You no good at all." He started shaking his head. "Sorry, sorry, sorry, piece of man with grey skin. Leave you here in this forest, yes, I do that."

Tau was angry then, and tired of being toyed with and insulted by this little thing. Who was he, this imp, to judge him? He started breathing more heavily and deeply. He started to move across the branch when suddenly he heard the thud of something behind him and felt the large branch move under his feet. He turned around to see a gorilla three times his size.

The gorilla's eyes peered at him as it snarled, then suddenly it charged toward him. Tau turned and ran, quickly coming to the end of the branch, forcing him to jump to the next one. Then he jumped down to a branch under him, and the gorilla pursued.

Tau was scared. The thought of this animal ripping him apart ran through his mind. His fear consumed him to the point where he thought he would be sick. All he knew was that he needed to get away. He continued to run across the giant branches when he felt his body stretch and change shape. The leopard in him came out again. He ran toward the imp, through the trees, running from branch to branch while still evading the gorilla behind him.

"Oh my!" shouted the imp, and then he darted off.

Tau's speed as a leopard was an easy match for the imp. His newfound agility made it easy for him to follow the imp from branch to branch across the large trees of this forest. But Tau was tired of this game. He followed the imp back through a doorway and into the tunnels. The imp stopped against the wall, seemingly cornered. Tau lunged at the creature. The imp ducked, the doorway in the wall shimmered, and Tau went through. He landed, splashing down in several inches of water.

He rolled over in the water, all wet, and looked up to see the imp poking his head out of the tree.

"Haha." said the imp. "Me still got some moves!"

Tau's body returned to normal. "Quit toying with me you little monster! I have better things to do than to spend all day chasing after you!"

"You no have better things to do. You chase for purpose. Me make sure you belong where you go."

"I wish people would stop talking to me about purpose. I thought you could help me find the White Forest. If you can't help me, leave me alone."

The imp cocked his head to the side and pointed. "White Forest, there over mountains."

Tau rolled over and looked far across the field at the mountains against the horizon. "What? That's them over there? Are you sure?"

"Sure, I am sure; over mountains. Now I leave you."

"Wait, you're leaving?"

"Job done now. Bye bye, Amotekun."

Before Tau could say anything else, the imp was gone; it scurried back into the magical doorway of the tree. Tau started to go after him but relented, only placing his hand up to the tree. It was hard, normal; apparently the small moment in time that it functioned as a doorway had passed. Funny little thing, he thought to himself.

He turned back, looking at the snowcapped mountains behind him. He was alone again.

XIV "HI"

The water felt heavier with every step. It was just over a foot deep. The only thing that kept Tau moving was the snowcapped mountain range at the far end that never left his view. They were as he had seen them in his visions. He was focused on getting there. His anxiety fueled him. He thought of the little imp that had brought him there. It had toyed with him, but eventually it brought him to the right place.

Large patches of green lilies and grass floated on the surface of the water. Tau walked in between the patches of green, along the many paths that separated them. Progress felt extremely slow. For a while, he could not tell if he was getting closer to the mountains ahead of him at all. He wondered if this was some magical place where he could walk forever and ever and never get to his destination.

He also wondered about what terrible things could be lurking around under the surface of the water. He already had been tied up by a giant spider, and just yesterday, almost eaten alive by some monstrous worm. He did not want any surprises in this marsh. He spent a great deal of time looking into the water, pushing the plant life away as he walked; staring intently into the water that was too murky to see his feet.

His legs felt tired. Not only did it take great awkward effort to walk through all this water, but the soil at the bottom was soft. Time and time again, his feet sank deep into the mud. For every step, he overcame the earth's efforts to pull him under. He wanted to rest, but he did not. After several hours, he finally made his way to the edge of the wetlands.

He reached the base of the mountain in the early evening, with a few hours left until dusk, and started making his way up. He kept wondering how cold it would be at the top where the snow had blanketed the peaks. He certainly was not dressed for it, and he hated the cold. He wished he had not left his cloak.

He rested for a second and contemplated how cold it would be, and how hard the mountains would be to climb.

"Stop complaining," Chad said. "And keep moving."

Tau nodded and proceeded up the mountain, finding places to grab where he could and little paths here and there where he could walk. He began to hoist himself up to a ledge when he was disturbed.

"Hi," a squeaky high-pitched voice called to him in his left ear.

"What?" Tau said, startled. He turned to see a tiny white bird about an inch and a half in length, hovering above his shoulder. "Hey c'mon, you're going to make me fall."

The bird flapped its wings as fast as a bumblebee, hovering and moving from side to side.

"Hi," it said again.

"Hi, yes, great, a talking bird."

"Hi."

"Yes, hello, I hear you. If you don't mind, I'm trying to climb this mountain and it doesn't help with you buzzing around my head." Tau finally pulled himself up to the ledge.

The little bird followed.

"Hi."

"Is that all you can say?" Tau asked, moving his head from side to side, following the bird.

"Hi."

"Well, you're the lucky one, you've got wings, and you could probably fly up to the top. I have to do this the hard way." He stood up and began following a steep path upward.

"Have you been up there? Do you know what is on the other side?"

"Hi."

"Hmm, I'm not sure if that is a yes or a no."

At the end of the path, he was forced to climb again. The tips of his fingers stung and his forearms were so tired they felt as if they were about to burst. Then the little bird stopped flying, perched itself on Tau's shoulder and closed its eyes.

"Hey, are you sleeping?" Tau peered at the bird and took notice of the bird's chest heaving in and out. "You are sleeping! Humph, it figures."

He continued climbing, grunting as he spoke to himself, "Bird's got wings, but he sits on my shoulder while I do all the work. I still don't see why I'm the one out here climbing mountains, chasing imps through trees, and talking to birds that can only say one word. I bet Chega isn't climbing mountains right now. He's probably having a party, sipping on twilka berry juice, making googoo eyes at a girl that I helped him hook up with."

Then Tau noticed little snowflakes on the ground. With all the climbing he had not noticed the cold air at all. In fact, he was still as warm as before. He began to notice the color of everything around him. The little patches of grass were white. Then he noticed a few leaves bundled, caught by a rock, and they were white too.

He picked up one of the leaves and examined it. It was a dingy white with a black stem. He found another leaf. It was not white, but grey. It crumbled in his hand like a dead leaf. Then he realized that from a distance, this all looked like snow. But it wasn't snow. It was the grass, the plants, and the leaves. It was all white.

"Hey, this stuff isn't snow at all," he said to the bird. "It's foliage. That's why I'm not cold. It's not cold here."

"Hi." The bird woke up, yawning.

"Oh, you're awake now. Done with your nap? I've never seen foliage that's grey and white. It's usually green, or brown and orange. This is very odd."

"Hi hi!"

"That's two 'hi's'. Does that mean yes?"

"Hi."

"Okay, does that mean no?"

"Hi hi hi."

"I'm so confused. But you're a cute bird. Come on, let's go."

"Hi."

It took about 2 more hours for him to reach the top of the mountain; the little bird following him the whole way. He stood up and looked out across the land he had crossed. It was beautiful and the sun was setting in the distance.

He could see so much of the world from there, almost as if he was seeing all of it. He could see forests, rivers, grasslands, and other mountains. The longer he stood there, the more these elements of the earth seemed to take form on a spiritual level. "Orishas," he whispered under his breath.

He felt a strange connection, and he thought he could see each of the spirits of God. There was Shango, in a dark cloud far away with lightning bolts flashing though it. There was Oshumare, in a rainbow set over the hills. There was Osain, the Orisha of the forest. There was Oko of the harvest, Oya of the winds, Oshun of the rivers, love, and beauty, and Obatala, the father of all human kind; they were all there before him. It seemed like he saw all of the Orisha's except Yemoja, mother of the sea. He could not see her at all, but he also could not see the ocean.

For a brief moment, Tau experienced a kismet sensation, though it was most unlike him to think of anything in terms of destiny; especially regarding himself. He took in the view. The bird still sat on his shoulder as if it was enjoying the view along with him. He turned and looked at the other side of the mountain, where he was headed, and there he saw the dense white forest.

Still shining in the diminishing sunlight, it was spectacular. The entire forest was encircled by a mountain range. The leaves on the trees were white, forming almost a complete canopy over whatever lay beneath. Their trunks and branches, like the leaves he had found, were perfectly black. Everything in the forest looked to be painted in black and white. A hawk circled overhead, completely black on top, and the underside, all white.

"I would have to guess that this is the white forest. This is where I need to be!"

He looked down the side of the mountain.

"It's a long way down. I'm too tired, and the sun has almost gone. What do you say we camp here tonight and make our way down in the morning?"

The bird hopped off his shoulder and began flying again. "Hi."

"Of course, I'll be doing all the work. There are enough branches and twigs up here to start a fire."

Striking fire rocks together provided enough sparks to get some kindling of dry grey dead grass burning. He added more twigs and wood until it grew, then sat back against a rock and stared into the ever-changing flames for a while.

He looked above him, at the sky and the stars that blinked on one by one as the sun fell below the horizon. Soon there were millions sparkling above his head. A half-moon sat against this twinkling background, giving light to the peaks and a faint glow to the white trees below him. All along the little bird stayed with him.

"I'm going to have to give you a name if you're going to keep hanging around. "

The bird sat on his hand while he lightly stroked its back with his finger.

"I thought about calling you, 'Hi hi,' but that seems a bit too easy and frankly it sounds stupid. What about Wingy? Yeah, I think that works. I think I'll call you Wingy."

Wingy flapped his wings for a moment. "Hi."

"First thing we have to do tomorrow, Wingy, is find some food. I'm so hungry. Don't worry; I'm not putting bird on my menu. Besides, I doubt a little thing like you would fill me up."

Wingy suddenly jumped up, "Hi Hi,"

"Oh, I'm sorry, I was saying I'm NOT going to eat you."

"Hi." The bird flew off.

"Wingy! No, I'm sorry. Is it the name? I can call you something else if you want!"

Wingy was gone.

"Great, now I'm alone again. Not that I was really with anyone. I've been talking to a bird. And now I'm talking to myself. I don't know which is worse."

Tau sat there for a while waiting for Wingy to come back, turning the wood in the fire, hoping that he had enough for the night.

Wingy came back and dropped a small bunch of white grape-like fruit right before him.

"Oh, you went to get food."

"Hi."

"Thank you so much." Tau began eating the fruit. Wingy flew off again. Before long he was back with more, and then off again. Ten times he went out into the darkness and came back with more fruit for Tau to eat. It was not enough to fill his belly, but it was enough for the moment.

Before long, Tau fell asleep. His dreams recapped the journey so far: his uncle rushing him from the village, that terrible looking spider, Anansi, the music wielders, and the Red Barrier City.

He awoke suddenly during the night. He looked at the fire still burning. Its color seemed much more pale than usual. Beyond it, he saw three sets of eyes peering at him. They looked like they belonged to large cats of some sort.

He jumped up quickly, turning around to grab his weapon. When he turned back, the animals were gone.

A dream? He wondered. "Wingy, did you see them?" Wingy, however, was perched on a nearby rock, fast asleep.

Tau walked around the fire, shaking. His eyes and head

moved in all directions, looking for the animals. He saw nothing, not even tracks. "It must have been a dream," he said to himself, "so why are you shaking?"

With no luck at finding anything, he sat down again next to the rock. He could not calm himself enough to fall asleep. For the next hour, he kept getting up and walking around his camp, looking for something that was ready to eat him. Every sound caught his attention. It was not until day break that the sun lit the peaks enough for his fears to subside.

Little Wingy awoke as soon as the warm sunlight hit his body, flapping his wings and flying off of the rock. Yet Tau was just falling back to sleep. He did not fully awake until mid-day.

"I see you're awake," Tau said.

"Hi."

Tau kicked dirt onto what remained of his smoldering campfire. "Well," he said to Wingy, "looks like I slept most of the day. I should really be getting on with my journey. You coming with?"

"Hi."

"Yeah. That's what I thought."

Going down this side of the mountain was much easier than climbing up had been. There were paths and level plains for him to walk on. For most of the way he could walk by foot instead of clinging to the side of the wall like he did for much of the time on his way up. He found more pathways to lead him down to the bottom. All the while, he marveled at the size and the beauty of the white forest. The tree trunks were ten, twenty, even thirty feet thick it seemed. White, black, and grey vines twisted around them. The white leaves flourished from all the numerous large branches that protruded from the trunks.

The trees twisted up high into the sky and caught beautiful rays of sunlight bouncing off the white leaves and leaking through the gaps. So many fruits were new to him, yet there were some he would have recognized had it not been for their color.

All of them were covered with different designs of white, black, and grey.

He took notice of a banana tree with pure white bananas. With his blades, he quickly climbed it and plucked one from its bunch. He sat in the tree, peeled the banana and ate it. He listened to the sounds of the insects and the animals around. He was not scared at all; he was calm, at peace. After two more bananas and another forty minutes of enjoying the scenery, he climbed down again.

As he walked, he noticed distinct paths. It was apparent that someone traveled there, and often. Before long, Wingy joined him again, flying over and perching himself on Tau's shoulder. Tau began to see man-made objects: a wheelbarrow, a cart with a broken wheel, a bird-house, and artwork stretched from one tree to another hanging above him. Finally he came to a very large tree with a stairway that wrapped around the trunk as it went up.

"Maybe this is it, Wingy."

"Hi," Wingy responded.

"Yeah, I know, hi. You've got my back if something goes wrong, right?"

Wingy said nothing.

"Oh, it's like that now, is it?"

He started walking forward when he saw movement off the right of his peripheral vision. He snapped his head in that direction to see a white leopard with black spots sitting before him.

"Okay, maybe not," he said as his heart began racing. He stepped backward and saw more movement. Another leopard slowly walked toward him and then sat down. Tau froze and looked around. Another leopard came, and then another. Soon, in every direction, leopards surrounded him. They all sat about thirty feet from him, looking.

Tau slowly grabbed both of his blades. "Wingy, remember that part about having my back? I think now would be a good time."

Wingy hopped off of his shoulder and began buzzing frantically around his head.

"Hi, hi hi hi hi hi hi." he said over and over again.

"Shhh." Tau tried to calm him. "That's not what I meant."

The leopards slowly moved in a little closer. Most of them stopped at about twenty feet away from him, but one continued to approach him. It walked around him, sizing him up. Tau did not know what to do. If he tried to attack it, surely the others would waste no time tearing him apart, making him dinner. And it was probably way too late to play dead, not that that would work with any wild cat anyway; he would still be dinner. But they had not eaten him yet, so his best chance seemed to be not to anger or frighten them into mauling him to death.

Slowly, very slowly Tau knelt on the ground. He placed his blade on the ground also, trying very hard to control his fear and his heavy breathing. As the leopard continued to walk around him even closer, it touched its nose to Tau's skin, sniffing at him all over. Every inch of Tau's body was trembling. The leopard came around to his face and stared him in the eyes. Tau wanted no confrontation with the animal so he put his head down and closed his eyes, trying not to cry.

Several moments passed while Tau feared his demise, and then he felt the oddest thing. The leopard put its paw on his shoulder. Tau opened his eyes to find that he was no longer staring at a leopard, but at a woman. She was standing above him, bending over slightly to bring her hand to his shoulder.

"Who are you?" the woman asked, not in a particularly inviting tone.

Tau looked at her but did not answer. She was dressed in some sort of white, two-piece skin garment. It did not cover her arms, nor her stomach, and only came half way down her thighs with a slit on the left side. She wore a black sash of sorts around her waist and sheathed on each side were blades shaped just like the ones he had. Her face was beautiful yet strong. Her eyes looked upon him with interest. Her body was perfectly fit as an athlete, or a warrior. And her skin, her skin was as dark grey as his!

Tau's fears gave way to immense curiosity. "You're like me!" Tau shouted as he lunged toward her and put his arm around her. The other leopards started to dart toward her, until she put her hands up to stop them.

"It's all right," she yelled to them. "I don't think he is here to hurt us."

Tau released his grasp from around her. "Hurt you? Why would I hurt you?"

"Who are you?" the woman asked again. "How did you get here? Where do you come from?"

"I think….I come from here."

"Hmmm?" she responded in a low tone.

"My name is Tau. I have traveled very far to get here."

"From where? How far have you traveled, boy?"

"From Makazi, a small village, ma'am, on the other side of the world, not far from Ufalme."

"Ufalme?" she said. "That is far. How long has the journey taken you? How did you get here? Who else knows that we are here?"

"I didn't walk the whole way. I traveled throughout the secret trees of the tree imps."

"Tree imps?"

"Yes, and no one knows that you are here. I didn't even know that you were here!"

Tau had not noticed the change, but as he looked around, he saw that all of the rest of the leopards had taken human form. The men and women pressed in closer to him, curious, but seemingly no longer threatened by Tau. A very fit man approached him. In fact, all of them looked to be in great shape.

"Tau, did you say?" the man asked.

"Yes, sir. Tau Zaire."

My name is Kato, and the woman you have been talking to is Kamaria, my twin sister. Of those of us that are left, she is in charge. I'm out ranked by a simple ten minutes of life. Tell me, how is it that you have come to know of this place? How did you know to come here?"

"It is very hard to explain, but something called me here. I've been having visions. Visions of the White Forest, and these snow covered mountains that surround it."

"What you see is not snow."

"Now I know, but before, in my visions, I thought it was snow."

"So you have come to discover where you came from?" Kamaria asked.

"I came to make the visions stop, because they are painful. But if this is where I am from, then I have come for that too."

Kamaria and Kato looked at each other for a moment.

"So, is this where I am from?"

"It would appear so," said Kato. "Tell me Tau, who are your parents?"

"I don't know my real parents; I was found by a man when I was a baby, and raised by him."

"What about the others?" asked Kamaria, sounding urgent. "Have you seen them? More of our kind?"

"No, ma'am, I've never seen anyone like me before, not until now. You are the first of my kind that I have ever seen."

Kamaria put her hands on either side of Tau's head, staring into his eyes. She tightened her grip on him and said very firmly as if she was trying to make him tell the truth, "Who sent you? Where are they?"

"I don't know what you mean! Where is who?"

Kato quickly moved between them, grabbing her arm. "He does not know. Calm yourself. Anger will not get the answers we need. Kamaria, the boy has never seen anyone of his kind before," he said to her in a calm yet intent manner.

Kamaria seemed briefly upset. Without a word, she yanked her arm from his grasp and walked away from the group.

"Don't worry," said Kato. "Her actions have nothing to do with you. There is much going on here that you do not yet know about." He kept his gaze on Kamaria as she walked away. For a moment, he was lost in thought, and then he broke his own silence. "For now, let us welcome you to our home in The White Forest. We call it, The Amotekun City. We are the Tribe of Leopards."

"The Tribe of Leopards," Tau repeated. "Amotekun? The imp used that word. What is it?"

"It is us. We are also known as Amotekuns."

"And I am one of you?"

Kato gave a smile. "I am corrected then. Welcome home."

XV HOME

Tau met the rest of the tribe and was taken on a tour of this beautiful forest they inhabited. It all appeared well managed, as if they took great pride in their landscaping. The bushes were nicely cut and shaped. Many distinct paths led in different directions throughout the plants and the grass of the village, some trailing off, twisting and turning beyond where he could see, while others were short trails that ended at vegetable patches or stopped right at the door of one of their huts. The huts blended well with the rest of the forest. They were made from vines and sticks that were packed tightly together. Most of the huts were round, with domed roofs and wicker doors decorated by different cloths.

Some trails led to stairways that twisted around huge trees as they went up. High above them, there were bridges connecting one great tree to another, and many of these were hidden from the ground by the white leaves of the trees. Decorations of wire, stick, vine, and cloth stretched high across the paths between the trees in different pleasant artsy fashions.

Tau even came upon a patch of mimicking plants; their only difference from the ones he had seen before was their white flukes, black stems, and white leaves. He, of course, took the liberty of playing with the plants as Juran had showed him. First he got one to mimic him, and then he watched as all the rest joined in. He liked those plants. He would be sure to bring some back to his village when he went back.

He marveled at the taste of a particular black fruit, tasty indeed, yet not quite as tasty as a twilka berry. Still, he took it upon himself to eat three large ones. He would have thought that a place where everything was black, white, and grey would look terribly dismal, but it did not. It was as beautiful as any place he had seen with plentiful bright colors. It was so beautiful that it did not seem real.

"How is it that everything here is without color?" he asked Kato.

"Why is the sky blue, or the grass green elsewhere? It is simply their nature. As it is our nature to have grey skin."

"My skin was not always grey. It was brown like everyone else's. Well everyone outside of here. It would only turn grey when I got sick. I think people were afraid of me because of it."

"It was not their fault. People are afraid of what they do not understand. It is in our nature as humans. As far as your skin not being grey before, I have heard that tends to happen to children that grow up outside the forest."

"You mean the children that grow up here are grey all the time?"

"Yes. By the time they are a month old. And so is that why you left? Because the people feared you?"

"Yes, that and a boy died. He drowned in water. They blamed his death on me, and then I turned into a leopard right in front of them."

"Oh my, I'm sorry to hear about the boy."

"He was my best friend."

"Why did you turn? Did you want to frighten them?"

"I didn't want to, it just happened. I cannot control it."

"You cannot control when you change?"

"No, I have done it, but I don't know how."

"Well, we will have to fix that, won't we! No point in having the power to shift and not be able to control it. Give it a try."

A quick white mist suddenly formed around Kato as he changed his shape from man to leopard.

"Wow," Tau said, astonished.

Kato ran out ahead of them off of the path about thirty meters, and then turned around to look at Tau. The white mist wrapped around him as he changed back to a man. "Come," he yelled.

Tau closed his eyes tight as the others watched him. He strained with all his might, but nothing happened. He sighed, disgusted with himself. "I can't!" he yelled back.

"Try again." Kato yelled.

Tau tried again, this time harder. He tried to remember how he saw himself before as he ran as a leopard with his view down low, seeing his legs and paws stretch out in front of him. Again, nothing happened.

Kato changed to a leopard and ran toward him before changing back again. "I see you straining as hard as you can."

"Yes, very hard, but it doesn't work."

"Perhaps because you are focused on your muscles. It is not your muscles that change you, but that part deep down inside you that no one else in the world has."

"What part is that?"

"Oh, I'm afraid that is not something I can simply spell out, for you have nothing to relate it to. But it is inside you, and it is that which will control your shifting. You have done it before."

"Yes, but as I said, I don't know how."

"Well, how did it happen before?"

"The first time, I don't even remember. I was chasing a boar, or it was chasing me, I'm not sure. The second time, there was a mob in my village that was after me; they were all trying to get me. The third time, I was away from the village and some men were after me, trying to capture me. And the Fourth time was just yesterday, I was trying to follow a tree imp. We were in this thick forest, high in the trees and out of nowhere, I saw this huge gorilla, not far from me at all. It came at me, and as I fled, I changed."

"Hmmm, so all the times that you recall, you were fleeing?"

"Yes."

"Frightened?"

"Not simply frightened. Scared for my life."

"Well, then we may have something."

"You mean I...."

Kato jumped and pointed at the ground with a terrifying look on his face, "SNAKE! It's going to kill you!"

Tau jumped back in terror. "What? Where?" He peered all over the ground in search of the thing. "I don't see it!"

Kato chucked. "I'm sorry, I'm sorry. It was necessary. There is no snake. Haha."

Tau clenched his hand upon chest; his heart was beating so hard he thought it would break right through his ribs. "Why would you do that?"

"Oh, come now, young Tau, I was testing a theory."

"So what are you saying? I have to be afraid to change. I don't like that theory at all."

"It is not the fear that causes you to change. But it was the fear that has connected you to the part of you that does. I'd like to try some things to get you to change and when you do, focus on that connection, it is very important. Focus on that feeling that happens deep inside you when you change. Once you can pinpoint that feeling, you will be able to pull from it whenever you want.

Tau felt something terrible in the pit of his stomach. "I'm not going to like this, am I?"

Kato grinned at him," Probably not."

* * *

Tau could not see anything. His body trembled with apprehension.

"Stay put," Kato said to him from a distance. "Don't move unless I say."

But Tau's anxiety was getting the best of him. He slowly

reached his hand up to move the blindfold enough to get a peek.

"Don't touch it!" Kato yelled to him.

Tau jumped and put his hands back to his side. From what he could tell, Kato was not close to him; at least twenty or more yards away by the sound of his voice. What was Kato doing? The few minutes he stood there felt like hours. He waited and tried to imagine what could be in store for him.

Soon, he heard a light rumbling. It was getting louder. No, it was getting CLOSER.

"Now, boy! Pull the blindfold off!"

Tau did not hesitate. He yanked the blindfold off as quickly as he could, and there, before him, he saw the source of that rumbling; a huge white ox with jet-black horns was heading his way. Tau froze with fear, as the large animal came closer to him, gaining speed, and getting so much bigger in his view.

"Do something, boy! Don't stand there!" yelled one of the men standing nearby.

Fortunately, Tau's instincts took over and commanded his feet to move. He turned around, opposite the ox, and ran. Tau was afraid, and this time, like before, he was afraid for his life. Surely, he made friends of these people, and they would not let this beast trample him to death; but "surely," meant nothing in this moment. All his brain knew was that he needed to get away. He needed to get away or he would die!

The other's watched closely as Tau ran for his life. Then, he changed. He became aware of a glowing white mist surrounding him, and in an instant, he changed to his leopard form. The ox gained speed, but Tau gained even more. He ran alongside the fence, quickly putting distance between himself and the ox.

Everyone cheered with hoots and hollers. "That a boy, Tau! You've got it now!"

Kato, pulled on a rope connected to the ox and slowed its pace until it came to a halt. "Come, Tau. Come back!"

Tau heard Kato's words and saw that the ox had stopped

chasing him. He ran back to Kato and spoke. At least he tried to speak, but nothing came out but a cat-roar.

"Now change back."

Tau looked at Kato curiously. He wanted to ask how, but again, only the sounds of a leopard came out. After a few moments, he was wrapped in that glowing mist and back to his human form. "That thing almost killed me!"

"Yes," Kato said with a grin, putting his arm around Tau's shoulder. "But it didn't. And you changed."

"Yes, I did change, didn't I?"

"And you will find that changing to a human will be much easier than changing to a cat."

"But why is that?"

"You have been a human your whole life, so you already know what it is like. It is easy to get back to that familiar place."

"But I couldn't speak."

"No, not in your cat form, you can no more speak than any other leopard."

"So, you guys.., we, can't talk to each other when we change?"

"We don't talk, but we communicate. You will understand soon enough. Now, can you do it again? Did you focus on that feeling like I told you?"

"Focus on what feeling? I was focused on not getting killed!"

"The whole point, my boy, was for you to understand that part inside you that makes you change. If you didn't do it, then you know what that means."

Tau sighed. Unfortunately, he knew exactly what that meant.

Tau was still scared, staring into the darkness of the black blindfold.

"Don't worry, Tau." He heard Chad speaking to him. "At least you know what to expect this time. At least you know that it will be an ox and Kato has it tied to a rope. He'll neve· let it trample you to death. This time, it will be easier. Remember, focus on the feeling."

Tau nodded to Chad's words. They comforted him a bit. He waited to hear Kato's call to take the blindfold off. Tau already knew his plan: "Okay, when I take it off, don't even wait for the ox to get close, turn and start running. Then when I change, focus on the feeling." He repeated it back to himself over and over while he waited. He wanted to do it right this time and not have to go through this silly ordeal of almost getting trampled again. This time he would be ready.

This time, however, the rumbling noise was more vigorous and louder than been before. Tau could feel the vibrations moving through his body. Did Kato forget to tell him to take the blindfold off? He reached his hand up to take a quick peak.

"Wait!" Kato yelled, "Wait…wait…wait…NOW! Take it off!"

Tau took it off. This time, the ox was much closer, almost on top of him. And there was not only one, there were four! Their feet kicked up a cloud of dust as they dug into the dirt. Their faces looked fierce, as if they possessed a personal grudge against him. Tau did not wait. He took off running and like before, he changed.

The crowd roared, "You did it again, Tau!"

He looked over to the fence where he saw Chad sitting with his thumbs up. Tau smiled.

They pulled on the ropes once more to slow the oxen, while Tau ran to the end of the fence and then back toward them. This time he changed in mid run and came to Kato.

"Yes!" I did it again! Did you see!"

"Haha!" laughed Kato. "Yes, we all saw. Now, can you do it again?"

"I could try."

"The feeling boy, did you focus on the feeling? If not, we've got many more oxen!"

"No, no." Tau answered quickly. "I felt it, and I remember."

"Good. Now concentrate on that feeling. Remember, it's not a muscle that does it."

Tau replayed what had happened in his head. He was blindfolded. He was all ready to see one ox, but then there were four. He turned and ran for his life, and then this odd sensation from within him occurred.

"We're waiting, boy."

"Give me a minute," he pleaded.

He closed his eyes again and shuffled his feet on the ground. That feeling. It was as if something fierce yet simple bubbled within him, an instinct that he could not quite describe. It encompassed him from the inside out. He was not remembering the sensation; he was actually feeling it again. He opened his eyes and found himself on all fours. He looked at his front paws, then turned and looked at his body, all white and covered with black spots. He had done it again, without any fear this time. He looked at Kato and growled.

Kato and two other men changed as well. Kato gave him a look. Although Kato said nothing, Tau seemed to understand what he wanted. "Follow us," a message came to him, not in words, but as a simple understanding. The leopards raced away, and Tau followed. They raced through the thick of the forest avoiding the pathways, through and around bushes, jumping over logs and large rocks. Tau followed. They raced across a stream, over a small hill, and used their great claws to climb a tree. Tau followed.

When they changed back to men, so did Tau.

"C'mon Tau, you're doing great!" They ran halfway across a bridge and then changed back again to leopards. It took Tau a little time to remember again, and the bridge swaying high in the treetops did not help his concentration.

Still a human, he kept running, to the other side and when he got to the end, he paused. "Remember the feeling, remember the feeling," he said to himself until once again, he changed.

Tau saw Kato, halfway down the tree already, looking back at him. Tau felt another instinctive communication coming from Kato, "Hurry up."

Tau hurried after them and continued using his cat body to run across the forest. He liked this feeling. He liked being this animal, so strong and so swift. His senses were working better than ever before. His vision was not only better, but also quicker. His eyes were able to sense the terrain ahead of him. He could better smell the aroma of the forest, the trees, the grass, and the flowers. His hearing too was more acute; he could hear the wind in his ears and the footsteps of those running ahead of him. He could pinpoint the location of their steps, even before seeing their bodies.

He could even hear a rabbit or a squirrel or something rustling in the grass behind him. He turned to look, and realized that it was no squirrel at all. It was another leopard. The leopard pounced upon him. He lost his footing and went sliding across the ground, rolling over and over. He lay there on the ground with dust hovering around him to see a leopard walking up to him. It was Kamaria. He did not know how he knew, but he knew.

She changed right before him and stood there with a smug grin on her face. "You should be more careful to pay attention to your surroundings. If I were someone else, you could have been killed."

Tau changed back into human form and cowered in front of her. She waited for him to speak, only to hear nothing. What could he say? What the heck is the matter with you? He thought of saying that, but did not think it would go over very well. Kato and the others ran over to them and changed back to their human form.

"Kamaria!" said Kato, with obvious reservations about her actions. "Why?"

Good, Tau thought, someone is sticking up for me.

"If the boy wants to be one of us, he must learn to fight like one of us." Kamaria said, seemingly determined to provoke something.

"He IS one of us."

"Then let him prove it." Kamaria pulled out her blades and stared Tau in the eye. Her feet shifted over the ground, changing and readying her balance.

"Must he do it now? Let the boy eat and rest first. Perhaps tomorrow, we will learn of his fighting skills."

Kamaria began to slowly circle around Tau. "Battle does not wait for you to eat, or rest. Battle takes you as you are."

Tau saw Kamaria's body and attitude. He listened to the sound of her words, and knew that she was going to strike at him.

Kato asked, "Can you fight, boy?"

Tau hesitated, "Yes." He said yes, but did not want to fight.

"Then ready your blades," said Kato.

"But...." Tau protested.

"I said ready your blades!"

Reluctantly, Tau pulled out his blades, one in each hand. He looked at Kato, and then over to Kamaria who looked at him as if he were prey.

"And if you are not ready," Kamaria continued, "the battle will not only take you, but it will send all those around you to their deaths!" She swung her blade down toward Tau. He brought his blade up to meet hers and the clank of the metal echoed throughout the forest. White, black, and grey birds fled from their trees, taking to the air. The sound of the fluttering wings caught Tau's attention. When he turned his head back, his face was met with an elbow. Kamaria immediately followed that with a blow to his gut from the hilt of her blade.

"Okay," Tau coughed, "stop! I don't want to hit a girl."

Kato put his face in his hands and shook his head. "Dear boy, you really should not have said that."

An angered and insulted Kamaria went to work on him. She swung her blade with hard blows; the kind that tired Tau's arms every time he blocked them. She kicked him and punched him. He blocked many of her blows, but the few that got through, hurt! He went on the offensive, swinging and punching, lunging at her. She was quick to move, block, and parry.

Kato finally stopped the fight, moving between them.

"Okay, the boy has had enough." He approached Kamaria, and gently grabbed both of her arms. "Does he really need to go through this?"

"When it comes down to it, dear brother, this boy may end up getting us killed. He is not up to the fight. You will be the one picking up his slack. Now unhand me."

Kato let her arms go, "Sometimes you go too far, sister."

Kamaria looked him in the eye with disgust. She whipped her blades down at the ground. Both of them stuck firmly into the soil. She gave Tau one last look of disapproval, then walked away.

Kato helped Tau to his feet. Tau was breathing heavily, still frightened of her.

"Are you all right?" Kato asked.

"You mean, besides the pain and humiliation?"

"Heh, yeah, besides that."

"I guess I'm okay." He wiped a small amount of blood from his face. "Why doesn't she like me?"

"Oh, it's not you Tau. Trust me, it's not you. Like I said,

there are things going on here that you do not yet know about."

"Maybe if I knew, then I would understand why she hates me."

"Let's just get you cleaned up, and then you should rest. Dinner will be in a couple hours. Then, we can tell you more about what has happened here.

They walked for a moment before a smirk ran across Kato's face. "You want to hear something funny, Tau?"

"Sure."

"My mother was the only person to call Kamaria by her second name, *Aweena*. Do you know what that means?"

"No. What?"

"Gentle."

Tau laughed, trying hard to limit the movement of his aching chest and stomach muscles. "Never would have guessed that in a million years...."

XVI DINNER

The sun was going down when Kato led Tau up a spiraling wooden stairway that circled around one of the huge trees near the center of the forest. The doorway into the hollow trunk was covered by a series of long blankets draped in front of it, which they pushed aside to enter a spacious room. The walls inside the tree were light gray, yet it was the abundance of color that first touched Tau's senses. The interior was decorated by several cloths of colorful linen and painted wooden sculptures placed along the edges of the room. Tau sat down on a thin square beanbag in front of a large mesab, a handmade wicker table with the base made in the shape of an hourglass. The round top was covered with a large dome. This table was big enough for five people to sit around comfortably, and there were 10 mesabs spread throughout the room.

Candles lit the area, placed in hollowed out sections of the wall and lined with dark fireproof clay. Eight metal towers, five feet tall, were placed evenly, with flat tops where larger fires burned, not from candles, but from a mixture of wooden chips covered in fire sap that allowed a large flame to burn for hours.

Ten women holding large pitchers of water and a metal bowl entered the room, one to each table. One of them leaned over to Tau with an inviting smile. "Your hands," she said. Tau held his hands out over the metal bowl, and she poured soothing warm water over them for cleaning. The water only bathed his hands, but he could feel the pleasant sensation moving up his arms and throughout his body. The metal bowl underneath captured the excess run-off water.

The domes of the mesab tables were lifted and a thin layer of flat unleavened bread was unrolled across most of the surface. Finally food and drink was brought to the table. There were a variety of dishes, not served on plates, but placed in separate piles all over the thin bread. There were 8 different kinds with different colors, all with inviting aromas, which triggered Tau's salivary glands to work in excess. He was ready to eat.

The dishes were various mixtures of beans, meats, and vegetables, all cooked with exotic spices. "Careful of that red one and that yellow one," said a man next to him. "They are very spicy! Personally, I love them, but they may be too much for you the first time."

Tau nodded.

"There is so much color in here," Tau said, grabbing a piece of bread and picking up food with it."

"Ha, nothing is ever simply black and white, my friend, said Kato."

"Are you liking the food, Tau?" asked Taj, sitting at the same table.

"Yes, it is very good. I want to try everything!"

"Feel free. Is this place much different from your home?"

"Very different! Yes, this is very good."

"Will you be staying with us then?"

"I don't know. I'd like to go home. But things aren't the same there. I do miss my Uncle though. And I miss Chad."

"Is this Chad a friend of yours?" asked Kato.

Tau's eyes dropped to the floor. "He was."

"You are welcome to stay or leave as you please."

"It is so far though. And I feel like I have come for a purpose, like I am supposed to do something."

"It could be that you are supposed to learn where you are from. And you have."

"I guess so."

"Perhaps tomorrow, we will continue to give you some training. Soon you will be able to change as fast and as easily as we do."

"I would like that. It's wonderful to be able to use this power.

I want to be able to control it. Um...where is Kamaria?" Everyone he met in the Amotekun City was in the room eating, except for her.

"She is around somewhere," Kato replied. "She has been in a saddened state of mind for quite some time now."

"Why?"

The air in the room stiffened. People began shifting in their seats and looking around uncomfortably. It was obvious that everyone's mood had changed.

"She lost someone very close to her and it haunts her every day."

"Oh."

The room was silent for a while more. Tau diverted his attention to the crackling sound of the fires upon the metal towers.

"Tau," said Kato. "Here there are twenty-six of us. I don't know if you can tell, but this forest supports far more than that. A year ago, our numbers were more than a hundred."

"What happened to them?"

"All we know for sure is that they have been taken. We don't know where or why."

"That's horrible."

"Yes, it is," said Taj. "All of our attempts to find them have failed. Footprints were the only sign of them; footprints that led into the sea.

"Yet these boats must have been massive. They usually take thirty or more of us at a time. Those of us that you see now were not here the last time they came. We were still out searching. That was three months ago," said Kato.

"Were they large in numbers? You could not defeat them with a hundred people?"

"They brought with them a demon. A demon in the shape of a large man, seven feet tall, but made out of crystal. His eyes glowed with a white-blue fire, even during the day. And they were cold. I could feel the coldness as it stood right in front of me. It felt like it was sucking the energy right out of my body. There was also something terrible about this creature that took our power away."

"You couldn't change?"

"Not only that, but our essence of being. We were weak. Our strength and agility was nothing near what it normally is. No, we didn't stand a chance."

"Who were the people that took them?"

"They are the Brood, but a faction that I have never seen before. The red painted design on their black masks, necks, hands, and clothing.... I'll never forget it."

"The Brood! They also came to my village, the day I left."

"So then you do know of them."

"Oh, yes. So what will you do now?"

"We don't know."

"Next time they come, we will go with them!" Kamaria said sternly as she entered. She brought tension into the room as everyone again stopped eating.

Kato stood up. "Go with them? What do you mean?"

"I mean, brother, that it seems that the only way we will find our people, is if they take us to them."

"That doesn't make any sense."

"We have looked for them and found nothing. This is the only course of action that will lead us to our people. The next time they come, we will put up a fight. But in the end, we will let them take us."

"But Kamaria, it's..."

"I have spoken. My decision is final!" She began to walk out.

"And if they are all dead?"

Kamaria stopped for a moment, but said nothing.

Kato got up from the table and walked over to her. "Kamaria, you are making rash decisions for all of us. Why do you continue to act as if you are the only one who has lost someone?"

"And why do you continue to act as though you have lost nothing? Perhaps you have already found a suitable replacement."

"What does that mean?"

"I see the way you have warmed up to the boy. This Tau," she said pointing in Tau's direction without even looking. "He is not your son. Your son is gone, with the others."

There was a moment of awkward silence as everyone looked at Tau. Kamaria walked out of the room. Kato returned to the table.

"Is everything alright?" Tau asked.

"No, Tau," Kato said calmly. "Although I wish it were. I am glad to welcome you. But it appears that this may not have been the best time for you to have come home. Eat."

"I don't think I am hungry anymore." Tau suddenly felt like the center of attention. The pressure of every eye in the room pressed in on him. He slowly stood up from the table. "I think I'll go outside for a while."

"Tau."

He heard Kato call in a soft voice, as if he was going to stop him from leaving. But he did not.

Tau exited the room and looked down over the wooden railing in time to see Kamaria descending at the end of the staircase. He did not like her. She walked with a proud, stern, straight back, as if she was better than everyone else. Her attitude offended him.

"Don't be so hard on her, Tau," he heard Chad say.

"Look at her," Tau replied. "Who does she think she is?"

"Think about it, Tau. These people have had more than half of their village taken away from them. Not only has she lost someone dear to her, but she probably feels responsible in some way."

"You may be right, Chad. And now, she's got the weight of

an entire people's future on her."

"I bet you somewhere in there, Kamaria's got a heart, just like the rest of us."

Tau followed her down the stairs and across the forest. She disappeared behind a stand of trees, and he hurried to catch up. For a few moments he could not find her. In the night, the White Forest emitted a glow from the reflected light of the moon. Many of the white leaves and flowers reflected an orange light from the various fires. Under the moon, he saw her on top of a small mountain. The moon was bright, hanging in the air right behind her, creating the most beautiful silhouette of her kneeling on the ground. Tau wondered how she had gotten up there so fast.

He was making his way up the terrain when her method came to him. She had changed! Tau closed his eyes and focused, managing to change after a short time. Not short enough for him. He wanted to learn to do it instantly, like the others did. He looked forward to further training tomorrow with Kato. At the moment though, he could use his leopard form to tackle this terrain more efficiently.

He scaled it with ease, jumping from hill to rock, his agile body making way across the uneven surfaces upward to the top. In the distance, he saw Kamaria. She was singing, looking out to the sky. The melody was soft. It sounded somewhat sad, or maybe it was the quiver in her voice. Was she crying? Tau changed back to his human form and moved in closer; too close.

Kamaria stopped singing. "Who's there?" she yelled and changed into a leopard, ready to defend herself.

"Um, it's me," said Tau.

She growled and then changed back to her human self. "What are you doing sneaking around? Do you want to get killed?"

"No, ma'am, really I don't."

"Then why are you bothering me?"

All of a sudden, Tau did not know. Why had he come up

here after her? It was not as if they were getting along or anything. She always seemed as if she would bite his head off at any second. But part of him wanted to make some sort of connection with this woman.

"I agree with you," he said. "About going with them next time they come to take you."

"That's surprising. I don't think your new friend Kato is in agreement at all."

"That's understandable too. He doesn't want the whole tribe to die. And I understand you lost someone. This may be the best way to find out where they are."

"What do you know about loss, boy?"

"I lost my best friend. And I'm so far away from home that it is possible that I'll never return."

"Then you plan on staying? Do you think you are one of us?"

"I AM one of you."

"When it comes down to it, will you fight for us?"

"I'm still here, aren't I? I will do what is necessary."

She walked over closer to him and stared deeply into his eyes. "We will see."

Then she left.

XVII DORO

The sleeping chambers varied. Some were huts on the ground. Others were structures built high above, connected to or carved into the trees; smaller versions of the dining hall. Since the abductions, all the inhabitants of the White Forest slept in the latter. They were the most hidden; best fortified, and could fit the largest number of people at once.

No one dared to sleep alone anymore. Tau was put in a room with Taj, Kato, and a few of the other men to keep him safe. Besides, it was obvious that he and Kato were connecting, as Kamaria so plainly pointed out.

The night was calm. The White Forest was filled with the familiar sounds of crickets, birds, owls, and various other non-threatening wildlife making their chirps and calls to each other. The only actual bad sound was Taj, who made the most horrific snoring sound whenever he rolled onto his back.

Most of the people awoke with the rising of the sun. Their breakfast consisted of a light meal of fruit and hot grain and everyone drank two cups of water as soon as they woke up. They walked through the forest picking the fruit right from the branches. Tau turned to having that nice white fruit he ate the day before. He would have loved to take some of the seeds back to his village, if he ever went home, but Kato told him that they would not grow anywhere else.

Kamaria seemed to be a bit nicer that morning than she had been before. However, she did not actually say anything pleasant directly to Tau. There was no, "Good morning Tau, how was your sleep?" or anything like that. But she also did not make it a point to be mean either. Tau understood what Kato meant about it not being about him. Kamaria isolated herself from everyone. She often walked alone.

It was time for Tau to continue his training, and he was looking forward to learning. He was not only looking forward to learning to control leopard abilities better; he also wanted to learn how to fight. It was odd. He had never wanted to learn how to fight before. He regretted trying to ignore all the lessons that Uncle tried to teach him over the years. Now, there was a spark that went off inside of him that told him that he needed to learn. He still did not think of himself as a fighter, yet when he had fought the worms during the silent rain, he realized that somewhere inside of him there was a warrior. Maybe Uncle taught him something after all.

Unfortunately, that day, his skills would not be sharpened by training, but in actual battle, for the Brood's army pressed in.

Kamaria felt it first. She walked up the mountainside in her leopard form in an attempt to be alone, when unintentionally she changed back into her human form. Every attempt she made to shape shift back to an animal failed, and then she realized it had to be the demon. She remembered the feeling from the first time they came. No one was able to shift, and those that were already in leopard form were forced back into being human. She ran to Kato and the others as the army was closing in. "They are here!"

"I know," said Kato, "I see them. Come, Tau, stay close to me."

All of the leopard tribe had gathered to be spectators of Tau's training. They moved close together and watched as the army approached.

"Scatter!" Kamaria commanded.

And they did. Many of them ran in different directions up the trees, ropes, and stairs, already showing signs of the demon's proximity. Tau was feeling fatigued, and he realized that the others must all be feeling it too. A few of them stayed on the ground with Kamaria and Kato.

A man with a shaved head led the army. He was dressed differently than the soldiers. He carried a short staff with a skull on top. He wore ropes made of bone that crisscrossed his torso and a long cloth cape on his back.

Behind the leader was the demon, exactly as Kato had described. He was huge, robust. His body, arms, and legs were much thicker than that of a normal man. He was made up entirely of a light blue crystal with bright points of light at his joints. The demon had no feet. A ball of light blue flame sat at the bottom of his legs and though he barely left any tracks, a loud thump could be heard when he walked.

Twenty men from the Brood army rushed past the bald man and the demon to attack. The leopard tribesman on the ground met them with their blades. It was all so sudden; swords and metal clashed, echoing through the forest.

The tribe blew darts from the trees while the Brood's army shot arrows back up at them. Then, from all directions, about twenty more of the Brood's army suddenly appeared and joined in the attack. Normally the Leopard Tribe was swift and evasive, but their efforts were slow, and lacking their full capabilities. They became even slower as they tired.

The man with the skull on his staff did nothing but watch. He and the demon stood still while the rest of the troops went to work.

Kamaria seemed to have more strength than any of them. She fought off three men at a time, killing them. The Brood still came, swinging with their swords.

Kato killed a man, but was wounded in the process. Tau went over to him to help.

"No, boy, save yourself."

The Brood Army was winning, capturing the leopard people one after another in nets and tying them up. Kamaria came to Kato's aid.

"You see, brother, as I thought. They are more interested in capturing us than killing us."

"Perhaps," said Kato.

Tau was standing with his blades in hand next to them, ready to ward off two guards closing in to apprehend Kato. Kato pulled Tau down to the ground to keep him from fighting. Kamaria stepped in front. She held her blades high, breathing heavily, and engaged the two guards.

It was not long until most of the tribe were captured and bound. The bald man with the staff grinned and came closer with the demon, as if to enjoy the show.

Kamaria was the last one standing, still fighting.

"Kamaria, give it up," said Kato.

"Not yet."

Another guard approached her. It took all of her might, but she blocked his attacks and sent him crashing to the ground.

"That is enough," said the bald man with the staff. "I can't have you killing off ALL my guards, even if I do enjoy the entertainment."

Kamaria turned to him defensively and raised her blades. "I could kill you next. Then we would all be entertained."

"I don't think so," said the man.

He raised his short staff. In the eyes of the skull were diamonds which started to glow. A white energy beam came from it, engulfing Kamaria. This beam seemed to weaken her even more than simply being in the presence of the demon. She fell to her knees.

"That's better," the man with the staff said, walking over to her.

"Who are you?" she asked, struggling. "What do you want?"

The man looked around, watching his army round up the Leopard Tribe. He smiled.

"I am called Hatari. And what I want is all of YOU."

"What have you done with my people?" she asked while having her hands bound.

"That is a question that I promise will be answered."

"I should have killed you first!"

The demon reacted to this threat; he stepped forward and leaned close to her face.

"Don't touch her," yelled Kato.

Kamaria looked at the Demon.

"I'd like to introduce you to Doro," said Hatari. "He has very unique abilities."

"You have stolen our powers with this Demon."

"Very smart. Much easier this way. Get them up."

All twenty-seven of them were tied to a long rope. All of their weapons were taken away from them and left behind. The Army walked them single file through the forest with Kamaria at the head.

"By doing this, you have sealed your grave," she said to Hatari as she walked past him.

Hatari smiled.

The group walked to the edge of the mountain and up one of the easier trails. Kato and Tau were tied nine people back from Kamaria.

"I hope she knows what she's doing," Tau whispered to Kato.

"I hope so too," Kato replied.

They were halfway up the mountain on a thin ledge. There was barely enough room for some of the Brood men to walk beside their prisoners to keep them in check.

Then it happened again, that terrible piercing noise inside Tau's head. He had thought that he was done with these painful episodes. He had made it to the White Forest, what else was there? What did it want? Then he remembered that he had given the vial away to that stupid imp, which meant that he did not have a way of stopping it this time!

He fell to the ground, disturbing everyone in the line.

"What is wrong with him?" one of the guards asked.

"I don't know," said Kato.

"Get up, boy!" the guard said, kicking Tau as he rolled on

the ground. "Playing around won't save you!"

Tau did not respond to him. He barely even heard him. Instead, he rolled right off of the cliff. Everyone connected to him on the rope was yanked. They tried to pull him back, but his thrashing around worked against them.

"Cut him loose!" someone said, "or he's going to pull everyone over!"

They cut his rope and tried to pull him up again, but Tau slipped down the mountain, onto the cliff below.

Kato screamed as he saw Tau fall. He turned toward the guard, rammed his head into his chest and pinned him against the rock behind. Another guard came and pounded Kato on his back, knocked him to the ground, and followed up with another blow to his back, then three more to his face.

Hatari came to their position. "What has happened here?"

"The young one, my Lord, he went crazy and almost pulled the others over. We cut him loose."

Everyone looked at Tau lying on the ground; still.

"Go and see if he is alive," Hatari told one of the guards.

They waited as the man made his way down to Tau to check and see if he was breathing, or if his heart was still beating. The man looked up at Hatari and shook his head. "Dead sir!"

Gasps were heard from The Tribe, especially from Kato. He looked up at Kamaria with the look of, "this is your fault!" Kamaria said nothing.

"If he is dead, he is of no use. Let's go," commanded Hatari.

The man checking on Tau caught up to them as they continued to ascend the mountain. They made it to the top, and then back down the other side, leaving behind the lifeless body of Tau.

XVIII FACES

"Wake up, Tau." He vaguely heard Chad calling to him. "Come on, Tau, wake up."

He thought he saw Chad standing over him. He quickly sat up, snapping out of his sleep. Chad was not there.

A wave of dizziness washed over him and a searing pain rushed to his head, causing him to fall back to the ground. He looked up to the ledge he had fallen from, vaguely remembering his episode that took him over the edge. The stinging pain all over his body reminded him of the impact of the fall.

Wingy buzzed erratically around his head, back and forth. Then Tau suddenly remembered everything that had happened. They came, as Kamaria had said they would. They came and they took everyone away. He stood up, still off balance, again feeling dizzy, and found himself falling against a nearby rocky wall. He took another moment to let his strength return to his body and his vision return to normal. He looked back at the wall of the cliff and then made his way up to the place he had fallen from to look for tracks.

"Wingy, did you see them? Did you see which way they went?"

"Hi hi," Wingy said, buzzing around in his usual manner.

It did not matter. So many of the Brood had come, and so many members of the tribe had been taken, that their tracks were easy to find. The ground where they had walked was tremendously trampled and disturbed.

When he found them, would he be without his weapons, he wondered as his hand reached down to grab his blade that was not there. The Brood had collected all of them from the Tribe and left them in the village. He was sure that sooner or later he would need his. He ran back to the village and found it void of people, as he had expected, but part of him was hoping someone would be there. He looked at the array of weapons lying on the ground, swords, knives, spears, and many curved blades similar to his. After finding his own, he sheathed them and headed back toward the side of the cliff were he had last seen his people.

He followed their tracks up the side of the mountain, to the top.

From there, he could see the vastness of the ocean. "Yemoja!" he said. "You are beautiful." He decided that he must be on the other side from where he originally came in.

He followed the tracks down the mountain and further as the ground turned to sand. All the tracks lead into the ocean. They had obviously traveled by boat. How was he supposed to follow them across the ocean?

Why had he been brought here? Why did he have the visions? Was it so he could see the last of his people taken off? It did not make sense. Once again, he was alone. Once again, he was the only one of his kind. He balled his fists in anger and knelt on the coarse wet sand. The waves barely lapped onto his legs before they receded out again.

And then, once more, it happened; that sound that he hated. He knew he should not have given that vial to the little Imp. Because of it, he had no way of dealing with this pain. However, to his surprise, it did not hurt. He felt a slight ringing in his ears, but it was not painful. And this time, he could feel something pulling him back toward the mountain, back toward the White Forest behind it. Again he saw a vision, but not one of white-capped mountains. This one was of a strange, large hole in the ground, lined with black vines and branches with added specks of white that went down into it. It was all black and white, like the forest. He quickly got himself up. Why he was being called back to the forest; especially since everyone was gone?

The ringing in his ears stopped, and so did the vision and the sensation that something was pulling him. Great, he thought, now when I want the vision to stay, it goes away. He focused hard to keep the memory of what it looked like. He climbed up the mountain and back down the other side, making his way back into the forest, with Wingy keeping him company the whole time.

Suddenly, Wingy flew off ahead of them. He started flying in a small circle all the while yelling, "hi hi hi hi hi," over and over again. Tau got the impression that Wingy wanted him to follow. So he did, running after the bird. Wingy flew away again. It was hard for Tau to keep up; he jumped over and around logs and dodged in and out of trees.

Perhaps he was running too fast, for all of a sudden he ran right up to an extremely large hole in the ground. He almost fell over into it, but at the last second, he reached over and grabbed onto one of the black branches that went down into it. It was the hole he had seen in his vision. It seemed much bigger, at least fifty feet across. Or maybe it seemed bigger because he had almost tumbled into it.

He lowered himself and hung at the side of the hole, looking down. The hole was so deep that he could not see the bottom. The outer edge was lined with black branches that went down into the unknown darkness. The branches were so densely packed together that he could not even see the color of the ground or rock behind them.

Now what? he thought to himself.

He again saw Wingy, who gently landed on Tau's shoulder.

"You again! Thanks very much for NOT warning me about the hole. I almost fell right into it."

"Hi."

"So, if you knew to bring me to this hole, do you know where I go from here? Or was it a coincidence? Hurry up. My arms are getting tired. It's either back up, or further down."

The bird said nothing.

"Okay, back up then."

As he started to climb up, Wingy hopped off of his shoulder and began to fly down lower into the giant hole.

Tau sighed. "How did I know that you were going to do that?"

Tau followed the bird farther down. Then, when the bird flew around to the other side, Tau followed. He climbed around the hole, shifting sideways from vine-to-vine and branch-to-branch. Soon, Wingy once again sat upon his shoulder.

"Don't tell me you are tired. I'm the one hanging on for dear life in a hole that I can't even see the bottom of. Look, I thought you were showing me where I'm supposed to go. I thought you were..."

Tau felt a breeze hitting his face. It was not coming from above or below him; it was coming from behind the branches somewhere in front of him. He reached his hand through; there was no wall behind. "Wingy, you're a genius!" He smiled at the little bird.

Tau anxiously began pushing the branches and vines aside to reveal a cavern. With a bit of effort, he swung himself inside. The room was made from carefully placed square rocks of mostly the same size that were fashioned together in a precise manner, showing careful craftsmanship. It was not a very large room, only about twenty feet wide, eight feet high, and forty feet deep. Tau pushed more branches and vines aside in order to allow more sunlight into the dark room. The walls also had markings on them. He could read the word Amotekun amongst various other scribbles he thought to be of the *first tongue*. Simple images caught his eye of outlined men. In the middle of them was the image of a leopard sitting, and facing forward.

Tau walked up to the image of the leopard and rubbed his hands across the etched drawings, wiping dirt from the wall. He looked to the floor and noticed paw print impressions in the rock; they started way back at the entrance and went all the way up to the wall in front of him, directly under the image of the leopard.

He took some time to clean all of the dirt packed into these impressions on the floor. They were single tracks, as if one leopard actually had left them long ago. Then he noticed that one of the tracks was cut off at the wall. The rest must go under it, he thought. It was then that he realized that there was a doorway of stone, a doorway for leopards!

It took him a while and some concentration, but he managed to change shape into his leopard form. It still felt odd to him to be walking on four legs. He walked over to the track impressions in the ground and matched them exactly with his own paws. When he got to the wall, a small door opened large enough for a leopard to comfortably walk through.

The door led to a dark tunnel. When Tau stepped inside, vines of light attached to the walls suddenly became illuminated. At first, he thought this was another thing that he had not seen before. Then he remembered being in the tunnels of the tree imps, where there were vines like these. He was so busy chasing the imp that he had barely noticed them.

As Tau began moving through the tunnel, he looked behind him and noticed that Wingy was no longer following. Then the door slid down shut. I guess it is just me then, Tau thought.

He continued down the tunnel until it opened up into another chamber. It was smaller than the first room, yet made out of the same dark brick. This room was circular, with many drawings etched into the walls like the other one. In the center stood a two-foot high round stone stoop, and sitting on top of that was a stone sculpture of a leopard. The head of the leopard was stretched upward; its mouth was hollow, as were the eyes.

The room was lit softly by more of those strange vines that stretched their way across the ceiling. Tau walked around the room in his leopard form a few times. It seemed to be a dead end. But if it was, then what was he supposed to do? Finally, he transformed and stood as a human.

"Hello!" he called out. "I'm here! Is this what you wanted?

Is this where I need to be? Well, I have come. Now what is it that you want with me?"

Suddenly, he felt a small rumbling throughout the room. The ground shook, sending vibrations through his feet and up his whole body. Small bits of dirt and sand fell from the cracks of the brick ceiling. The light from the vines dimmed to almost nothing. Tau's heart began to quicken with fear. Frantically, he looked all around him, and then he saw some of the writings on the wall light up. One after another the glyphs all around the room lit up and then dimmed. Tau hesitated as the luminous vines went dark until the room was almost pitch black inside. Then a white light lit up the eyes of the stone leopard on the stoop. Light came out of the leopard's mouth as well, until all of a sudden something emerged from the mouth of the statue.

It was like shiny metal water. A six foot stream of a substance that looked like silver water all lit up from the inside was moving around the room, circling. It made the strangest noise that sounded like a snake hissing from underwater. Tau did not know what to do. He did not know if it was friend or foe, but it certainly held his attention.

He took a deep breath and tried his best to dig up whatever courage he had inside. Finally he spoke. "Is it you? Are you the one that summoned me?"

The thing floated around the room, and then slowly came right toward him. It stopped about two feet from his face. The tail end of it got shorter, making the front end of it much bigger. Then the shiny liquid metal formed the face of a man. It did not stop at one face, it continually changed its shape into another face, and then another. The faces were of different men and women all with the same shiny liquid metal quality.

It spoke, in not one voice, but many. Some of them men, some of them women, some of them children, some of them spoken in a whisper, but all the time speaking in unison. The voice also spoke the words "I" and "we" simultaneously.

"Yes," the voice said, "I/we have summoned you here, to this temple. We/I stopped your heart in order to save you from being taken by the Brood."

"I was dead?"

"Not dead."

"Are you one person, or different people?"

"One and many are yet the same. Your mind is not capable of understanding the differences." The face once again stretched out to a long thick pool, moved around behind Tau, and then formed into a face again. Tau did not feel as if his question had been answered at all.

"Well, who are you?"

"We/I are/am the Keeper(s)."

"The Keepers of what?"

"We/I are/am the Keeper(s) of the power of the Shape Shifters. Keeper(s) of the Leopard Tribe. It is because of me/us that you exist."

"Then you should know that the Leopard Tribe is no more. They have all been taken except me."

"We/I are/am aware of what has happened to the Tribe of Leopards."

"Then what about me? Why am I here?"

"You have been chosen to save them. It is why you have been summoned."

"Me? I can't save anyone; I'm one person! I am not even a warrior. If you need someone to catch a fish, I'm your man, but I can't save anybody. I couldn't even save Chad. You've chosen the wrong person. You would have been better off choosing Kamaria, or Kato or...."

"No, we/I have chosen correctly. If you do not save them, then no one will. It is why you were born."

"Wait...why I was born? Did you know that all of this would happen way back when I was born?"

The faces continued to change and the voices spoke as if it

was cycling through several people. "Then, now, and what will be is all the same. I/we know it as one."

"That's a lot of stuff," Tau said under his breath. "Then you must be pretty powerful. Why don't you save them? You could do it!"

"I/We am/are the Keeper(s)."

"Does that mean you can't save them, or you won't save them?"

"I/We am/are the Keepers(s).

"So what now, then?"

The liquid stretched out to a different spot and then began forming faces again. "On the night of tomorrow, a red star will appear. You must go to the sands at the base of the mountain. Travel south until you see the rock that shouldn't stand, yet does. From there, you shall swim out to the sea until your image covers the red star's reflection in the water. It will be a very long swim. Once you have done so, you must swim down into The Deep until you can't anymore."

"What?" Tau said, feeling a bit confused and aggravated. "Keep on swimming down? That is suicide!"

"It is what must be done to save your people." With that, the faces stopped and the liquid metal thing stretched out, circled the room once more, and then disappeared back into the mouth of the stone leopard. A second later, the vines on the ceiling lit up again.

"What!" Tau shouted in anger. "That's it? I don't get any special weapons or anything? Hello?"

There was no answer.

*   *   *   *   *

THE ROCK THAT SHOULDN'T STAND, YET IT DOES.
Tau played the Keepers words over and over and over

again as he walked along the shore. He also mocked them, "on the night of tomorrow." Who talks like that? "We are the Keepers." How is that a way to answer my question?

The wet sand, close to the incoming waves, was easier to walk upon than the rippling loose dry sand, which sucked at his feet and made them slip with every step. At least the wet sand was firm.

The night was clear. The stars were numerous, but he could already see the big red star that the Keepers had spoken about. It hung in the sky like it *wanted* to be found. He knew he had to find the rock.

He was terribly concerned for his new friends. He already started to think of them as family. He even missed Kamaria, as stern and unpleasant as she was. It was his focus on all of them that kept him going through the night to find this strange rock.

He began to think that he might have missed it. But when he finally came upon it, there was no mistaking this giant boulder sticking out of the ground. It was rectangular shaped, reaching the height of about sixty feet. It looked as though it was oddly balanced on the tip of one of the corners, as if at any second, it would fall over. Perhaps they chose the right name for it after all.

He walked over to the rock, and looked at the red star above. Now, it was time to swim out there. It still did not make sense to him, swimming to the reflection of a star in the ocean. But he had seen a lot of things that did not make sense lately. He was finding out that there was a lot about Madunia that he had not known, and even more that he did not understand. Maybe this was one of those times when he should listen and trust. Besides, why would the Keepers lie to him? From what they had said, their purpose was the security of the Leopard Tribe.

He dove into the water, swimming straight in line with the rock and the star. He kept a good pace, as not to tire himself out. It was a good thing too, for he swam for about two hours before he actually found himself moving atop the star's reflection in the water. Okay, so they were right so far. He reached his hand up, pooling a small bit of water in it, and, to his surprise, he saw the reflection of the red star as if he was holding it. He looked around, treading water for a while, but there was nothing but deep, dark, ocean as far as his eyes could see. He was not afraid of drowning; he was a sea-man. However, he was concerned that he might become something's late night snack, so he decided not to waste any more time hanging around.

He took one deep breath, and dove into the water. Down he went, hardly able to see a thing. The light from the moon penetrated the surface only enough to give the water a slight glow. Even that was fading as he went deeper. He could only go so much further before he gave up, desperately heading to the surface for a breath of air.

"There is nothing here!" he screamed out in a rage. There was so much emptiness around him that no echo returned, his loud voice carried away by the sea. "Why would you send me out here? Does it amuse you to watch us die?" He lay on his back for a moment, catching his breath. "Chad I'm sorry! I can't do it. There is nothing here! You died for nothing!" he yelled out into the empty night.

He kept still, floating on the water, staring at the red star directly above him. "I should go to sleep, right here. I should end it. I'm tired of this. I give up. I'll let go and drown, like you did, Chad. I deserve it. Uncle, Uncle, I failed. I don't know what I am doing. They have sent me here to die. I'm sorry Uncle.

"Deeper." The voices came to him. "You must go deeper."

"Deeper?" he yelled. "There is nothing down there!"

He did not get a reply. "Fine! Is that what you want? You want to watch me kill myself? Will that make you happy?" He continued to yell as he splashed his hands against the water in disgust. "But if I die, and Chad's not there, I'm going to be really upset! You hear me! REALLY...UP...SET!"

Okay, he told himself, this time I'm going down, and I'm not coming up. I will leave my fate to Yemoja, queen of the ocean. You can do it, Tau. No one in the village can hold their breath as long as you and no one can dive as deep. Now DIVE!

He took numerous deep breaths, forcing the air in and out of his lungs. Finally he took one last huge breath of air and dove back into the sea. He headed straight down into the blackness, taking the strongest strokes that he could. He could feel the water pressure building in his ears until they started to hurt. He squeezed his nose with his fingers and blew into it to compensate, feeling the relief of the pressure equalizing within him. Before long, the water was too dark to see anything. Not even a faint glow. He couldn't even see his arms and hands as he swam. He hoped that his brain was correct in telling him which way was down, but there was no way he could be sure. He continued to move through complete blackness. The water became colder, even heavier. He could feel its pressure and weight all around him. Fear overwhelmed him. He knew that this was the place where he was going to die. He thought of Chad, and how horrible it must have felt to drown. As the pressure in his chest grew, he knew that he would soon know exactly what it was like.

Then, he noticed that he could see his hands. He thought he was imagining it. He waved them in front of his face to be sure. Yes, he could see, barely. Somewhere, there was a light. It came from in front of him, deeper down. He had to go deeper. He started to run out of breath, but the light... something was there. He must get to it. He was struggling against his lungs. They wanted air. He felt the worst tightening sensation in his chest that he had ever felt in his life. His lungs felt like they were about to burst; they burned. This was deeper than they ever had been before and they had had enough. His lungs convulsed, trying to force him to breathe. He fought hard against them as he began a fight with his body. With every second his body jerked, and his lungs clenched trying to force a breath. It was terribly painful. Terror struck through his body. He was not going to make it. This must have been what Chad went through. Maybe this was how Tau was supposed to die for letting Chad go. He was never going to reach the light. It was too far. He reached for it. He was a strong swimmer, but his body was past its limit.

"Yemoja, is that you?"

He felt the terrible burn of water entering his lungs. Then the light faded as Tau closed his eyes and passed out.

LEOPARD SPOTS ARE CALLED
ROSETTES

XIX NYAMI

NYAMI

"How far is the tunnel now?" General Jelani turned his head slightly to allow one of his maidens to pick his hair while asking one of his diggers the question. They stood next to a hole being tunneled beneath the Red Barrier. The man was short, brawny and covered with dirt. The scratches and abrasions all over him were probably from his mistreatment and scraping up against the rocks in the soil. His voice was the opposite of his appearance; frail, not as in weak, but more in the way of timid, as if the man had no backbone.

"We have gone over two hundred yards, General."

"And still, the barrier continues?"

"Yes, we assume that it is one big sphere. It does continue all the way underground. By the angle, I would say that there is as much underground as there is above it."

The General scratched the hair on his short goatee under his delightful grin. "Let us leave the assumptions to someone else. I want this tunnel to go completely to the other side. Then, I want you to start another one to cross it. I want these tunnels to be big enough to send some machines down there and room for people to work them."

"It will take some time, sir."

"Time is something that we do have, my friend. Make it happen."

"Will do, sir." The digger bowed to him, then turned to speak to his own men about continuing the work.

"Now then," the General directed his attention to a messenger woman standing by. "I want to hit this bubble from all angles. Send word to the Brood. I require a way to get to the top of this thing. I'd like to put some people and some machines up there. None of our Movers can fly something that high. We could build huge scaffolding, but if there is an easier way, I'd like to try it. I have heard of certain flying machines. Have you ever seen one?"

"No, sir, I have never seen one, but like you I have heard of something of the sort. However, I am not sure if they really exist."

"Well, I would like to find out if they do, and if anyone has access to such a thing, I would imagine that it would be the Children of Montok."

"Yes, sir, I will deliver the message. I will be as swift as the wind itself."

"If they haven't got a machine, please ask them if they have a beast or giant bird or something else that can do the job. I need to get up there."

The messenger pointed up into the sky, "Perhaps, General, your request is being answered, yet not in the way you might have hoped. She comes...."

General Jelani followed the woman's finger up into the sky. There were few times when the General lost his charismatic grin, this was one of them.

In the distance he saw them. At first, they looked like one huge black shadow traveling through the sky. As they got closer, he could see the wings flapping vigorously against the wind, blocking out the blue sky behind them. Perhaps fifty or more black owls came their way. The city became quiet as more and more people became aware of their approach and stopped to look. The faces of many people who stood there watching showed a mix of awe and fear. Others ran to their houses or whatever structure they could find nearby.

The owls quickly engulfed the common areas of the city, disturbing everyone and everything in their path; yet, in general, they flew quietly. The beating of their wings did not make the loud flapping sound of most other birds. It was only when the birds were right upon them that General Jelani heard the sound. They came in like locusts, weaving in and out of people, circling around the inner perimeter of the great city. People did their best to cover their heads as the numerous black owls swarmed by them, forcing some of the people to dive to the ground.

"You may not need to leave after all," the General told the messenger. "Why don't you go home? Spend some time with your family."

"Yes, General." The messenger bowed and then ran.

General Jelani stood there, watching the swarm of owls come his way. As they approached, he fluttered his cape out, kneeling on one knee with his head down. One of his maidens made a quick effort to straighten his clothing as much as possible, and then both of his maidens knelt behind him.

The owls soon converged into one spot in front of the General. They all came together; merging into one another until at last a woman was formed. Nyami, one of the Children of Montok; she was the only woman, the only sister. Her skin was as dark as coffee. Her black hair consisted of thin braids that draped across her shoulders and flowed more than halfway down her back. Her dress was as white as her hair was black. It draped all the way to the ground and loosely fit the contours of her thin body. Her eyes, slightly slanted, only added to her already beautiful face. She carried with her a black and silver staff with a black onyx crystal at the top.

"Welcome back to your city, M' Lady. How may I serve you?" said the General, respectfully, without lifting his head.

"You may rise, General."

"Thank you, M' Lady."

"I would speak with you." She did not wait for his response. She began walking and expected him to follow. He did, but only after he waved away both of his maidens.

"I am looking for a boy, General. Have you seen him?"

"There are many boys that roam through here, M' Lady. They are the sons of your workers. Which boy is it that you speak of?"

"You would make no mistake about this boy, General. He is grey-skinned."

"Grey-skinned? I have only heard of such a thing in stories. You are right as usual, M' Lady. I would have remembered something such as that."

The General lied as well as he could. He did not know how Nyami had found out about young Tau. One of the inhabitants of the city may have seen him. Surely none of his trusted guards would have breathed a word.

Maybe one of Nyami's owls was spying on his city. No matter how she had found out; he wanted to make sure that she considered her source to be wrong. He did not want to give the boy up. Hagga had told him that Tau was very important.

While the General pondered this, Nyami said, "You wouldn't lie to me, would you, General? You wouldn't be hiding such a boy from me, would you?"

"Why would I do that M' Lady? What of this child? What is important about him?"

"All you need to know is that he is an enemy of the Brood. He is to be captured and delivered to me on site. Alive!"

"As you wish, M' Lady. I will instruct my guards to keep an eye out for him. If he is here hiding, I assure you, we will find him."

"Good then. Now, tell me, who is the owner of this hut?" She stopped walking, giving a grimacing look at the hut to which she pointed.

General Jelani knew the hut. It belonged to the thief that had escaped his village not long ago. What could Nyami want with it? "It belongs to one of your laborers, M' Lady. He is not a specialist of any kind, only an extra pair of labor hands."

"Then it does not belong to a sorcerer?"

"No, not that I am aware of, although sometimes people do hide their true identities."

An owl flew from inside the hut and landed on her shoulder. "Come," she told the General as she walked inside.

He followed. The hut was nothing special. It was a poor man's hut made of several long sticks that created the walls of one room spanning ten feet across. The bed was only a bunch of blankets spread out on the dirt ground. The tree stump off to the side was used for an eating table so short that its owner probably sat with his legs crossed while eating.

A two layered shelving unit pieced together with miss-matched legs and shelves was positioned against the wall. On the top shelf sat a candle, stuck to the wood by its own wax. There were obvious places where other candles previously had burned themselves out altogether. The bottom shelf was cluttered with different tan cloths, all with writing on them.

Nyami entered the room and stood there a moment with her eyes closed. Then she went over to the bedding, pulled it up, and dug her hand into the dirt below. It was not long until she pulled out a small sack and emptied an assortment of gems onto the stump-table.

"Explain this!"

"M' Lady, plenty of people hide their valuables. I would even encourage it."

She reached down, grabbing a one-inch peridot. "This, General, is a pure-grade crystal."

The General shook his head. "Excuse me, I had no idea."

"To whom does this belong? I want him here, now!"

"M' Lady, the man you seek is a thief. He fled two days ago to the south. My troops have gone after him but alas, they have lost his trail. I am afraid that the name he gave us was a false one. Now that I know that he was also a trader of illegal pure-grade gems, we will double our efforts!"

Of course the General DID know where the man was. He also knew that the man traveled to the west, not south. He could have also easily told her about the man's accomplice, still here in the city, but he did not. He would handle the matter himself, and punish them accordingly. He knew that no matter what punishment he gave them, Nyami's punishment would be ten times worse.

Nyami's slanted eyes burned bright with a white glow. She reached her hand out toward the General, conjuring up the power of the wind around her arm. She thrust the wind forward, knocking the General back against the wall and onto the ground. The frail wall of the poorly built shack collapsed though the entire hut did not fall. The General dug his fingers into the dirt, gathering his strength as he looked up at her.

"Perhaps you have forgotten certain rules, General, so let me explain them to you: Low-grade, mid-grade, and high-grade crystals may be used by the people for trade, for decoration, or for whatever they wish. But no common person may possess a pure-grade crystal for any reason. I will only allow pure-grade crystals to be used by sorcerers. Even they may only have what they require for use on their staff weapons. Anything else will require special permission. Is that clear?"

"Yes, M' Lady," said the General as he picked himself off of the ground.

"Maybe we should check in on you more often, to see what kind of city it is that you are running here. Do you run this city, or do the thieves and smugglers?"

"Please forgive the oversight, M' Lady. I know that all sorcerers have the power to detect pure-grade crystals, some more than others. None of the sorcerers in the city are as powerful as you are. Their crystal-grade detection is not as strong as yours. They were unable to find the crystals as you were."

"I am not looking for your petty excuses General." She began to walk out of the door. "Get your house in order. If you cannot, you will be replaced by someone who can." She exited the small hut.

The General bowed with sarcasm. Before he followed her out, he took a moment to inhale deeply to try and relax, hoping that her visit would be a short one.

As he exited, he saw Nyami standing over one of the young girls in the village. With so many people in the village, it was hard for him to remember everyone, but the name Mya suddenly popped into his head. She was about 5 or 6 years old, he figured. She wore a one-piece dress, which left her arms exposed. Originally, it had been white, but use and age had dirtied it so that, even when clean, the whole thing was a dingy yellow.

The young girl raised her arms up to Nyami, as if she wanted something. The General wanted to yell out to her, to tell her to get away from that witch, but he did not. He stood there, wondering what exactly was going on between the two. He hoped that Nyami would not extend her cruelty to a young child.

He could see Nyami's lips moving, speaking to the young girl, though he was too far away to hear what she was saying. What could it possibly be, he wondered. He figured that anything

Nyami said would be nothing but poison.

It was then that he made up his mind to do something to intervene. He took a step forward. Nyami looked over at him, and so did the little girl. He paused. Suddenly, Nyami burst into numerous black owls again and headed for the sky.

The General was more than happy to see her leave. His grin returned to his handsome face. He looked at the little girl again. She was being consoled by her mother, who had just run to her aid. He would have to be sure to warn both of them to stay away from Nyami in the future, before the young girl's curiosity got her into trouble.

This was his city. It was his job to protect the people in it, but he needed to do it carefully. The last thing that he wanted was to be fired. For one, being relieved of employment from the Brood usually came with a great deal of pain, if not death. But besides that, it was in the people's best interest for him to stay in control of the city. He thought the people were better off with him in charge. Who knew how someone else would treat them? He was walking a fine balance of allegiance to the Brood, and to his own morals.

Then he realized that after all of that, he had forgotten to ask Nyami about the flying machine.

As he looked up into the sky where the last glimpse of Nyami was seen, he felt the hairs on his neck stand up. He felt a sudden shift in the wind and he looked to the east. His eyes squinted in terror at the sight of the Thread coming his way. Great, he thought to himself. Roll one boulder moves out of the way and another one rolls into its place.

XX MYA

Mya loved fire. She would stare at it for extended periods of time, lost in the ever-changing flame. Even the small flame currently burning atop the little candle in her hut captured her attention for a half hour. Not only did she love the warm yellow and orange glow of the flame, she loved how it danced with the slightest bit of wind. She was fully aware that something so beautiful also possessed the power to destroy. In fact, that fact intrigued her even more.

It continuously burned away at the wax, changing its shape. People feared fire, but everyone needed it. She often brought her hand as close to it as she could to feel the heat up against her skin. At times, she even stuck her finger directly into the flame for a second until the burning pain caused her to yank it out. For some reason, she felt that being a part of the flame for a moment was worth the pain that followed.

This time she looked over her shoulder at her mother at the other side of the hut, to make sure she was not watching. Her mother would never allow her to burn herself, but Mya did not care. She could not resist connecting with such elegant power.

The six-year-old girl did not even tremble as she leaned in to place her finger into the flickering heat. In less than a second, the pain was too much. She yanked her finger back and quickly placed it into her mouth to soothe it. She would not dare show her mother or her father that she had hurt herself. They would not understand. They never did. So she sat there on the ground with her finger in her mouth and continued staring at the fire.

"Mya," her mother called out to her. "Go find your brother and tell him that the food is ready."

Her mother's voice was nothing more than a faint whisper to Mya, who was still concentrating on the flame. She made no motion to show that she heard anything.

Then the flame suddenly went out. It was replaced by a wisp of smoke that trailed its way upward into the air. Mya's mother's face came into view with a grimacing look, and Mya realized that it was her mother who had blown out the candle. She was a bit disturbed by this, but her mother had gotten her attention.

"Mya, please go get your brother and tell him it is time to eat. We gave him money to go buy grain from mister Ulu. Tell him to hurry up. Okay?"

Mya stood up and stared at her mother for a second. She looked down at the candle, and then began to make her way out of the hut.

It was a regular day in the Red Barrier City. Their hut was on the inside of the dirt walkway that circled the dome. There were people everywhere going about their usually daily activities, whatever they were; shopping, carrying things, pulling carts, pushing wagons, leading animals, and working. Though the city was a place of continuous activity and movement, Mya found it quite boring. She did not know why and could not understand it, but she did not like this place, not one bit. She found no joy in her life, living with her parents and her brother. She continuously entertained thoughts of leaving.

She made her way down the walkway around the dome to Brother Ulu's shop. He sold all sorts of grain. From time to time he also had an assortment of beans, but it was rare. Usually people came to him because they could be sure they could get whatever grain they needed.

His shop was mostly exterior. On top of the wooden bar was where he kept samples of his grain, and then behind the bar was where he kept bags of much larger volumes of the stuff. Mya's brother, Luwen, was nowhere to be found.

"Hello, Mya," said Brother Ulu. "Tell your mother and father that I still have the grain that they wanted and that he can pick it up any time." Then he looked at her for a moment. "What am I saying? When you see them, point them my way."

Mya looked at him for another second then walked away. If Brother Ulu was telling her that her family's grain was still there to pick up, then that meant her brother had not been there to buy it yet. She knew of a place where her brother might be.

She walked down the wide walkway a bit more and then turned down between two huts and behind them toward the outer edge of the city limit, by the fence that surrounded it. There were usually very few people by the edge. All of the huts, stores and structures faced inward.

There she saw her brother with three other boys. They were all sitting around a small table playing a game of, "jewel and cup." The game was one for gamblers. Three cups sat face down. The stone master would place a stone or jewel underneath one of the cups. Then he would quickly rearrange the three cups while the player carefully tried to keep watch of the one cup that the jewel was under. Once the jewel master stopped moving the cups, the player then attempted to guess which one the jewel was under. If the player guessed right, he won money. If he guessed wrong, he lost money. Simple.

"Mya," her brother Luwen greeted her with a worried look on his face. He shook his head and placed his face in his hands. The other boys' faces were filled with smirks and glares of pride. "I've lost almost all of our money. Mom and dad are going to kill me," Luwen continued.

"Hello Mya," said the Jewel Master in a condescending tone. She looked at him blankly. "Have you come to play as well? All are welcome."

She did not pay much attention to him. She looked her

brother in the eye and pointed in the direction of home.

"Did they send you to get me? Is it time to go home?" Luwen asked.

Mya put her finger up to her open mouth.

Luwen looked at her, then at the sun's position. "Time to eat?" He sighed. "But I can't go back! They will kill me."

"Well, if you've got nothing else to play with, Luwen," said the Jewel Master, "then I guess we're done here. Maybe you can win your money back another time."

Mya pointed back to the direction of home again. Luwen reached into his pouch one last time and pulled out one more jewel. It was a red high-grade gem, much bigger than any of the ones he had played with so far. He took a moment while he rolled it around through his fingers.

The Jewel Master's eyes opened wide. "Maybe you do have something to play with after all. What grade is that?"

"It's a high grade jewel. I promised myself that no matter what, I wouldn't play this one," Luwen said in a low voice.

"Hey buddy, you HAVE to play that one. You could win back almost half your money with one that size. You DO want to win your money back, don't you? You have to play to win, buddy."

Luwen looked at Mya for a moment. Then he reached his hand out to place the jewel on the table. Mya grabbed his arm firmly before he could put it down and again pointed in the direction of home.

"No, I have to try."

"Yes Mya, let him try," said the Jewel Master. "You never know, he could win it all back. I'll tell you what, play the big one. If you win, I'll give you ALL your money back." He reached into a pouch and pulled out the twelve small jewels that Luwen had already lost and put them on the table.

"All of them?" Luwen asked eagerly.

"Yup."

"Okay, then."

Luwen stared at his sister; Mya made her face look grimacing and serious. She did not want him to play anymore; she wanted him to come home. Soon, Luwen's strength overcame hers and he put the jewel on the table.

Mya tugged strongly at his shirt to pull him away, but still he resisted. "Mya, I have to. I have to at least *try* to win our money back." Then he placed one of the cups upside down covering the jewel.

The Jewel Master smiled. "Okay, then. Looks like we have ourselves a game!" He went to work with the cups, moving them around one another. "Are you following?" he asked.

Mya watched as Luwen did his best to keep his eye on the one that his jewel was under. Then the Jewel Master stopped for a second and lifted up a cup, showing the jewel. "It's right here, boys and girls, is everyone keeping track?" He put the cup down and continued the game.

Luwen still kept watch on his cup. Mya too was watching, trying to follow, concentrating very hard. Then she noticed a strange feeling she had never felt before. It was almost as if she could feel where the jewel was. It was pulling at her, through the cup. Somehow she could sense it. Then suddenly, it shifted, as if it was pulling at her through a different cup. She was confused for a second. Her eyes never saw the jewel move; yet that feeling was now coming from a different cup.

Being able to sense a jewel was something that sorcerer's did. It was not a talent for common people such as Mya. Still, even someone that would grow up one day to be a powerful sorcerer would not be able to do any type of jewel sensing until their teenage years, and that would come with practice and schooling. Here she was at age six, and somehow this talent happened upon her with no training whatsoever. But she was quite sure. She could sense it as if she was looking right at it.

The Jewel Master stopped. All three of the cups were in a

line. "Okay, Luwen. Where is your jewel?"

Luwen reached out to grab the one on the left, but Mya gently grabbed his hand.

"This is the one, Mya, I know it."

Quickly, Mya moved his hand on top of the middle one.

"Are you sure?"

She pointed to it.

"You have to be sure, Mya. I could have sworn it was the other one."

She firmly pointed to it again. Then Luwen flipped the middle cup over, revealing his jewel. He let out a deep sigh of relief as a smile grew across his face.

He stood up and grabbed Mya, hugging her. "Thank you little sis!" Then he went to the table and gathered all of his jewels, placing them into the pouch.

"Hey! Wait a minute!" The Jewel Master stood up in anger. "That's not fair! Give it back!"

"Give it back?" Luwen replied. "You said that if I won, I could have it all."

"Yes, but I was playing you, not your weirdo sister!"

"I'm not giving it back. I won it!"

"Then I'll have to take it!"

The Jewel Master rushed over and grabbed him, quickly putting him into a headlock. The other boys stood up as if they too wanted a piece of the action. One of them went over and started tugging at Luwen's pouch, which was firmly clasped in his hand.

"No!" Luwen shouted.

The Jewel Master started to squeeze tightly around Luwen's neck, partially cutting of his air. It was apparent that Luwen was having trouble breathing. Then the boy that was trying to free the pouch from Luwen's hand began punching him in the stomach.

All the while, Mya stood there and watched blankly. She watched as if it was not even happening in front of her. Her brother was being beaten up, but she was not concerned for him, though she knew that she should be. She was more intrigued than anything. She wondered how long Luwen would be able to hold on to that bag of jewels before he would let go, and how much harder the boy would have to squeeze and for how long before her brother died. How much more effort would it take for the boy to snap Luwen's neck, like when someone snaps the neck of a chicken, a common site in the city. She wondered what it felt like to be the Jewel Master in that moment. ...To have someone's life right there in her hands, at her mercy. The amount of power and control the Jewel Master had over her brother at that moment sparked an overwhelming sense of curiosity.

The struggle caused Luwen's pouch to fall from his hands to the ground near Mya, then she heard a man call out to them from afar. "Hey! What's going on back here?"

Immediately, the Jewel Master looked at the man coming from around the hut and threw Luwen to the ground. "Let's go, boys."

Luwen reached his arm out to break his fall. He let out a horrible shriek. "My arm!"

Mya watched him eying the pouch on the ground. Just as the Jewel Master went to pick it up, Mya reached her hand on top of his. As soon as her hand touched his, he quickly yanked his hand back from a shock.

"Ouch!" he said grabbing his hand with the other. He looked at Mya with disturbing curiosity.

Mya heard the spark. She also felt it, yet it was not the least bit painful to her. She took a moment to look at her own hand.

"You can keep your stupid money!" said the Jewel Master, and then he and the boys quickly left.

The man came rushing over to them. "Are you okay? What has happened here?" He reached down to help Luwen to his feet.

"Ow!" Luwen screamed. "My arm! I think it's broken."

"What's your name, boy? Where are your parents?"

"Luwen. My parents are at home. It's not far."

The man picked him up. "Let's get you home then." He looked at Mya for a moment. She was standing there, seemingly unaffected by all of the chaos. "And what's your name?"

"That's Mya, my sister."

"Then I suppose you should come too, young lady."

Mya followed the man carrying her brother through the crowds as Luwen pointed the way. Their mother was outside their hut as they approached. She immediately came running over to them."

"Oh my! What has happened?" she asked.

"I'm not sure, ma'am. It looked like he and a couple of boys were fighting. His arm may be broken."

"A fight? Broken arm? We must get him to the medicine man!" She turned her attention toward the hut. "Kulo! Come out here quick. It's Luwen, he's hurt!"

Their father came out of their hut. He was a big man, muscular. Most of his work in the city consisted of digging and carpentry. "What happened?"

"The boy was fighting. He may have broken his arm! We have to get him to the medicine man."

"Here," said Kulo. "I will take him. Thank you, sir."

"No problem, I hope the boy is all right," the man replied.

"Come, Mya," said her mother as they trekked around the dirt walkway, through the crowds, toward the medicine man.

Suddenly, Mya noticed a commotion among the people. Everyone began to scatter in all directions as they looked up into the sky.

Kulo stopped as he too looked toward the sky. "Nyami is coming!"

They began to move faster.

Soon the numerous owls were upon them. Kulo quickly moved into the medicine man's hut carrying Luwen, followed by their mother, but not Mya. She stood there without fear in the middle of the walkway as the owls flew by her. Others covered their head and bodies for protection, but not Mya. She spread her arms out and welcomed them. She closed her eyes and let them fly across her body, feeling the wind from the flapping of their wings and the feathers as they brushed across her skin.

"Mya!" her mother yelled, rushing to her, covering her from the birds with her arms. "Get in here!" She pulled Mya through the cloth covered opening of the medicine man's hut, knelt down by her, and held her by the shoulders. "When those owls come, I want you to stay away from them, and the lady that will follow. Do you understand?"

Mya slightly cocked her head to the side. She wondered what the big deal was. She liked the owls. She knew they were a part of the woman, Nyami. She liked her too. She felt close to her. She never understood why people feared her. She was pretty, and Mya admired her power. If only she could have power like that, she could fly off wherever she wanted, whenever she wanted. She could leave this place that was constantly filled with people. The city air was always filled with the noise of builders, animals, and the sounds of hundreds of people talking during the day.

"The boy has broken his arm," said the medicine man as they reentered.

Mya's mother left her up against the wall while she dealt with the matter of Luwen's broken bones.

Mya watched the drama of her parents and the doctor discussing what needed to be done about Luwen. For several minutes, she stood by while constantly glancing through the crack between the cloths in the doorway. The walkway was empty. Then Mya gasped when she saw Nyami again walking on the walkway. Mya looked back at her parents who were focused on Luwen and then slipped out of the doorway.

She walked up to Nyami and stared up to her. Nyami stared back, but for a few moments, neither of them said a thing.

Then, softly, Nyami spoke. "What is it you want, little one?"

What did she want? Mya wanted to go with her. She wanted Nyami to take off to wherever she was going and take her with her. She raised her arms up into the air as a baby does, wanting to be picked up, then gestured with her eyes toward the sky.

"No," said Nyami. "You cannot go with me."

Mya dropped her hands. Then she raised one back up and reached for Nyami's hand. Nyami seemed hesitant, but she reached her hand out, and Mya grabbed hold of one of her fingers. An almost imperceptible smile crept onto Mya's face.

Mya's attention was broken for a second as she looked back at General Jelani coming out of the hut.

She looked up at Nyami, who gently pulled her hand back from Mya's. "Perhaps, some day."

Then instantly, Nyami burst into dozens of owls and flew away. An overwhelming sense of rejection developed inside Mya. Why did the lady refuse to take her with her? Somehow, a part of her felt as if she was SUPPOSED to go, yet this woman denied her request. Mya had seen Nyami a few times before, and each time, she felt an indescribable connection to her. While everyone else tried to stay away, Mya wanted to be closer. She became angry inside, frustrated. She gnashed her teeth together and tightened every muscle in her body.

It was then that her mother came to her again. She scowled deeply at Mya and grabbed Mya by the face gently with both hands. Mya peeked up at her from under her anger-turned eyebrows.

"Mya, honey, what is it?"

Then, Mya heard a terrible crackling sound from the sky. Not ordinary thunder. This sound was specific, recognized immediately by anyone who had heard it before. It had an abnormal rumble to it, accompanied by the strange sound of sizzling static. Mya and her mother looked up to see the Thread.

Unlike a storm, the dimensions and edges of the Thread were

easily definable. It was to the east of the city and small at first, perhaps a hundred feet wide. It hung in the air beneath the clouds, irregularly shaped and as thin as a windowpane. Inside, sparks of white, black, and grey continuously blinked all over it while lighting flashed from end to end.

It grew bigger as it came closer, headed directly for the city. As the people began coming out again after Nyami's departure, they were placed back into a state of panic. This time, they frantically began to cover up, tie down their belongings, and lock tight their doors. The ones who were smart enough to prepare for storms placed objects of importance inside of holes that had been previously dug into the ground.

All in all, it was a moment of chaos and panic. Whether they personally had experienced the Thread before or not, for the most part, all of the people had heard of it. No one knew why it came or where it would come next. No one knew exactly what it would do each time it appeared. But everyone knew that it was to be feared. In no time the fear tuned to screams that could be heard throughout the entire Red Barrier City.

"Come, Mya!" she heard her mother say as she felt a tug on her hand. She did not move. She watched the Thread as it moved in.

Her mother did not waste time; she picked Mya up and ran toward the medicine man's hut, dodging in and out of the chaos of people running all around them. "We must get to Luwen and your father!" her mother screamed.

By the time they got close to the hut she saw her father carrying Luwen back the other way toward their home. "It's the Thread! Get them to the house!" He screamed to her mother loudly against the sound of the wind that was picking up and the odd crackling sound of the storm.

More odd effects from the Thread began to affect the city. Bolts of lightning struck the ground, throwing up spurts of dirt, dust, and rocks that flew into the air like mini explosions. The earth shook, throwing people off balance and causing them to stumble or fall to the ground. In some places where the lighting struck, instead of small explosions, it caused the surrounding area to freeze, instantly covering surfaces with ice. Mya was intrigued by the oddity of it as a bolt of lightning hit a fallen woman on the leg, causing the leg to be encased in ice.

The effects were sporadic. Here and there, a small tornado as hot as fire touched down for a brief second and then disappeared. One second, the ground rumbled and opened up, then the next minute the hardest of rains ever conceived came crashing down on a small area. Mya and her family were forced to the ground by a short burst of pounding rain, and then it stopped. The parents scrambled up, still carrying their children, and continued to make their way toward their home. While her mother carried her, Mya looked upward toward the heart of the Thread. She reached her hand out to it, intending to touch it if she could.

Suddenly, and without warning, one of the huts, not very well put together, exploded from within, sending panels of frozen wood flying everywhere. One of them hit her father in the back as he ran, carrying his son. He stumbled for a second, but continued on, finally reaching their hut.

Their hut was strong. Even though the walls were anchored several feet deep into the ground, it was still made of wood. Once inside, Mya's father latched the door and wrapped the connections tight with rope. Then they all sat huddled together, listening and waiting for this storm to pass.

"It will be alright," Kulo said with his big strong arms wrapped around both of his kids and his wife.

There were moments when they did not hear any wind at all; then there were other moments when the wind was so strong that it seemed like it would lift their hut right off of the ground. The sounds of people screaming and yelling from both nearby and far away came to them through the noise of the storm. They heard crashing sounds of structures falling over, the cries of animals, the rumbling of the shaking ground, and always, the odd crackling lightning sound that only the Thread could provide, rarely accompanied by thunder.

Their whole hut shook again, followed by the cracking sound of icicles forming. Mya looked up to see the corner of the building being encased in ice. Everyone trembled with fear, waiting for this all to pass and hoping that they would make it through alive; everyone except Mya.

She was not scared. She looked around at the rest of her family, again simply curious about their panicking and curious about the destruction around her. She understood their fear, even if she did not share it. She found herself staring at one of the lit candles as it flickered constantly from the wind that penetrated through the beams. She became lost in the flame and soon forgot about everything that was happening around her. Before long she became so calm that she fell asleep. Moments after that, the Thread disappeared into nothing.

XXI THE DEEP

Water. Tau was under water. Or, more accurately, there was water above him. It filled the ceiling, covering every inch of it. Then he realized that it did not just cover the ceiling, it WAS the ceiling. The only thing behind the water was more water.

"Yemoja!" he said as he sat up. Tau looked around the room to see that the walls were also made out of water. The floor was made of marble with blue, white, and black swirled into it. Although he had never seen this sort of marble floor before, his brain understood that it was there, that he could walk on it, that it was real.

But the ceiling and the walls did not seem real at all. The watery walls curved upward in this round room and met at the top to form a dome. What was this place? Where was he? The last thing he remembered was drowning. He could still feel remnants of the pain in his chest.

He began to examine the bed that he was in. It was comfortable, made of a spongy material. There was a silky sheet over him with green and white patterns of swirls, which he began to pull back.

His focus quickly shifted from the bed, back to the ceiling and the walls made of water. What kept the water from falling in and drowning him?

Besides the bed, the only other things in the room were two pillars by the doorway, each about four feet high. They had different color crystals on top of them that gave off light. The other light in the room came from several spots along the edges of the floor where it met the watery wall of the twenty-five foot room. Yet again, his thoughts and his gaze drifted back toward the water around him. How was it held there? What stopped it from falling into the room?

"Hello?" he yelled out, but received no answer in return. He walked over to the wall; the wall made of nothing but water, and studied it. It was not stagnant. It rippled from end to end. Beyond the surface, Tau could see lights in the distance. Closer to him, he could make out shapes, and movement through the water. There were fish, large and small, swimming around. Then he made out what looked like a man swimming about a hundred feet or so from where he was. Soon he counted five people swimming. One was circling overhead. The others were circling in all different directions around the room.

Tau studied these men for a moment, not sure if they were there to help or to hurt him. Perhaps they were the ones who had put him here. Suddenly he noticed something peculiar about all of them. From what he could tell, there were fins of some sort protruding from both of their legs, and from their arms as well. Odd, he thought. Must be some sort of *water folk*. Once again, something that he only heard about in stories was right there in front of him. Was he in the ocean?

"Hello," he yelled out, waving his hand, trying to get their attention. Eventually, he did. One of the seamen looked right at him. The swimmer's eyes peered right into Tau, which actually scared the crap out of him. He stepped back from the watery wall to wait for this strange man to come toward him. Instead, the man swam away.

Tau was discouraged. Against his own better judgment, he put his hand up to the wall of water and touched it. For some reason, he expected something unexpected, or not to be able to touch the wall at all. But he could. His fingers went right into it. It felt like…water. He pulled his fingers back, and to his surprise; there was not a drop of water on them. Next, he put his entire hand into it, moving it around, feeling the cool water run across his fingers and across his hand, watching the extra ripples that he made in the wall with his movement. Being this deep under the surface, he would have thought the water to be a lot colder than it was.

Well, he had gone this far; next, he placed his face into the wall and opened his eyes. He could taste the salt in the water. He moved his head back and forth until finally, he leaned all the way into the wall and his whole body went through it. Tau had spent a lot of time in the water in his life. This time, the water felt very strange and so different.

He swam away from the room and then looked back at it, wondering how all that water did not simply fall in. He could not tell exactly how deep he was; only that he could not see the surface. Looking upward revealed only blackness. He looked back down at the room he had been in, and the rest of the long corridor it was connected to. The corridor was a fully enclosed tunnel and extended until it connected to another small-bubbled shaped junction with water for a ceiling, like his room. He stayed in place, treading water, looking at the whole system of rooms and corridors and lights spread out across the ocean floor.

He looked out at another one of the seamen. He would have swum over to him, but his lungs told him not to. He was not a man of the sea, though, until now, he had always thought that he was. He hoped he could get back into the room, where he could breathe. Quickly, he made the short swim back to the room and stuck his head into it, taking in a good breath of air. The rest of his body stayed in the water, only his head, chest and arms were inside the room.

Suddenly he realized that he had made the stupid mistake of coming in too high! He tried to use his arms to swim backward into the water. All he really did was wiggle around enough for him to fall out of the water completely and into the room. His body fell all the way through the wall, and he crashed to the floor.

It hurt. He felt pretty stupid, telling himself that next time he would make sure to come in a lot closer to the floor. Of course, as he rolled over, he had another thought which made him feel even more stupid. He should have tried the door!

Picking himself up, he went over to the doorway, noticing

that he was not wet. He felt his perfectly dry arms and clothes. He should have been soaked. He had been totally submerged in water.

Reaching the doorway, he could see down the connecting hallway, but there was something shimmering blue stretched across the threshold. He touched it and this time his hand did not go through. After a few taps and pokes, he realized that he was not going to get out that way. There was some kind of barrier of light across the doorway. Perhaps he was right the first time. He would have to swim out to one of those men. Maybe they could tell him how he had gotten here.

He did not have to. He turned around to see one of the men coming toward him, swimming through the water. Beyond the wall, there were more men swimming around in the ocean. A shiver of fear sparked through his body. His instincts told him to grab his blades. Who knew what this man was coming to do to him. What if these sea creatures ate people? He certainly was not in the mood to be someone's dinner! Then again, seamen probably ate fish. That would make a lot more sense, although it was possible that the man may have a pet; some huge beastly sea creature, and maybe IT ate people.

His weapons! Tau searched, but did not see them. They were not in the room either. Someone must have taken them from him before placing him here. This is a prison, he thought.

The man came out of the water and through the wall, coming feet first, and landing on the floor. Now that's the way to enter the room, Tau thought to himself. It was all so elegant; clearly this man had done this before. He had twelve fins; three on each leg coming out of the side, one bigger one up by each thigh, and two smaller ones down by his calves. The ones on his arms were the same way; one larger one coming out the side of each bicep, and two smaller ones down by his forearms. All of them were green, despite the brown color of his skin. The only difference was that the fins on his right arm were wrapped around a short staff about a foot long. At the end of it was a circle with different green and white crystals in the middle.

Once the man came into the room, his fins wrapped themselves tightly around his skin. They were thin, and when wrapped, they looked more like a nicely painted design than part of his body. Most of his skin was dark brown, yet there were long streaks of green paint that curled and twisted at the end of the design. It was hard for Tau to understand how a man who had just been in the water came out perfectly dry, but he accepted it.

"Um, hi." Tau was the first to speak in a timid voice, not sure if he should be speaking at all.

"Who are you?" the seaman asked in a demanding tone.

"I am Tau. Mister....?"

"I am Captain Tawn. I've come to determine why you are here."

"I don't know. I woke up in this room. I don't know how I got here."

"I meant what you were doing in the middle of the water?"

"Oh, that. It's hard to explain. I was told to follow the red star and swim...."

"Are you a shape shifter?"

"Well, yes."

The man's face became a bit more grim. "As I thought. You will remain here." He turned around and went back through the wall, entering the water as the fins on his arms and legs unfolded. He made a waving gesture, then six more seamen quickly came closer, encircling Tau's room as the seaman swam away with his body waving through the water in a fast fish-like movement.

"Wait," Tau yelled. "Am I a prisoner?"

Captain Tawn did not answer. He kept on swimming until he was out of view. The rest of the men swimming around the room remained.

Great, Tau said to himself, a prisoner underwater.

He remained there for some time, yet he had no idea exactly

how long. He had no way of telling time since he could not see the sun. The minutes seemed to drag, with each one that passed making him even more anxious than the last. He studied the seamen swimming outside the room almost as if he was some sort of prey.

"What do you think they are going to do?" Chad asked him. He was standing next to the wall while curiously poking his fingers into the water.

"I don't know, but that Captain Tawn guy did not seem happy that I was a shape shifter. Maybe I should have said that I wasn't."

"No. No sense in lying about it. They would have figured it out sooner or later."

"You're probably right. But there is nothing I can do now but wait for him to come back."

"You could do that. Or, you could try the door again."

"Right!" Tau said. "There has to be a way to turn that light barrier thing off."

Tau went back to the door and studied the crystals sitting on top of the pillar with their luminous glow. He fiddled with them for a moment and noticed that they moved. They did not come off the pillar, but they did slide around. With a little more fiddling, the blue light barrier at the doorway flickered for a second. "Ah, maybe this WILL turn it off!"

He messed with the crystals on the other side for a moment, and then played around with both of them at the same time. Then he felt water dripping on his head. He looked behind him, into the room. It was raining!

"Uh, Tau," said Chad seemingly very concerned. "I think the ceiling is falling in."

"I know! I see it."

"What did you do?"

"I don't know," Tau became frantic. He returned to the crystals and continued to move them around.

More water came in, faster. The room began to fill with water. In a short time, the water had risen to his ankles.

At last, the clear blue shield flickered again until it was gone altogether. He smiled as he reached his hand out to confirm what he had done. It was gone.

"It's coming in faster, Tau!"

"Don't yell at me, this was your idea!"

The water continued to pour into the room.

"Run, Tau, Run!"

Quickly, he ran down the corridor to the other end until it turned. He rounded the corner and then peeked back around it to the room he had been in a moment before. Within seconds, the entire roof caved in. The water came rushing down the corridor all at once. Eyes widened in fear, he turned and ran.

Down the hallway he sprinted as the water followed, filling up the space in the corridor where he had been seconds before. He came to another room, much smaller than his prison and continued through the doorway on the left then down another one; the water was still after him, getting even closer. At the end of the hallway he saw a girl. He yelled out to her as he ran her way, "The water! It's coming. It's coming!"

The girl stood by the doorway, watching Tau as he ran towards her and the water that followed, filling up the hall. Quickly she moved around the crystals next to the door. The blue light barrier came on.

"No!" Tau yelled as he came to her at the end and pounded on the light barrier. "Why'd you do that? Now...."

The water violently filled the corridor, engulfing Tau and the girl, stopping at the barrier. It was fine for her; she skillfully dove into the water as it came smashing against her, unwrapping her blue fins from around her arms and legs. Tau, on the other hand, felt the blow of the water as it knocked into him. Then he was underwater, holding his breath.

The girl looked at him curiously, watching him panic while

he held his breath. "Can you breathe?" she asked him, her voice sounded almost as clear as if it had traveled through the air.

Tau looked at her strangely as if she had asked the dumbest question in the world. After another moment, she spoke again.

"Don't worry," she said.

He felt a certain pleasantness as he looked at her. With the hallway filled with water, he should have been panicking. He should have begun to search for a way out so that he could breathe. But he didn't. He just looked at her kind face.

Her skin was medium brown which was also painted with lines and swirls. Except instead of green, her paintings were purple. He could not tell what sort of fabric she wore around her body; it was tight fitting silver two-piece garment, which covered her chest and some type of shorts.

She had a small staff or wand attached to her arm, the same as Captain Tawn did. The top of it was encircled with a mesh of different colored crystals in the center. When she grabbed his arm the crystals lit up for a moment.

The next thing Tau knew was that he could breathe.

"See," she said, smiling.

The water was all around him, but it was no longer touching him. She had created a bubble of air that encircled him. Not actually a bubble shaped bubble, but one that followed the contours of his body exactly, like a one-inch suit of air. Again, Tau was perfectly dry.

"I take it, you can't breathe under water?" she said.

"No, not at all," Tau said, still breathing heavily. "Thank you. How are you doing this?"

"Easy, I moved the water away from you."

"I suppose that makes sense," Tau said, feeling confused. "Thank you, anyway. I was in the room back there and then I accidently made all of the water come in."

"What do you think you were doing, collapsing water into the tunnels like that? Especially if you can't breathe."

"It was an accident. I didn't mean to."

"You didn't change either. Are you not Shark Folk?"

"I don't know what Shark Folk is. I don't even know how I got here."

The girl squinted and studied him. "So if you can't breathe under water, and you are not Shark Folk, then what are you doing here?"

"I told you, I don't know how I got here! I just woke up here."

"No, no, that's not what I mean. I mean what were you doing so deep in the middle of the ocean? I found you. You were almost dead."

"It's a long story."

"There will be time to tell it later then. First, we'd better clear these tunnels of water before my father finds out what you have done. Follow me."

"Wait," Tau said. "I don't even know your name."

"My name is Amanzi," she said with a smile.

"Well, I'm Tau."

"Well, Tau, do you mind if we clear these tunnels of all this water now before my father flips his lid?"

"Oh, yeah. Sure…."

Amanzi turned away, swimming back down the tunnel in the direction that Tau originally had come from. Tau started after her.

"You must be a Dry Lander then," she said. "Still, I don't know if my father is going to be happy about this or not. I'm going to have to…."

She reached the other end of the tunnel. When she turned behind her, Tau was not even close. He was trying his best to swim after her, but he was only halfway through the tunnel. Amanzi shook her head and waited for him to reach her.

"Is that as fast as you can swim?"

"I'm the fastest swimmer in my village."

"Probably not saying much; a village of Dry Landers, no

doubt. That's not going to cut it down here in The Deep. You'd better stay close, or you're going to be fish food." She swam across the threshold and into the corner room.

"Fish food?" Tau asked, following behind her.

Amanzi fiddled with the pillar at the doorway, moving the different colored crystals around. A force field came up between the room and the corridor. "Yeah, you know, fish food, shark bait, squid chow, meaning, something big and nasty is going to eat you. She fiddled some more. Tau watched as the water drained out of the tunnel behind them.

"Did you say eat me?"

"Stay close. Don't go wandering off or anything."

"No problem."

Amanzi started across the room and then looked back at Tau. "I'll tow you, it will be easier."

"What do you mean by t...?" Tau felt his body being thrust forward. Amanzi was swimming to the door and Tau, without any effort of his own, was following behind her.

They crossed into the next tunnel and Amanzi once again put up the force field and drained the water out of the room. She continued this, towing Tau along with her until they were all the way back to Tau's original room.

"This is the place," said Tau. "This is the prison I was in."

"Prison?" Amanzi asked as she moved the last crystal into place. The water slowly drained to the sides of what was before a dome of water. "You might want to make your way to the ground."

"Oh, right." Tau said as he swam to the floor.

"I'm not an expert on prisons," Amanzi said, pointing at the pillars in front of the door, "but generally, I don't think they put the controls of the door on the inside."

"Sure felt like a prison."

"And hopefully, that is not where you will go. The guards are coming."

"Should we run?"

"What? No. That would be stupid."

Two guards swam toward the room. They both entered through the invisible barrier with a look of contempt on their faces.

"Amanzi!" one of them shouted. "What are you doing with the prisoner?"

"See," Tau whispered to her. "I told you it was a prison."

"Shhh," she told him, then turned her attention to the guards. "Prisoner? He is not a prisoner. I bet you don't even know who he is."

"That is to be determined. He tried to escape."

"Um, no. That was me," said Amanzi. "I'm sorry, it was an accident. I wanted to come in and I hit the wrong switch and, oops! All the water came rushing in. I almost killed him. He could have drowned to death. Please don't tell my father. I fixed it all back."

"What do you mean, killed him? The boy is Shark Folk. He is a spy."

"I'm not Shark Folk."

Amanzi shushed him. "He is not a spy, and he is not Shark Folk. He is a Dry Lander."

"Hmm," said the guard. "This is not for me to determine. He will need to be questioned by your father."

Amanzi sighed. "I know. But at least let ME take the boy. He seems nice enough."

"WE will take him. You can come with us. That is the best that I can do. And we must bind his hands. In case he tries to escape."

"Escape? How can he escape? He'll drown if he isn't with one of us, so where is he going to go?"

"And what if he is lying to you, and he IS Shark Folk. Then he's a spy that you helped escape. I'm sure that your father wouldn't be too happy about that!"

"No sir, I guess he wouldn't."

The other guard began binding Tau's hands behind his back with a string of seaweed-like vines.

Tau was confused; he struggled against the guard's actions. "I'm not a spy. I'm not Shark Folk. I'm looking for my people."

"What people, Tau?" Amanzi asked.

"I'm looking for the rest of my people, Amotekuns. They were all taken!" He struggled in his bindings, trying to get free.

"If you keep struggling, boy, we'll kill you and ask the questions later."

Tau surely did not want that. He kept his mouth shut and kept still.

Amanzi was not so quick to follow. "Kill?" She yelled. "That's too far. He's only trying to scare you, Tau. No one is killing anybody!"

"Young lady, do you wish to come with us or not? If you are going to be a problem, we will leave you here."

"I'll come with," she said. "I'm the one who found him in the first place."

The guards led, making their way over to the edge of the room, to the wall of water. If these people have hallways, why don't they use them? Tau held his breath and moved into the ocean; then resumed breathing when he realized he did not have to hold his breath at all. Again, someone moved the water away from his body, creating a bubble of air for him to breathe in.

They rose upward, clearing the height of the dome. More of the city revealed itself to Tau. There were many lights, mostly beautiful blue, green, and white lights coming from everywhere. The city spanned out as far as he could see on the ocean floor. There were several long hallway-like structures like the one he had been in, connecting all of the larger compartments. However, not all of it seemed to be continuously connected. His section was separate from everything else and they were not moving away from it; they were headed toward the center.

It was a dome, much larger than all of the others. It had hallways connected to it from several angles. Again, Tau wondered why they did not use the hallways to get to where they were going. However, at least this way, he was able to see more of the surrounding city.

The large center dome was protected by a force field. They could not simply make their way in through the sides as they did his prison room. Instead, they entered through the side of one of the hallways connecting to it. This hallway too, on the inside and out, was made of light blue, white, and black colored marble. It was as if someone took a large brush and lightly swooshed the colors together.

"Where are we?" Tau asked once they entered the dry air of the hallway.

"This is the Main Hall," answered Amanzi. She took a deep breath. "My father will be in there."

"Why does the look on your face make me nervous?"

"Probably because HE makes ME nervous."

They left the hallway and entered the Main Hall. Like the others, there were pillars at the door, except these were black. Other black pillars were placed along the edges of the large room. At the top of all of them were various colored crystals emitting soft-colored light. There were statues placed all around, made of stone and marble that represented different kinds of sea creatures from The Deep: an octopus, a dolphin, an eel, a starfish, and several others.

Ahead of them was a platform with ten stairs. More guards were at the side, and at the top, a man sat on a chair with a grim look on his face. His skin was slightly darker than Amanzi's. The fins wrapped around his legs and arms shone with bluish silver. He sat there stroking his short black and white beard as the man in front of him spoke, though Tau was too far away to make out what he was saying.

"That's my father," said Amanzi, "otherwise known as

Soldier Prime. The man he is talking to is his Captain, second only to my father."

"Sshh," the guard whispered to Amanzi, giving her a glare.

Amanzi's father looked up at them, then held his hand up for the Captain to stop speaking and gestured to the guards to bring Tau forward.

Amanzi, Tau, and the two guards moved closer.

"Is this him?" asked Soldier Prime.

"Yes sir," answered the guard. "We have suspicions that he is Shark Folk, but..."

Amanzi quickly butted in, "Oh, but he isn't Shark Folk father. He said he was..."

Soldier Prime raised his hand again to silence her. He stood up from his chair and walked slowly down the stairs, keeping an eye on Tau the whole time. Tau shifted, feeling unusually uncomfortable. His hands were still bound, and that did not help. He worked his wrists slightly against the vines.

Soldier Prime looked over at Amanzi in disappointment. She got the message, and lowered her head.

"Who are you boy? Where do you come from?"

Tau swallowed a lump in his throat. "My name is Tau, Tau Zaire. As to where I come from, that is a long story. For now, I would have to say, The White Forest. Amotekun City."

"My guards seem to think you are Shark Folk."

"Sir, I don't even know what that is."

Soldier Prime looked at Tau, keenly rubbing the side of his chin. Tau felt like he was trying to read his mind. "The lion of the river."

"Yes sir, that's what my name means."

"So you consider yourself to be a man of the water? Like us."

"No, sir, not at all like you. I mean, I can swim pretty well for a normal person, but not at all like you."

"And you've never heard of Shark Folk?"

"Apparently I am what Amanzi calls a Dry Lander."

"Then what are you doing here?"

"I am looking for my people. They have been taken somewhere by the Brood. They were put in large boats and taken across the sea."

"Then you are enemies of the Brood?"

"Isn't everyone, sir?"

Soldier Prime chuckled. "Not the Shark Folk. If what you say is true, then count your blessings that you don't know of them."

Tau nodded.

"Of course you could be lying and may be a spy, even if you are not one of them. You could be working for them. Who knows what tactics they are willing to use against us?"

"Sir, I assure you, I am not."

Soldier Prime glanced over to his daughter, "Amanzi, Amanzi, Amanzi, what am I going to do with you? You brought a stranger, a Dry Lander, to our city with no regard as to who he is or what his intentions are."

"Father, he would have died, and I..." Once again, the hand of silence.

"You are in luck, boy," said Soldier Prime as he looked at a large flat square crystal on his wrist. "I have no time for this. I have real problems on my hands to deal with pertaining to the Shark Folk. I'm trying to stop an impending invasion, and a war. It just so happens that I know who your people are. Your grey skin gives it away. It also happens that I know where your people have been taken."

Tau opened his mouth in disbelief. "You do!"

"Yes, the Amotekuns. You see, the Brood have traveled by sea, and there is not much that goes on in the sea without my knowledge. They have been taken to a place called Goree Island." He paused for a moment, looking at Tau. "I'm not sure if you will like what you find there. If I were you, I'd stay clear from that place."

"But sir, I must go. I have too."

Soldier Prime nodded. "If you insist. It's your life. Let the boy's hands go."

The guards proceeded to untie them. Tau massaged his wrists vigorously.

"We could get you there, but I'm afraid there are two problems involved. One is this conflict with the Shark Folk. I can't let any of my guards leave the city right now. The second problem is that we are people of The Deep, and we do not let ourselves get involved with the affairs of Dry Landers. Other than that, you are free to go. It is a pretty simple trek to Goree Island. It runs right along the path of one of our trams."

"But father, he still won't know the way," said Amanzi.

"No, he won't. That's why you are going to go with him. You brought him here, so he is your responsibility."

"You want me to take him?"

"You seem generally concerned about the boy, and it is a short journey. You shouldn't have any problems if you take the Tram. And that way, you will have the Tram operator to accompany you as well. Once you have taken him, I do want you to come right back."

"I can do it. I will take him, and return promptly."

"I'm sure you will." Soldier Prime began his way back up the stairs. "Now, I am sorry, but I have some very important matters to deal with. I wish you well on your journey, Mr. Tau. And I wish you the strength to overcome whatever you find there." He turned back around to look at Tau. "I guarantee you will need it."

Soldier Prime looked up for a moment and shouted into the hall. "Give this boy back his weapons. He will definitely need them."

A guard came to Tau and handed them to him. Tau nodded.

Amanzi bowed to her father, and then nudged Tau to do the same. "Bow," she whispered.

Tau bowed and then began to follow Amanzi back down the hallway.

"Oh, and Amanzi," said Soldier Prime. "What is the rule?"

Amanzi cleared her throat. "Never interfere with matters on the dry land."

Soldier prime nodded. "I will expect you not to forget that."

With another bow, Amanzi and Tau left the room. They swam through the water. Actually, Amanzi swam, while Tau followed in tow, safe inside the air bubble she provided for him.

"Hey, Amanzi! Who's your friend?" Tau heard another girl's voice from behind them. He noticed contempt on Amanzi's face, and she rolled her eyes as she spoke to him.

"Stay…quiet," she told him.

As they turned around, two girls met them. They looked a bit older than Amanzi. The biggest difference was that they were heavily decorated with makeup designs on their faces. They both wore sparkling necklaces that twinkled in the light. Even their clothes were much fancier than what Amanzi wore.

"Hello Zola, hello Zuri," Amanzi said in a monotone voice.

"So, who's the boy?" Zola asked.

Zola and Zuri swam circles around them in opposite directions, eyeing Tau up and down with false, coy smiles.

"Probably her new boyfriend," said Zuri. They both giggled.

"I doubt it," said Zola. "Amanzi gets a boyfriend? That will be the day!"

Amanzi rolled her eyes again. "His name is Tau. He is a Dry Lander."

"Oh, it all makes sense now," Zuri giggled. "It figures. Her new boy isn't even from here. What are you doing in The Deep, Tau?"

"I'm looking for my people, the Leopard Tribe."

Amanzi nudged him in the side.

"Well, Dry Lander, I don't know if you have noticed, but there are no air-breathers down here. Perhaps you could try looking on land somewhere. That would make a lot more sense, haha."

"Not too smart, is he, Zuri?"

"No, not at all, Zola. But he is a bit cute for a Dry Lander. I'll tell you what, Tau, if you want to get yourself a girl of The Deep, find yourself a real woman." She came a bit closer to Tau and batted her eyes, obviously trying to entice him with a small amount of flirting. "Amanzi doesn't quite represent how a real woman of The Deep is supposed to be. Hehehe."

"Stop it!" Amanzi yelled. "He's a visitor, and I'm helping him. That's it. Why don't you two go fix your makeup or something? You have no idea what you are talking about!"

"Oh my, Zuri," said Zola, "I think that we have made her angry."

"Oh yes, Zola," said Zuri, "I think we should leave before Miss Feisty starts swinging weapons at us. She is a fighter you know, like the boys."

Zola and Zuri swam off together, giggling. Amanzi quickly sped off in the other direction, forgetting all about Tau.

In moments, Tau felt his water bubble collapse in all around him. He was suddenly immersed in water and tried quickly to hold his breath before all of the ocean water rushed into his lungs. Through the midst of hundreds of bubbles, he could see Amanzi trailing off. He tried to swim after her, screaming as loud as he could. He began to choke on the water. Was this how Chad felt when he died? Was this what he went through?

Amanzi heard his voice through a gurgling of water. She quickly turned back to grab him, immediately placing the air bubble back around him. "I'm sorry," she said, "I forgot about you for a second."

Her tone did not sound sorry at all. More like she was angry. "C'mon, *fish fodder*."

Tau was relieved to have his air back. He coughed and coughed, feeling himself once again being dragged through the water as Amanzi towed him. This time, he was moving faster than ever before. He watched Amanzi swim through the water with a stern demeanor. Even her way of swimming was angry.

"Who were those girls?" Tau asked.

He did not get an answer. Amanzi kept swimming ahead.

"Amanzi?"

"Not now!"

Tau got the hint. Apparently he was just along for the ride. He got the sense that Amanzi wanted to be alone. Of course she could not be, because she had to babysit this air-breather. She swam vigorously through The Deep. They moved through a large school of hundreds of fish. Tau swatted at them as if they were hundreds of locusts flying all around his body.

The blue tint of the water darkened as they left the lights of the city. The light from Amanzi's staff glowed, but still, the eeriness of the dark ocean was getting to Tau. He felt completely vulnerable. He was fully aware that everything down here was a much better swimmer than he was. And without Amanzi there to protect him and give him simple things like air to breath, he would be, as she so plainly said, *fish fodder*.

Soon, when the glow of the city behind them fully diminished, Tau noticed a green glow from ahead. They came to the edge of a sharp cliff, and there in the distance Tau began to make out the familiar shape of an extremely large dome.

Unlike the other one at the Red Barrier City, this one was green, but it was the same size. It lit up the ocean as the only source of light where they were in The Deep. A few shapes of people circled it. Probably guards of some sort. Their bodies were small and dark, backlit against the bright green dome, and they were swimming slowly around it.

Amanzi stopped at the top of a cliff and locked her eyes on the dome. Tau drifted downward to her, sitting next to her on the ledge. He looked at the dome, then back to her, noticing how much she was engulfed in its light.

"It's pretty, isn't it?" she asked calmly. "I come here sometimes to think, to get away. Don't you ever want to get away Tau? Leave everything behind?"

"Those girls," Tau said. "They really got to you, didn't they?"

"My sisters? Yeah, that's the way they are. I'll never be like them. Don't think that I want to be."

"Sisters? They're your sisters?"

"Yup, two sisters, they're twins, and one brother. My brother and I get along quite well. But Zola and Zuri have never liked me."

"Why?"

"Because they want me to be like them. But I don't want to be like them. All they care about is being pretty and having some boy chase after them. Our city is on the brink of war with the Shark Folk, and their biggest concern is whether or not to match their fins to their cheeks, or the right rock to sit on all perky-like for the right guys to swim by."

"But you do paint yourself, don't you?" Tau asked. "You have that purple design all over you."

"No, this isn't a design," she said, pointing to one of the swirls on her arm. "This is part of me. These patterns grown naturally."

"Really? Wow, that's nice."

"Thank you," she responded.

Tau thought for a moment. "What about the ones on Captain Tawn, and your father. Are they natural too?"

"Yes. All of my people have them."

"I find that really strange but at the same time beautiful," said Tau.

"I'll try not to take offense to the, 'strange,' remark," she said.

Tau realized that he probably had said something that he shouldn't. He desperately wanted to move the conversation along. "Um… so why don't your sisters like you?"

"They don't like me because I'm not like them. I'm not pretty."

"But you are, um pretty." Tau tried his best to talk around the lump in his throat.

"You're just saying that."

"No. I mean you don't have the entire make up and clothes like they do, but who needs all of that? You are much prettier than they are." Tau could not keep eye contact. His gaze traveled downward to the rocky surface that he sat on.

"I suppose I may as well find a boyfriend then."

"So you don't have one? A boyfriend."

"Are you even listening to me?"

"Yes."

Amanzi shook her head. Then both of them were quiet for some time. They sat there, looking at the bright green dome.

Tau stole peeks at her from time to time out of the corner of his eye to see if she was peeking back at him, but she was not. He sort of felt stupid for saying that she was pretty. But why should he feel stupid? She WAS pretty, but she did not know it. Tau could not figure out for sure if she really did not think she was pretty, or did not care to be.

There was more silence. Tau took notice of all of the little sounds in the water that seemed to become louder the longer that the silence went on. Whatever the sounds were, they were strange. Some of them were just the sounds of moving water. Other sounds he heard, like clicks and whistles, he figured were from various animals of The Deep. None of them made him forget that he was sitting next to a very unhappy girl.

"So what is it that you want to be," asked Tau.

"What do you mean?"

"You said all your sisters wanted was to be pretty, and you say that is not your thing. So…what is your thing?"

"Far be it for them to read something. Or learn anything at

all. I like to know how things work. We are on the brink of war, and I want to learn how to fight. Our lives may depend on it someday. If I had my way, I'd be in my father's army; something with a purpose. I want to make a difference"

"I see." There was silence again as Tau's eyes drifted back toward the dome. "I see why you come here. There is something about the light. It's soothing."

"You feel it too?"

"Yeah. This is the second one I've seen. I saw a red one, on dry land. But seeing it here under the water gives it a much more wondrous look. The glow, it's different."

"And I suppose the Dry Landers don't know what they are or where they came from either?"

"Not a clue. All they know is that one-day it wasn't there, and the next day it was. They are trying very hard to get in though. They are using machines, weapons, sorcery, anything they can think of, with no luck."

"Same here, except, we have not tried so hard to get inside. We keep watch over it, but we trust that Mami Wata will let us know what it is in time."

"Mami What…?"

"Mami Wata."

"Who or what is that?"

"If there was no Mami Wata, there would be no us. It is her spirit that guides us, and it is her spirit that has brought us into being."

"Mami Wata, Mami Wata, Mami Wata," Tau said over and over again. "Heh, sounds funny."

Amanzi laughed. "Don't make fun. She is very important."

"I'm not saying she is not, I like the way it sounds; Mami Wata, Mami Wata, Mami Wata, Mami Wata, Haha."

Amanzi giggled again.

"You're laughing! That's a good thing."

"Yeah, thanks."

"Hey, are we allowed to go to the dome, or whatever you guys call it?"

"We call it the green dome, and sure we can go over too it. Why wouldn't we?"

"I figured because of the guards I saw swimming around...."

"No, no, no. They are there in case something comes out."

"Okay. I'd race you, but there is no point in that."

"Haha, nope. Come on, *shark food*. I'll take you."

She jumped up from the cliff, taking Tau along with her. When they were over the dome, she brought them downward, letting Tau move under his own power for the last few feet. This dome felt like the other one, spongy and gelatinous, yet firm. Tau leaned into it, looking at the green light bouncing off of his hands and body. Looking upward, he saw the light fading into the darkness of the sea.

"Sometimes," Amanzi said, "you can see something moving inside there. But I can never make it out."

"Yeah, like the red one."

"Makes you really wonder what is going on in there."

Tau ran his fingers across the soft outer shell. "I'm pretty sure one day we will find out. I hope it will be a good thing."

"It will be, I can feel it," she said while pressing her face all the way up against it. "One day," she said.

"We should probably go soon."

"Yes. I must take you to the Tram.

XXII THE TRAM

Amanzi jumped up from the dome and began swimming. With her power to control water, she towed Tau along the way. At first, it was a bit unnerving for Tau, having no control of his movements. But by this time, he was used to it. He still angled his body forward as if he was doing all the work. He mimicked Amanzi's dolphin-like movements through the water as if he was actually doing the swimming himself. It was the same way all of her people swam, with an elegant fluid motion so that their bodies undulated up and down to move forward.

Soon, Tau could see the lights of the city once again. Amanzi brought him over the series of corridors, rounded rooms and towers that made up the bulk of this grand water community. He noticed more structures on cliffs of different heights, built into the rock, each one spectacularly luminous. Then they went downward to a round structure at the end of one of the hallways. A series of long rows of crystals, each about one foot wide, sprouted out from the edge of the room about eight feet apart. Ten rows of two crystals led off in four different directions in the room as if to lead to it or otherwise, to lead away, like landing strips. This was the Tram station.

They entered the room through a doorway with no door; there was no visible barrier, yet like the water in his prison room, the water was held back from entering. On the inside, like all the doorways Tau had seen so far, there was a white pillar next to the entrance with an assortment of crystals on top.

Inside, there were benches and chairs made of a bluish marble. More light blue crystals lined the ceiling, lighting the interior. At the far end of the room were three men and two women sitting at a table, busying themselves with some sort of square board game with different colored pieces of stone. Of all of the chairs and benches in the room, this table was the only place that was occupied.

The men and women looked up at Amanzi and Tau as they entered as if pleasantly surprised. One of the men stood up to greet them. "Hey, if it isn't young Amanzi. What brings you to the Tram?"

"Hello, Kofi. Hello, everyone, this is my friend, Tau. He is a Dry Lander."

They all stood up and nodded their heads. "Hello, Tau."

One of the women stepped forward. "A Dry Lander? How delightful! How did you come to be in our city?"

"It's a long story, ma'am."

"Well, at least you are polite, and a handsome young man. Although I'd have to say that I have seen Dry Landers before, but I have yet to see anyone with such grey skin."

"It is a trait of my people, ma'am. The Leopard Tribe."

"Don't bother the boy with silly questions, Fatuma. Let them be about their business. Are you taking a tour of the city, boy, or have you come to use the Tram?" asked Kofi.

"We've come to use the Tram, Kofi," said Amanzi.

"Good. Then we'd be glad to take you. It has been mighty slow here over the past few weeks. At first, when talk of war with the Shark Folk spread, it was busier than ever. Then after the first week, it all came to a halt. Talk of war has made people less apt to travel. Last year at this time the place was thriving with folks, all sitting down waiting for the next Tram. But now, we haven't had a traveler here in over two days. Not sure why we need five operators sitting around. It seems that all we have to do all day is play game after game of Shax. Do you play Shax, Tau?"

"No, sir, I never heard of it."

"Well if you ever have the time, come around here and I'll teach you a thing or two about it."

"Haha," Fatuma laughed. "Kofi is even a worse Shax player than he is a Tram operator. I've won the last ten games in a row, which if I remember correctly, gives me seniority to operate the next Tram ride. It looks like I'll be the one to take you."

"Eh," said Kofi in disappointment. "She's right, it's her turn. Which of the cities do you need to go to?"

"Not one of our cities, Kofi. We need to go to Goree Island," said Amanzi."

"Goree, you say. Not much there from what I know of the place. Besides, that's a place for Dry Landers, Amanzi. I don't think your father would approve of that."

"I'm not going to the land. I just need to make sure that he gets there safely."

"Now, that we can do," said Fatuma "It is not far off from the Tram route of the Eastern City, but unless I hear otherwise, young lady, you will be coming back with me."

"Understood, ma'am."

"Okay then, no need to hang around here. I'll give you guys some time to brush up on your Shax skills until I get back, haha."

Fatuma led Amanzi and Tau over to a section of the room where the floor slopped downward into a smooth ramp. It extended beyond the reaches of the room above, further out into the water directly between the two rows of crystals.

The ramp merged into a rounded canal in the ocean floor about eight feet wide. The rows of crystals lined the side of the canal every twenty feet. Above the canal was a shaft of air ten feet high, making one big long tunnel. This air tunnel also followed the canal as far as the eye could see.

"I take it that you cannot breathe under water," said Fatuma.

"No, I can hold my breath for a long time, but breathing, I cannot do," Tau answered.

"Then Amanzi, I'll take care of the Tram, and you take care of him."

"Don't worry Fatuma, we've been doing it all day," Amanzi responded.

"Yes, I'm pretty used to it by now. Except for the time that

Amanzi forgot about me and I almost drowned."

"Amanzi!" Fatuma scolded.

"It was an accident. Won't happen again!"

Fatuma raised her arms upward as the small crystals on her staff began to shine. She slowly moved her arms downward, and then a large sphere of water entered the air tunnel from the ocean above and was brought down to the floor of the canal. Tau looked at the way the lights of the light blue crystals from the canal bounced off of the rippling surface. He was in awe at this large bubble of water.

"Now we step in," said Amanzi.

"We step inside that sphere of water?" Tau asked.

"Of course," said Fatuma. "That is the way it works. Here, I will go first." The sphere seemingly swallowed her up as she stepped in. Her image became distorted by the waves and motions of the water inside. Next went Amanzi, holding Tau's hand. She pulled him in right after her. He held his breath as he entered, even though Amanzi was quick to make sure that his air bubble was intact as soon as he came inside.

He took a moment to think about where he currently was: inside a thin layer of air all around him, inside a sphere of water, inside a tunnel filled with air, at the bottom of the ocean. It was like magic within magic, within magic.

"Here we go," said Fatuma as she reached her arm forward. The water-sphere lifted off of the dry ground a couple of inches and began moving forward. Tau watched the columns of illuminated crystals on the side zoom by faster and faster, and he heard a very low hum. He also noticed a small eel swimming close to him in the water-sphere.

"Um, Amanzi, there is something in here."

"Oh, that's an eel, it's not so big. You're not afraid of it are you? See? Look."

She stretched her arm out to the eel. It coiled itself around her arm and moved upward toward her shoulder.

"No, not afraid. A bit startled, maybe. I didn't expect to see anything in here."

"It happens sometimes," said Fatuma. "Sometimes things get trapped in the bubble when I bring it down. One time I accidently trapped a giant whale."

"Really?" Tau asked.

"No." Fatuma giggled.

"There you go, little buddy," said Amanzi to the eel. She used her power to control water to move it out of the water-sphere and back into the ocean above. Tau continued to be amazed by everything the Mar-Folk did.

"How does all of this work?" he asked.

"As you probably already know," said Fatuma, "we have the power to control water. Amanzi, even as we speak, is using her power to keep a pocket of air around you so that you can breathe. As we swim, we not only move through the water, we also move the water around us. It allows us to move even faster. This water Tram is another example of our power over the water. The crystals on the side of the tunnels aid us, as do the crystals in our staffs, and the crystals we keep in several of the rooms throughout the city. They amplify our power."

"So the crystals keep the water out of the tunnel?"

"Precisely. If you were to move far enough ahead of us, you would no longer see the crystals glowing. They are always working, to keep the air tunnel, yet it takes so little energy that the glow is extremely dim; only visible if you were right on top of it. As we move through the tunnel, they glow brightly as their power is used in conjunction with mine to swiftly move us through. In this manner, we can move much more quickly than simply swimming."

"So why do you need Tram operators? Can't Amanzi do what you are doing?"

"That's a pretty good question. Shows that you are paying attention. I like that. While we all have power over the water, I have been specifically trained to do this task with these crystals. It takes practice to feel them out. Sure, Amanzi could do it, but again, not nearly as fast or as well as I can."

"Besides," said Amanzi, "It's probably best right now for me to keep you breathing."

"Please do," said Tau.

"Here, try this." Amanzi went to the front of the water Tram and stuck her head out of it. "Come on," she said putting her face back into the sphere. "It's fun."

Tau was hesitant. He was wondering how easy it would be to fall out of the bubble, like he had fallen back into his prison room. He cautiously moved to the front and stuck his head out of the water sphere; into the air tunnel.

"Wow, this is great," he said. "It feels like we are moving so fast this way." He watched the glowing crystals as they moved quickly by them. Tau was surprised at how dry the ground was below them. It did not have a spot of water on it. He looked to the sides and at the water above them at all the fish that were swimming within his reach.

"Weeeeeeeeee!" Amanzi screamed out.

"Do you do this all the time?" Tau asked.

"Sometimes. They usually don't let us."

Tau felt a tug at his body pulling him back inside.

"That's enough of that," said Fatuma. "If you fall out, it will be on my head."

"I wouldn't have let him fall, Fatuma, I had him. I wanted to show him some fun."

"Which is why I let you do it in the first place. Believe it or not, your safety is my responsibility. So from here out, you stay inside."

"It's okay," said Tau. "It was fun while it lasted. How fast can this thing go?"

"Would you really like to see?" asked Fatuma.

"Sure!"

"I normally don't do this, but since you are new and I haven't even been out on the Tram in a while, I'll humor you. Amanzi, you help me out the best that you can. We'll see how fast we can get this thing moving."

"Oh, I've never run a Tram before, Fatuma," said Amanzi.

"I'm running it, you're helping out. Feel the balance between the water and the crystals and pull us through. Any help you can give me will make us go faster. Ready?"

"Yes."

"Here we go."

Fatuma's staff glowed even brighter as they sped off much faster than they had been moving before. So fast the rows of crystals on the side almost looked as if they were one continuous light. The path of the Tram followed the contours of the ocean floor precisely. As the terrain changed, so did the track to match it.

They zoomed around mountains, up hills, and down through valleys; all the while, Fatuma kept control and Amanzi did her best to help her move faster. Tau was along for the ride, and he was enjoying it. Soon they started up a huge hill and Fatuma began to slow the Tram.

"Ease off for a moment, Amanzi," she said. "This part is tricky. Let me go at it alone for a while."

Amanzi let Fatuma take total control again as the Tram slowed, coming to the top of the hill. Tau noticed why, for on the other side was a sharp steep drop straight down.

Fatuma sped it up again as they went downward. Tau could not help but to let out a loud, "whoa," as he felt the sensation of his stomach moving into his throat. He grabbed onto Amanzi to be sure that he would not fall out of the water-sphere all together.

The bottom of the cliff rounded out onto level ground again and Fatuma allowed Amanzi to resume helping her with speed; and they went faster again.

"See," said Fatuma. "That's what an Operator is for. You

have to really learn how to keep inside the tunnel through all the twists and turns and drops like that. Otherwise you could fly right off the track. It takes skill, my boy! I know this Tram and track like the back of my.... something is wrong!" she shouted. "Stop! Amanzi Stop!"

Fatuma struggled to bring the Tram to a halt. Every muscle in her body clinched tighter, but it was not enough. The water-sphere of the Tram smashed up against a boulder that sat in the tunnel directly in their path. Water splashed everywhere.

The three of them also were thrown against the boulder and fell into the canal on the ground. Tau found himself drenched in water although the air-tunnel was still intact.

"Is everyone all right?" asked Fatuma.

"I think so," said Amanzi. "Tau?"

"What happened?" Tau asked, picking himself up off of the ground.

"I'm not sure," said Fatuma as she also stood up. She looked around the tunnel and at the large boulder in the way. "When did this get here? We could have been seriously hurt. That's the last time I let some kids talk me into breaking the rules. It is reasons like this that we have to be careful. You never know what can happen. We really should not have been going that fast."

"Can we go around it?" Amanzi asked.

"The tunnel in front of us has collapsed. Perhaps it continues further up. Stay here for a second. I'll be right back." She walked into the water on the side of the tunnel and swam away.

"How are you doing, Tau?" Amanzi asked.

"My shoulder hurts, but I will be all right. Heck, if you only knew all the strange things that have happened to me over the past week, you'd wonder how I'm even alive. This doesn't even compare."

"I'll be looking forward to hearing all your stories."

"Has this ever happened to you on the Tram before?"

"Never. But I don't ride it all the time like Fatuma. Perhaps she has dealt with this sort of thing before. She'll know what to do."

"Hey," said Fatuma poking her head back inside the tunnel. "Can you two move?"

"Yes."

"Yes."

"Come on then, I want to show you something. We have a bigger problem than I thought."

She moved back into the water and they followed. They swam up above the Tram, looking at the boulder and the rest of the track there after.

"This is no accident," Fatuma said.

"What do you mean?" Amanzi asked.

"I mean someone has done this deliberately. Look at the boulder on the track. At first, I supposed that it could happen accidently, but there are no cliffs or hills nearby for a rock that size to fall from. And it would take a mighty current to move a boulder like that into place. Now look beyond the boulder. Much of the canal has been destroyed. That is man-made destruction. And even if all of that was some sort of coincidence, none of the crystals are lit beyond the boulder, not even a little, and I put my face right up close to it to check."

"What does it mean?"

"It means there is yet another break in the track somewhere down the line. These crystals should shine as we get close to them. That is how they are designed, but they only do so if they are connected to the source; to one of the stations on either end. No, someone has destroyed the track here, and then again somewhere down the line. Who knows how far down?"

"Shark Folk," Amanzi suggested.

"Yes, that is what I am thinking. They are up to something. I must go back and report this. We have to go back."

"Go back? But we've got to be close to Goree Island by now."

"We are, but this is a matter of security. This has to be reported immediately. The Shark Folk have deliberately taken actions against us."

"Tau needs to find his people," Amanzi explained.

"Yes, ma'am. We haven't told you the whole story, but I must get to my people, as soon as possible. I fear that they are in far worse trouble than you are. I have to get to them," urged Tau.

"I don't know," said Fatuma shaking her head. "This does not look good."

"Fatuma," said Amanzi. "Why don't you go back to the city and tell my father what has happened here. If it is as important as you say, then you must go back now. But let me take Tau to the island. It is what we have come for."

Fatuma thought for a moment. "Okay. You two go. But Amanzi, after you have taken him to the island, you come back to the Tram. Do your best to make your way down the tunnel. I will send someone else back as soon as possible. Oh, and Amanzi…."

"I know, I know, keep to the water and don't get involved in Dry Lander affairs."

"Yes. Travel safely. I wish you luck, Tau, and hope that you will be able to visit The Deep again."

"Thank you," Tau responded. "I wish you luck as well."

Fatuma quickly swam back to the air-tunnel and created a water-sphere for herself. Within moments, she had sped away.

"So I guess that we go it alone from here?" asked Tau.

"Yes, it's better that way. I didn't want to tell her, but there is a cave nearby here. It may be coincidence, but I need to check it out."

XXIII CHILDREN CRY

Never before had Tau ever experienced the ocean like this. There was so much to see, and while each moment provided him with something more spectacular to watch, Amanzi did not seem to notice at all. She was moving with speed and urgency, like a fish running from danger. All the while, Tau marveled at all of the sights along their path.

It was morning. The light rays of the sun burst through the surface like shiny swords piercing the water. Before, Tau's record for being below the water's surface was about eight minutes. Now, he had been further out and deeper than ever before and as far as his record for time, well it had been a whole day.

He took notice of all the living creatures around him. There were so many different kinds of colorful fish, large and small. He saw eels, turtles, huge stingrays, and beautiful giant jellyfish, some of them fifty feet long. There were vibrantly colored reefs in a world of their own, thriving with life. Tau added these sea creatures to his long and continuing list of new things. The starfish swam propelling themselves almost like squid, and large sea horses changed color once frightened. He saw bird-fish that were as comfortable swimming in the water, as they were flying in the sky above. How nice, Tau thought, a creature that lived on land, air, and water

"Where are we going?" he asked, concerned at the nature of Amanzi's urgent stride.

"It's up ahead," she replied. "It is much easier to show you than to tell you. I hope no one has gotten to him."

She did not stop moving until they arrived. She perched behind a protruding boulder on some very rocky, uneven terrain and pointed ahead of them in the distance to a large column-like structure. It was a natural, rounded, long column of rock about fifteen feet across. At the top of it was a much more grand rock structure. It looked like the column was holding up a small mountain under the sea.

"That's where we have to go," said Amanzi.

Tau saw the structure that she was referring to. But what really concerned him were the objects swimming around it; at least a dozen huge water beasts circled the column. They even looked big from where he was. They were fifteen-foot long, flat creatures with a dozen tentacles coming off of their sides.

"What about those big things swimming around?" Tau asked, appropriately.

"The migas? Yeah, well, we have to get past those. I knew they would be here. We put them there to protect what's inside."

"So wait a minute. You guys purposely tricked giant monsters into protecting whatever it is inside, and now we are going to try to get past them."

"Yes. We keep this place a secret, but with those things there, who in their right mind would go wandering in? There is an opening in the side of the column near the bottom. If we can make it in there, we are home free. Then we swim to the top. They are too big to make it inside."

"More like too big to get past. How do you plan on doing that?"

"Well, if I were alone, I could do it with no problem. I'm much faster and more agile than those things. But I've got you with me now, so we'll have to come up with something."

"I should have gone back on the Tram. Why didn't we bring Fatuma with us? At least we would have someone to help."

"Oh, no. We couldn't have done that. She doesn't know about it. We put the migas there to keep people away, but really it's the fact that this place is a secret that keeps it safe. I shouldn't even know about it."

"Then how do you know about it?"

"I'm the daughter of Soldier Prime. Sometimes information

comes my way. Even secrets."

"What secret?" Tau asked. He still did not know why they were here.

"Our greatest warrior."

"What? Is he trapped inside?"

"Too hard to explain," said Amanzi. "Like I said, it would be easier to show you."

"Okay, so we still have to get inside without getting eaten. I'm guessing those things have no problem eating people, whether those people are from land or sea."

"You're right. But I think I know how we can get in." Amanzi thought for a second then continued. "I may have to leave you. How long can you hold your breath?"

"I don't like where this is going, but about eight minutes. Er, seven, let's say seven. No, make that six. I can hold my breath for a good five minutes."

"Oh, I see. Before, it was, 'look at me, my name is Tau. I can hold my breath for eight minutes. I can hold it longer than anyone in my village.' How did you get down to five?"

"Being careful, that's all, until you tell me what is going through your head."

"Well, like I said before. I'm pretty swift and agile, not to mention the fact that I can hold them off by controlling the water around them, something that the Shark Folk cannot do. And they are actually air breathing mammals, not fish, so the Shark Folk can't control them. I figure that if I can lure them away, then you'll have time to swim into the column. The only problem is that if I get too far from you, I won't be able to keep your air bubble."

"So you want me to hold my breath all the way over there and up the column?"

"Yup."

"That's crazy!"

"It shouldn't take you five minutes, not even as slow as

YOU swim."

"Sure, but what if something goes wrong? I could drown."

"Here, take my watch," she said as she removed a flat crystal from her wrist and handed it to him. Tau had noticed it before but had not paid much attention to it. "This way, you'll know how much time has passed. Make it to the column and swim to the top. There is a cave up there; plenty of air. I'll be back before you get there."

Tau studied the watch for a moment, the slightly curved rectangular crystal with a smooth surface. It had a green glow emitting from it with many bubbles inside that seemed as if they had some sort of organization to them; some of them moved, some of them did not. "I have no idea what I am looking at. How do you tell time with this? It just looks like a bunch of bubbles moving around."

"Yes. It IS a bunch of bubbles moving around. Look, twenty four hours in a day, right?"

"Um, right."

"Okay, then, these show your hours here, these show your minutes and then seconds here. Simple."

"Okay, sure. I guess. But how will I know when the air bubble is going to go away? If I'm going to hold my breath, I'm going to need to take in a lung full of air first."

"Oh, yeah. I hadn't thought about that."

"It's because you breathe water. You don't know what it is like to have to hold your breath."

"I'll flash my wand six times. Um, two sets of three, like this," she quickly demonstrated to him, holding out her arm and counting. "One, two, three, pause, one, two, three."

"Better make it nine," Tau suggested.

"Okay, nine then. Like this, one, two, three, pause, one two three, pause, one two three."

"Are you sure about this?"

"Absolutely. Perfect plan."

"Yeah, perfect for you. You breathe water."

"Hey, I don't have it easy either. I have to evade and fight off the migas."

"That doesn't make me feel better. If something happens to you, I could drown. Even if I make it in there, but you don't, I'd be trapped in that cave forever probably."

"I wouldn't worry. You'll die of starvation long before forever comes."

He stared blankly at her. She gave him a coy smile.

"We going to do this or not?" she asked.

"I guess so."

"Swim as fast as you can, or you'll be…"

"I know, I know, migas' dessert."

"Something like that."

Amanzi swam off in a hurry, toward the column and toward the migas. Tau's anxiety grew. He could feel his heart beating faster and faster, which was not good for somebody who was about to have to hold his breath. He watched her move closer as the details of her body faded to a silhouette against the clear blue water.

Her intent was to provoke the migas. She used her power to thrust a current of water toward them, knocking them back. A few of them came after her as she quickly swam to the side, dodging their charge.

She swam right to the densest region of them. When it looked like she had the attention of all of them she swam up, looped around, came back down, and the migas followed. For a moment, one of them was able to grab her. It spun her around, twisting her closer to it. Tau feared for her. How could she volunteer to take on those beasts? When she got close enough, she made one quick cut to the migas' eye with her knife. It let her go and she swiftly moved away from it.

He looked at the watch, still learning how to use it as the seconds went by. He was quite intrigued by the thing.

He watched the light on her staff. Every time she moved the water, pushing the beasts back, it glowed. Each time, he anxiously got ready to hold his breath and move in. Then he saw the signal. As Amanzi started to move further away, bringing the migas with her, she flashed the light. One, two, three flashes of light, then a pause, three more and a pause... Tau began breathing in and out rapidly, short breaths in, and long breaths out, trying to prepare his lungs, getting them ready to take in the deepest breath ever taken. His apprehension grew. What was he doing? Was he ready for this? He had not been afraid to be under water since he was young. He thought of himself as a master of it. But this could be too much for him. This was going to be the test of all tests.

"You really ready to do this?" Chad asked him with apparent doubt.

Tau nodded, afraid to waste any breath on speaking.

"Then get ready, my friend..."

Three more flashes. Tau took a deep breath. A few seconds later, he felt the coldness of the water splashing upon his body. The air bubble was gone. He expected it to happen, but the sensation of the water crashing down on him completely took him off guard. He felt trapped and as the ocean engulfed him, a terrible sense of claustrophobia swept through him.

"What are you waiting for?" asked Chad. "Get going!"

Tau nodded, and then started toward the column, watching Amanzi trailing the migas away, twisting and turning through the water, using her powers to push them away from her whenever they got close.

He looked at the watch; one minute had passed, and he was nearing the column at the bottom. He circled around it, trying to find an entrance with no luck. He swam upward while rounding the column when a migas unexpectedly met him. The beast's mouth opened wide with all of its teeth preparing to tear into him.

Tau jumped back in time with a short yelp, letting loose a ton of air bubbles. He yanked out his blades and frantically swiped at the animal until he felt one of them connect with the Migas's tentacles. Another tentacle tried to grab him, but Tau did the same, slicing at the tentacle until that nasty migas yanked it back.

It was not a mortal wound, but the migas apparently did not like the feeling of steel slicing through its flesh at all. It backed off from its attack and headed off way from Tau. So much for the thought that Amanzi had lured them ALL away. Tau became increasingly concerned that there could be another one upon him at any second. He needed to get inside. Here in the water, he knew that everything was faster and more deadly than he was. He felt much like a fish out of water.

Two minutes passed. He continued looking for the entrance to the column, searching with his eyes and his hands, moving along the rock. He could not find one. He began to doubt that Amanzi knew what she was talking about. He looked around for her, but she was nowhere to be seen. It made him panic even more, but he continued to search the column for an open hole.

He looked at the watch. Three minutes passed. Still, Tau held his breath. Finally he found the entrance. It was plenty big enough for him to swim inside and luckily, not at all big enough for one of the migas to fit through. He gladly moved in, feeling a bit safer, and hoping that he could easily make his way to the top. For a moment he paused to see if he could catch any glimpse of Amanzi. He still did not see her.

The inside of the column was dark at first, but as he looked upward, he could see light. Good, there WAS something to swim too. Then he noticed that the light was moving. To be more correct, there was something in the water moving around in front of the light!

Four minutes passed. He continued upward, feeling the tension build in his chest, as his lungs began to struggle. He was going to need some air soon. Under these stressful conditions, his body was not as efficient in doing without air as it usually was.

His heart was beating way too fast.

He cautiously swam up the column. He felt trapped inside this vertical tunnel, knowing that the only way out was to reach the top or to go back down the way he had come in. As he got closer to the top, the light brought into detail these strange shapes moving around in the water. They were migas!

So much for the idea that they could not fit inside; these migas were much smaller than the others. They could fit through the entrance as easily as he could. Amanzi had said nothing of these; though he did not have a choice. All he knew was that he had to get past them to get to the air above. He pulled out his blades again and carefully moved toward them.

Five minutes with no air. He was suddenly fighting his body. His lungs tried to pump, but he struggled against them as hard as he could as the tightness in his chest increased. His hands shook, and he could barely control his weapons. He remembered drowning, just a day ago, the pain, the burning of his lungs as they filled with water, his lungs fighting for something to take in while his muscles convulsed to push the water out. For some reason, every time he was near death in the ocean, his thoughts moved back to Chad, and what it must have felt like in the last moments of his life.

At first he wanted to move through these little beasts cautiously, but his new plan was to swim through them with speed, swinging blindly at everything around him and hoping for the best.

Before he knew it, he felt the water move away from him as once again the air bubble was back. He looked down the tunnel to see Amanzi swimming upward, toward him.

"Amanzi!" he yelled, taking huge wonderful breaths of air. If his lungs could speak they would have thanked her over and over again.

"Told you!" she said. "Piece of cake."

"Piece of cake? I thought I was about to die! I didn't see

where you were and look!" He pointed up to the smaller migas. "We can't go up; we have to get out of here!"

"Oh my," she said. "I didn't know they were in here, but don't worry, these are the babies. They won't attack you. Move slowly, and you should be fine."

"Move slowly? Through those? There are at least thirty or forty of them!"

"Yes, slowly. They don't even have teeth when they are that small. Come on. We'll go together."

Amanzi swam up to Tau's level, and slowly they began to move up the tunnel. They swam right through the swarm of the baby migas. Tau felt their bodies slither against his as he ascended. Each touch sent a shiver down his spine. He felt like snakes were crawling all over him, and he wanted to scream.

One of them slithered down his back and curled its body around him. "It's got me! It's got me!" he screamed and thrashed around.

"No! No! You're fine," she assured him as she aided in pulling the thing off of him.

But he had scared the baby beast. It swam round toward his face and let out a loud shriek, "EEEEEEEEEEEEEEEEEEEE!"

After the one screamed, others followed, thrashing wildly until all of the little babies were letting out horrible sounding shrieks.

"They're freaking out," said Amanzi.

"They're freaking out? I'm freaking out!"

Then they heard a loud thump against the side of the column. It sent ripples through the water inside hard enough for Tau to feel. More loud thumping followed, over and over again, until the pounding noise was constant.

"What is it?" Tau yelled.

"It's their parents!"

The adult migas' had heard the call of their children. They responded with a deep roaring sound. They swam fiercely, ramming the column with their large heads. One of the adults tried to stuff itself into the entrance. Its large body became lodged, and it shook vigorously, trying to make its way inside. Another one, not far below them, was able to ram the column so hard that it made a hole big enough for its nose to fit through.

"They're breaking in!" yelled Amanzi.

"Yes, I see it! I see it!"

The migas began sticking their tentacles through the holes, grabbing and swatting at them. Amanzi and Tau continued to move around the tunnel, slashing at them, cutting off tentacles, which were replaced by more coming through the hole. Still other migas were trying to come in head first.

The young ones continued to scream, swarming all around Amanzi and Tau. Another loud thud, and a migas made another hole in the tunnel, trying to break through with its face. This time it happened right in front of them. The large beast backed up and then rammed the hole again, making it even bigger. Tau watched as it backed up yet again and started its run for another ramming. He could tell that soon, this thing would break its way inside.

"We have to move!" Amanzi yelled. "Hurry."

Her wand started to glow as she moved the water all around Tau and pushed him upward as hard as she could. Tau felt himself being thrust toward the opening at the top; he was about ten feet from it, when his air bubble collapsed again.

He looked around frantically for Amanzi. The migas rammed the hole one last time, smashing though it and into Amanzi. It apparently knocked her backward against the other side of the column up against the hard rock. She was knocked out cold, which immediately collapsed the air bubble around Tau.

Unlike before, Tau was not at all ready for his air to be taken away. As the water came back upon him, he was busy inhaling. His lungs burned worse than ever as the water rushed into them. Immediately, he choked on it, feeling like he was drowning. He desperately made his way up the last ten feet of water at the top and pulled himself onto the dirt surface.

He lay there coughing and wheezing in terrible pain as his body tried to force the water out. He inhaled deeply, clutching his chest, crawling around on the ground as he leaned over and looked back into the column of water. Amanzi appeared to be dead, floating in the water. Part of her was wrapped in the tentacle of one of the adult migas. Right above her, a Migas was squirming around in the hole that it had made, trying to make its way through to her, and still others continued to pound their way into the rocky tunnel. The little ones still swarmed around shrieking and screaming, apparently calling out to their parents to come save them from these strangers.

"Amanzi!" he said to himself in between gasps. He took a small moment to catch his breath and stop coughing, but he knew he had to go back and save her. He stood up, and, with both his blades in his hands, he dove back into the water.

He did not worry about the babies since he knew that they could not hurt him. But he readied himself as he came to that large adult that was making its way inside. Tau swung as hard as he could at the beast, wounding the topside of it with several cuts. Soon it backed itself out of the hole. He was not going to wait for it to come back, or for another one to come and take its place. He cut Amanzi loose from the tentacle holding her, then sheathed his blades and grabbed Amanzi under her shoulders, lifting her up.

Tau carried her through the water and through the swarm of baby migas until he reached the top. He pulled himself out of the water, then Amanzi, and laid her on the ground. She did not move.

"Amanzi!" he cried out to her. "Amanzi, wake up!"

She was breathing, which was a good thing, but it was very slow. Still she did not wake up. He sat on the ground and laid her across his lap, waiting and hoping for her to wake up, or move, or anything.

He gasped and sighed, now looking around the room when

his attention was brought to the far wall. There, suspended on the wall, was a sleeping man incased in crystal.

XIV SAVIOR

The room glowed with an amber light, but not from any fire. Several one-foot long crystals lay evenly along the base of the wall of the irregularly rounded cave, casting a soft elegant glow. Illuminated vines stretched across the ceiling and on the upper part of the walls, curving and twisting, providing more light to the room.

The floor varied from grey rock, to black dirt, and was covered with long green grass and flowers such as African violets, lilacs, stapelias, and Ashanti bloods. Each flower was bright and brilliant, and they covered most of the floor. It all looked tended to, as if it was someone's personal garden.

There was a clear patch of soft soil directly under the man encased in the crystal. He looked as if he was either dead or asleep. He had bright blue fins that were wrapped around his legs and arms. He wore no shirt on his muscular chest, but his form fitting pants looked as though they were made from shiny blue and silver fish scales that captured the light in the room brilliantly.

His salt and pepper beard was long enough to touch his strong chest and was connected to his mustache above it. The gray and black hair on his head was long as well, and though it was thick and full, it was swooped back behind him. He looked, if nothing else, peaceful.

His skin was very dark, and his patterns were made of gold; a fitting color for a man that emanated greatness. Tau had wondered what other colors naturally developed across these people, but gold was not one that he had thought of before. Perhaps gold was save for people of great importance.

Tau looked toward the man, his eyes watering from tears, holding Amanzi in his arms. After Chad, he just could not be responsible for another friend dying. Perhaps there was something this man could do. There was obviously something powerful about him.

"I don't know if you are this Mami Wata that Amanzi spoke of, but if you are, then I know you have great power. Please, please, don't let Amanzi die. I haven't known her long, but I know that she is a good person, and she doesn't deserve this. I do. She was only saving me." He leaned down, squeezing Amanzi tight. "Come on Amanzi, you have to wake up!" Over and over again, he said in soft voice, "Please wake up, please wake up, please wake up, please wake up..."

Tau noticed the slight sound of trickling water. A small stream of it began to flow out of the top of the tunnel where Tau had entered the room.

Amanzi made a slow movement toward the water, pointing her finger out to it. The water moved along the ground then flowed up to her finger. It spread across her hand, her arm, and across the rest of her until her entire body was completely covered in a thin layer of water. Tau felt her chest expand as she took in a giant deep breath.

Her eyes cracked open, to Tau's delight. A smile stretched across his face. "Amanzi!" he cried. "You're okay!"

Amanzi blinked her eyes and looked around the room in confusion.

"It's me, Tau."

"Tau?" she asked in a soft, unsure voice.

"Yes. It's me."

Suddenly Amanzi sat up. A look of terror spread across her face. "The migas!"

"It's okay," Tau said, assuring her of their safety. "We are safe now. We're in the cave."

"How?"

"The migas knocked you unconscious. I pulled you out. I didn't know if you were okay or not, but your Mami Wata helped you," he said, pointing to the man on the wall. "I begged him, I begged him to make sure you were all right."

"You begged for me?"

"Well, not begged. I asked him," Tau said, feeling a bit bashful. Amanzi, seeming to see right through him, smiled. She looked over at the man on the wall. "Tau, that's not Mami Wata. Mami Wata comes to us as woman."

"Oh. Well I saw him cover you with water and bring you back."

She looked at the layer of water on her skin. "Oh, that. I did that."

"You?"

"It is something that my people do when we are out of water. See, when you are in water, we keep a layer of air around you. Sometimes when we are out of water, we like to keep a layer of water around us. It feels better. We also do it to help heal ourselves when we are out of water. I probably did it without even thinking about it."

"Then no one helped you? Not this guy, and not Mami Wata?"

"Oh, I wouldn't say that. We never know when Mami Wata helps us. It could be every day. Her spirit helps all of my people. She is queen of all that is in the sea."

"Like Yemoja?"

"Who?"

"Uncle always taught me that Yemoja was the soul of the sea."

"It could be. They could be the same person, or different souls. Sometimes what seems different to us is the same to them. One may be the mother, the other the daughter; who knows? But you don't have to completely understand them to respect them."

"So what about this guy?"

Amanzi slowly stood up. Tau instinctively helped her. Then she walked over to the man in the crystal. She knelt before him in the dirt patch and then stood up again. "This is Behan'zin, one of our greatest warriors. I came because I needed to be sure that he hadn't been taken, or destroyed."

"How long has he been here?" asked Tau, moving over to stand beside her.

"I'm not sure. A long time. Way before I was born."

"Why is he in here hanging on the wall?"

"It was a terrible time for my people. We were in the middle of a civil war. At the same time, we were in a war with the Dry Landers."

Amanzi paused for a moment. She walked foreword and put her hand on the crystal containing Behan'zin. He was hanging so high on the wall that her hand barely reached past his foot. "Not only was he a great warrior, but he was also a wise and peaceful man. He taught us the error of our ways. He brought the civil war to an end and peace to our people. He also negotiated a truce with the Dry Landers. It is why we do not interfere in the affairs of Dry Landers today. Once peace settled among us, Behan'zin felt that his talents would be wasted living a regular life. He asked to be encased in crystal until he was needed again. He was a great man, a selfless man. He didn't even need to live the life of peace that he so greatly fought for."

"How will you know when to bring him out? Who decides?"

"Mami Wata will let us know when the time is right. Hopefully it will be soon. I think something is wrong with the sea."

"What do you mean?"

"I'm not sure, I've tried to explain it before, but people think that I am crazy. I can feel it though. It's like the ocean is sick or something. When he was around, there used to be sky-whales. They said their songs could be heard throughout the sea, but no one has heard them since he has been gone. And then there is this war with the shark folk. It's going to happen; I just know it. We will need him again soon.

"These Shark Folk, they share the waters with you?"

"Yes, but they are shape shifters. They are humans that have the ability to change into sharks. They live on both the land and in the sea. Lately the tensions between us have been growing. No one is exactly sure why. Some say it is because of simple greed over territory. Some say it is because they want to control the green dome. Others think that it is because they have been joining forces with The Children of Montok."

A fire burned in the pit of Tau's stomach. "Yes, The Children of Montok, also known as the Brood. I know of them well. They are the ones who chased me out of my village. They are the reason why I am here. They are the ones who have taken my people to Goree Island. I must get them back." Tau walked closer to the body of Behan'zin. "I don't get it."

"Get what?"

"Look at him. He is exactly what you described. He looks like a great man, a man to entrust the fate of a whole people to, a man that can move mountains, a man with great power, a man that is almost a god."

"Yes, he is. He has enormous power. He is a Water Crafter."

"What's a Water Crafter?"

"You know that my people and I can control water, but a Water Crafter can truly use the power of water to do miraculous things. I have personally never seen anyone use the art of Water Crafting. I don't know if there is still anyone that can."

"How is it different from what you do?"

"With Water Crafting, one can use regular water to create *white water*, to talk to spirits, *blue water,* which can freeze to create ice, and *gold water,* which can make one invincible. And those are just a few of them. There is also *red water* and *black water.* With all of this power, he became our savior."

"Savior." Tau put his head down. He walked away from the wall and took a deep breath. "Savior? That's what a savior is supposed to look like, Amanzi. Like him. Not like me. I don't understand at all. How can I save anyone? I'm not strong like he is. I'm not a great warrior. I don't have the special powers he does. I'm not smart. I can't negotiate peace treaties. I thought I was a good swimmer, but compared to you, that's not even true. You tell me how I am supposed to be a savior! I shouldn't even be here. I want to go back home with Uncle. Life was good there. I'm not selfless. And I don't want to be anyone's savior."

Amanzi walked over to him and put her hand on his shoulder. "You saved ME."

"That was different."

"You have a lot bearing down on you. Know that you don't carry it alone. You have been chosen, Tau, for a reason. It doesn't matter if you understand or if you can even see what that reason is. Those that watch over us can see far more than we can. You should know that the gods have a plan, and it is simply up to us to take our part in it. You must believe in yourself. I believe in you."

Tau looked at her. The layer of water still surrounded her body, shimmering against the light as it rippled across her skin. "Maybe you are right," he said, staring into her eyes. "I do know one thing though. I don't care what your sisters say. You're one of the prettiest girls I have ever seen."

Amanzi bashfully smiled at him. They spent another moment staring at each other with smiles that simply said, "I care."

"You know," said Tau, uncomfortably changing the mood. "You said that the Shark Folk are shape shifters. I never told you that I am a shape shifter too."

"You are? You mean you are Shark Folk!"

"No, not Shark Folk at all. Here watch."

Tau took a couple steps back from her. He closed his eyes tight, trying his best to remember his new skill. A white mist circled his body and in the next second, he was standing before her on all fours in his leopard form with a tan coat and black spots. He ran across the room and then back to her.

Amanzi jumped back for a second and then smiled. "All this

time, and you never told me this."

Tau turned back into his human form. "Well, we've been busy. And there is not much use for it in the water."

"What's that like? To turn into a cheetah?"

"Leopard," Tau corrected.

"Leopard."

"It's actually pretty cool. I can run really fast. Not a lot of room for it in here, but what is hard to describe is my heightened sense of agility and balance. Not to mention my other senses like eyesight, smell, and hearing.

Amanzi thought for a second, "what happens to your clothes, and your weapons? They just disappeared, and now that you are human again, they are back."

"Hmmm, I don't know. That's a really good question. I never thought about it. I didn't think to even ask when Kato taught me."

"You're clothes and weapons just disappear and you didn't think to ask one question about it?"

"No. I've just learned all of this myself. I guess I was all wrapped up in the magic of it all. Finding out you can change into a leopard and that you are from a whole race of people that can do the same is a pretty big deal. I've grown up my whole life not being around my people, the Tribe of Leopards, and as soon as I did find them, they got captured. Everyone except me."

"See, that only proves that you are the one for the job. The gods saved you, and you alone."

"Yeah. It was easy for the Brood. All they had to do was look for the people with the grey skin. I don't know what they want us for, but it isn't right, being hunted down for the color of your skin."

"You're right. A man can't help what people he was born to, nor what village. All he can do is decide what kind of man he is going to be, regardless if he has grey skin or not. And you, Tau, I think you will be a great man."

Tau gave an uncertain nod. Then he switched his gaze from the man to the vines in the room. I've been seeing those vines lately. What are they?"

"You mean the life-vines?" she pointed.

"Yes."

"They're vines…that give light."

"Then, shouldn't we call them "light-vines?""

"Maybe. But they are alive. So they are called life-vines. They can be used for many, many things. Mostly, people use them for the light though."

"I can't believe I have never seen them before. There is a lot that I have seen lately that I have never seen before. I never realized there was so much outside of Makazi."

Amanzi walked back to the column and looked deep into the water with the baby Migas still thrashing around.

"We have made them angry. It's going to be hard to get out of here."

"We're going to have to come up with a plan."

Amanzi sighed. "Please say we don't have to do it right now. "I'm too tired to think. Way too tired to go fighting off monsters again."

"No. We should rest for a while. You should sit down."

"Good idea." She walked over by Tau and sat next to him.

"How close are we to Goree Island?"

"Very close actually. It won't take us long to get there."

"I think it's amazing how you can control water like that."

"We are born with it. We are sorcerers. But you have a power too. Your people are also sorcerers. A different kind."

"Yes, but nothing like yours. I'd love to borrow your control of water, even for a little while. It would be great."

"Oh, I could do that, but it wouldn't be good."

"Oh, no. I was kidding. But you really could?"

"It's been done before, but very rarely. And only to someone else with some kind of sorcerer's blood. Only problem is, usually that means that we are about to die. Any one of us that has lent our power to someone else has died after doing so."

"That doesn't sound good."

"No. Like I said, it is rarely done."

"I'll settle for having you tow me through the water."

"Haha. I have to, or else, you would be migas' cuisine."

"I'm so tired right now; I would be an easy meal."

"Then let's not go anywhere until we take a good long nap. It's probably well into the night by now. What time is it?"

Tau looked at the watch. "Uh… It's…"

"Still can't read it?"

"No, I got it. 10:18." He started to take it off of his wrist. "Here, you should take it back."

"No, that's okay, you can keep it if you want it. But if you get too far from me, it will stop working after about ten minutes or so."

Tau scrunched up his face, "Why? How does it work?"

She moved to him to point at the watch as she talked. "Inside the crystal is basically water. And since we control water, it only works around us."

"So you are making the time go by?"

"No. More like, it is just powered by us. I really don't know how the thing works. I don't actually make them."

"Oh, I see."

"But the way it works is just like your time. What do you call it? Palm-time?"

"Yes."

"I've always wondered why they call it that."

"Palm-time?"

"Yes."

"Oh, I think it comes from an ancient king when it was invented. He would place one of his palms out toward the horizon, straight in front of him. That would be the hour one. Then he would place the other hand on top of that one for the second hour. He would keep doing that and get to the hour six straight above him. Then he would go back down toward the horizon behind him until he reached the hour twelve. Then he would do the same thing downward past his feet at the hour six again and then back to the original horizon. That would complete a full circle with twenty-four hours in a day. Oh, and each of his fingers would be twelve minutes."

"Does that work for everyone? I mean people have different sized hands."

"It works well enough."

"Wait, you said that hour six was above you. But straight above you would be twelve."

"Oh. Right," said Tau. "For some reason, they switched that so that noon would be hour 12 at the height of the sun."

"Making midnight hour 12 at your feet."

"Right."

"It's a bit weird, but it makes sense. Gotta keep time somehow. May as well use the sun. Although, it is not very exact."

"How exact do you need to be?"

"Well, we can count things exactly by the seconds, at all times."

"How do you do that?"

"The drip."

"The drip?"

"Yea. "It's in a cave. The cave shows us time by the drips. Every second, a drip drops. And then there is another drip that drops every minute. There are all sorts of different drips in there. People call it the cave of time. Or sometimes the time cave. It just so happens, the drip gives us twenty-four hours too."

"Wow, that's weird. And it always works?"

"Yup. It's down there working right now. It's been there since as long as our people can remember. I think that it is Mami Wata that keeps the drip going. I should take you to it one day."

"I'd be glad to go. But if we are going to do that, I have to find my people first."

"Yes. And speaking of time, it's probably time for us to get some sleep."

"Agreed."

XXV RAW COMFORT

The body of Behan'zin was the first thing that Tau saw when he awoke. At first, looking at him made Tau feel inferior, and all that came to his mind was self-doubt. However, after a moment, looking at Behan'zin gave him confidence in himself.

He glanced around for Amanzi, but she was not there. He stood up and looked around the room; still she was not there.

"Amanzi," he called out while rushing over to the water column. She did not answer. He strained his eyes to look as far down the column as he could, but it was empty. Not even the baby migas were there.

Worried, he looked back a Behan'zin, on the wall. "Where is Amanzi? Did something happen to her?" He half expected the great savior to jump down from the wall and answer him, but his body remained the same, motionless in his deep sleep.

Tau looked back into the water, thinking about how long he could hold his breath. Would he have to dive down into the water to look for her? He would only get so far. He walked over to a rock and sat upon it, thinking the worst, imagining sea monsters coming into the cave and taking her while they slept. He quickly tried to push these notions out of his mind.

He looked at the watch she gave him, trying to figure how much time had passed, but there was no light coming from it. It was black. He tapped and shook the thing but still it did not come on.

After a while, he noticed that the watch suddenly show again with its green light. Again, he could see the bubbles inside. Then the feint sound of splashing water focused his attention to the water hole, where Amanzi emerged. He smiled.

"Hope you are hungry," she said cheerfully.

"I thought something might have happened to you. Where

did you go?" Tau said, relieved.

"To get us food," she said climbing out of the water. "I didn't want to wake you." Then she held up two large fish.

"How long were you gone?" he asked. "I tried looking at your watch, but it turned black."

"Oh. If I'm to far away from it for too long, it will turn of. It came back on when I got closer."

"Oh. That's neat. I was wondering what was wrong with it. Well, what happened to the migas?"

"They're gone. I suppose the parents didn't find this place safe anymore. I'm going to have to tell my father that they are no longer there to protect it. He'll know what to do." She laid one of the fish next to him. "Here, this one is yours."

Tau looked around the cavern. "What are we going to cook them with?"

"Cook? No need to cook. We'll eat them raw."

Tau turned his face in disgust. "Do you always eat them raw?"

"No. We usually cook our food. But when we need to, we eat it raw. That's what took me so long. Had to find the right ones."

"I guess I will try it."

"You'll try or you'll be hungry."

Tau waited to see how she would eat her fish. He pictured her biting right into its face, but she did not. She pulled out her knife and cut the head off. Then she sliced the belly and gutted the fish. After that she carefully cut under its skin and peeled it off.

"Are you going to eat?" she asked. "Or are you just going to watch me?"

Tau smiled and then repeated the same steps with his fish until the meat was attainable. Both of them cut pieces off and he watched her watching him as he placed a piece in his mouth. Her eyes beckoned for a response from him.

"Well?"

It was not what Tau was used to, but it was not terrible either; perhaps because he was so hungry. The texture was mostly soft with minimal resistance to his bites. He could taste the distinct flavor of the fish and a slight saltiness to it. He nodded his head to her.

"Glad you like it."

"I do like fish. I eat it all the time. But we never eat it raw back home."

"What's it like?"

"My home?"

"Yes. You've seen my home. What's yours like? Were you born there or have you lived a bunch of places?"

"I was born there." Then he thought for a moment. "Actually, that's not true. I don't know where I was born. But I was raised there from a baby."

"How could you not know where you were born? Don't your parents know?"

"I only have one parent, Uncle. Actually, I call him that, but he's not even my real uncle. I never knew my parents. Uncle found me when I was a baby."

Amanzi stopped eating and developed a distraught look on her face. "He just found a baby?"

"Yup. As the story goes, he found me in a basket on a river. He said that I was crying so loudly that I had the lungs of a lion. That's how I got my name, Tau Zaire. It means, 'lion of the river.'"

"Wow. You would think that leaving a baby in a basket on a river wouldn't be a safe thing to do." She gestured toward Tau. "But here you are."

"What about your parents?" he asked. "I guess I've already met your dad. "He's...well...stern. I pretty much hoped he wasn't going to kill me. Is your mother nice? And were you born in the same place where you live now?"

"My mom is a wonderful woman, although she can be difficult at times. Especially lately. I was born in the Eastern City. We moved to the West City when I was young, when my father became Soldier Prime. I think there is something bad going on between my parents, but I don't know what. My mother goes back to the East City quite often."

"Is that a bad thing? What's wrong with the Eastern City?"

"There is nothing bad about it. It's a great place. We are from there. My grandparents are there, and other members of my family. Mother has friends and the whole life she had before back there. We have gone back and forth many times to visit."

"So if there is nothing wrong with it, then what makes you think something is wrong with your parents?"

She has been going a lot lately. She goes alone, and doesn't take me, or my sisters, or my brother, or my dad. And she goes for long periods of time; which isn't normal. She's been gone for three weeks now."

"I'm thirsty," said Tau.

"Thirsty? Oh. I didn't even think about it. If we were back home, I could get you some fresh water. But I don't think there is any around here. We'll have to find some when we leave."

"It's okay. I think I'll be all right for now." He placed another chunk of salty raw fish into his mouth. "So, you miss your mother?"

"Yes. But it's more than that. It's the feeling that something is wrong, and not knowing what it is."

"Uncle used to tell me that in life, you can never have all the answers. He said that it is the search for the answers that is the real journey of life."

"In a way that makes sense. Of course, if you look at it another way, it's extremely complicated."

"Heh, yeah. I always hated when he talked like that. But then sometimes something would happen, and then I'd understand. Like meeting you. I was sent away to find answers about myself and my people. I don't have those answers yet, but I'm glad that I had to look for them because now I've met you. And being with you is…comforting."

"That's sweet."

"And sometimes, you just have to do nothing. Don't even think about it."

"How can I not think about it?"

"I don't know, but not knowing and thinking about it will leave you wondering the worst. Maybe it's not as bad as you think. Maybe your mother is just tending to someone else's problems over there." He took a deep breath. "When you were gone just now, going to get us food, I didn't know where you were. I thought something had happened to you. Terrible things ran through my head that involved you getting eaten by sea creatures. Eventually I had to just relax, quit thinking those crazy thoughts, and wait. Then all of a sudden, there you were, smiling. And everything was okay."

"You're so right. Sometimes, I do think the worst."

"Well don't do that," he said calmly. "Don't think the worst."

"Okay, but can I tell you something?"

"Is it the worst?"

"I'm only telling you because I want you to know what I've been thinking. Not because I'm actually thinking it now, because I'm not."

"Um…okay."

"What if?" she took a long pause, "what if it's me she's running away from."

"See, that is exactly the type of thing you shouldn't be thinking."

Amanzi quickly stood up. "I know. I know. But sometimes I think what if the reason why she keeps leaving has something to do with me. She's been so distant. Maybe I'm not the sweet little girl that she wanted; maybe I ask too many questions about the world that we live in, or maybe she expected me to be a different person, a better person. Maybe…"

Tau stood up and grabbed her hands, interrupting her. "Hey," he said calmly. "How long have you been doing this to yourself?"

"Doing what?"

"Placing blame on yourself for your mother's issues. You said it yourself; you don't know what is going on with her, so why make yourself the villain? You don't deserve that."

"I'm not even sure why I'm telling you all of this."

"It's okay. I'll listen to whatever it is you have to say. But you shouldn't make yourself the bad guy. One thing I know about you for sure already, is that you are a great person. Probably the best that I've met yet."

"You're just saying that. You can't really know."

"I know that you are smart. You figured out how to get in here. I know that whatever skills it is that you and your people possess, you are a master. I mean, you handled those migas like nothing. I also know that you care…about everyone. I don't know your brother, but it looks like your sisters only care about themselves, but not you. You care about everyone. You're not only worried about your mother, but you're worried about the fate of all your people and this war. You even went out of your way to make sure that Behan'zin was okay, because you know he matters. So despite all this drama going on in your head, Amanzi, you are a good person."

"Thank you," she said and leaned in closer to him. "I believe in you, too."

Neither of them said anything for a while. They stood there holding hands, with her head on his chest until Amanzi spoke again.

"Sorry about that. I didn't mean to get into all of that."

"This conversation certainly did take a turn."

"Heh, yea, it sure did." Then she quickly broke away from

him.

"What are we doing? I've just been going on and on about my mother, while your entire tribe is out there somewhere. You have to find them."

"It's okay, we can take our time," Tau assured her.

"No," she said. "We should go. That is, if you are ready."

"Okay then," said Tau as he grabbed her hand, then they walked over to the water hole in the ground. "You first."

Amanzi smiled and dove into the water. Tau took one last look at Behan'zin, hoping that during his stay there, he had absorbed some of his greatness. Then he followed after her.

XXVI GOREE ISLAND

Tau and Amanzi surfaced at virtually the same time with the island in view in front of them. The mid-day sun, high in the clear sky, shone brightly on the almost golden sands. It felt strange to Tau to be above water again. He had not realized how accustomed his mind had become to being under the sea. Only a couple of days had passed, and yet the cotton clouds that hung silently in the sky seemed almost like a long lost friend. He turned to Amanzi who suddenly spit out a long spout of water from her lips.

The sight brought him to the taste of salt water on his own lips. "Yuk," said Tau.

"What?"

"The saltwater on my mouth, I hate it. It's the one thing that I don't like about the ocean. There is no salt in the lake where I'm from. I don't see how you can stand it."

"Tau, I live in salt water, all day, every day. I breathe in it."

"How do you breathe, anyway? I don't see any gills or anything."

"Oh, we have them, they're just inside. When I spit the water out just then, I was emptying my cavity to start breathing air again. It's this air that is strange to me; all that dryness. Like that sand on your island over there."

It looked much like any other island. The bright sands stretched over one hundred feet inland and as far as they could see around the island. Behind that was a tree line that looked to be the start of a thick forest.

Goree Island was made up of two parts: the main island, which was extremely large and directly in front of them, and one other island that was small enough that almost the whole thing could be seen at once. There was a channel that separated the bigger one from the smaller one.

The smaller island had strange looking large structures attached to it. Once they got a bit closer, Amanzi recognized them for what they were, but Tau had never seen anything like them before in his life.

"Look how big those boats are," he said.

"When they are that big, they call them ships."

"I have heard of great ships, but I have never seen one before. You?"

"Oh yes. They are often used by Dry Landers to transport things across the water."

"And inside, can you put things inside it too?"

"Yes, a lot of space inside."

"I bet if it was empty, you could put about a hundred people in there."

"Maybe, but not very comfortably."

"Still, it would explain how they could take so many people at once. And they have three ships." Tau studied the area and the two islands for a moment. "I'll bet everyone is on that larger island."

"Agreed," said Amanzi. "Then they keep the ships over here to keep people from escaping."

"That makes sense."

The smaller island, where the three ships were docked, was for the most part open land. Beyond its beach the land was flat with very few trees to hide behind.

The sands of the larger island extended for about a hundred feet before changing to a thick forest; the obvious choice for where his people might be, if they were there at all. Tau thought that the shoreline was too wide. It would take them quite some time to make their way to the tree line. It was too open, too easy for the guards walking across the sand to see them.

They decided to make their way around the island, to somewhere where they could hide more easily once they were out of the water. They swam toward the channel that separated the two islands. There was no bridge, but there was a large flat structure of wood tied together lying on the small island just before the channel. Tau thought that perhaps if someone pushed it or pulled it across the channel, it could be used for a bridge.

The guards were of the Brood. There was no doubt about that in Tau's mind. He had seen those black masks with red paint on them enough times, and each time the sight of them made his whole body cringe.

Amanzi and Tau stayed underwater as they made their way through the channel to move around to the other part of the island. As they neared the channel they came to an underwater net blocking their path. It was made from rope with several thousand sharp teeth woven into it.

"So much for going this way," said Tau as he grabbed on to the net with his hands. "What do you suppose this is for?"

"I don't know," said Amanzi. She too was feeling the net, pulling at it to see how strong it was. "I wonder how far it goes."

"It looks like we will have to go around the other..."

Suddenly, the water around Tau felt increasingly hot!

"Look out!" Amanzi screamed as she grabbed Tau and yanked him back.

A red shark came at them from the other side of the net. It bit into the net trying to get at them, and then quickly let go as the teeth from the net pierced into its mouth.

"Whoa. Thanks," said Tau.

"It's a red shark!" she said. "They aren't terribly big, but when they attack, they glow and heat up all the water around them. It boils small fish in an instant. I suppose the net is to keep those things out."

"It looks more like it's there to keep them in," he said. "I'll bet the whole channel is filled with them, to keep people from trying to swim from the main island to the smaller one with the boats. I guess we'll have to take the long way around."

"Okay, but if we run into any more nets, let's stay clear of them."

They circled the island, staying under water most of the time, only coming up now and then to check the layout of the shore. Soon the sandy shoreline ended and they came upon an area where the ocean water met right up to the black rocks, forming a small cliff. At the top of the cliff was an immediate tree line that started the forest. They carefully surfaced in front of the rocks, then grasped on to the side of them to stay above water, checking their surroundings for any hint of the Brood Army.

"This looks good," said Tau, eyeing the layout of the cliff. It seemed like a suitable way to enter the island.

"Tau," said Amanzi in a timid voice.

But Tau kept talking. "We should easily be able to climb that."

"Tau."

"Once we are at the top, we can hide in the trees as we make our way onto the island."

"Tau."

"Once in the tress, I'll change to a leopard. I'll be harder to see that way, plus I'll be able to hear, see, and smell much better."

"Tau."

"Don't worry, if we get into trouble, I'll make sure not to leave you behind. I'll stay at a pace where you can keep up. Otherwise I'll leave you in the dust if I'm a leopard. Ha, this time, we will be on MY turf!" he said smugly.

"Tau!" Amanzi shouted firmly. "Listen!"

"What? What is it?"

"I'm not going with you."

Tau stared at her blankly.

"Did you hear me? I'm..."

"Not going with? What do you mean? Is it because you'll be out of the water? You can do that water thing where you cover your whole body, can't you?"

"Yes, I can do that, but that's not it."

"Then why?"

"You know why. It's forbidden. I can't get involved in your affairs on dry land."

"But who would know?"

"It's not that simple. You heard my father tell me, and you heard Fatuma. My job was to get you this far, and I have. That's all I can do."

Tau's eyebrows curled inward in anger. He had hoped that Amanzi would be with him for much longer. For some reason, he had assumed that she would. Of all the people he had met on his journey, he felt the closest to Amanzi. "But I need you. I can't do this alone."

"You don't need me, Tau. You are about to embark on a very important task, and I know that you will make it through."

"So that's it? Two days, and then you're gone?"

"Two wonderful days, Tau. I'm glad that I met you and that I could be a part of your life. We will see each other again. I know it."

"Then this is goodbye?"

"For now, yes. You have to climb that cliff and fulfill your destiny. I have to return home."

He stared into her eyes, and then his gaze trailed off over the water for a few seconds as if he had fallen into a trance.

Amanzi touched his shoulder. His eyes whipped back, locking onto hers.

"Goodbye, Tau."

"Goodbye…Amanzi."

She turned around and dove beneath the water. Tau waited for a while and let himself sink below the surface of the water as he watched her disappear in the distance. He knew she had really left when his air bubble suddenly collapsed upon him and still, he stayed under water to see if she would come back.

Soon he surfaced again. His body was wet and Amanzi was

gone. It took a few minutes for him to accept it, but then he turned and slowly swam toward a better spot to climb the rock. He found the perfect access point, mapping out in his head how exactly he would climb to the top. It was not until he was almost there that Amanzi surfaced again right in front of him.

"Amanzi?" Tau asked, confused.

"So….," she said rolling her eyes upward and sounding uncertain. "There is something that I've wanted to ask you."

"What is that?"

"Have you ever kissed a girl before?"

"Well, um...I..."

Before he could get his sentence going, Amanzi grabbed him and pressed her lips right up against his. Tau was surprised. He kept his eyes open at first, but then closed them and with his arms he squeezed her as tight as she was squeezing him. They held it for quite some time as they both sank below the surface of the water. And still they did not part. After a long while, Amanzi kicked her legs and they rose to the top again. She let go and their lips parted. She smiled at him.

"The answer is YES," she said smiling, and once again turned and dove back into the water. This time, she was gone for good.

XXVII THE ESCAPEE

HATARI

Tau climbed the cliff, stopping before he entered the tree line at the top. He turned around to look at the water, Amanzi's home. To him, she was as beautiful as the sparkling sunlight that danced across the surface of the sea like millions of tiny diamonds. His thoughts were of her and how this very odd journey allowed them to meet, even if only for a short time.

He looked at the watch. He was glad she had given it to him to remember her by. He looked at the soft green glow and all of the bubbles moving inside of it. Then he noticed the light begin to fade until it went black. Another reminder that she was gone.

"You'll see her again," said Chad standing next to him.

"I hope so."

Tau smiled, then turned around and plunged into the dense forest before him. He wanted to take his blades out and cut a pathway through, but he knew he needed to be as quiet as possible. And so he moved slowly and carefully amongst the trees.

He made a few attempts to change into his leopard form. Surely, it would be easier to infiltrate quietly through the trees if he was a stealthy cat. Unfortunately, it did not work. He was not sure if it was his inexperience at the task of shape shifting, or if it meant that there was a much more serious problem.

He came to the conclusion that it was not him. He had been getting the hang of changing. The obvious conclusion was that the crystal demon was near, somewhere on the island. As much as he hated that idea, it probably was a good thing. Perhaps it meant the Leopard Tribe was near as well.

The birds were numerous. He could hear them singing and calling to one another. He looked above at the canopy of trees that did its best to blot out the harsh sunlight, but welcomed the warm air. It was damp, and he needed to dry his clothes, still wet from being in the water.

The terrain led him up a hill, and he kept notice of the sun's position so that he did not get lost. However, he did not quite know where he was going; he only wanted to make sure that he continued to go deeper inland.

"There she is, men! We're gaining on her! Don't let her get away!"

Standing at the top of the hill, Tau heard the voice shouting not too far from his position. It must have been coming from somewhere below him. He scrambled to see through the thicket, trying to figure out who the voice was and where it came from. There, down a steep cliff, he saw Kamaria running along a pathway like her life depended on it. Seven or eight seconds behind her were six guards of the Brood in pursuit.

Tau knew he had to help. He turned the other way to meet up with her as she rounded the hill. He ran toward her, almost too fast, barely managing to keep himself from tumbling.

Kamaria flew by without even seeing him. He came out to

the path and called out, "Kamaria!" Then he started after her.

Kamaria turned for a moment and stopped. "No boy, don't come any further!" She ran toward him, frantically waving her hands. "Get off of the trail!" Kamaria dove at him, only a second too late. A net sprung out, catching both of them, tangling their arms and legs until they fell to the ground.

Kamaria tried desperately to find the way out of it, but there was no time. The guards were soon upon them.

"Good work, boy," said Kamaria in a disgusted manner. "You've gotten us trapped."

"I didn't mean to," said Tau. "I thought you were in trouble. I didn't know they set a trap."

"No, boy," she said firmly, "I set the trap for THEM!"

"Oh."

"I thought you were dead," said Kamaria, as if his being alive was a bad thing.

"It's a very long story."

"I've been on the run for two days, getting the upper hand on this scum, and in one second, you have managed to get me captured again."

All Tau could think to say was, "Sorry."

The guards came up to them, panting and out of breath. Kamaria had run them dry of energy. The head guard looked at them trapped in the net and smiled. Among the guards present, he was the only one not wearing one of those black and red menacing masks. The look of his face was menacing enough, and he did have a few red painted marks across one of his eyes. His knotted, untamed hair sprouted out from all sides. "All that running for nothing," he said. "Now, you are back where you started. Take those weapons from the boy."

Kamaria looked at the guard with sharp eyes through the holes of the net.

The guard smirked. "You know, a pretty woman like you needn't run away. I could make things very easy here for you…for the right type of payment."

Kamaria smiled, "It pleases me to look upon your face, Saah. And I'm glad that you enjoy mine, for it will be the last thing that you see when I run a sword through your heart."

Saah stood up, pulled out his sword, and placed it directly under her chin in one fluid motion. "If I kill you now, then I needn't worry about that, will I?" He removed his sword from under her chin, and instead of killing her, wacked her across the head with the side of it. "You WILL learn respect." He turned towards the other guards. "Get them up," he said as he sheathed his sword. "Let's make our way back."

The guards got Tau and Kamaria out of the net, and then bound them to one another. They were both tied to a rope that the guards pulled as they walked.

"Again, boy," said Kamaria. "Thanks." She then shrieked at the sting of a whip cracking across her back.

"Quiet!" Saah yelled.

Tau flinched at the sound, and even more so at the way that Kamaria reacted to the pain. He had never seen her this way before; at the mercy of others. Even when they had been taken before, at the Amotekun City, it seemed to be by her will. In this circumstance, she seemed totally at the mercy of this Saah, and had no choice but to endure the pain of his whip. And it was all Tau's fault.

Saah was the obvious leader of these men. He walked with his head high. His posture spoke of leadership. The others obeyed him without question. As they trekked through the forest, all it took was the raising of his hand to stop the party.

The other men looked at him as he studied the sounds and smells of the forest. They seemed to be waiting for him to tell them what to do next.

"Down!" he commanded.

And they did, pulling Kamaria and Tau to the ground with them. Not Saah though. He stayed standing. As Tau looked at

Saah out of the corner of the top of his eye, with his head down, he began to hear a slight screeching sound. The sound got louder and closer until it was met by the hard crunch of Saah's hand. He caught a flying blood snake coming at them.

These snakes more glided than flew, but sometimes they swooped down from high in the trees for their attack on their prey. Rarely were they deadly. A person would have to be attacked by a few of them or have a severe allergic reaction to their venom to die. Yet one was always enough to drop a grown man to the ground, then feed on his blood for a few minutes until it had had enough. Anyone bitten could be sick for days.

Saah looked at the creature in his hands, wiggling it around, and then crushed it in his fist. Almost immediately, Tau heard the sound of another screeching blood snake flying toward them, which Saah caught as well, leaving the thing to the same fate as the other.

Saah threw them to the ground and then gestured forward. The men rose, pulling up Kamaria and Tau along with them, and continued on.

In another hour, they arrived at the camp. The forest ended suddenly, as they emerged from the tree line to a wide-open plain of reddish dirt and mud. There were several different terraced levels of it, all which looked to be cut, carved, and landscaped by man. In many parts of the land, there were huge deep holes, most of them too deep to see what or who was inside. It was probably all part of the forest at some point, but presently it was a huge field of dirt and digging. Spread throughout were numerous tents made of cloth, animal skin, or giant leaves, all of which were built on wooden frames.

The seriousness of the situation unfolded as they came closer. Tau was appalled at how horrible the scene was! There were people everywhere. Grey people, like Tau, working, moving, carrying, pushing, and digging. Standing throughout was the Brood's Army, keeping watch, pointing, commanding, pushing, snapping whips, and yelling.

Tau caught a glimpse of a boy who looked terribly exhausted, pushing a wheelbarrow full of rocks through the very soft red dirt. He staggered from side to side as if he was walking in pain, taking uncertain barefooted steps in the mud. A guard walked slowly next to him, seeming to be amused by the boy's despair. As soon as the boy stumbled and fell, the guard struck him with a glowing rod and ordered him back up. The boy's body shook in obvious pain, then made eye contact with Tau while getting back to his feet.

It was a sight that Tau had nothing to compare to. Kamaria looked back at him as if to say, "Now do you see?" And another look that said, "Thanks for bringing me back to this."

They trekked through the camp, noticed by all. Tau made it a point to look into the large holes. Inside there were more of his kind, standing in ankle deep muddy water. The real surprising thing was that most of them were kids his age or younger. This was the first time he had seen any of the Leopard Tribe children. Part of him was happy to see them; another part of him was so saddened at their obvious dire situation that he wanted to cry.

He became aware that everyone took notice to him. In fact all the work slowed and heads turned as he walked among them. He was obviously a stranger. All eyes were on him and Kamaria as the guards led them through the camp.

Saah pushed Kamaria forward, causing her to stumble to her knees. The onlookers gasped as she fell to the ground. "See that," Saah said to another guard. "She's their strong one. I'd bet you a high-grade ruby that these people hoped she got away. It's worth it, having her escape for a while only to be caught again." He smiled with pride. "You can see the hope within them being crushed."

Kamaria wobbled back to her feet, and as they continued to walk, the rest of the guards throughout the camp began to clap. One after another, more of the guards joined in on the clapping until they were all clapping in unison at her recapture. Tau noticed the gloating on all of their faces while the faces of the slaves dropped to further despair. It was like the Brood was putting on a show to let all the Leopard Tribe know that their icon of strength and hope was now subdued and under their control again.

On a distant hill, the highest point in the whole camp, there stood a two-story light yellow stone structure. It was crude, made from very large slabs that leaned awkwardly together as if it had been put together in a hurry. At the top level was a large window, which gave a perfect view for someone to look over the entire camp in efforts to monitor all if its activities. Saah looked up to the window as a dark shadowed figure came to it. The figure nodded and so did Saah before ordering the guards to cut Tau and Kamaria loose.

Saah grabbed Kamaria by the arm and walked her over to another guard. This guard too, was one of the few that did not wear a mask on his face. His black head was perfectly contrasted by his short white Mohawk. He nodded and smirked at Saah as he approached.

"Togar! And you said I wouldn't catch her," Saah said proudly, returning the grin. "Being part of the Brood's army, you should never doubt our success. You have a lot to learn."

Togar smirked at Kamaria, looking her up and down. Kamaria locked her eyes on his, not showing weakness.

"Kamaria," he said.

"Togar," Kamaria responded in a soft calm voice, with eyes that seemed to be meant to kill.

"Your attempted escape proved nothing but the fact that you cannot get away."

Kamaria did not respond. She continued to glare at him in contempt.

"Perhaps some time in a cage will help you to rethink your acceptance of your condition."

"It isn't the conditions here that I despise as much as it is you."

Togar raised his hand and backhanded her as hard as he could. Tau lunged forward, held back by guards as Kamaria fell to the ground.

Saah chuckled. "Perhaps you have learned a great deal already, Togar."

"From you, Master Saah."

They were still the spectacle of the camp. Most of the captives continued to work, yet they kept glancing at Kamaria furtively. One man in particular, from inside of a large ditch not too far from them was being held back as well, not by guards, but by his fellow younger comrades. He looked Togar in the eyes while Togar smirked back at him.

Saah too took interest in this man's behavior. He looked him in the eye as he grabbed a fist full of Kamaria's hair, tugging at the back of her head. "Welcome back," he whispered to her with his eyes locked on to the man's. "Put her into the cage," he said, and then pushed her forward.

Guards picked her up and dragged her over to a wooden cage, throwing her in. One of the guards pulled out a metal piece, made for all four fingers to fit through. On the rounded end of it, were six different color crystals about a half-inch wide; keys. With his hand gripped through it, he placed the green crystal against a rounded impression on the lock of the cage. Green light illuminated for a second and then clicking sounds were heard. Then they opened the door.

Saah walked over to Tau, grabbing him by the arm. "Orientation is immediate here, boy." He violently dragged Tau over to the man who had lunged to help Kamaria, still being held back by some of the younger Leopard people, and threw Tau into the ditch. "Show this boy what to do. He'll be part of your sect." He paused for a second, and then continued. "Oh, and you might want to know that you have him to thank for Kamaria's capture."

The man looked strong, but used a crutch to walk due to his crippled left leg. The crutch was a simple one made from a single branch that forked at one end. He said nothing; he only glared at Saah while the boys in the pit grabbed hold of Tau.

"We'll take care of him, sir," said one of the other children slaves.

Saah nodded and walked away. The children helped Tau to his feet.

"Stand quickly," one of the boys said. "Don't show them any weakness."

The crippled man took his eyes off of Saah, directing his attention back into the pit and at Tau.

"Is it true?" the man asked Tau. "Are you responsible for her being captured again?"

Tau was reluctant to answer, but he did anyway. "Yes. But it was an accident, I…"

"Say no more. He only told me that so that I will treat you harshly, and I will not fall into his trap. Who are you boy? I've not seen you before."

"I am Tau. And…."

"Tau? Kamaria spoke of you. She said that you were dead!"

"It's very complicated,"

"So it seems. My name is Dwe." Then he turned to the rest of the kids. "Everyone, this is Tau; he can meet you all individually in time. I'm sure he has quite a story to tell us about who he is, where he comes from, and how he got here. I, myself, would like to know…"

"Work!" They heard a voice yell to them and the sound of a whip snapping against the ground.

"Come on," said Dwe. "We can talk softly, but we must work. The guards won't hesitate to strike you. Those glow rods pack an awful sting."

With his crutch, and one good leg, Dwe jumped down into a lower section of the open pit mine, splashing into the muddy water. "Come on boy. A young man like you shouldn't have any trouble getting down here."

Tau jumped down. The water was only ankle deep but still, he was not looking forward to getting himself as muddy as the others looked. Dwe handed him a round bowl-like object about a foot across, with very small holes at the bottom.

The other kids paid close attention to him with blank stares and with slow waves of their hands, making Tau feel uncomfortable. He felt like a spectacle. "Hello," he said to them slowly. "I... I'm Tau."

"Hello," they replied.

A young girl, somewhat around his age, approached him with even more curiosity. "Are you one of us?"

"Yes," Tau replied. "I believe I am."

"Where do you come from?"

"Hey, new kid," one of the guards shouted from above, "this isn't a party. Pair up with Dwe like you were told and have him show you what to do."

Tau looked at the guard, wondering what kind of harsh face he was making behind his mask. The mask looked mean enough; it was doing its job by intimidating him. He definitely did not want to make the guards angry. He nodded to the girl, and then positioned himself next to Dwe.

"You already trying to make enemies of the guards?" Dwe asked.

"Who's that girl?"

"Heh, time for that later, Tau."

"Why are you the only adult in this pit? And where are most of the other adults?" Tau asked.

Dwe lifted up his bad leg and patted it with his hand. "Ever since I hurt the leg, they put me here. Usually they keep most of the male adults in the mines in the mountain, and the women on the other side. It is much harder labor. When it is time to do more digging out here, they will generally use adults to do it too. But for the most part, they keep the young and the wounded here. The work is pretty simple. Put the sifter down. Get some mud and water into it, and sift sift sift until you find something good."

"What am I looking for?"

"Diamonds. That's what they want. The Brood, that is. They brought us here, now all it seems that they want us to do, is to get them diamonds."

"That's it?" Tau asked, confused.

"Yup. Here, try it."

Tau put some mud and water into his sifter and went to work. "But why us? I mean, why only us?"

"Who knows? Perhaps because we have been isolated for so long, that everyone has forgotten about us. We won't be missed." Dwe looked over his shoulder and then leaned toward Tau. "But don't worry. We will break free of this soon enough. You must always be ready. But the time is not right yet. Don't do anything hasty or stupid or you'll wind up like..." He paused for a second, looking up toward the ground level.

"You were going to say Kamaria."

"Keep working. You've got the hang of it already. I'll show you what to look for when I find something."

"Is that what happened to her? She wouldn't wait?" Tau continued. "What is with her and that guard, um, Saah?"

"Don't get me wrong. Kamaria's strength is one of the things that I love about her. But I fear that she will make things worse for herself. I fear that sooner or later, they will have her killed, or *taken*."

"I saw you," Tau said. "When Saah knocked Kamaria to the ground."

"Yes, for that moment, my emotions got the best of me. Good thing that these young ones were smart enough to hold me back."

"So you know her well?"

"Of course I do. She's my fiancée."

XXVIII THE TAKEN

"There you go Tau, that's a good one," Dwe encouraged him.

The day carried on long and hot. The sun bore down on him like a constant blanket of heat. Tau welcomed the thought of dusk as he could see the sun nearing the horizon. The work was tedious, and it did not take long before he understood why the people were so muddy; they purposely covered themselves with the mud to keep the harsh rays of the sun off of their skin.

He stayed in his hole, ankle deep in the muddy water the entire time, sifting through the clay and rocks. He was beyond annoyed at the small rocks and pebbles that continued to become lodged between the bottoms of his feet and his sandals. That aggravation was only slightly balanced by the fact that he made some progress.

"Now we'll have to go up and give this to our sect master, Togar," Dwe said.

When he climbed out of the pit, Tau saw Togar walking nearby with Saah, and another man that he recognized. The first time he had seen him was in the Amotekun City, when the Brood came to take his people away. Hatari. Tau would never forget the contours of Hatari's baldhead; or the decorations of bone and feathers that he wore.

"That's Lord Hatari," Dwe whispered to Tau, as he too climbed out of the pit. "And don't forget the LORD part when you speak. He's Onoc's brother; both of them are Children of Montok. Make sure you show him respect. At least fake it. He is the wrong person to show any type of contempt for. Trust me, Tau, I'm not telling you to like him, or any of them. I plan to kill them all as soon as we have the chance. But for now, keep your feelings to yourself. The Children of Montok don't like being made fools of."

There was a commotion coming from Hatari, Saah, and one of the leopard slaves. Tau could not hear the words, but Lord Hatari did not seem happy at all.

Suddenly, the man rushed toward Hatari, as if to strike him down with his shovel. He raised it high into the air; his scream, a war charge, traveled throughout the camp and caused everyone to take notice.

Saah pulled out his whip and struck the man with it. Hatari raised his short staff. The diamond eyes in the sockets of the skull began to shine, and a beam of light shone into the chest of the man. The man slowed and then dropped to the ground.

"Did you see that?" asked Dwe.

Tau only nodded.

"He has reached into that man and taken some of his energy."

Hatari then closed his eyes, clinched is fists and inhaled.

"See, the man's energy has now moved into Hatari, making him stronger. You can see his gratification."

Hatari reached down and grabbed the man by his hair. "I don't know if you were trying to be brave, or simply suicidal, but you have dared to try and assault me? For that, you will become one of the *taken*."

Hatari looked up into the main building at the top of the hill. The dark figure stood in the window, watching the whole thing. Tau still could not make out the details of what he looked like. All that he knew was that when he asked Dwe about the large dark figure that stood watch in the window, Dwe simply answered, "Lord Onoc."

Hatari nodded to Onoc. Seconds later, the crystal demon, Doro, came walking into the camp. Doro's blue fire shone brightly from his eyes, his mouth, from the cracks in his elbows, and from the bottom of his legs, where his feet should be. He stomped through the camp until he reached Hatari, Togar, Saah, and the weakened man lying on the ground. "*Take* him," Hatari said.

Without hesitation, Doro reached out with his blue crystal hand, and picked the man up by his throat. The man struggled to get free of Doro, trying to pry his hand off, without success.

An older woman came running to Hatari's position, screaming as she dropped to her knees. "No, please Lord Hatari. Don't let the Demon *take* him!"

"Get back old woman!" Hatari snapped. "Or you will join him. No man, or woman, is exempt from punishment."

Two guards held the woman back while she cried and sobbed, begging for Hatari to let the man go.

"Proceed," he said to Doro.

Doro brought the man closer to him. His eyes became brighter as a blue mist emanated from the man and entered into Doro's face. The mist became thicker and thicker until a ghostly image of the man came out of him and into the demon.

The man's eyes turned completely blue. Even the whites of his eyes were blue. His hands dropped to his sides and his entire body went limp. Doro dropped him to the ground.

"Get up and get back to work," Hatari yelled at him. The corpse-body stood up, looked at Hatari with an empty gaze and slowly walked away.

"*The Taken*," Dwe said to Tau. "That demon has ripped that man's soul out of his body. It has happened to a hand full of us so far. He may as well just kill him, taking a man's soul and leaving a hollow shell is just the same."

Tau had no words, no questions; he stared blankly, as if his soul had been taken too. Hatari, Togar, and Doro, came walking nearby when Dwe called out to them. "Lord Hatari."

"What is it?" Hatari asked as if he was being bothered yet again.

"This boy," Dwe replied. "Look at the size of this diamond. And only his first day." Unlike his fiancée, Dwe spoke with more respect to his captors than Kamaria was willing to do.

He spoke with a low calm voice that simply said everything, "matter-of-factly." He never cowered before them, but tried his best to look them in the eye with every encounter.

"Bring it," Hatari said to him, holding out his hand.

Dwe stood up, leaning his weight onto his crutch in the process, and handed him the large diamond.

Hatari took a tight grip of the diamond and closed his eyes for a moment. "Hmmm, a pure grade crystal. Good job, boy."

Hatari looked at Tau, who could hardly take his eyes off of Doro. He could not wrap his head around what this thing was. Simply being near to the thing scared him.

"Do you like our demon friend, boy?"

"No sir. I mean yes sir. I mean….I don't understand the question sir."

Hatari laughed. "I think the boy is scared of you, Doro."

Doro let out a grunting hum.

"Stand up, boy. What is your name?"

"Tau."

"This is a fine diamond you have fetched, Tau. I'll need you to get as many more like it as you can."

"Yes, sir."

"Why do you look familiar? Do I know you?"

"Yes sir," said Tau. "From the island. From here." He hoped Hatari had not remembered him from the White Forest. He was supposed to be dead.

"Are you sure?" Hatari asked, focusing his eyes deeply into Tau's."

"Yes, it has to be, Lord."

"Hmm, back to work." Hatari started to turn and walk away when Dwe butted in.

"Lord Hatari!"

Hatari turned.

"I wanted to ask of Kamaria. It is a particularly hot day. I would like to bring her water."

"Ah, Kamaria, the trouble maker. Master Saah, has this woman had a drink today?

"No, she is suffering punishment for trying to escape."

"Agreed. Yet it is a hot day. We cannot let our strongest die. We need them the most. Go ahead; get the woman some water, but only one cup, and no food until tomorrow. I want the people to see her suffering."

"Thank you, Lord Hatari."

"No," said Hatari. "Not you. Let the boy do it."

"But Lord…"

"I said to let the boy do it. He is the one that found the stone, not you, correct?"

"Yes."

"Then let him do it. How old are you boy?"

"Sixteen, sir," Tau replied.

"Sixteen? You're a bit small for sixteen. You know, if you're sixteen, you should be pushing wheelbarrows in the mountain."

"Perhaps, since he is small, Lord Hatari, he should stay here, in the pits," said Dwe.

"Perhaps you should hand out all the jobs," Hatari replied. "Perhaps you would like mine?"

"No, my Lord."

"Good then. Is it all right with you, SLAVE, if I go about my business? Is there anymore that the SLAVE needs from me?"

"No, sir."

"Good then. Since he started here, he will sleep in your tent with you. But while there is work, he will be in the mountain."

"Yes, Lord Hatari."

"Boy, get the water, then get yourself to the mountain."

"Yes, Lord Hatari," Tau complied.

"Back to work." Then Hatari, Doro, Saah, and Togar walked away.

When Tau walked toward the rickety wooden cage, he fixed

his eyes on Kamaria lying in the corner like a limp doll. She was asleep; her body was taking in huge deep unsteady breaths, as her slumber did nothing to cure how exhausted she was. Her breathing stopped and her eyes flew wide open as Tau approached. She quickly turned around to his direction.

Tau was startled. He jumped back, spilling half the water out of the brown clay cup.

"Oh, it's you," she said in a dry raspy voice that struggled to get out, once again, not sounding happy at all to see Tau. "What is it you want now? Have you come to *save* me again?"

"I....I came to bring you some water." They both looked down at the spilled portion of it. "I'm sorry. Didn't mean to spill it."

"I'd rather die of thirst than to take *your* water?"

"Wow, lady. Really? I think you are going a bit overboard. Don't you?"

Kamaria squinted at him. "Give me the water."

"Here."

She took the cup and drank. Tau stood there, not knowing what to say next, but wanting to make conversation.

"I'm working with Dwe, your fiancée."

Kamaria finished drinking. "No fiancée of mine."

"But I thought...."

"Dwe is weak. I know that now. The man refuses to fight against our oppressors. He does whatever they command of him, without question. The man has lost his backbone. I refuse to marry a man such as that! A man that is weak!"

"Could be. Or it could be that he knows when not to fight. I don't think you're doing anyone any good causing so much trouble."

"What do you know? You've just gotten here."

"I know who you were back in the White Forest. I know that Lord Hatari calls you the troublemaker. I know that you are the only one being punished, hungry, inside of a cage. And I know that they have managed to take our strongest, and made her look weaker than anyone."

"Yes, you know this because YOU put me here, remember."

"Oh, yeah, sorry about that. But what were you planning to do anyway? Keep running around the island? They would have caught you sooner or later."

"Maybe, but I would have killed many more of them first. What's it to you? Why have you come here? Why come to the island? You were free. You should have left all of this to us."

"I came because it was your order that said we would have to all be together to be free. But I have also come because I have spoken to The Keepers in the temple."

"You? The Keepers have spoken to you? The Keepers speak to no one."

"Well, they spoke to me."

"What did they say?"

"They sent me here. They said that it would be my job, no, I think they said, my *destiny,* to save all of us."

"Hahaha. That's funny. Go and fetch me more water, boy"

"Lord Hatari said only the one cup."

"He's no Lord of mine. And what, you'll do whatever they say?

"For now. Yes."

"Who are you to save anyone? You're not even truly one of us. You don't know what it means to be an Amotekun."

"That's true," Tau admitted, reluctantly. "There is much that I don't know about myself and about our people. But that is why I have people like you and Kato to help teach me. I don't know where we come from. I don't know what a normal life is like for our people. I don't even know what happens to our clothes and weapons when we change. Really, what does happen to our clothes and weapons when we change?"

Kamaria chucked. "Your ignorance will surely get us all killed. I'm not sure why the Keepers would even think of choosing you. But if they did, then tell me young one, what is your plan? Or should I call you, young savior? What is this grand idea that you have to save all of us?"

"I don't know." Tau put his head down. "But having you caught and put in the cage would not have been part of it."

"I sit in this cage because for days I ran and fought. I no longer had the strength to fight. Give me a day to rest, and I promise you that more will die by my hand. I see no fight within you, Tau. I suppose that The Keepers have chosen wrong, and we are all doomed."

"All I'm saying is when and if the time comes, it would be better for everyone if you were strong and ready, and if you didn't take it upon yourself to do things alone."

Tau walked away, leaving her in her cage. He was astonished at himself. He had never spoken to anyone that way before. In a way, it was downright disrespectful. She was right though. If he was supposed to be the savior, he would have to come up with a plan. So far, he didn't have any idea what it was. What could he possibly do that would be different from anyone else? "Everyone rise up, destroy the enemy, and run away." This plan was going to need some work.

XXIX HANDS LIKE INK

Tau went to the mountain, passing the guards, the pits, and the slaves working them. He was still a stranger to them, piquing their interest as he walked by. What he really wanted to do was get to know the people, his people, especially some of the kids his age. But their current situation did not allow for that. He took it upon himself to give gentle greetings to everyone, waving, saying, "hello," "hi," and "good day."

One guard shoved a slave into the mud right in front of Tau. Tau smiled at the guard and the man, saying "hello," and waved as he walked past them. "Is that the cave mines over that way?"

The guard nodded and pointed. Tau sensed that his nonchalant attitude was throwing everyone off guard. For the moment, it was his way of dealing with his fear and the uncomfortable feeling that this situation brought upon him.

At the entrance to the cave were two guards. Tau glanced up. They always looked so sinister to him, especially since he could not see their faces behind those wooden masks. But he watched as both of their eyes locked on him when he approached.

"Excuse me, I'm, supposed to…"

"Get in there, and grab a wheelbarrow," one of the guards snapped.

"But I don't know where to…."

"They'll show you." The guard made a gesture inside.

Tau moved between them as he entered. He felt a sudden shove on his back and the next thing he knew; he was face first on the ground.

Tau heard both guards snickering at his tumble. "That's for the back talk, boy. Haha."

He got up, feeling all sorts of embarrassment, and continued.

There was a lot of noise coming from inside; clanking, hammering, talking, but it was the screams and yells of pain that made him cringe. He heard the sound of a grown man screaming out in agony, echoing from inside. He could not help but to wonder what was happening to the man. What sort of terrible things were the Brood doing to him?

"Hey," another guard called to him. "Come here."

"Yes, sir."

"Follow."

They went deeper into the tunnels. Tau began to see many people chained up along the walls. Suddenly he knew where all of the adults were. Mostly men, they hacked and chiseled at the dark walls of rock. Like most of the people he had seen so far, all of them looked exhausted. Their faces and skin gave off a shiny luster from all of the sweat on their dark grey skin. Large chunks of rock lay all around them. In those chunks, Tau could see more of what they were after; the diamonds shining and twinkling in the flickering light of the fires. Tau imagined the screaming he heard before coming from each of the men that he saw. He shuddered.

The guard brought him to a wooden wheelbarrow. "All you have to do is fill this up with the rocks you see lying around..."

Another young boy came down the tunnel with his wheelbarrow filled to the top. It looked heavy. The boy locked eyes with Tau for a moment as the weight in his wheelbarrow caused him to go slightly off course and almost hit the wall. He quickly corrected himself and moved on. Everyone's reaction was the same. They ignored the boy who had stumbled, and stared instead at the stranger, this newcomer, Tau.

"Like him," said the guard.

"Then what do I do with them?"

"Don't interrupt boy, unless you want the whip." Then the guard pulled out his glow rod and brought it near Tau's face. "Or my favorite," he continued as his mouth curled up into a smirk, "the rod."

The glow rods were short staffs a foot long with a mesh of crystals at the top all stuck together in the shape of a sphere. There were life-vines that crisscrossed around this bundled sphere of crystals as if they were holding them together. The crystals inside glowed, giving off light, while the life-vines were covered with little pale blue lights that looked like millions of ants of light running across the vines. The top and bottom of the rods were separate parts, and when the top half was pulled out an inch, turned one-quarter turn, and then shifted back down, the light was turned on.

Tau's eyes focused on the glowing light.

"You take them out of the caves, empty the barrow, and then come back for more."

"Where do I empty them?"

"Around on the other side of the mountain. Once you are outside, ask someone where you are supposed to go. You think you can handle that?"

"Yes, sir."

"You'd better. Now, get to work. I can't stand here all day and answer your questions. And I hate kids."

"Yes, sir."

Tau looked at the man for a moment.

"Wait a minute," the guard said. "What is that, on your arm? Let me see it."

"This?" said Tau as he brought Amanzi's non-functioning watch closer. "Oh, nothing. It was just a gift from a friend."

The guard grabbed him by the arm and studied the watch. "You need better friends, boy. This thing is worthless."

"Yes, sir."

"Well, get to work!" the guard snapped.

Quickly, Tau grabbed the wheelbarrow. He moved to the nearest man and began placing the rocks the man had broken off of the wall into the wheelbarrow. He tried to be polite, making light conversation with everyone, making sure he introduced himself. Most of the people were not up for much conversation. Still, he tried.

Once his barrow was full, he began to make his way back to the entrance, trying to remember which way he had come in. There were so many different tunnels throughout the mine that it was easy to get lost. He walked alone down one of the tunnels that curved to the left up ahead of him. Soon, he noticed a faint blue glow against the wall in front. He also felt a slight vibration in the ground beneath his feet, which he began to hear as it got closer. Thump thump thump. He stopped and waited to see what was coming from around the corner.

It was Doro.

Tau let go of the wheelbarrow. It dropped to the ground off balance and tilted to the side, spilling rocks everywhere. He did not even notice. He was completely focused on Doro's large blue crystal body coming toward him. Somehow, in these tunnels, he seemed larger than before and much, much more frightening as everything in his vision faded to black except for Doro.

Tau took a step to the side. He wanted to make sure there was plenty of room for Doro to get through. He was also hoping that Doro would not even notice him snug all the way up against the side of the wall. He was wrong.

Doro looked at the spilled wheelbarrow, and then his eyes of blue fire locked on to Tau. He walked right up to him, hovering. Tau felt the slight breeze of a cold wind coming from Doro as his body stole any heat out of the air around him. It took every ounce of Tau's strength not to pee on himself.

"Pick them up" Doro said in the deepest of menacing voices.

"U...Um," Tau stuttered, surprised that this thing could talk. "It...It was an accident. I dropped it."

Doro leaned in closer to him. "Know this boy; here, we deal with accidents very seriously."

"Y...y...yes, sir." Tau's eyes were about as wide as they

could get. Blinking was a skill momentarily lost. He tried his best to control his erratic heavy breathing for fear of hyperventilating.

Doro stood there staring into Tau as if he was intensely curious about him. "I will enjoy *taking* you someday." Then he walked away.

Tau fell to the floor, catching his breath. Somehow, this experience had been more frightening than the giant spider. Still shaking, and in a panic, he righted his wheelbarrow and put the rocks back into it. He started walking all the while looking behind him, hoping that he would not see any sign of Doro ever again!

He was wasting so much thought on how scared he was of Doro that soon he realized that he was completely lost. Great, he thought. How could I be so stupid? He wandered around for a while, trying to get back on track, until one of the guards yelled at him.

"Hey! What are you doing here?"

Tau swallowed. He did not want to tell the guard he was lost for fear of being scolded. If they took accidents very seriously here, he was sure it would be the same for stupidity. There was no explanation for being where he was, however, so he found the truth jumping its way out of his mouth.

"I'm lost. I'm trying to find my way out to dump these rocks."

"It might take a moment to figure out these tunnels boy. But I suggest you do it quick. The Brood doesn't take well to anyone slowing up progress."

"Yes, sir."

"But since you're here, I have a job for you. You see that cauldron?"

Tau's attention was diverted to a slave pushing a wheelbarrow of dirt and rock past him.

"Hey, boy," the guard smacked him in the face. "Pay attention. Lose focus again and you'll get the sting of my rod."

"The cauldron, sir! I'm listening."

"And don't talk smart! Grab some bowls and fill them. I'll show you where to go."

Tau filled three bowls with whatever that brown, thick soupy stuff was, and held them in his arms.

"Is that all you can carry? The last girl could carry eight. You going to let a girl out do you?"

"No sir," he said as he set the bowls down and filled more.

A young girl walked by him, carrying a large sac over her shoulder. She was his age, average looking, and of course was as dirty as everyone else, except this girl was one of the *taken*. Her eyes were all blue. Her blank face looked as if she was in a coma, or dead. These people really freaked him out. But Tau said, "hi," just to find some hint of a person inside there. He even smiled at her, hoping to get some sign of emotion in return. The *taken* girl paid no attention to his greeting or the wave of his hand.

"You're a cheery one, aren't you," said the guard to Tau. "That won't last long. You don't see anyone else smiling around here, do you? Not even me."

I can't see you smiling because you've got the mask on. The thought went through Tau's head. He was not stupid enough to say it out loud.

"No point in trying to wave to her anyway. There is nothing there. Watch. The guard yelled out to the *taken* girl, "Hey, slave, stop."

The girl stopped. He took his glow rod and waved it in front of her face. The girl paid no attention to it or them; she just stared blankly ahead with her all-blue eyes.

"Yoo-hoo, you in there?" the guard asked the girl, snapping his fingers in front of her eyes and lightly slapping her on the cheek.

"See, nothing. They don't even blink. But they do obey. You'll end up like her if you become a problem. So make sure you do as you are told; nothing more, nothing less. And by the way, that's the girl whose job you are doing right now. There was an incident and well…well, this is what happens around here."

They came to a small room. It was as dark and dirty as the rest of the caves, yet this one had weak, elderly people lying around.

"Feed them," said the guard. "You'll have to make another trip to get them all. Let me know when you are done. And don't take forever."

"Yes, sir," Tau nodded.

The people in the room glanced over at him as he came in. "Hi," he said.

"Such a lovely boy," a woman said in a quivering voice. She was sitting closest to him, leaning up against the wall. He turned his lip at their dreary presence, covered in dirt, their frail bodies dressed in simple cloth. Their matted grey hair looked white compared to their skin, and also looked as if it had not been tended to for quite some time. "What's your name, boy? Have I seen you before?"

"No ma'am. My name is Tau. I'm new here."

"But I haven't seen you before. Not here, not ever. How is that possible?"

Tau, rolled his eyes. "It's a long story, ma'am. Are you hungry?"

"Well, I'm hungry!" said a man not far from her. "She'll talk 'til your ears pop off your head. Come closer."

Tau moved over to him as the old man stretched out his decrepit hands to touch him and feel his muscles. "I used to be strong like that, long time ago!"

"The food, the food, pass us the food!" said another old women.

"Oh, yes, right away," Tau responded.

He passed out the six bowls, but there were five more faces staring at him, waiting for food. They had the look of hungry orphans. "Oh, I'll have to get more."

"Hands for bowl!" said another one of the old men, raising

his hands into the air. He was crouched down, sitting against the wall. He was the only one who had seemed not to pay any attention to Tau since he came in. Even now, the man did not look up at him. His eyes stayed focused on the ground while he spoke, "bowls and stuff!"

"Quiet!" yelled another. "Let the boy leave, Ink!"

Tau slowly backed his way out of the room and headed down the tunnel until he met up with the guard again. Then the both of them proceeded back to the cauldron.

"Did you have fun with the old and crazy?" the guard asked him.

"What's wrong with them?" Tau asked.

"Like I said, old and crazy. Not much use for anything, but we are told to keep them alive, so we do. If I had my way, we'd let them starve or push them off into the ocean."

"That's a bit cruel, don't you think?"

The guard pushed Tau up against the wall. "Listen to my words, kid, I'm not here to be nice. I'm here to keep you in line. Now take the rest of those bowls in there."

Tau was beginning to think that he had a knack for making people upset. Perhaps he should keep his mouth shut.

He returned to the old people with their food. He hated the sight of them, sitting on the dirt floor or lying like rag dolls across stone benches. They were in no way neat when they ate, either. There was already food smeared on their faces and caught in their hair. The sauce dripped all over them and onto the floor. Pity overwhelmed him. At least they were being fed. However, it did seem odd to him that the Brood would go through the trouble of keeping them alive when they were of no use.

He passed out the remaining bowls. Ink, the old man crouched up against the wall, still did not look at him. It was almost as if he was *taken,* yet his eyes were not blue, and he did seem somewhat responsive.

"Here," Tau said as nicely as possible. The man kept his

head down, staring at the ground, which seemed particularly odd to Tau. "Are you hungry? Do you want some food?"

The man still did not look, but held his hand out, high above his head. "I saw them. I saw them all flying around. Flying around the sun, like me."

"What is wrong with him?" asked Tau. "What's he talking about?

"Sometimes we have no idea. Sometimes he goes on about nothing!" yelled another, obviously aggravated by the old man.

"Did you call him Ink before?"

"That's Ink."

"Hello, Ink. Can you hear me? The food is right here; grab it."

Ink continued to hold his hand up in the air. Tau decided to place the bowl in the man's hand, but when he went to let go, the bowl almost fell over.

"Ink, you have to hold it or it will fall. Do you understand?"

"Before changed to now," said Ink.

"What do you mean?"

"As big as you were small."

"Don't worry about him," said an old woman. "I'll feed him. Give me the bowl."

"Are you sure?" asked Tau.

"Sure, sure, boy, now go away. Ink and I have a long past together. I can figure him out better than anyone."

"Does he know me?"

"Can't be sure if he was even talking to you, boy. Can't be sure of anything he says. You best run your feet. You're not supposed to stay all day in here. The last girl got in a lot of trouble doing that. Hey, how did you get a girl's job anyway?"

Tau sighed. "Okay, I suppose I'll see you folks later."

"Probably not until tomorrow. They only feed us once a day."

Tau turned to walk away, but Ink grabbed his arm. This

time, for the first time, Ink looked Tau directly in his eyes. Tau flinched, tensing up every muscle in his body, trying to pull away without hurting the old guy.

"Do better! Kill the Demon!" Ink said to him before letting go. His eyes were fixed on Tau's pupils with meaning and intent. There was an imperative sternness in his voice. Tau fell to the floor and quickly scurried back up to his feet. He hurried out of the room, making his way back down the tunnels to the cauldron.

The guard was there. This time there was another slave woman also at the cauldron, stirring it with the very long wooden ladle.

"What's the matter boy? Old folks get to you? Heh," said the guard.

"No, I'm okay. They are...a little strange, that's all."

He was lying. They were not a little strange. They were a lot strange; especially that Ink. What did he mean by "kill the demon?" The words seemed self-explanatory, but did not make sense in Tau's head. The guard showed him the route out of the mountain, saying "Learn it. I'm not showing you again," Ink's words were all Tau could think about. But this time, he made sure to keep track of where he was going so he did not get lost.

Once outside, he was shown around the mountain to where he was supposed to dump the rocks. This section consisted of mostly adult women. They had huge hammers and sifters much like the one Dwe had. He heard the CLANK of the hammers as the chained women sweated away, smashing the rocks. Others sat down with the task of more delicately chiseling away any rock with obvious large diamond pieces embedded into them. It seemed that the Brood wanted as many large pieces as possible.

He was nice as usual to everyone that he saw. And as usual, he felt he was an odd stranger to them that sparked particular stares. He did find out that he had been the talk amongst the slaves. Everyone had heard of him, although, who he was exactly was still a mystery to most, even after he told them of his upbringing in the Makazi village.

The guards were always watchful. Thus, it was hard to strike up long conversations with anyone. He could only give them small bits of information about his life. Still, many people were too exhausted to have much conversation anyway. The women on the outside smashed so much rock that their bodies were becoming numb. Moreover, relief from the hot sun was unheard of outside the mountain. At least they received water regularly. Poor Kamaria baked in the heat, cramped in her small cage with hardly any water at all.

Tau spent the rest of the day on wheelbarrow detail. He went into the caves, filled his barrow, pushed it out, dumped it, and then repeated this over and over again. Each time, the wheelbarrow felt like it was getting heavier and heavier. As his muscles tired, he was reminded of the boy he saw when he first came to the camp, the poor boy that was pushing the wheelbarrow while staggering the whole way. This was Tau's first day. Who knew how long that boy had been there and for how many days, or weeks, or months, and how many fully loaded trips the boy had taken. Tau remembered the look on the boy's face, so tired, so distraught. Tau knew that sooner or later that would be him.

The guard was right; it did not take long for Tau's smile to disappear. Soon, he did not bother to be extra nice or to give proper greetings and waves to the people as he passed them. He felt himself turning into them, and so quickly. He wondered how long he would be here. How long would the Brood keep his people in slavery? A hopeless answer crept into his mind, "until I set them free." An answer, that at the moment he could not come to terms with.

It was not until later in that evening that Tau found a reason to smile again. He was doing his regular job of picking up rocks and putting them into his wheelbarrow when he came down a new tunnel. It seemed the same as the others at first, the men in chains pounding away at the hard walls of the caverns, when he saw a familiar face.

"Kato!" He did not dare shout it, but he was very happy to see him. Tau held back his desire to run over and hug the man.

"Tau," Kato acknowledged him. He leaned away from the wall, almost instinctively, to move toward Tau, only to be stopped suddenly by his chains. The thick of Kato's predicament moved through Tau, dropping his shoulders from a hint of pity.

"Come closer, Tau," Kato whispered.

Tau carefully looked over his shoulder, and then moved his wheelbarrow in next to Kato. He dropped to his knees next to him and slowly began to place rocks into it.

"It is good to see you, boy. Until the recent rumors of your arrival, I thought you were dead. How did you get here? Did they come for you?"

"No. I appeared to be dead because The Keepers made it look that way. I went to see them in the temple and then they sent me here to save you. To save everyone." He continued placing more rocks into the wheelbarrow, still looking around for any guards that no doubt would be against them holding an extensive conversation.

"The Keepers?"

"Yes. I know, apparently it's a big deal."

"A big deal, and you should add, a great honor."

"Yes, but I'm not sure what I can do alone."

"You are not alone, Tau. Stay confident in yourself. If the Keepers have put you on a path, then it is for great reason. No one has spoken to them in three generations."

"How are you?" Tau asked, not as an arbitrary question, but out of real concern. Kato looked very different than he remembered. Now, when he spoke, it was almost as if there was a quiver in his voice from extreme exhaustion. In one word, Tau thought he looked horrible.

"Honestly Tau, these people, the Brood, they are monsters. They treat us like animals. They make us work unthinkable backbreaking hours. It's terrible." He placed his head in his hands and then looked back at Tau. "You know where I sleep?"

"Where?"

"Right here. They are too afraid of the men to unlock our chains and move us, so we just stay here, all the time. I work here, eat here, and sleep here. We will only be able to take so much more of this. If the Keepers truly have sent you here, then thank the spirits for it."

Tau did not want to show what he was feeling. He was feeling too much pity for this man that he thought so highly of, this man who had taught him how to be who he really was, part of the Leopard Tribe.

It was easy for him to hate the Brood. Time after time, again and again, they had proven how vile they were. What gave them the right?

He knew what his uncle would say. *"Power should be used to better thyself and the world. Those who selfishly use it otherwise, those that would use it to suck the life of others around them, are already dead inside. And their souls will never forgive them."*

He forgot to pay attention to his rocks. He was picking them up too fast and soon his wheelbarrow was full. Therefore, if a guard walked past, he would look as if he was having a conversation with Kato, and that was not good.

"You should probably go Tau. You shouldn't be caught idle for too long. Promise me that you will be smart. Don't do anything stupid, okay."

"I promise."

"Oh, and promise me that you will come back and see me from time to time."

Tau smiled and nodded.

*   *   *   *   *

By late evening, every inch of Tau's body ached. He was pretty sure that he had never done so much physical work in a single day in his life. He staggered to the tent he shared with Dwe, Kofi, and Hondo, being the first to make it back. Within seconds, he was fast asleep.

He managed to get a few hours of sleep until sometime late in the evening when he heard the murmur of voices and commotion. Dwe, Kofi and Hondo were all kneeling at the opening of the tent, barely peeking out.

"What is it?" Tau asked.

"It's her," Dwe reluctantly responded.

"Who?"

"Nyami."

Tau could not make her out. However, he could barely make out some shape flying in front of the moon. To him, it looked like a fuzzy black line moving through the air in the distance.

"How can you tell?"

"I've seen her come before. She travels like a flock of deadly owls."

"I've heard of her. She is part of the Brood, isn't she?"

"Of all six of the Children of Montok, I believe she is the worst. This is her third visit here. The first two times, she didn't leave without making some drastic changes. Some of us died."

"Yes, I remember," said Hondo. "She made everyone work harder. Some of us died in the rush."

"So the stories of her are true?" asked Tau. "Can she control the wind, and the owls?"

"No, she IS the owls," Hondo corrected. "You should see her when she comes apart and then back together again."

"You seem terribly worried," said Tau to Dwe.

"Come," said Dwe. "She is landing."

Tau watched the flock of black owls come together near the main fort at the top of the hill. The guards around her all kneeled or bowed as she approached them. Apparently one of them had not bowed to her satisfaction. Nyami used her power of the wind to knock him back off his feet. Even from afar, the way that her eyes glowed white when she used her power was intriguing. All Tau could say was, "Wow!"

"I told ya," said Hondo. "If you could have evil and cool in the same place, it would be Nyami."

Dwe squinted tightly and grabbed Hondo by the arm. "Evil is never to be admired no matter how cool you THINK she is. Do you understand, boy!"

"Yes," he answered.

Nyami walked into the fort and out of sight.

Tau watched Dwe close the flap on their tent and sit back, apparently in deep thought. He looked up at Tau whose constant gaze was still upon him. "Yes Tau, I am worried; only because she has come so few times. Each time she has come, she has only stayed a few days, but while she is here, something chaotic happens." He pointed to his knee. "Part of me wants to know what it is they are planning. Why is she here this time, and what is their overall purpose?" He peeked back outside the tent for a moment, looking back at the fort. "If only we could be there listening to what they were saying."

"Well, why don't we find out?" said Tau.

The others looked at him. "What do you mean by that?" Hondo asked.

"That fort has windows. Has no one thought to sneak over there to find out what it is they do in there?"

"Tau," said Dwe. "I'm sure someone has thought of it, but it would be pretty dangerous. No, not dangerous, stupid."

"It could be done though! All someone would have to do is sneak over there, get up to the ledge, and listen in."

"And who would be silly enough to do something like that?"

"I could do it," Tau assured him.

"I know you feel a certain responsibility since your talk with The Keepers, Tau, but that doesn't mean balancing your life upon death."

"We are already balancing upon death. You said that every time she comes, people die. Who is to know if it is going to be you or me?"

"Even if someone should go, it should be me. I cannot let you endanger yourself. It wouldn't be right."

"Come on Brother Dwe, no offense, but with your leg, you would have a hard time getting around without getting noticed. I'm smaller, I know how to be stealthy, and you said it yourself; it's a lot easier to move through the compound at night than it would be to try and escape from it."

"Tau..."

"And yes, like it or not, I do have some responsibility to the tribe, one that was given to me. The Keepers sent me here for a reason, and I should find out what that reason is."

Everyone was silent for a moment, looking at Brother Dwe. Soon, he nodded his head. "Okay. I suppose that you ARE the savior."

"And I'll go with him!" Hondo added.

"Me too," said Kofi.

"Now, what makes you two think that I would let you go with?"

"Well," said Kofi, "it's too dangerous for someone to go alone."

"And besides," said Hondo, "someone has got to hoist him up to the window."

Brother Dwe shrugged.

XXX PRACTICE ROUND

Kofi and Hondo struggled to hoist Tau up to the ledge. It was wide, with plenty of room to move around, and plenty of space for all three of them.

"Come up," Tau whispered down to them.

"Someone is coming!" said Hondo. The moving shadow from the glow rod gave the guard away long before he had gotten to them. He was right around the corner and would be at their position in a moment.

"Get me down!" Tau scratched his throat, from trying to yell and whisper at the same time, giving it the oddest feeling.

"No time," said Hondo. "Lay down or something. Better for us to flee." The two boys ran, leaving Tau alone on the ledge.

They were right; it was too late for him to jump down. He'd probably hurt himself in the process. Then he would really be caught. And who knew what they would do to him.

As predicted, the guard came around the corner. Tau lay down on top of the ledge as quickly as he could, hugging his body against the crack were it met with the wall. To his advantage, the wide ledge shadowed him from the light. Even with his slight glance upward, the guard could not see him.

Tau did not know that for sure. He listened to the footsteps on the ground until he heard the guard walk away. When the light finally faded, he peeked over the edge of the ledge to make sure, but all he saw was the darkness on the ground that lay before him.

Then he heard voices coming from the window above him. He picked himself up enough to peek inside. There was a lot more going on than he had expected.

There was one large wooden chair with a decorative cloth laid across it and another cloth lying in front of it. Tau could only assume that Onoc was the man that sat in it. His stern demeanor overshadowed even Hatari, who also was present, standing a couple of feet in front of the chair and facing it. Nyami stood beside Hatari, while Doro stood next to a wall nearby. Aside from these major players, there were four guards as well as six of the *taken* standing there like statues with their blank blue eyes.

"Tomorrow night will be the final ritual," said Onoc. "Think of tonight as a practice round. We need to be sure. Soon, we will have the power of all the shape shifters, and with all their powers combined, we will gain access to all of the Barrier Cities."

"I trust in you, brother," said Nyami. "It was your insight that gave me the power of the owl, making me more powerful than I ever was before. Yet, I wonder how it is that you know the secret to the Barrier Cities."

"Nyami, before I answer that, could you explain to me how it is that you command the power of the wind, or how you can shift into not only one owl, but many?"

"It is simply a part of me," she responded. "How I do it cannot be explained. It would be like telling how it is that I can move my hand."

"KNOWING is one of my gifts. As you well know, I simply understand things. And when I foresaw that you would be the perfect candidate for the power of the Eagle shape shifters, I knew the power would not be exact. Though I did not know that instead of shifting to an eagle you were given the power to shift into an owl. Still, the basis of the power is the same."

"And you brother," said Hatari. "You gathered that you would be the perfect candidate for the power of the Leopard Tribe?"

"Yes. Eventually, we will split the power of all the Shape Shifters between all of our brethren. The power of leopard, ape, snake, and shark will be ours, just as the power of the eagle has been given to Nyami, though changed to an owl form. The fact that Nyami can split herself into so many has been an added bonus. I gather that we can all expect similar effects; slight differences in the powers that we gain."

"Once we all have the powers, then we will have access to the Barrier Cities?" asked Hatari.

"Yes, and all that they have to offer. By then, we will control all of Madunia."

"And you, Hatari, with your power of absorption, may be able to have the power of all five! But you must be patient. It may take some time."

"Are you sure that we will be ready for tomorrow's ritual, for your transformation?" asked Nyami.

"Yes, and frankly not soon enough. I'm tired of dealing with these people of the Leopard Tribe, stuck on this island. Everything about them irritates me. We need to get back to the mainland of Madunia and continue to conquer more territory. But first, we must make sure everything goes according to plan tomorrow.

The cages that encircle the ritual grounds are plenty strong enough to hold all of the Leopard Tribe. As far as the *taken* are concerned, they are never a problem. They will do as they are told and stand inside the ritual circle."

"And I am prepared to do my part," stated Nyami. "I will split myself fifty different ways and fly around the circle with the diamonds."

"Doro," Onoc waved him closer, "you are the key. This won't work without you. Once the ritual begins, it will be up to you to absorb the energy from ALL of the Leopard Tribe, so you must *take* every last one of them. Only then can you redirect their energy to us. And this is very important, once the ritual has been started, and Doro's transfer of energy begins, it cannot be interrupted for any reason. Stopping the ritual may have unforeseen consequences. Is that understood?"

Everyone nodded.

"For now," he continued, "we must practice the ritual with only a small few." He gave Nyami a secretive look out of the corner of his eye. Nyami nodded, with her eye keen on Hatari as if she knew something that he did not.

On the floor of the room, there were four circles. Three of them formed a triangle with one of those circles directly in front of Onoc's chair. Lines were drawn from each of those circles with diamond dust to the center of the triangle, where the fourth circle was drawn.

They each moved into position; Onoc occupied one of the circles, Hatari another one, and the six *taken* were crammed into the third. Doro took the remaining circle in the center. Nyami stood to the side.

"Slaves, begin your chant, *Obenga sodden. Agassi moga emdua gendo. Ngandazi mbatto neziba. Obenga sodden. Agassi moga emdua gendo. Ngandazi mbatto neziba. Obenga sodden. Agassi moga emdua gendo. Ngandazi mbatto neziba.*"

The *taken* slaves joined in. "*Obenga sodden. Agassi moga emdua gendo. Ngandazi mbatto neziba.*" Nyami knelt in the corner, far away from them, and bowed her head. A strange lump grew out of her back until a piece of her emerged into a black owl. Another one followed immediately, then another. The owls flew over to a barrel in the corner, grabbed a large diamond with their claws, and then flew over to the ritual circles. Each of the owls did this until twenty of them were flying around the ritual circles, continuously circling everyone except Nyami and the guards. Nyami continued to kneel on the floor.

The chants continued. The birds continued to fly. The diamonds they carried began to glow brighter and brighter as the birds flew faster and faster.

Doro's fiery eyes and hands began to glow brighter as well. Light blue strands of energy began to form in the area of the ritual circles. Hatari twitched, his body jerked for a moment until a mist began emanating from his body and into Doro. Then the mist moved from Doro, to Onoc. For a while, there was a continuous stream of energy moving from Hatari, to Doro, to Onoc.

From outside the fort, Tau gazed through the window at the

flickering white and blue light. It was an amazing spectacle as light poured into the night sky. People from around the camp took notice. Finally one big flash of blue light was seen. Inside the fort, a light blue foggy mist was left over. It slowly dissipated as Tau continued to look inside the room. The birds dropped the diamonds before returning to Nyami's body.

Hatari dropped to his knees. "I feel weak," he said, barely able to stand back up. Again he fell, this time being caught by one of the guards. "What has happened?"

Onoc inhaled as if he had been given a burst of energy. He looked over to Nyami and nodded. "I'm sorry brother, but it was necessary." He walked over to Hatari, grabbing his other arm to help him stand. "How do you feel?"

"Necessary?" asked Hatari. "What do you mean?"

"I needed your power to perform tomorrow night's ritual."

Hatari pushed Onoc away and lifted his staff. "I have been betrayed!"

"Your powers will not work, Hatari."

"It was not a betrayal brother," said Nyami. "It was necessary."

"Nyami, you too? Why?"

"He looks weak," said Onoc. "Sit him down."

The guards tried to move him to a chair, but Hatari shoved them away. Even that simple movement seemed to tire him. He sat himself down.

"Why, brother? Kill me now, or I will destroy you in time! I promise you that!"

"I know what I have done to you seems as if you have been betrayed. But I have done you a marvelous favor. Hatari, you were given the southern territories to gain control of. I've seen that Ufalme and all of its districts have been particularly hard for you. If you do what I say, you will be as powerful as ever, and like I said before, able to take the power of ALL the shape shifters, not only one."

"What do you mean? I won't listen to your lies."

"Deep in the forbidden expanse lies a mountain with crystals and jewels that are in perfect combination for someone of your talents. I have started your powers from zero so that they may better infuse you with your full potential. But you had to start from nothing; that is the only way. I needed to take all of your power away so that it could come back to you even stronger."

"You expect me to sit here while the two of you continue to conspire against me? How long is it that you expect me to stay in this mountain?"

"You will gain some of your strength and powers back shortly. I was very careful to explain to Doro not to do anything permanent or deadly. It will take many years brother, but trust me, it will be worth it. There are plenty of ogres there with strength and vigor, waiting for someone to organize them into doing something useful. Use their strength to protect you, and to mine for you the crystal that will aid you in gaining strength, as we have done here with the Leopard Tribe."

Nyami came closer to Hatari. She put her hand on his shoulder to console him. "We love you brother. Trust that Onoc has done nothing to harm you."

"Then why keep it from me?"

"Would you have voluntarily agreed to such a thing? To have your powers temporarily removed?"

"Of course not!"

"Then there is your answer."

They were all interrupted by the sound of an owl making a *"whoooing,"* noise as it flew in through the front window. In its claws, a necklace dangled with a crystal on the end. The bird flew to Nyami, dropping the necklace to her, and then landed on her shoulder. Nyami smiled as she turned to Onoc.

"She brings good news brother. We know the location of the Music Wielders. She has brought us proof of their whereabouts." Nyami placed the necklace into Onoc's hand, and he held it up to study it.

"What is it?" Hatari asked.

"A necklace," said Onoc. "One crafted by the Music wielders." He smiled. "After we leave this island, we will personally get to the Music Wielders make them bow to our will, or kill them all. Tomorrow, Nyami, after the ritual, you will find them. But do not engage them until I can gather a proper army at their location. These people who have eluded us so far will be controlled, or destroyed. They possess far too much power to be untamed."

"I will send her back out to their location now to keep watch. They are too far for my owls to keep a mental link with me."

"Proceed," Onoc said and nodded.

The owl left Nyami's arm and flew out of the window.

"Tell me brother," Hatari said to Onoc. "Why is it that when you depleted me of my powers, they flowed into you?"

"I do not nearly possess all of your power, Hatari; only a hint of it. You are skillful in many things, perhaps the most powerful of all witch doctors. What I needed was your power of absorption. The ability you have to take in the energy, or the essence of another. You are similar to Doro in that way, although Doro is capable of reaching much deeper; he can steal people's very being right out of them. I need your power to help me absorb what he takes from the Leopard Tribe. Only then will my minions and I be able to have their power. I will choose nine of my men to join me: Saah, my most trusted of all the guards, Togar, one that I do not necessarily have the same trust for, but serves his purpose, and seven others."

"These men," asked Hatari. "Are any of them in this room now?"

"No."

Hatari grabbed Onoc by his shirt, pulling him closer to whisper into his ear. "I hope none of these men in the room are your favorite, brother. They have seen me weak, and I cannot allow that."

Hatari let Onoc go, and immediately stood up. He looked at the guard to the left of him, the one that caught him when he fell, and shoved his staff through his chest. Onoc nodded to Nyami and the three of them quickly killed all of the remaining guards in the room.

"Not quite the action that I would have called for, Hatari, but you are probably right. No one should see any of the Children of Montok when they are weak. Nor should they know the story of our necessity to take your powers."

"Ha!" Nyami, laughed. "That was fun."

"Perhaps, Hatari, we should take this a step further. I'll give you a few men; leave the island tonight. Should any unforeseen trouble happen tomorrow, I don't want any of the guards the wiser that you don't have your powers."

"There are only three ships brother," said Hatari. "If I leave tonight, that would leave you with two. You won't have enough room to carry all the guards and the slaves away from the island. Do you plan to stay?"

"Haha, no. We will be done with this island. As for the ships, we'll have plenty of room. After tomorrow's ritual, all of the Leopard Tribe will be either dead or as useless as the rest of the *taken*. Either way, they will be of no more use to us. They can die on this island locked in the cages for all I care."

Nyami's head turned toward the window. Tau quickly ducked down, not sure if he had been seen. He did not wait to find out. Quickly he hung down from the ledge, dropped the rest of the way, and ran off into the night.

It took a little ducking, dodging, and being careful to move from one shadow to the next, but he managed to get himself back to his tent. He darted in, disturbing the other boys. Tau then peeked back outside.

"Tau!" said Hondo. "We thought something terrible happened to you. What happened?"

"Shhh!" Tau whispered back to him and continued looking outside. There was definitely some sort of scuffle going on. The guards were moving around more than usual. Hatari, Nyami, and Onoc stood at the top of the hill outside the fort, talking to Saah.

Glow rods started coming on. Guards walked up to various tents and opened them. Then Tau saw one of the guards heading toward their tent. He darted back inside.

"They're coming. Quick, act like you're sleeping."

By the time the guard opened the flap on the tent, everyone was still. The guard moved his glow rod into the tent, panning it around the room to get a good look. Soon he closed the flap and was gone.

Hondo waited a while before he said anything. "Tau, what's going on?"

"I think they saw me," Tau whispered back.

"In the window?"

"Yes."

"What did you see?"

"Hondo, it's terrible. By tomorrow night, we'll all be dead!

*   *   *   *   *

"Surely we must do something!" Hondo cried inside the tent to Dwe with no regard to how loud his voice was getting. Tau explained what he had seen and heard from outside the window. The news, of course, was not taken very well.

"Quiet!" Dwe demanded with a harsh whisper. "Of course we will do something, but yelling at the top of our lungs is not helpful." Dwe peeked outside of the tent, to see if any of the guards had been alerted by Hondo's voice. Then he ducked back inside. "And we mustn't let the Brood know that we know of their plans. We will get the word out to people, but quietly."

"We should find a way to let Kamaria out of her cage," said

Hondo.

"Surely, but not even Kamaria can take on the whole army. Most of our strongest and most capable warriors are chained up inside the mountain. I can't have you children rising up a rebellion only to get you killed."

"My dad. Where is my father? He would know what to do."

"I have not seen Brother Kato since the day he arrived. I'm sure that he is in the mountain caves somewhere."

Tau turned his head quickly. "Kato? Did you say Kato? Is he your father?"

"Yes," Hondo cried.

"I know Kato, and I have seen him, today."

"You've seen my father? Where?" Hondo asked earnestly.

"As Brother Dwe said, he is in the mountain, chained up with the rest of the men."

"Are you sure it was him?" Kofi asked. "How do you know him?

"When I first came to the White Forest, he was there. I ate with him. He taught me how to change into my leopard form. I know him."

"You must take me to him!" Hondo insisted.

"We can't do anything until morning, Hondo," said Dwe. "The last thing that we want is for everyone to be getting up in the middle of the night to tell everyone else the news. Too easy to get caught that way."

Hondo put his head down in disappointment.

"Well, what does Tau think?" asked Kofi.

"Me?"

Everyone looked at Kofi as if to say, "why Tau?"

"Yeah. He is supposed to be our savior, right. I mean, The Keepers DID send him."

Everyone was looking at Tau. Suddenly, he felt a great weight upon him.

"Yes," Dwe agreed. "If it is true, then we must look to you.

At the very least, hear what you have to say on the matter."

Tau swallowed. He did not want to say anything wrong. He certainly did not want to come up with an action that would cause anyone to get killed. "I think…" Everyone leaned in closer. "I think that at day break, when everyone wakes up, we slowly spread the word. So that everyone knows. I can move around a lot, where as you guys are stuck in the pit. I will get opinions from everyone. But I agree that we must somehow get free sometime before tomorrow's ceremony."

Tau could not believe anything was coming out of his mouth that made sense. He did not actually have a plan yet, but he did have an idea.

"But we are on an island, and the only way off is by those huge ships. We'll have to find someone that can drive them." He paused for a moment while everyone listened. "Oh! And I know of people that can help. The Mer Folk. Perhaps they can help us. They are the people of the sea who helped me to get here. I'm sure they can help us in some way. The only problem will be finding some way to contact them."

They all kept looking at him, waiting for more.

"That's all I have, for now."

Dwe squinted. "All right, Tau. You come to me tomorrow, within two hours of the start of the day. Tell me what you have learned."

Tau nodded.

"There is something about you, young Tau, that I can't deny. I for one would have never chosen you to lead a battle. But The Keepers have picked you, and I cannot deny that. So, I will look to you in our time of need. I hope you can handle that."

"Yes, sir," Tau said firmly, although he felt very unsure.

"But know this, leg or no leg, when it comes down to the moment, I will fight to the death for my people, and I will be behind you all the way."

Tau nodded again.

"For now boys," Dwe continued, "I want you to get some sleep. I need you to be well rested for tomorrow."

XXXI THE PERFECT PLAN

Three hours until daybreak. Dwe, Hondo, Kofi, and Tau, lay inside the tent. Tau was awake. He was plagued by the thought of this whole *savior* thing. He was finding it hard to breathe, unable to cope with the pressure. It was as if, with every passing minute, another layer of tension built up inside of his head.

At first, he had been told that he was the savior, but he had no clue where his people were, or what to save them from. Finally, he knew the enemy, he knew his people's situation, and he knew what would happen to them should he fail. To top all of that off, it was happening in a few hours. It was almost time to act, and he still did not have a clue of what to do. Last night, he did a good job of stalling. His plan so far was to wait until morning and then ask everyone else what to do. Yeah right, some plan! Tau rolled over to find Hondo's eyes wide open. He too was awake.

"Do you really know where my father is?" asked Hondo.

"Yes."

"Can you take me to him?"

"I don't think so, Hondo. The guards will know if you are supposed to be there or not. And trust me, they are far from nice."

"What about now? Can you take me now?"

"Now?"

"Yes, it would be easier now anyway, always easier to move during the night. And there will be fewer guards inside the mountain. They have to sleep too, you know."

"I don't know. I don't think Dwe will let us do that."

"He doesn't have to know."

"Hondo, I....."

The boy started tearing up. An uneasy quiver came to his voice as he spoke. "Please Tau. It has been months since I have seen him. And who knows if I will see him ever again. I don't even know if he knows about mother."

"Your mother? What happened to her?"

"They killed her!"

If there was ever a time that Tau felt empathy, it was then. Poor boy, Tau thought. He knew what it was like to lose someone. After all, he was not sure he would ever see Uncle again; the only father that he had ever known. If he had the opportunity to see him right now, he would do it, no matter what the cost was. No doubt, young Hondo deserved the chance to see his father.

* * * * *

Tau was having second thoughts as he led Hondo through the dark passages of the caves. It was darker than earlier, with fewer lit torches hung along the wall. He took extra care to focus on each tunnel and cavern as they traveled. He wanted to make sure that he knew where he was going, because this would certainly be the wrong time for him to get lost.

Hondo kept himself close to Tau, and both of them took soft careful steps through the twisting caverns. Finally, they came to Kato. He was asleep, laying right there in the same spot where he had worked all day. He looked peaceful. Given the amount of work that Tau knew he had done throughout the day, followed by all the backbreaking work he would have to do in the morning, it seemed almost wrong to wake him. But Tau knew that no matter how tired the man was, he would be absolutely elated to see his son.

Hondo brought the torch close to his father as he whispered to him, shaking him by his shoulder.

Kato's eyes opened wide. "Hondo!" He reached out to hug

Hondo in his arms.

"Father!"

Tau watched while Kato hugged his son so tightly he looked as if he might break him. They pulled back, immediately. Kato checked Hondo for any broken bones or wounds that The Brood may have given him.

"Are you all right, boy? What are you doing here?"

"Tau told me he saw you, father, so I had to come. I had to come see you!"

Kato looked at Tau, standing directly behind Hondo, for the first time. He smiled. "Tau, if anyone could have done this, I should have known it would be you. But you know you shouldn't have. It's too dangerous, for both of you."

"We had to come," said Tau. "There is so much to tell you, about tonight."

"What do you mean?"

"Yes, father, we must tell you. You will know what to do. Kamaria is locked up, and by the night, we could all be dead."

"All dead? Hondo, Tau, what are you talking about?" Kato grabbed Hondo by his shoulders and took a second to look both ways down the tunnel. "Quickly, it is important, you must tell me, and then the both of you must get out of here before the guards come. Most of them are sleeping now, but they still have patrols."

Tau saw Chad standing in the middle of the tunnel. "Hey, Tau," Chad said. "Don't you think you have somewhere else to go? I mean while you are in the mountain, you might as well go see, you know who..."

"You're right, I should go see him." Tau said.

"See who?" Kato asked him.

Tau looked at Kato and Hondo sternly. "Ink. I have to go talk to Ink."

"Go?" Hondo asked, surprised. "But Tau, we must tell my father about…"

"I know. You know everything that I do. You tell him. I will come back for you. Trust me, it's important. We don't have much time."

Before they could call Tau back, he hurried away.

"He's down here. Come on," said Chad.

"I know, I remember. I'm trying to watch out for guards. You don't want me to run into them, do you?"

"Certainly not! Oh, and one more thing..."

"What?"

"I know you are trying to spread word to everyone that you see, but I don't really trust these old people to keep their mouths shut. Not that they would do it on purpose or anything, they..."

"Yeah, I get it. Perhaps it is best if they didn't know anything."

He entered the room where Ink and the rest of the elderly people were kept. Tau attempted to wake him quietly. Unfortunately the old man yelped as soon as Tau touched him, disturbing the others that were sleeping around them.

"Ink, what did you mean before when you said to kill the demon?" Tau asked him in a whisper.

"Kill the demon, life is there!" said Ink.

"Sssshhh," Tau jolted toward him. "We don't want the guards to hear us." He paused for a second to look around him. "Do you mean Doro?"

"Like her," said Ink.

"Like who?" asked Tau.

Ink pointed his finger at Tau's face. "Her eyes."

"What's he talking about?" Tau turned to ask the other elders in the room.

"Who knows what he is talking about? We told you, that one is crazy."

"Ink," said Tau, "what are you talking about?"

"Not my eyes. Two eyes."

"Eyes?"

"Eyes, eyes, eyes; she's still in the eyes." Ink pointed into

Tau's eyes. "There she is."

"What else, Ink? Tell me something else besides eyes?"

"Hands, hands, hands!"

Tau took a deep breath, trying to figure out if Ink was crazy, or if there was something that actually made sense somewhere in there.

"What about hands, Ink? Whose hands?"

"Hmmm, hands!" Ink raised up his hands. "Your hands... my hands. My hands...her hands."

Tau looked at the man's hands and then at his own. Inks hands were obviously older and more decrepit looking than his, but Tau noticed a small similarity between them. Tau's middle finger, ring finger, and pointer finger had very slight curves to them. It appeared that Ink's fingers curved the same way. Tau put his hands side-by-side Ink's and put them up to Ink's face.

"Are our hands the same, Ink?"

Ink nodded. "Same hand."

An inquisitive smile warmed up Tau's face. "Does he have any children?" Tau asked the other elders in the room.

"He has his daughter and son, Kamaria and Kato," said an old woman.

"Kamaria is his daughter!" Tau exclaimed as his head began putting pieces together. "But that means..."

"No, no, no," said one of the old men. "You forgot about the other ones. His son died at 18. It was a terrible sickness. And there was his other daughter, the one that married, the one that left. She and her husband...they never came back."

"Another daughter?"

"Yes."

"Who was she? I thought you all stayed in the city. Why did she leave? Where did she go?" Tau asked frantically.

No one answered. The old folks murmured amongst themselves.

"Secret baby," said Ink, pointing to Tau, smiling in the most ridiculous fashion. "Safe baby places."

Tau looked at the dark black walls barely lit by the torches. Was it his imagination, or was it turning blue? No, it was not his imagination at all. "Quick! Lay down!" he whispered to everyone. "Quiet!"

He thrust himself up against the wall near the entrance and watched as the walls became bluer by the second. Then he could feel the small vibrations in the ground and the wall that he leaned against. There was no doubt in his mind. It was Doro. He held his breath as Doro came near the entrance and then continued to walk past. Tau exhaled with a sigh of relief. He hated that monster. The last thing that he wanted was to come face to face with it again.

Hondo and Kato! He envisioned Doro meeting up with them. Doro was coming from that direction. He had to see if they had met the terrible fate of the cold fire demon. He scuffled back up to his feet and walked over to Ink who was already fast asleep. There was no need to wake him up again. Tau did not have the time to chat.

"I have to go, Ink," he whispered. "But I think that I understand." Tau took one last look at the old, frail man lying there with a single cloth over his mid-section. "We will talk again."

As he walked the corridors, he was even more alert than before, franticly and constantly checking in front and behind him for sounds of people walking, or for any light from a torch, or a glow rod, or worst of all, from Doro. As much as he wanted to hurry, his pace was slow, and he was very careful to check around corners and down tunnels before he proceeded.

He was careful not to wake anyone. He passed by many of the adult men who were chained up, like Kato, right there where they worked. If he only had the keys, he could set all of them free. A possible plan, he thought to himself. Then, he saw the light of a torch lighting the walls of the tunnel in front of him. It was moving toward him, and he panicked. Quickly, he turned around the other way, only to hear the voices of some other guards coming toward him. He had nowhere to go. There were no nooks in the wall for him to hide in, nor was there another corridor for him to turn down. He looked down at the men chained up against the wall, on either side of the tunnel. As quick as he could, he gently placed himself between two of them lying on the ground.

He slightly brushed up against the man next to him, which woke him out of his sleep. The man opened his eyes and scooted back. Tau put his finger to his mouth, indicating that he wanted the man to be quiet. He did not have time to explain. All he could say was, "Sssssshhhhhhhh," as quietly as possible, followed by a look out of the corner of his eye that he hoped said, "danger!"

The man nodded. They both put their heads to the ground and in the next few seconds, a patrol of two guards rounded the corner and walked past them. The second patrol came, moments after that. They too walked past Tau with no problem and continued their patrol as usual until they were out of sight. Tau waited a short moment, and then hopped to his feet. "Thanks," he whispered to the man. "I have to go."

The man sat up, concerned and confused. "Wait, are you Tau?"

"Yes. How did you know?"

"The people, they talk about you. What's happening?"

"I don't have time to explain it right now, sorry."

The man nodded. Tau started to walk off and then turned back around to the man and leaned over to him. "Today is the day. Be ready when the time comes." Then he left the man again, and finally he found his way back to Kato and Hondo.

"Where did you go?" Hondo asked, sounding extremely concerned. "We thought something happened to you."

"I had to talk to old Ink," Tau replied.

"Ink?" asked Kato. "What about him?"

Tau stared at the both of them for a moment. "We should go.

I've seen two patrols and Doro."

"Yes," said Kato. "You were right to come here, but you two should go."

"Did Hondo tell you everything?"

"Yes. And these Mer Folk, if you can get to them, do you think they will help us?"

"I hope so."

"Then go. Hondo will explain to you what I have told him."

Tau nodded. "Come, Hondo, let's go."

Hondo and Kato hugged one last time. "Soon, son, we will see each other again."

Tau grabbed Hondo's hand. As soon as they turned around, before they even realized it, they ran right into the arms of the guards. Unfortunately, one of the five guards was Togar.

They grabbed the two boys before either of them could think or react. They both screamed, struggling against the guards as they brought them back around the corner.

Kato cringed at the sight of his son in the hands of the Brood.

Togar smirked. "And what would be so important for two young boys to go running around the tunnels so early in the day?"

"My son," Kato said tugging against his chains. "He wanted to see me. I have not seen him for months."

Togar shook his head. "This is not a family reunion. You are slaves. What you want isn't up to you."

"Father!" Hondo screamed, still struggling.

"Be calm, son."

Other slave men began waking up from all of the noise. They too, of course, were still chained to the wall. They watched this spectacle before them of Kato, the guards, and the two children. Togar walked forward, close to Kato, yet not close enough for Kato to grab him.

"You know the penalties for disobedience. And so does your son."

"Yes, Master Togar," Kato agreed. "Do what you will with me, but please leave my son alone."

"You know," said Togar, "in the end, it's really not going to matter much."

"Then you will spare him?"

Everyone's eyes turned as a blue light began to bounce off the walls. Everyone knew who it was. Again, it was Doro. He walked in and said nothing. He stood in the center of the tunnel. The men along the wall did their best to stay as far from him as possible, hugging up against the side of the corridor.

Tau could suddenly feel the temperature drop. He was still not used to seeing this beast. He had dodged him minutes ago, only to be confronted by him again. He could not believe his luck. For some reason, whenever he saw Doro, he felt this horrible sickening feeling in the pit of his stomach. He felt sorry for bringing Hondo into the caves despite his wanting to see his father. If they were all going to be killed, then it was not really worth it.

Togar brought his glow rod close to Kato. Tau could faintly hear the sizzling of energy running through it. The glow rod was about an inch from Kato's neck, lighting up his skin and the contours of his strong face.

"Do what you want with me, he says," said Togar, mocking Kato. "Hmm, that could be anything. You know, part of me doesn't care much for Onoc's rules of keeping as many of you alive as possible. I could kill all three of you. Then again, Doro came all this way." He smiled, looked at Tau, and then stood up. "You're the new boy, aren't you?"

"Yes, sir," Tau said, quivering.

"I prefer Master Togar."

"Yes sir, Master Togar."

"You see, these other two know the rules; they have been here long enough. But I suppose I can show you a bit of leniency." He looked Tau in his eyes, and then looked along

Tau's body as if measuring him. "Doro," he said and then paused again, looking back into Tau's eyes. "*Take* him."

A shock ran through Tau's body, that awful feeling in his stomach became worse until he noticed that Togar was not pointing at him, he was pointing at Hondo.

Doro did not hesitate. He put his large hand around Hondo's shoulder. It was almost large enough to cover up half of his chest.

"No!" Kato cried out. "Don't do it!" He lunged forward with all his might. The loud CLANK from the tightening of his chains echoed in the chamber. There was no way he could reach them, although he tried as hard as he could. "Let him go!" Kato screamed while he continued to struggle against the chains and shackles. The metal tore at his skin, blood trickled to the floor as he tried desperately to squeeze his hands and feet through their braces.

Togar thrust his glow rod into Kato's chest. He yelled as the rod hit his skin. Tau watched the small sparks flicker upon contact while Kato could do nothing but scream.

"Kato!" Tau yelled. He too began struggling harder. It took three guards to hold him. "Hondo!"

Four of the other slave men in the area were also yelling at the guards to let the boy go. All of them pulled on their chains, trying to free themselves from the wall. The guards struck them all with glow rods to calm them. Tau tried to cover his ears to the sound of their screaming.

All they could do was watch as the blue mist flowed from Hondo into Doro's eyes and mouth. His body twitched as at last a blue outlined image of him came out of his face and disappeared into Doro's, and then his body went limp.

"I'll kill you!" Kato cried out.

"I think not," said Togar. Once again, he thrust his glow rod up against Kato, whose eyes were streaming tears.

Every ounce of strength in Tau's body wanted to fight for Kato, but there was nothing that he could do. He could not believe his eyes. How could this be happening? He felt more intense rage building up inside than he had ever felt before. Suddenly, he yanked his arms free from the guards, punched the both of them so hard and fast that they hit the wall behind them and yelled out, "ENOUGH!"

Everyone stopped and looked at him as he stood there panting. Togar walked toward him with a confused look on his face. "What was that?" he asked.

"My name is Tau. I have been sent here by a higher power. Let my people go, or you...will...suffer!"

Togar took another step forward. He turned his eyes upward as if to look for something to suddenly fall from the heavens. "You, boy, have got to be the stupidest person I have ever met." Then, with his hand, he knocked Tau to the floor.

The guards stood over him. Togar walked over, rising up his glow rod with a disappointed look on his face. "Attacking a guard?" He sounded surprised. "New kid or not, you will regret doing that. And perhaps your screaming will teach the others what will happen should they ever raise a hand against us!"

Togar reached his glow rod out to Tau's chest. He lay on the ground, feeling the pain of it and crying out. Togar stopped for a moment, looking at his guards. "Come on men, this is a group session."

The guards looked at each other, and then pulled out their glow rods as well, turning them on. All of them attacked Tau at once, all over his body. Tau could not believe the pain; it was like nothing he had ever felt before. As if millions of heated ants of energy swarmed him. He screamed and yelled louder than he ever had before. He wanted to tell them to stop, but his mouth could not form the words, not even to beg them. Soon it was all too much, and Tau passed out.

XXXII FAMILY MATTERS

Tau woke up with a sudden violent jerk. The pain of the glow rods still lingered throughout his body. He did not have much room to move. He noticed that he was in a terribly uncomfortable position. His neck was angled, twisted up against something hard. The glare of the sun pierced his pupils like knives, so he raised his hand to shield his face. It took quite a bit of blinking and focusing for him to be able to see anything clearly.

Great. He had landed himself in a cage again, outside, on the edge of the camp. He grabbed one of the bars to test its strength, tugging on it with his weak arms. It was definitely strong, although the way he felt, anything would have felt strong. He sat up, trying to rub the crook out of his neck when Kamaria spoke to him.

"Getting yourself jailed!" she said while clapping. "Good job. This all part of your great plan?"

Tau sat in the cage across from Kamaria. He did not look at her, yet he could feel her eyes piercing into him, judging him. Once again, he was embarrassed by simply being who he was, and to feel this way in front of someone like Kamaria made his shame seem that much worse. He certainly did not want to tell her that this was the second time in about a week that he had woken up in a cage.

"You know," she continued. "You've got quite a pair of lungs on you, boy. I heard you screaming before daybreak. The whole camp heard it. Too bad you are not a Music Wielder or you could scream us all free."

"I don't have a great plan," Tau admitted.

Kamaria leaned forward, grabbing the wooden bars with both of her hands. "Is it true, what I have heard? About tonight?"

Tau looked up at her dried face and her cracked lips. "Yes. I heard them talking about it last night."

"What do you plan to do?"

"I can't do much from in here."

"And if you were out?"

"Still not sure. I do think that perhaps I could enlist the aid of the Mer Folk."

"From The Deep?"

"Yes."

"Hhmm," she said, sitting back again against the cage. "They are a powerful people."

"You know of them?"

"Only things that I have heard. But I do not believe they involve themselves in worldly affairs."

Tau sighed. "I know. But I have a good friend down there, and I think she would help. Of course, it doesn't matter now."

"I thought you were supposed to be our savior. Saviors don't give up. Let me tell you a little something about leading. If you want people to follow you, then they can never see you give up."

"So you're on my side now? I thought you did not even like me."

"It's got nothing to do with liking you. It has to do with what I think is best for my people. There is no doubt about it, kid," she ran her fingers across the bars of her cage, "we are definitely on the same side."

"Can I ask you a question, Kamaria?"

"I got nothing else to do till noon, when they let me out of here."

"Is Ink your father?"

"That old kook?" She laughed and nodded her head. "Yes, yes he is. He actually should be ruler of the whole tribe, though everyone agrees that he is in no condition to rule anything. So it falls to me. I take it that you have met him."

"Yes, in the cave mines. He's in a chamber with a bunch of other old folks that the Brood considers useless."

"Well, at least he is still alive."

"What about your sister?"

Kamaria's face became more attentive. It was like Tau had asked her a question of an extremely personal nature; one that she never expected anyone to ask her, especially Tau. "My sister? Why do you ask?"

"What was her name?"

"Cella."

"Can you tell me about her?"

Kamaria's eyes trailed off for a moment. "She was strong like me. In fact, we were a lot alike. But she had a way of making people laugh. That was something that I always envied about her." Kamaria's eyebrows drew together and her lips tightened. "Then she went crazy and left, and took her husband with her. We haven't seen them since. I'm not sure if I've ever forgiven her for that."

"What do you mean, she went crazy?"

"You sure ask a lot of questions, kid."

"Trust me, it's important."

"She probably got it from old Ink. Who knows what a father can pass down to his child. She claimed to have visions; claimed to hear voices in her head. At first, they were small and few, then after a while, they consumed her. She couldn't think. She insisted on leaving, going where the visions wanted her to, figure out what they wanted her to do. So, she left. Like I said, she went crazy."

"She wasn't crazy," said Tau.

"It sounds crazy to me, kid."

"The same thing happened to me. I lived on the other side of Madunia. I had visions, visions that brought me to the Amotekun City. Cella didn't leave because she was crazy. She left because the Keepers probably gave her visions to keep her baby safe. She left to give birth to me."

Kamaria's face contorted with astonishment and curiosity.

"What are you saying, Tau? That you are Cella's child?"

"Yes. Ink said that when she left, she gave birth to a secret baby and that I was that secret baby."

"Ha. You should know, you can't pay attention to anything that Ink says."

"That's what people think, but you just have to pay MORE attention."

Kamaria's face went blank for moment. Her eyes were locked onto Tau's face, but it was if she did not see him at all. She lacked any expression whatsoever. Then, out of nowhere, she burst into an uncontrollable laughter. Her laughter turned to a deep, horrible cough.

Tau looked at her, hoping that she was not suddenly going to die. Soon, she got control of her cough and fell silent only to start laughing again moments later.

"All this time, and you are my sister's son... my nephew! You see, she still can make me laugh. Haha."

Tau was not sure what was exactly funny about the situation, but joined in with a slight laugh as well.

"Well, boy, say hi to your Auntie Kamaria. I can see it now. It's in the eyes. Hahaha."

"That's what Ink said."

"Have more respect, Tau. To you, he's Grandpa Ink! Hahaha." She laughed until she started coughing again.

The sound of Kamaria's laughter came strangely to Tau's ears. It caught him completely off guard, though he welcomed it. It was a side of Kamaria he had not seen before, even if she was going slightly mad from lack of food, thirst, and the terrible effects of staying out under the sun for days.

A guard apparently had noticed her coughing, because he came over with a bowl of water for each of them. "Here," he said. "You are in luck. We were told that no one goes hungry or thirsty today. There will be food for you soon." Then the guard walked away.

They both began drinking. Tau could not believe how good the water felt in his mouth, or how soothing it was to feel the cool wetness move down his throat. He could only imagine how thirsty Kamaria was.

"What do you think that was about?" Kamaria asked Tau. "This is more water than they gave me for the entire day yesterday."

"You see," he responded, "Onoc wants everybody strong for the ritual tonight. Something about stealing all our energy and abilities."

"So, nephew," Kamaria spoke between more pleasant drinking. "How are we going to get out of here? We are all sure to be doomed tonight if what you say is true."

"Well, Dwe is making sure that everyone knows. He is formulating a time to attack. He is also trying to find someone that can drive those giant ships."

"Dwe? My Dwe?"

"Yes, ma'am."

"So, the coward is helping you. I'm surprised he is in favor of any movement against the Brood."

"Dwe is no coward, Kamaria. He is all for fighting. But he knows it should be at the right time. Fighting is more than brute force. It is also tactics and cunning thought. He was never against fighting; it's the timing he has had a problem with."

"Oh, and now the timing is right?"

"Now, we have no choice. And Dwe believes in me. I'm still not sure what to do, but Dwe is ready. He is ready to fight."

Kamaria thought deeply for a moment. "I've been a fool to treat Dwe the way that I have. And perhaps I owe you an apology."

"Thank you."

"No thanks is necessary. Getting results will be plenty thanks enough. If what you say about the Keepers is true, then they have chosen you for a reason. You must believe in that."

"I do."

"No, I don't think you do, not yet, but you will. You must!"

There was a silence between them for a moment. Tau slumped down into his cage. He knew those words were supposed to encourage him, especially since those words came from Kamaria. He tried to let them sink into his mind, although there were many layers of doubt deep within him. Still, given the choice, he would pass on this savior thing to someone else if he could. If his destiny were up to him, he would rather be back in his village fishing. He missed the times before this whole *getting Chad killed and turning into a leopard business.*

"So, these Mer Folk," Kamaria continued. "Tell me more about them."

Tau not only told her about the Mer Folk, and about Amanzi, he told her his whole story. He told her of his visions and the awful pain that accompanied them. He told her about Hagga the shaman, Anansi, the music wielders, and even Juran the Animan. He was as detailed as possible. For the first time, he could see Kamaria finally look upon him as if he was a person, and for the first time he felt that she too had begun to believe in him.

XXXIII PURSUIT

Kamaria and Tau were quiet for the rest of the morning. Tau watched her fade in and out of consciousness despite their being well fed, as the guard had promised. When noon came, they watched the guard walking toward them to let her out.

"When it happens, Tau, it will be quick. Be smart, and don't make a move until the right moment. You'll know when. Save yourself and find the Mer Folk. Don't worry about anyone else, especially me," Kamaria said softly. "Use the green one."

"What are you talking about?" Tau asked. "When what happens? What are you going to do?"

The guard came to her cage, knocking on it with his rod. "You. Saah wants to see you."

Kamaria winked and then whispered to Tau, "I'm doing what any leader should do: what I think is right for my people."

She moved slowly as the guard dragged her out of the cage. "Not so tough now, are you?" said the guard.

Kamaria smiled at him, "I'd like to thank you, sir, for the food. If it weren't for that, I might not be able to do this...." With great speed, she tackled him to the ground. She quickly grabbed his rod from his hands and in the commotion snatched his keys off of his belt. As she struck the guard with the glow rod, she quickly buried the keys in the dirt in front of Tau's cage.

Tau began to reach for them but she shook her head, "Not yet."

Again she struck the guard with the glow rod, holding it against his body for longer than anyone should endure. His screams of anguish were too loud for anyone on the island to ignore. Everyone could see what was going on. Other guards rushed toward her. She gave one final blow of the rod, hitting the guard across his face so hard that she cracked his mask. Again, she looked at Tau. "Oh, I wasn't quite as weak as I let on."

Then she quickly ran toward the pits. Another guard approached her only to be met by the rod as she swung it with all of her might, knocking the man off of his feet. She did not stay to try and finish him off.

She reached Dwe's pit, diving onto the ground, sliding until half of her body was hanging over the edge. Dwe was on his way out of it to see what all of the commotion was about when he saw her.

"Kamaria!" He yelled as he limped over to her. "What has happened, what have you done?"

"I am a fool, my love, and I wanted you to know that I do love you. And if you can believe in the boy, then so can I. Don't make any moves until he comes back." She grabbed him and quickly pressed her lips up against his.

They were suddenly interrupted, as the guards yanked Kamaria backwards by her legs and dragged her across the dirt.

"He will save us. You shall be free!" she yelled to Dwe.

"Kamaria!" he yelled desperately as he pulled himself out of his pit in an effort to go after her.

Tau was in awe. He could not believe his eyes as he watched Kamaria being attacked by the guards. Then, suddenly, he noticed that everyone was watching Kamaria. No one, not one of the guards or slaves was looking his way. If he was going to get away, now would be a good time. He frantically searched through the red earth in front of his cage to find the keys that Kamaria had so skillfully hidden moments before. His hands were shaking. He placed the green key to the lock and opened the gate. He headed straight for the tree line, making it without being noticed by anyone.

Once hidden there, he turned and looked at what was happening behind him. Everyone was in a ruckus; the guards had their hands full trying to keep the slaves in line without having a full-blown riot break out. Dwe was on his stomach. Three guards held him firmly to the ground by striking him with their glow rods. Meanwhile, Kamaria still fought with all her might against four of the other guards.

With quickness and determination, she forced a sword out of one of the guard's hands; using it to kill two of the others. She would not stop. She was like a machine gone mad, and nothing could shut her down as one guard after another fell at her feet.

It was not long before Tau saw Doro and Saah headed to the site. Saah was quick to throw out commands to every nearby guard to keep the situation under control, while Onoc continued to watch the whole thing from the window up high in his fort.

For a moment, it almost seemed as if the Brood would lose control of the people in this situation, as anger and chaos spread throughout the camp. Then suddenly, people found themselves enveloped by a flock of black owls. They spread throughout the camp, blinding people and scratching the slaves with their talons as they flew by. Everyone shielded themselves, diving to the ground, even the guards. The birds finally flew toward Kamaria, swarming all around like a tornado setting upon her. Tau could see scratches from the owl's claws on Kamaria's face, neck and arms, as they sliced into her skin over and over again. She swatted at them, but their numbers overwhelmed her.

Helplessly, Tau watched this swarm of birds surrounding Kamaria like a tornado. Soon, she fell to her knees, then to the ground, trying to cover herself with her arms and to prevent herself from being ripped to shreds. The tornado slowed. The birds merged together to form Nyami once again.

Kamaria looked up at her from the ground, breathing heavily in a dire pant, covered in cuts and blood.

"This ends now," Nyami said.

Kamaria was too stubborn. As quickly as she could, she jumped up and ran toward Nyami at full speed. She roared like a raging lion intent on killing its prey.

Nyami was quick to react. She reached her arm out in front

of her, thrusting a strong wind blowing that slowed Kamaria's movements. Kamaria struggled against it until it finally blew her the ground. Nyami's shoulders bulged for a moment as two large owls sprouted from her body. They flew over to Kamaria lying on the ground and landed on her chest, digging their talons deep into her skin. Kamaria grunted but let out no cry of pain.

"So stupid," Nyami remarked. She looked over at Doro and nodded her head. Doro walked over to Kamaria. Dwe still lay on the ground. He struggled at the sight of Doro approaching his love.

Doro grabbed Kamaria by the neck, lifting her into the air. She kicked her legs fiercely as though trying to fight him, connecting with his large hard chest with no result. Doro was ten times as strong as any man or woman. His cold, fiery eyes began to glow even brighter. Kamaria began to shake, struggling against him.

A light blue ghostly figure emerged from Kamaria's body. It stopped for a moment, turned toward Dwe, and seemed to smile before entering Doro's body.

"Noooooooooooo!" Tau yelled, still standing at the tree line. Of course, the moment that he said it, he knew he should not have, for his voice flowed throughout the entire camp. Heads turned his way, including Saah and Doro. With a simple gesture Saah sent guards running across the camp toward Tau at the tree line.

"You've done it now," said Chad. "I think you should run!"

Tau did not waste any time. He ducked into the forest and ran. He moved swiftly through the thick of the forest and tall grass, winding in and out of the many trees. His instincts told him that he would be much better suited to turn himself into a leopard. It would certainly give him the speed and agility that he needed to keep himself far ahead of the troops. Though he tried, it still did not happen. He knew it was because of Doro. With that demon anywhere on the island, his newfound shape shifting abilities were useless.

He was not sure where he was going. His only thought was to move straight away from the camp and eventually he would have to emerge at the edge of the island. Then, suddenly, Tau felt his foot being caught on something. He lost his balance, falling head first onto the ground, rolling in the dirt and grass until he felt himself being hoisted up into the air. He had again fallen into one of Kamaria's traps. Except this time, he was not completely inside. He was not sure if the fall helped him, or aided in his capture, but only his foot was caught, entangled in one of the holes on the outside of the net. His body swung back and forth, and upside down, six feet off of the ground.

Mad at himself for only being free for a short time before he found himself once again caught, he leaned upwards, looking at how his foot was caught in the rope. If he tried hard enough, he might be able to get himself free. Then, he heard voices of the Brood coming his way. He reached up with his hand until he could grab the part of the net wrapped tightly around his foot.

He pulled at it as hard as he could before he felt a terrible burning sensation coming from his stomach muscles. His body dropped, once again swinging upside down in the net. He needed rest, if only for a moment, before he would try it again. His body had felt weak ever since he got to the island. He did not know or understand how Kamaria showed so much strength.

"Tau, they are coming!" exclaimed Chad. "You have to move!"

"I'm trying. I'm trying!" he shouted.

The voices made him panic. He fumbled with the net and his foot trying to get it loose. Soon, he grabbed on to the net with both of his hands, trying to take all of his weight off of his foot so that it was not pulling on the net at all. He yanked, pulled, and twisted the net until, finally, his foot came free. He dropped to the ground as controlled and quietly as possible, and then rolled to the side just in time. Tau lay on his stomach on the ground and watched as a patrol of three guards walked right past him. They stopped at the hanging net for a moment, looking around.

They were not more than ten feet away. He lay on his stomach with his hands perched firmly into the soft soil. The sun was blazing hot back at the camp. Here, under the shade of the trees, it was not much better. The humidity of the forest made for sweltering conditions. Tau blinked vigorously as sweat trickled down from his head and began to sting his eye.

He could feel a few ants crawling across his fingers and even worse were the flies, or were they mosquitoes? He was not sure, but they buzzed around his head while he tried to shake them off.

The worst thing was the nastiest two-inch wide millipede slowly dropping down a mere foot and a half in front of him. If it was not for the long body and countless legs, Tau would have thought it was a spider, for it was lowering itself by a long strand of silk from its backside.

The thing was about a foot long. It was brown with bright orange spots all over it and a kind of slimy exterior that reminded Tau of the bullfrogs back home.

He caught a shriek trying to leap from his mouth. Everything else in his vision blurred as his eyes focused on this creature in front of him. Somehow the creature knew he was there. It stopped its descent right at the same height as Tau's face and curved its body up to meet his eyes.

Tau took a moment to look at the guards again and saw that they were busy studying the area of the trap. The creature arched itself over toward Tau's face. It was too much for him. He rolled back, swinging at the creature. It jumped back as well, quickly lowering itself on its web. It began spinning around, faster and faster, while still lowering itself until it was spinning itself into the dirt, burrowing into the ground.

That ugly thing was gone, but Tau's quick movements in the brush caught the attention of the guards. He quickly scurried back, still keeping himself low to the ground. He moved fast, jumping behind a tree, then peeking back to see the guards' progress.

Ahead of him, he saw a mimicking flower. As he looked around, he noticed they were everywhere, mixed into the forest all around him. This gave him an idea. He took a moment to crouch down in front of one of them to get its dancing started. Then he quickly moved far away from it, ducking behind another tree.

"There he is!" one of the guards shouted.

Tau looked over to see that his deception had worked. The guards mistook the movement in the flowers for him. Soon, with so many of the flowers moving in the bush, the guards became confused, hacking and slashing at every movement that caught their eye. With the guards occupied with the flowers, Tau figured it would be a good time to slip away from the area all together.

He ran through the thick of the trees, fighting against his tiring body. It had been a while since he had heard or seen any of the guards. Then a figure showed up in front of him fast enough that he did not have time to stop. He tried, digging his feet into the ground so hard that he tumbled over. There he lay right at the base of Doro!

Doro grabbed him by the neck. Tau struggled as Doro lifted him off of the ground. Tau could not breathe. He tried to pry Doro's hand off of his neck as he had seen many others do before, but Doro was far too strong. Tau was surprised at the temperature of Doro's hands. He always thought that his body would feel as cold as ice, but it was not. It was the same temperature as any object around. Yet Tau could feel a cold breeze emanating from him as Doro brought Tau's face close to his own. It was like nothing else, staring into those blue eyes of fire; being only inches from this demon with the crystal face. He could see the sunlight refracting through Doro's blue body. Tau felt the coldness of Doro's being, like all of his heat being pulled away. He believed that at any moment, he would be *taken* or killed. He honestly did not know which one was worse.

He heard a crackling noise, the kind that wood makes when it breaks. They both looked down as the ground moved and Doro dropped down a couple of inches. Suddenly, the cracking sound got louder and Tau found both Doro and himself falling through the ground.

XXXIV DATE WITH A DEMON

Tau looked up with Doro standing over him. His glowing face was set against the background of a long dark tunnel leading straight up with the light of day far at the other end.

"I see you are not dead," Doro's deep voice rumbled inside the well. Tau could not decide if he was surprised or disappointed. His leg and his ribs delivered a jolt of pain as he tried to sit up. It was then that he noticed how small the space was that they were in. This small hole could not have been more than ten feet across. It was lined with dark brick as big as a foot in size each and was a completely enclosed circle.

To Tau, Doro seemed as menacing as ever, with his blue crystal shining against the darkness, and here he was, trapped in a hole with him. There was no escape. Tau stood up very slowly and carefully, holding the side of his chest. The monster stared at him, not saying anything. Tau wanted to look up again to see how far they had fallen. He wanted to look around to see exactly where they were. However, for the moment, his eyes were fixed on Doro, and Doro's eyes, if he had any, were definitely fixed on him.

The question was why? Why was Doro just standing there? His emotionless face felt more horrible, more terrorizing than anything. Tau feared that, if he took his eyes off of the beast for even one second, he would be attacked.

After a very long stalemate of looking at each other, Tau figured that he had to do something. But he could not do anything until he figured out what was going on with Doro, and how they got there.

"What happened? What did you do?" he asked the demon.

"I did nothing," Doro said, looking upward to the entrance from which they had come. "We have fallen. You would probably be dead if I wasn't holding you. If I had landed on top of you, I'm sure that I would have smashed you to blood."

"I'm sure you would have been real sorry if you killed me."

"No, I would not." Doro seemed to totally have missed the sarcasm.

"Are you going to?" Tau asked, leaning himself against the wall, almost pressing himself into it trying to get as far away from Doro as possible.

"Am I going to what?"

"Kill me, or *take* me?"

"Probably one or the other, at some time; whatever Lord Onoc decides."

That actually sounded like some good news to Tau. Doro did not plan on killing him in the well. He expected to wait to be commanded to do so. Even with that knowledge, Tau felt terribly afraid. Doro's empty eyes seemed to be locked in on Tau. For a moment, all Tau could hear was the sound of his own breathing as he tried to control his fear. His heart did not seem to be beating fast, but each beat thumped so hard he could feel it shaking every inch of his skin. His own fear twisted his stomach into an awful knot.

"So what do we do now?" Tau asked.

Doro tried to scale the wall. After several attempts, he came to one conclusion. "I am unable to get out."

"Um, you don't mind if I try, do you?"

Doro said nothing. He grunted and began a slow pace back and forth in the hole. The dark rocks reflected the blue flickering glow from his body as he neared them.

Tau turned to the wall and tried to get his fingers in the cracks between the bricks. No matter where he tried, he could not get enough leverage to climb out. He found a small space barely big enough to fit the tips of his fingers in. As soon as he tried to climb, his fingers burned from the sensation of his fingertips trying to carry his entire weight. He dropped to the ground.

"I don't think I can do it."

"I see." Doro said still pacing, slowly.

"I know,' said Tau impatiently. "You could throw me."

"Leaving you to escape, while I remain here alone."

Tau sat on the ground and watched the monster for a while. He still feared that, at any second, Doro was going to jump on him and send him to his grave. But for now it seemed that Doro was in the same situation he was in, trapped.

"It wouldn't have bothered you at all?" Tau asked.

"What?"

"If I died falling down here."

"What does it matter? If I died, I'm sure you would rejoice."

"No!" Tau shouted. "I mean, yes. I mean," Tau stood up. "That's only because...because of you we are stuck here. Because of you, we can't change shape, and you serve Onoc with no remorse for who gets hurt or who dies!" Before Tau knew it, he walked up to the monster, and Doro quickly put him in his place, snapping his head around, turning his cold eyes toward him. Tau quickly relented with a coward's stumble back to the other side.

"I wouldn't wish it on anyone. Death, that is," Tau continued. "Don't you have any feelings? Don't you care about anyone? Have you ever cared about anyone, or anything?"

"It does not matter."

"It does. It does matter!"

Doro turned and faced the wall. "I think I did have feelings once, back before this body. I was... human."

Tau's face filled with confusion. "You were human?"

"A long time ago. At least, I think that I remember having these... *feelings* that you talk about."

"What happened to you? How did you get like this?"

"What does it matter? When it comes time, I will destroy all of you."

"You said you weren't going to kill me right now, and we have nothing else to do, do we?"

Doro sighed. "I had a family; a wife, and a daughter. We lived in a small village in the northern lands. We were peaceful and kept to ourselves mostly." Doro seemed to be deep in thought. "Montok, the father of those you call your enemy, had recently come into reign. He already began taking over many lands, and our army consisted of no more than a dozen lightly armed guards.

A traveling wizard came to us. He needed food and shelter. He was an old man, tired, hungry, and worn. The hardships of his travels were blatantly apparent. We happily gave him food, shelter, and whatever he needed, in return, he placed his staff in the center of our village. He told us that while the staff remained, it would protect us and that soon, when the Brood came, it would calm their minds and they would not attack. He was right. When the Brood came, we talked them out of conquering our village and months later when they came back, we did the same. It was something about the power of this wizard's staff. Its red ruby had the power to enter the mind."

"So you were safe?" Tau asked anxiously.

"For a time. After a year, the wizard had to leave. My people were frightened. They knew the Brood would come back someday. We pleaded with the wizard to stay, but he told us that his debt to us had been paid and that he must move on."

"So when he left, they came back?"

"No. When he left, some of our warriors followed him, killed him, and took the staff. I was against it. According to them, the wizard's last words were, 'Bury me with my staff, for if you take it, there will be consequences.'"

"And they took it anyway, didn't they?"

"Of course. They placed it back where it had been in the center of the village. Three weeks passed and then it happened."

Tau leaned forward, in anticipation. "What?"

"We heard it while we slept; a loud menacing humming sound. All of us came out of our huts to see the red crystal at the top of the staff glowing brighter and brighter until it exploded. Pieces of it flew everywhere. For about 10 seconds we all looked at each other and then all of us, all at once, fell to the ground."

"What do you mean, 'fell to the ground?"

"We died. At least I think we died. I felt myself fall to the ground and the next thing I knew, I was hovering in the air, above my body. I didn't have shape or form, only my consciousness."

"Wow. You were like a ghost? The others too?"

"Ghost, spirit, phantom, I don't know. As for the others, I could see their bodies on the ground, but I couldn't see their spirits. It wasn't exactly sight, as you know it, yet it is the only word that you would understand.

I could only assume that whatever was happening to me was happening to them. I was terribly frightened. You have no idea what is like to have no arms, no legs; nothing but a mind. I could move though, with only a thought. I could guide my consciousness wherever I wanted it to go. There, on the ground I saw the body of my wife, Mila, and my daughter Ceti and for a brief moment, I thought I could feel their consciousness move through me, like their minds moved through mine. That was the last I knew of them."

"You never saw them again?"

"No."

"Well, maybe they are still here like you are. Maybe they are like you."

"Perhaps."

Tau shifted on the ground for a moment. "But that still doesn't explain how you got the way you are now."

"A couple of days went by and I remained the same. My mind without a body travelled through the village, trying to find some part of them. Then, I felt something calling to me on the ground, a piece of the wizard's red crystal. It was large. I was surprised a piece that large had survived. It seemed like it beckoned me to come closer. I couldn't resist it. For a long time my consciousness surrounded it as I could do nothing but look at it. I have no idea how much time went by. It could have been days or weeks, but at some point, it became a part of me. I could feel my body forming. It was painful; like a body of shattered glass forming around it." He put his hand up to his chest, "and still it remains."

Tau was beside himself. All this time he thought this crystalline creature had no feelings at all. He thought it had no heart. However, Doro was a man, and this man was saddened; a victim through no fault of his own.

"So, you do have some feelings."

Doro lifted his head up to look at Tau.

"But why then? Why follow Onoc? I've seen you treat people as if you were a monster. I've watched you *take* them."

"I care nothing for those people, for Onoc, or for anyone else. When Onoc first saw me, he knew that I was a man. He could see it. That's his power, you know, he *knows* things. Onoc understands like no other man, someone's potential. He understands how the strange powers of the world work. If anyone can figure out if my wife and daughter are still alive and if they can be saved, it is he. Makes no difference to me if the rest of the world suffers and dies, I need to find them."

"Your sense of allegiance for your family is twisted, probably because of what has been done to you. I know when you were a man, what you felt for them was love, but I don't think what you feel now is love at all."

"What do you know about love, boy!"

"I know that when you have love in your heart then you don't want to see destruction and despair. Real love is something that enlightens a person to be better and to look upon the world with mercy and understanding." Tau paused for a second; he was slightly disturbed that he sounded exactly like Uncle. "Whatever has changed you, whatever you are, it has twisted that love into something despicable, and now all you see is anger. You've done terrible, terrible things to people. I think that if your wife and daughter saw what you have become, they would be ashamed of you."

Doro became angered. He stood up. The blue glow of his body became brighter and he sucked all of the heat out of the air. Tau noticed the sudden change in temperature, feeling goose bumps all over his body and his hairs stand on end. The creature rose to his feet. Once again, Tau had said too much.

"What do you know about love?" Doro screamed. He swung his giant fist toward Tau who quickly darted to the side, evading. Doro's hand struck the brick, breaking large chunks of it loose. Doro turned around, his eyes meeting with Tau on the other side.

"No! I didn't mean..." Tau yelled out, trying to talk his way out of this. He reached his hands out in front of him, gesturing for Doro to stay back.

But Doro did not back down. He rushed at Tau again, leading with his fist and missing Tau by inches as he moved out of the way, rolling to the ground. Doro thrust himself with so much power that his arm penetrated halfway into the wall. He was stuck. The large bricks of the wall came loose and crumbled to the ground as water thrust its way into the room. This was no small trickle; it was a geyser of enormous pressure. The water came in so fast that all the bricks of the wall came loose, one by one.

Very quickly, Tau was up to his knees in water, and in no time, up to his waist as the water rose.

He continued to evade Doro as they splashed around in the water, being knocked down by the force of the geyser and trying his best not to get hit by one of these falling bricks that made up the wall.

Doro was not so lucky. His large frame was slow. The bricks fell on top of him, trapping his legs and his body so that he was unable to move.

As the water rose above Doro's head, he reached his hands

out until finally he grabbed hold of Tau's foot. Tau swam as hard as he could, but Doro held a tight grip, swinging him around under the water against one wall and then the other.

A few minutes passed since the last time Tau had taken a breath of air. He scrambled to get loose. Both he and Doro were under water, except Doro had the advantage of not needing to breathe. Soon, Tau's body went limp. He stopped all movement, letting his body float in the water. Doro stared at him for a moment, and then shook Tau by the leg he was holding. Doro released his grasp and let Tau go free.

Tau let his body float in the water but his slow, upward movement stopped. He needed to breathe and soon. He opened one eye to peek at Doro down below him, trying to free himself from the rocks one by one. Then he suddenly went for it, swimming to the top of the well until he finally was able to climb out.

Tau looked down to see Doro's blue body at the bottom of the well. Doro looked up at him and then Tau rushed off. As he left Doro behind, Tau wondered if the demon would be able to get out. For a moment, he felt sorry for Doro, despite his being a monster.

* * * * *

Why were the guards so relentless in pursuing him? Was it the same with Kamaria? He remembered when he had so elegantly caught up with her during her escape. The guards had chased her for days. He could not believe that she had put up with this for so long. Then again, Kamaria was Kamaria.

Eventually, he made it to the edge of the forest, where he stood on a high cliff overlooking the sea. The Brood was close enough to get a glimpse of him diving off of the ledge and to hear his splash as he entered the water. Two of them jumped in behind him.

Tau swam deep into the water, further than any of the guards could possibly go. He swam further around the island and surfaced slowly, far away from them, though he could still see them standing on the edge of the cliff, giving orders to search here and there. Then he continued his way to the other side of the island.

He went back to the same place where he last saw Amanzi. His stomach gave him butterflies at the simple thought of seeing her again. He was sure that by now she had made it home and back with an army of Mer Folk to aid him. They had to be somewhere around here beneath the surface, waiting.

For an hour, he treaded water, briefly dipping below from time to time to search through the clear water. He wandered over to a coral reef, vibrant with color. There was plenty of sea-life briskly swimming around it. He took some time to swim through a school of small fish, grabbed at a few starfish sitting on the ocean floor, and even found a large turtle to pet and swim with; anything to pass the time waiting for Amanzi and her people.

Soon, he became tired of swimming. He swam to the bank, hid against the side of a tall dark rocky cliff and waited. As day turned to night, the breeze shifted, bringing the cool air and causing his wet body to shiver. He curled up and tucked himself against the cliff and waited.

His eyes watched the water splash up against the rocks and as the light faded, it became harder to see in the diminishing light. He turned his gaze upwards to the stars and thought about the kiss that he and Amanzi had shared not far from where he was. But where was she? He knew she would come for him because she knew what was at stake. He knew that she was not allowed to interfere in the affairs of the Dry Landers, but he thought that the connection between them was stronger than any such rule. Perhaps he was wrong.

She never came. There was no sign of any of the Mer Folk. Tau's disappointment shattered his very soul. He was heartbroken.

He would have waited there for days, but he did not have that much time. The ritual was going to start soon. With one last look at the sea, he turned his back on it and walked back into the forest.

Once again, Tau was lost. He felt his purpose to be meaningless. Why even bother going back? He had no reinforcements and still, no plan. He dreaded going back to Dwe and his people without the help he had promised. Worst of all, Kamaria had been *taken* because she finally believed in him. All for nothing.

"Are you going to give up?" He heard Chad talking to him.

"I'm not giving up Chad. There is nothing for me to do. She was supposed to be here, I was sure of it."

"The Keepers never said that Amanzi and the Mer Folk were supposed to save the tribe. They said YOU were."

"But Chad, I can't. It's only me!"

"So, then you ARE giving up. Giving up on Dwe and Kamaria, giving up on Kato and his son. Giving up on me."

"Shut up Chad! You're not even real! You're just in my head. Get out of my head, go away, you're making me crazy!"

"Maybe I am real, maybe not. Maybe I come to you to aid you from the *beyond* or maybe I'm a part of you that knows that you have a job to do. It doesn't matter. You have a destiny before you, and you have to see it through. Maybe I'm the part of you that remembers that you trapped the demon in that well, and without the demon…"

Tau gasped. "That's right! Without Doro, the ritual can't take place. So there is a chance; at least that is something."

Tau used this small piece of good news to fuel him. He had to move on. That one little bit of awareness was enough to give him hope. He made his way back to the camp and tried to figure out his next move.

XXXV THE RITUAL

ONOC

Doro was there. Somehow, some way, the monster had escaped. Tau felt a sickening tingle in the pit of his stomach that made his whole body tremble. It was apparent that the fate of his people was still in jeopardy. He had a perfect view from the top of the hill, crouching next to the walls of Onoc's fort. If he did not know that all of this would bring an end to the very existence of all his people, he might think of the sight as being cool.

Four, elongated, curved cages circled the entire ritual encampment. There was a break between the cages that separated them, allowing one to walk from inside the circle to outside of it. Along the side of the cages were the Brood's guards. They formed a complete circle, all with their glow rods turned on. Tau clenched his fists at the sight of some of them sticking their rods inside the cages, giving a fiery jolt to any of the slaves that looked like they were not cooperating, or that hinted at the slightest inclination of revolt.

Inside the circle of guards were the *taken*. About twenty of them knelt in a large circle, equidistant from each other, staring blankly ahead toward the center.

Inside the circle of the *taken*, were two separate ritual circles connected by a line of writings and glyphs, probably in the first tongue, drawn in fine diamond dust and the smallest of diamond stones. Doro stood in one of the circles and in the other, Onoc and his trusted guards stood ready to commence the ritual.

Doro is the key, Tau thought to himself. If he could manage to push him outside of the circle after the ritual begins, or even better, kill him, then hopefully that would stop it. When he was busy eavesdropping outside of the window, he remembered Onoc being quite adamant about that fact. He also remembered Onoc saying that once the ritual was started, it could not be interrupted or there would be unforeseen consequences.

He moved carefully and made his way inside Onoc's fort. It was empty. All of the guards were down below, as was everyone else on the island; all there for the ritual. He made his way up the stairs and searched several rooms before he found a pile of knives, swords of varying length. Then, he smiled at the site of his own weapons. He had missed them. He had gotten used to having them at his side at all times. As he sheathed his blades, he looked over and noticed, lying on the table, the necklace that the owl had brought in to Nyami. It was Nyah's.

Sadness washed over him at the notion that, after the Brood was done with his people, they would be going after Chega, Nyah, and the rest of the Music Wielders. It was not right. As powerful as they were, they wished no harm to anyone. They did not have the thirst for power that drove the Brood to do their evil deeds. The idea of Onoc and the rest of the Children of Montok knowing where they were and seeking to destroy them made him angry. He grabbed the necklace and placed it around his neck. It was time to go and stop this ritual whatever it took, even if he had to do it alone.

The *taken* started chanting, "*Obenga sodden. Agassi moga emdua gendo. Ngandazi mbatto neziba;*" over and over again. Onoc looked at Nyami and nodded. Nyami suddenly turned into numerous owls which began flying along the circle around Onoc and Doro, picking up very large diamonds in their claws until all of them were carrying the sparkling gems.

Faster and faster they flew.

The slaves became frantic, trying to shake and break the cages from the inside. "Keep them under control!" Onoc shouted. The guards used their glow rods on them, to stop the mayhem. They stuck them through the cages time after time again. Shouts and screams of pain filled the air.

As the owls flew, the diamonds began to glow, not only the ones that they were carrying, but the ones on the ground and the diamond dust as well.

"Now, Doro!" yelled Onoc.

Doro's blue fire grew brighter. The ghostly images of all of the Leopard Tribe people in the cages began to emerge from their bodies. Tau watched the essence of the people in the cages being pulled out of them. They tried to struggle against it, but there was nothing that they could do. He watched the bluish outline of their souls being stretched and pulled by Doro until they finally entered him, and every part of his fiery blue body glowed fiercely.

Doro began channeling this energy to Onoc's circle. It flowed along the writing of diamond dust on the ground connecting the circles. As the essence of the Leopard Tribe's abilities flowed into Onoc, his hand changed back and forth from a human hand to a leopard paw. Tau saw that ghostly images of leopards were being superimposed over the faces of Saah and the other guards in the circle.

"It's now or never." Tau heard Chad's voice and he looked over to see Chad standing next to him.

"Right," Tau nodded. He took advantage of the fact that all the guards' attention was focused on the ritual. He ran between the gates and past the guards. He passed the *taken* that were kneeling on the ground and kept going straight to the owls that circled in front of him, too many to run through. He dove to the ground, sliding and rolling under them. Once on the other side, nothing lay between him and Doro.

Doro's back was turned to him. Tau pulled out his blades, jumped into the air and jammed them into Doro's back as hard as he could!

His blades bounced off of Doro's hard crystal skin. Tau fell to the ground as Doro turned to see him. Tau quickly got up and ran into Doro as hard as he could, pressing his shoulder into Doro to knock him out of his circle. Doro did not budge.

Tau swung his weapons again, chopping at Doro's legs and body. His blades could not cut through Doro's skin. They did not even chip or scratch him in the slightest.

Doro grabbed Tau, and his hand covered half of Tau's chest and shoulder. Then he lifted him into the air. The ritual continued. The channeling of energy continued. The slaves' souls were still being ripped from their bodies, and Onoc still watched the changes in his body as the energy poured into him.

"Doro, crush him!" Onoc shouted in a distorted voice that sounded very close to a leopard's roar. "Kill the boy!"

Doro looked deep into Tau's eyes. Tau felt like he was looking into the eyes of death itself. He struggled to move, to break free, but there was no way of overpowering a creature like Doro.

His crystal blue hand pressed hard against Tau's body. Tau's life flashed before his eyes in a mere second and the onset of failure overwhelmed him. He recapped his whole journey so far. His best friend had died for nothing. Soon all of his people would be dead; Kamaria, Kato, Hondo, all of them. And after that, the Brood would move to destroy the Music Wielders.

Tau thought about Chega and Nyah as he looked down at her necklace, and the echo gem, remembering how pure her voice was and what it did to the crystal. Then he suddenly remembered the power of the echo gem.

Tau started whistling. Nothing happened at first. His pitch was a bit off. Doro paused for a moment, as if curious about the whistling, while Tau continued changing pitches.

"What are you doing, Doro?" Onoc shouted. "Kill the boy!"

Doro was about to smash Tau with his bare hands when Tau hit the right note. The echo gem was activated. It came on with a glow and a light, high-pitched sound. The noise pierced through Doro's body with a jolt. He let go of Tau, dropping him to the ground.

Tau kept whistling, as loud and as hard as he could. He could hear Nyah's voice coming from the crystal. It was so elegant, so pure, and so crisp; Doro could not stand it. He grabbed his head to cover his ears. His body jerked around erratically much like Tau's had when he used to experience that piercing pain sent to him by the Keepers. Doro struggled and roared.

Onoc watched him in great concern. "Someone kill that boy!"

Saah started moving in the direction of Tau and Doro, but Onoc held him back. "No! No one in this circle may leave."

Some of the other guards readied their arrows, aiming at Tau from outside the circle of owls. The arrows flew, only hitting the owls that flew around the ritual between them and Tau. Many of them came crashing to the ground.

Nyah's voice grew louder. Doro still stomped around uncontrollably. Tau could hear the sound of crystal cracking and breaking as Doro's body began to split and crack in several places. Then, all of a sudden, Tau could see a bright red light inside Doro's chest. It pulsed, like a living heart. It was the ruby that Doro had talked about before. The ruby that his consciousness had hovered over; the one that had created him.

Tau reached over and grabbed one of his blades. He tore the necklace from his neck and wrapped it around the hilt. Slowly, he walked over to Doro and raised it as high as he could. Every fiber in his body wanted to kill this being; extinguish his bright blue flame forever. He looked into Doro's eyes. All he could see was evil and all of the people Doro had killed or *taken*.

"Goodbye, Demon," he said and then leaped into the air. With his blade held high, he brought it down with all his might, plunging it toward Doro's chest. It did not bounce off like before. This time, his blade made its way through one of the cracks appearing all over Doro's body. He drove it as deep as he could into Doro, cracking the crystal body even more until finally, it went straight to his red crystal heart. Tau could hear more sounds of crystal cracking and breaking. Doro's crystal ruby heart brightened, and then sprouted dozens of red lines that stretched throughout his body like blood-filled veins.

"No!" Onoc shouted as he watched these veins inside of Doro pulsating faster and faster. "You must not stop the ritual!" Doro's whole body vibrated with intensity. For a moment, Tau could see fear in those awful fiery eyes. There were sounds of more cracking and breaking as every part of Doro's body became unstable. As the demon exploded, a flash of bright light blinded Tau's eyes. He could see nothing but white.

XXXVI CROSSING THOUGHTS

At first, Tau noticed that all the sounds around him had deadened. Then he could hear the sounds of birds chirping in the distance. It was quiet, too quiet. So quiet that he could hear the soft rustling of a slight pleasant breeze against his ears.

Then, he noticed the most wonderful feeling of warmth all over his skin, like being bathed in sunlight. His eyes had not yet returned to normal, all he could see was whiteness, but he realized the most pleasant scent of summer air, and the sea. Although still blind, all of his other senses were giving him the sensations of a pleasurable peacefulness.

He felt around on the ground; grass, soft grass, lush short blades of grass full of moisture. The ground beneath was soft and giving to the touch. It was ever so comfortable.

Slowly, the bright light faded from his eyes. He found himself looking at the ground, at grass greener than he had ever seen before. And then he realized that it was daytime. He looked to the sky to confirm his thoughts. Yes, it was daytime. The sky was bright and blue with large fluffy white clouds. It looked wonderful. He felt wonderful.

But how could that be? It had been night-time. The last thing he remembered was plunging his blade deep into Doro's chest during the ritual. The Ritual! He thought to himself, my people! He looked around in a panic. There were no people. There was no ritual, no cages, none of the *taken*, no large hill with Onoc's fort atop it. But how could this be? There was no Kamaria, none of the Brood's guards, no owls, no red dirt, no pit mines, none of it. It was all gone.

All around him was a field of green grass and beyond that were large fields of wheat. In this beautiful sunlight they shone like gold. In the far distance were large rolling hills and close to him were beautiful towering baobab trees with a few thick green leaves. Beyond those, he could see to the horizon in every direction.

He was confused. Being here did not make any sense. He became conflicted. Everything was so nice. He wanted to feel joy, but he could not. Not while he knew that somewhere his people were being *taken* or killed. He felt that he should be worried for his tribe, but this wonderful feeling kept creeping into him. Everything felt so good, so right.

The sun's warm rays poured over his skin at the perfect temperature. It was if he could feel everything around him emotionally, and he loved it. This overwhelming feeling of love and happiness seemed to be coming from every aspect of this place.

Then, he turned his head to the most pleasant of all sounds, a young girl laughing. It was a familiar laughter. At least he thought so. It was the most pleasant sound he had ever heard. As he turned, his heart filled with warmth and joy as he saw a woman and a little girl, no older than five, running through the wheat fields. They both were smiling, laughing, happy; and so was Tau. Still, he did not understand. He did not recognize them, yet they both seemed familiar and filled him with so much obvious joy.

As he watched them together, still kneeling on the ground, a hand touched his shoulder. Tau looked up to see a man standing there. He was pleasant looking. A smile stretched across the short beard on his face. He was dressed in a fancy printed wrapping that came down to his knees from his waist. Another matching fabric covered only half his chest. His thick walking stick was as tall as he was.

The man spoke. "That is my daughter Ceti and my wife Mila." The man did not look at Tau. His eyes were focused on the woman and child in the field. Tau did not say anything because he did not know what to say. He still did not quite understand what was happening. However, he was starting to get an idea of who this was.

"You know, Tau." the man said, "I had totally forgotten the overpowering joy that they gave me."

"Doro?"

"Yes."

Tau's first instincts were to jump up to defend himself, to attack, to run, anything. But he did not. This place, wherever it was, was having some sort of effect on him. Quickly, a sense of calm serenity returned.

"I don't understand. What is happening?" asked Tau. "Why do I feel…"

"What you feel is me, Tau, or rather, what I felt on this day, the last day that I had with my wife and child. Luckily, it was a happy one. No matter what happens from here on out, at least I will have that."

Tau stood up. "You mean, this has nothing to do with me, this is what you felt?"

The woman picked up the little girl and tossed her into the air. The girl giggled even more as she floated upward and back down again. Once the woman caught her, they both looked over.

"Hi daddy!" Ceti said in a voice so pleasant that it made Tau's entire body tingle.

Both Mila and Ceti waved. Before Tau knew it, he found himself waving back to them. It was odd. Not like he commanded his arm to do it at all. More like his arm and hand took it upon themselves to wave back to them.

"Why did I do that?"

"You are doing what I did. Right now, you are me, doing what I did, seeing what I saw, feeling what I felt." Doro took a deep breath and looked around. "You are living a memory. It is not exact, for instance, over there, there was a pond." As he said it, the pond appeared. "But my wife and daughter, they are the true purpose of this memory. It is amazing how a man can be so overpowered by the ones that he loves. As for me, the feeling of joy that my wife and daughter gave me was indeed immense. As the demon I could remember this day, but the way that it actually made me *feel* completely evaded me."

"But why..." Tau started to ask as he turned his head to Doro, but he was gone. Tau did not spend any time looking around for him. He began walking toward Mila and Ceti, toward what *felt* like his family. His slow walk turned into a brisk run as Mila put Ceti down on her feet and she started her run toward him, her arms stretched out.

"Daddy!"

He quickly lifted her into the air.

Tau spent hours with Mila and Ceti. They ran and played in the fields of grass and wheat. They ate plums and twilka berries next to the pond. He enjoyed simply lying on the ground with Mila and holding her hand while together they watched Ceti run around in the sunshine, chasing butterflies with her purple dress fluttering in the wind behind her.

They threw rocks into the pond. At first, they threw them as far as they could, then they skipped them over the surface. Ceti had a hard time with it. Instead of bouncing off of the water's surface, her rocks plunged to the bottom as soon as they touched the pond. Tau gently grabbed her hands, placing a rock in them. With his hand on top of hers, he showed her his technique, showing her how to throw from low to the ground allowing the rock to skim the top of the water. He showed her the surface of the rock, trying to explain to her the dynamics of rock skipping.

After a few tries, her rock skipped several times over the water. She was so happy. Tau immersed himself in the smile that stretched across her face and in his own sense of pride. Another, "new," added to the list.

He lightly tossed another rock into the pond, watching the ripples as they spread across the entire surface. He walked closer to it, watching the waves as they rippled through his own reflection. It was not his reflection at all. It was Doro's. Well, the human form of Doro anyway.

"It was on this night that everything changed," said Doro.

Tau turned around to see Doro standing behind him. Tau looked around for Mila and Ceti. They were gone.

"Where did they go?" Tau asked, concerned.

"It actually wasn't them that left, it was me. I went back to the village a few hours earlier than they did."

Tau heard the sound of strong, violent winds. The rainbow disappeared, the blue sky turned grey, and he noticed the tops of the trees were bent over as far as they could, bowing to the strength of the sudden wind.

"What's happening?" Tau asked, suddenly worried.

"This is coming to an end."

"What do you mean?"

"Don't be alarmed. None of this is real. It is only a memory. And if I remember correctly, you've just shoved a very sharp blade into my heart."

"Oh, but I didn't mean to...."

"Heh, yes, you did. You did it for them."

Doro pointed toward the pond, back behind Tau. Tau turned around to see hundreds of people standing on the water. Their blank stares were terribly familiar. They all looked as if they were the *taken*. Tau turned his head from one side to the other, looking at how far the number of people stretched in either direction; all standing on top of the water. Some of them were people that he recognized from the Leopard Tribe.

"Are they...?"

"Yes." Doro's voice came from below him. Tau looked down to see Doro's reflection in the water talking to him. "All of the people that I have taken over the many years. There are so many, hundreds."

Doro's body rose out of the water until he was standing on top of it. Again, he was standing in front of Tau. This time, the hundreds and hundreds of people were standing behind him.

The winds picked up even stronger. In the distance, the mountains were being blown away. It was like they were turned into millions of pieces of confetti, and then carried off to the sky. He noticed the same thing happening to one of the trees very far from him.

Worse than that, some of the people on the far edge of the row were being blown away as well, like the mountains and the trees. Their bodies were being ripped into millions of pieces and carried away like statues of ash.

He looked at one of the people directly behind Doro. It was Kamaria. She stood there with a blank stare and blue eyes.

"Kamaria!" he cried out.

"She can't hear you."

"What's happening?" Tau yelled, watching the people disappear. Closer and closer the winds came, carrying off one person after another from all sides of the crowd. Whatever was happening, he figured that soon it was going to happen to Kamaria. "Make it stop!"

"I can't, Tau. You have done this. You are getting a glimpse of the destruction of all of this. But remember, you are not here. You've never really been HERE, because you are still on Goree Island, still in the ritual circle. Only a second has passed since you thrust the knife into my crystal heart. For a brief second, my consciousness is passing through you."

"A second? What do you mean a second? I've been here for the better part of a day."

"It may seem that way, but it has only been a mere second. Things happen so much faster in the mind."

Tau looked at the crowd of people, still being carried off into the wind. They were almost all gone. It was only a matter of time until Kamaria would be gone as well. A terrible worry and concern swelled through him. What had he done? He did not know that killing Doro would mean killing them as well. If he could, he would have taken it back, but what was done, was done.

"And them?" he asked. "Have I destroyed them?"

Doro smiled. "No, Tau, you have not destroyed them, you have freed them all. The *taken,* all of them shall be returned."

His words were followed by Kamaria's body being swept away, like fragile ash, and carried off into the sky. All of the *taken* were gone. If he understood Doro correctly, they were not really gone though. A sigh of relief swept over him. Then he noticed the wind taking away pieces of Doro as well. Suddenly he felt sorry for what used to be a Demon; sorry that he had killed him. He used to be a man, a man with a wife and daughter, a man who could love as much as anyone, if not more. Tau felt sorry for him, knowing that it really was not Doro's fault at all.

Tau walked up to him, suddenly realizing that he too was standing on water. He could feel the wetness beneath his feet. It was soft, and yet still hard enough somehow for him not to fall through.

"And what about you?" Tau asked? "Have I destroyed you forever?"

"No, Tau. You have set me free as well. You have given me another chance; a chance to search for my family, no matter where or how they exist. And now, I can do it without my mind and body being corrupted by a demon. Goodbye Tau. Goodbye, and thank you."

The final winds blew Doro away in millions of pieces. Tau watched them flutter through the sky until finally he could see no sign of them at all. Tau closed his eyes, waiting to be swept away like everyone else. But nothing happened.

The winds stopped and the sky once again brightened, leaving the sun open to warm up his body as before.

Soon he heard the sounds of the echo gem emanating Nyah's beautiful voice. He looked down into the water. There he saw the ritual. As if he was a bird soaring high above it, he could see the whole layout; the people in the cages, the circles, the guards, Hatari, Nyami, everything.

He could even see himself. He peered down closer to the image shimmering on the surface of the water. This has already happened. Only moments before, he had come to this place. Doro had picked him up. The song was playing. Tau watched Doro dance around in panic. He watched himself jump up and stab Doro right in his crystal heart.

Then he saw Doro explode: a bright blue mist spread out in all directions. It knocked everyone to the ground. Then, everything in the image went black. Tau tried his best to look even closer and suddenly the firmness of the water below his feet gave out. He fell, splashing into it. The water was dark, void, and in another second, he found himself on the dusty ground. It was nighttime again. He realized he was back at the ritual at almost the same moment that he had left.

He could not be sure he had gone anywhere at all. Perhaps it was a dream. Perhaps he had hit the ground and bumped his head. He looked over to see tiny pieces of Doro's light blue crystal body lying all around him, twinkling in the light of the fires and glow rods. By his feet, the tip of his weapon was stuck into the only large piece of Doro left, a chunk of his red crystal heart. Quickly, he removed the gem from his blade.

The guards got themselves up off of the ground. They went to the cages behind them, looking at the slaves who lay there motionless. Everyone's attention was drawn to the sound of a sinister laughing as the mist dissipated. There was Onoc and the guards that joined him inside of his ritual circle. They had all been changed. Not to leopards, but to black panthers. Each one was black with different blue patterns on his body.

"You see boy," said Onoc speaking from the form of a panther. "You're too late. Although I do applaud your efforts."

"No!" Tau cried out, looking around him at the bodies in the cages and the *taken* that were lying on the ground. "They're not dead! I thought that if I stopped the ritual, that it wouldn't work! I heard you say it. I killed the demon. It shouldn't have worked!"

"So, that was you at the window last night," Nyami said as she stood up, staggering and yanking arrows out of her body. Her white dress now had dirt and blood all over it.

"Are you hurt, sister?" asked Onoc.

"I will live brother, despite the terrible aim of your guards."

"Tau's head went down. "What will you do with me?"

"That's a good question," replied Onoc as he started to walk toward Tau in his panther form. "I could kill you now. Or I could leave you stranded on this island to live the rest of your days among your dead..."

Onoc stopped moving. His eyes bulged with fright. His face carried the look of both confusion and terror. Something was pulling him back.

Saah and the other guards that were transformed to panthers reacted the same way. "What is happening?" yelled one of them.

All of a sudden, in the circle where they had stood during the ritual, branches and leaves came twisting out of the ground. Yellow sparkles the size of grains of sand blinked all over the ground near them as a tree grew out of the dirt with a yellow glow all around it.

"Lord Onoc!" Saah yelled in fear, suddenly being pulled toward the tree. Then all of the panthers, including Onoc, were being dragged back toward it. One by one they disappeared into the tree as if it was swallowing them whole.

Onoc was the last one and the furthest from the tree. He dug his paws into the dirt, but there was no stopping it. "This can't be! The ritual wasn't complete! No! It can't be!" Those were the last of his words; soon he too met with the tree, and was pulled inside. The tree twisted back into the ground. All that was left were the dragging marks of their paws in the ground that ended at the circle.

The Leopard Tribe awakened all at once, as did all of the previously *taken*. It was not a slow rise. Their eyes flew open abruptly and they hopped to their feet. Tau was ready to shout out orders to everyone that awoke from their *taken* sleep. He assumed that they would be somewhat confused, and that he would need to give them some type of direction. However, he was wrong. It was as if those that were *taken* had been aware the whole time. In an instant, they were quick to take down the guards that were closest to them. More importantly, they were quick to grab the keys.

XXXVII THE LEOPARD TRIBE

It all happened quickly, executed like a thoroughly choreographed plan, which it was not. The Leopard Tribe was awake, and with Doro gone, Tau could feel a surge of energy, strength, and agility flow through him. By the look of the others fighting against the guards, they could feel it too. They did not hesitate to fight. The recently *taken* were not caged. They quickly shifted into their leopard forms and attacked the guards.

The guards were taken somewhat off guard. Since Doro's destruction, they had watched the rest of what took place in awe. The people within the cages grabbed the guards standing near them. They were pinned to the sides of the cages and quickly subdued.

"Take them all!" Kamaria yelled, as she overcame a guard with keys and stood in her human form. She threw the keys toward the cages and returned to her leopard form to fight, which she did expertly. One after another she took down the guards in her path.

The cages were all opened. The Leopard Tribe was free. They fought back against the guards, massively overpowering them with strength and speed. The added fear put the guards in a hectic, uncoordinated state. They hesitated as if waiting for orders. The threat of teeth, claws, and cat eyes seemed to overwhelm them. They were too slow to flee and too ill-equipped to fight.

"We must get to the boats!" Tau yelled while he too fought, meeting up with Kato.

"To the boats!" Kato repeated.

Everyone except Kamaria began to move toward the boats. She hesitated as her eyes became locked on Nyami's position at the top of the hill. She moved toward her, doing away quickly with any guard that stood in her path. Finally, she made her way to where Nyami stood and shifted into her leopard form, charging with vengeance. Her claws reached forward, waiting to slice into Nyami's body. Before Kamaria reached her, Nyami burst into numerous flying owls. Kamaria landed on the ground in the midst of flapping wings and claws.

The owls flew past her and through the thick of the rest of the fighters. Everyone guarded themselves as the swarming birds brushed past them in Nyami's attempt to flee. Kamaria managed to dig her claws into two of the owls. They dropped to the ground and disappeared into a black mist right before her. The rest of the owls gathered at the top of the hill next to the fort and converged back into Nyami's human form. She grabbed her arm as blood came from one of her wounds. A disappointed Kamaria looked up at her, as did Tau.

Nyami looked down upon them and raised her arms and staff. "You underestimate your importance to me," she yelled down to them. Then, once again, she burst into owls and flew away into the night sky.

Kamaria stood there watching her go as if she wanted to follow.

"Come, we have to get these people to the boats!" Dwe said to her.

Her angered gaze left the sky as she thrust herself toward Dwe, engaging him in a kiss.

"Let us go," she replied.

They continued to fight back the guards as they made their way around the perimeter of the island to the channel.

The few guards on the small island saw them coming. Quickly they pulled at the ropes of the bridge, pulling it out of reach from the large island.

"The ropes to the bridge are on the other side!" yelled Tau.

"We must make our way across the channel." said Kato, and started his way into the water.

"No!" Tau held him back, "the channel is filled with red

sharks. They'll eat us alive!"

"Then we must go around the channel. It is a longer swim, but we must."

"What about the sick and the elderly? There are plenty that cannot make it."

The tribe began gathering at the channel in a huge bunch. Strategically, it was a terrible position for them. It made it easier for the guards to overcome them. If they were going to battle, they needed to spread out.

Then Tau noticed movement in the water behind him. The water bubbled, swished, and swayed. It began to spread apart in the center of the channel. More and more of it gathered to the sides, forming two walls that were growing larger.

The green glow of his watch grabbed his attention. He looked at it eagerly to confirm that it was on. He couldn't help but to smile.

Soon, he could see the dirt floor of the channel as a pathway emerged with a towering wall of water on each side.

Tau eyes widened with joy, for in the middle of all of that was Amanzi, standing there with her arms reaching into the air. Her short staff glowed ever so brightly. Her fins wrapped themselves back around her body and a small amount of water came flowing back out of the wall covering her. Come on, shark bait, it's a lot of water, and I don't know how long I can do this."

"Amanzi!" Tau shouted cheerfully. He started toward her. "I thought you couldn't help us!"

"It's water, Tau, so I'm in my domain."

"Lead the people through," he told Kato.

"Tau! Remind me not to underestimate you ever again!" Kato said joyfully. "This way!" he yelled to the people.

Tau continued toward Amanzi when to his horror he saw something behind her. "Amanzi! Look out!"

A guard from the small island on the other side of the channel was making his way across. He came up behind Amanzi, pulled out his sword and before Tau could do anything, the guard sliced Amanzi down her back.

She dropped to her knees. The wall of water shook as if it was going to collapse. Tau took his blades out and sliced at the guard. The guard blocked it and Tau shoved him backward. The walls of water shook again, closing in closer to them, making the pathway much thinner as Amanzi dropped to the ground. The channel was beginning to fill back up. Tau felt the water rushing over his feet.

The guard swung at Tau, but he dodged to the side while the guard's own motion threw him off balance. He stumbled forward as part of his body fell into the wall of water. The guard screamed as three red sharks yanked him inside the large wall of water.

Tau rushed to Amanzi as Kato and some of the rest of the tribe got to them. "Hurry, get across!" Tau said to them. They ran past them, sloshing through the rising water, which reached almost to their shins. The walls of water were getting closer and closer together.

"Amanzi, are you okay?" Tau's voice quivered with concern. He knelt down in the water and held her in his arms.

"It hurts," she said with a frown, and then smiled. "But I'm glad to see you."

Many of the Leopard tribe moved past them to the smaller island. Tau leaned down and hugged her. "The water, Tau, I can't do it. I'm feeling weak."

"What about the rest of your people? Are they here?" Tau asked.

"No," she said. "It's just me. The water, it's getting heavy."

"Forget about the water! Don't die on me, you just got here."

"Tau, you must save your people. I can't hold the water back anymore, but you can."

"What do you mean?"

"You've got sorcerer's blood Tau, so I can give you my power. It won't last long, but it may be long enough to save you, and them."

"No, but that means.... but what you told me before.... I won't do it!"

"Tau, the water is filling back up and soon it will be deep enough for red sharks to swim in. The people will be killed, including us."

Tau looked at his people as they rushed through the rising water. The walls were close; the pathway was only about four feet across. Behind the walls, the red sharks started to glow in preparation to attack. They were able to barely stick their noses and teeth out of depths as the water around them sizzled from their heat.

Tau sobbed, "I won't do it."

"Yes, Tau, you will, you have too." Her voice trailed off.

"No! Don't"

She closed her eyes. Tau could feel a warming energy pouring into him. It was coming from Amanzi. Soon he could feel the water. He was aware of it, all of it. He could feel the walls around him. He could feel every step that people took as they splashed through the water, as if it was a part of him.

Amanzi unwrapped her fin from around her staff and placed it in Tau's hands. "Here Tau, it's up to you now." She let out a deep exhale and her arms fell to her side. Tau watched the shield of water around her fall off her body.

"Why did you do that?" he whimpered, holding her close to him. He felt the power of the staff in his hand. An angry Tau gripped it tightly and searched for all of the power inside of him that Amanzi had passed on.

In the crowd of people, Tau saw Hondo coming his way. "Tau! What are you doing? What is happening?"

"Take her to the boats, Hondo, quickly!"

"What about you?"

"Hondo, take her!"

Hondo picked up Amanzi and continued on.

The level of the water once again started to get lower and the walls wider and taller. Tau knelt on the ground with the brightly lit short staff held in the air. "Get to the boats!" Tau yelled. The others passed by him, walking on the dirt ground, as Tau knelt, steadily holding that staff in the air. They carried anyone that was sick, or elderly, or that had any trouble moving quickly on their own.

Soon, Kamaria came to his position with ten other tribesmen. She looked at Tau, who was crying. He could control the water around him, but he could not stop the tears from pouring down his face.

"Tau, what has happened? How are you doing this?" she asked.

Tau looked up at her, his eyes filled with tears, but he felt anger and determination.

"I'll explain later."

"The guards are coming. This is the last of us. We should go," said Kamaria

"Go ahead," said Tau. "I'm right behind you."

"You'd better be," she said as she patted him on the shoulder.

Tau could see the guards getting closer to them. He stood and began walking backwards. He saw Kamaria and the others shift into leopards and run toward the other side of the channel. He did not waste any more time. He ran behind them.

"Tau, hurry!" Kamaria shouted as she stood at the other side of the channel.

He could feel his feet splashing in the water as the channel began to fill up again. He dug his feet deep into the ground to thrust himself forward. As soon as he got to the other side, he stood next to Kamaria, as they and a few other tribesmen looked down the channel at the dozens of guards still trying to pursue.

"Tau, the water isn't falling fast enough. Some of them are going to get through," Kamaria said, standing ready to fight any of the guards that made it to the island.

Tau looked at the men almost upon them. "It should fall at any..."

Then, at once, the rest of the water came crashing down on the guards. They yelled and screamed as red sharks began seizing each and every one of them, glowing bright red underneath the water as they attacked. The guards yet to make it into the channel stood on the other side of it. There was nothing they could do, no way across. They had to let the Leopard Tribe go free.

XXXVIII CLEAR SAILING

The night was clear and the stars plentiful. The winds were kind to the two ships, yet strong enough to give them a decent velocity, pushing on the sails briskly to propel them across the ocean.

"Where is she?" Tau asked, moving through the crowds of people on board in desperate search for Amanzi. The deck was cluttered with the wounded bodies of the recently freed Leopard Tribe, many writhing in pain. He looked at all of the people being tended to on the deck while in search for her. "Amanzi!" he shouted.

Then he saw her lying across the floor with her eyes closed. A woman that he did not recognize sat beside her, tapping her forehead with a damp cloth. The woman looked up at him as he approached with enormous concern.

"You are Tau," the woman said definitively.

"Yes." Tau did not bother to ask her what her name was. The question did not enter his mind. At the moment, his only concern was for Amanzi. "Is she…"

"Alive? Yes," the woman answered.

"I thought she died. Will she be okay?"

"It's hard to tell. Kamaria has put her in my hands because I am a healer, though I have nothing here to heal her with. I believe that if she can make it through until tomorrow, then she will be okay. When we finally make it home, I have herbs that will help as well."

"I knew she was important to you," Kamaria spoke as she approached and crouched next to them. "This is the girl that you spoke of? The one from The Deep?"

"Yes, Amanzi," Tau responded while gently grasping Amanzi's hand. "She's the one who helped me find the island. If it wasn't for her, I never would have found you. But I did not want her to die for us."

"I think she is a strong one, Tau, and I believe that she will pull through."

Tau looked at the woman. "I believe you," he said firmly. "She will pull through."

"If it weren't for both of you," said the woman. We would have never escaped. It seems that you had a plan after all. Destroying that demon saved us. You both have done well, and we all owe you our lives, including me."

"Yes, we do owe you our lives," Dwe said as he approached with his limp.

Kamaria stood up quickly. "My husband!" she said.

She bowed her head and knelt before him in a completely submissive state. "Forgive me, my love, if I have shown you any disrespect"

Dwe looked around for a moment with a curious look on his face, and then gestured for her to rise. "You've never called me husband. We aren't even married yet."

"Only time separates that from the truth."

"And it is certainly not like you to bow before anyone. Tau, who is this woman we have brought back."

"I bow to ask for your forgiveness for the way I treated you. I should never have doubted you."

"Kamaria, there is nothing to forgive. Nor do you need to ever bow before me. I love you as I always have. We are free, and that is all that matters." He kissed her and they hugged each other tightly. For a moment, they were one.

Watching them embrace felt a bit intrusive to Tau, so he let his gaze trail off to the side until they broke. "Where is Kato," he asked. "And Hondo?"

Kamaria pointed to the other ship. "There, on that ship."

"Good, then they are okay."

"Yes."

"Will we be okay? Will we be able to sail home?"

Dwe gestured to a man standing at the helm and looking to the sky. "Do you see that man there?"

Tau nodded.

"That is Ngwetu. When he and his brother were first taken to the island, overcast skies threw their ship off course for a week. They can build small boats so when they got the chance to be on this ship, they paid as much attention as they could. Hopefully what they have learned will help us."

"I suppose that it's all we have. It will have to be enough."

Soon Tau looked over to see others coming toward them as everyone on the ship began to come near.

"I think they are here for you," Dwe said to Tau. "Let the people see who you are."

Tau looked at the woman nursing Amanzi.

"It's okay," she said to him. "I'll take care of her."

"If she wakes up, please give her this," he said handing her Amanzi's staff. He nodded and stood up, looking into the eyes of everyone that was looking at him. The people walked over one by one, bowing, nodding, and shaking his hand.

"Thank you, Tau."

"You have saved us all."

"We thank you so much."

"You are our savior."

"You destroyed the demon."

"This will never be forgotten."

"May our children's children praise you, Tau."

One by one they gave him praise. Tau was gracious enough to bow in response to each and every one of them. He was overwhelmed by their greetings. It felt like too much gratitude, more than he thought he deserved. But at the same time, it felt good. There had been too many times of doubt, too many times of not knowing what to do, and too many times of wanting to give up for him to be sure that he deserved this honor.

For a moment, he prided himself for keeping strong. He was

more than glad that somehow, through everything, he managed to keep up both his strength and his faith in himself. He learned undeniably how important it was for him to have faith in himself. So many times people had told him that if he did not believe in himself, then he would fail. He was proud to be the hero and at that moment, he felt like a hero.

He looked over to the side of the boat where he saw his friend Chad leaning against the railing, smiling and nodding at him. "Good job, Tau. I knew you could do it, buddy." Tau smiled and nodded back at him in return. Tau could finally see the purpose in the terrible sound that had contributed to Chad's death.

Soon the greetings subsided. Everyone relished in being all back together, free from the Brood. A delighted grin swept across Tau's face while he watched the people embrace each other in hugs and laughter. Kamaria and Dwe were nowhere to be found on the deck. Probably down below somewhere, Tau thought to himself, making the smile on his face spread even wider.

He leaned against the side railing, watching the bright moon glow as the reflected light danced upon the ocean's surface. He closed his eyes, listening to the water lapping up against the side of the ship and the whooshing sound that the huge vessel made as it pushed its way through the waves. Even the smell of the sea was calm and peaceful. He remembered how it felt to have Amanzi's power for a short time. He could feel the ocean. He could feel every part of the water. He could control it. What a wonderful gift Amanzi's people had. Tau took in a deep breath and let out a long sigh of relief. "Yemoja."

"Everything," his grandfather said, slowly making his way over.

"Ink, I didn't see you before. I thought you were on the other boat."

"Legs, stairs."

"Heh, yeah. I understand."

"Baby, home."

"Yes, I think I am home."

"Good, good," said Ink while patting him on the head.

"Though I think I will try to get word to Uncle, well my uncle who raised me, that I am okay."

"Baby, home." Another pat on the head.

"Kamaria said that my plan to kill the demon worked, but the more that I think about it, it was never my plan at all. None of it was. This was all a plan of a much higher power than me. I did not need to believe in myself as much as I needed to believe that there was a plan, and that no matter what happened, the plan was always there. I was only one part of it."

"Baby, home," grandfather Ink said as he put his arm around Tau.

"You know, Ink," said Tau. "It did all work out. And even though Amanzi is weak right now. I believe she is going to pull through just fine. I'm actually happy in this moment. I look forward to being a true Amotekun and learning all I can about us. Perhaps I'll even learn what happens to our clothes and weapons when we change. I don't suppose you would like to explain that to me?"

"Lights," said Ink.

"What do lights have to do with it?" Tau asked.

"Pretty lights."

Tau followed Ink's gaze into the sky. He thought perhaps that Ink was talking about the stars. However, he looked carefully at the sky, and he too saw dozens of little orange lights in the distance. "What is that?"

"Pretty lights."

Tau kept looking, and someone near him pointed out the lights as well. Fear gripped Tau's mind, because the lights began to look more and more like fire. A commotion grew loud as the people spoke and pointed and shuffled around.

Kamaria and Dwe came up from below deck. "What's going on?" Kamaria asked.

"Look!" said Tau. "There is fire in the sky, and it's coming this way!"

Kamaria studied the fire for a while. As the formation approached, it passed by the moon, and that's when she noticed them. BIRDS; owls to be exact!

"The witch!" said Kamaria. "Nyami has come back. And she carries fire with her!"

Soon it became clear that they were looking at probably fifty or so owls. They teemed together, carrying within their claws large branches flaming with fire.

"What do we do?" asked Tau.

"I don't know," said Kamaria. "We are helpless against an enemy from the sky. We have no bows. We should get the people below."

Tau ran up to the man at the helm of the ship. "Can you out run them, out maneuver them? Anything?"

"I am in no way a master of these vessels."

Tau looked around at all of his people. Kamaria had already begun moving them below the deck. The owls came closer. What he had not seen before was that a few of them did not carry tree branches, but carried buckets. Once they were over the ships, a black liquid poured out of them, dropping on the sails and all over the deck of both ships.

Tau squinted at the liquid for a moment, and then he realized from the smell of the black stuff that the owls were dumping fire sap on them!

Before he could scream out, the owls dropped their burning logs. Tau watched the fire fall from the sky and smash on the floor. The fire sap allowed it to spread instantly across the deck, up the mast, and continue on until in seconds the sails too were on fire. Panic and confusion spread even more rapidly than the fire as people scrambled to avoid the flames.

One of the burning logs went through the floor of the main deck as it hit, leaving the lower decks unsafe as well. Smoke and darkness added to the confusion as people from below began to emerge to the main deck once more. Each passing second proved to be more chaotic than the last.

Tau looked for Amanzi on the main deck, though he could barely focus. Everything was a blur, from the fires to the people running around screaming with no idea what to do. He called her name, asked people where she was, but in the confusion he could not find her.

The birds converged at the top of the center mast on Tau's ship to form Nyami. She looked down at them. A devious smile of pride stretched across her pretty, yet evil face. Tau looked up at her, and then shifted his gaze to Kamaria, who stood beside him. Kamaria's eyes too were locked onto Nyami, fixed as if tethered by a hard wire. Kamaria squinted and gritted her teeth.

Nyami returned Kamaria's glare. "The Children of Montok will rule this world. And we will wipe you off the face of it if need be!"

Kamaria grabbed a burning plank lying on the ground close by her. With both hands, she turned herself around, spinning, making three complete circles before she let go of the plank, hurling it upward in the air toward Nyami.

Nyami watched the burning wood come flying toward her and uttered one word, "Die!" She then burst into multiple owls, avoiding the wood completely.

It landed on a sail, lighting it on fire, before falling onto the deck, barely missing Tau. Kamaria went to him, grabbing him by the shoulders.

"Tau, we have to leave the ship! Tau, do you hear me? The whole ship is on fire! We must abandon it!"

But Tau did not respond. He gazed blankly, as if he was one of the *taken.*

"Help!" Tau heard a voice calling from behind them. A man was trapped under a board. He was struggling to get it off of his legs, yet was not strong enough to do it alone. Still not moving,

Tau watched Kamaria rush over to help the man.

Tau continued to stand there alone. He was totally immobilized. He could not move, speak, or do anything. All he could see was fire. He felt confused, as if his mind did not understand what was going on. How could this be happening? The yelling and screaming of the people became muted to nothing. He could no longer hear their voices, or the fire, or the sound of the wood cracking and breaking all around him. His body shut down. It was as if his mind closed the chapter of his being a savior. He had thought that the Leopard Tribe had been saved, he had thought that they were free, so what was this terrible thing happening before him?

The forward mast burned through halfway up from the bottom. It broke, toppling over, falling straight for him. Dwe was nearby. He called out to Tau as loudly as he could, but Tau still did not move. In a last attempt, Dwe ran and dove into Tau, taking him over the side of ship. The last thing that Tau remembered was entering the water.

XXXVIX THE KEEPERS KEEP

Tau found himself waking early the next morning, suddenly violently coughing saltwater out of his mouth and onto the beach. After he took a moment to catch his breath, taking in huge gasps of air, he remembered the fires and the chaos from the night before. "The ships!" he said while looking up and down the coast and then out to the sea. "My people!"

He soon realized that he was alone and somehow back at The Rock That Should Not Stand, back at the beginning, before he had even met Amanzi, or made it to Goree Island. "It was a dream," he said to himself. "None of it was real. I swam out from the rock, swam down deep into the water, and must have dreamed the whole thing. Amanzi wasn't real, Kamaria and the others on the island weren't real, none of it. It couldn't be real."

He looked down at his wrist. He still wore Amanzi's watch, and it was not lit. He had the watch, which proved that his journey had happened. But what were the odds of his ending up back here, next to the same rock? And if it was not a dream, that meant that...no! Where was everyone?

He sat on the beach for hours, waiting for someone else to wash ashore. No one did.

Perhaps they have all made it back to Amotekun City. Maybe I'm the only one that hasn't made it back yet.

He started the long walk to the White Forest. The walk back seemed ten times as long as the first time. He kept looking at the watch, hoping that the light would come on, hoping that Amanzi was near. But apparently she was not.

He looked for footsteps in the sand, for signs of anyone who had recently traveled back home. He found none. Of course, the tide could have easily come in and washed any of their tracks away. He walked far enough away from the water so that his tracks would not be washed away so easily.

He made it back to the white-capped mountains and climbed his way to the top. He paused for a while, looking out to the sea and then stared out at the familiar site of the White Forest. He took in a deep breath in anticipation as he went down the other side, hoping someone would be there.

But there was no one. Every tent and every hut was empty. Every tree and pathway was void of any signs that anyone had recently been there. He called out over and over to anyone that might be around to hear him. The only reply that he received was his own echo.

The forest was far too calm, far too peaceful. He watched as a gentle breeze nudged the children's swings, shook the wind chimes, and blew open the flaps of tents and unlatched doors. It was as if there were ghosts lingering around for the simple purpose of teasing him, sending him false perceptions that somebody was there. He had never felt so alone. Not even Wingy came by to bother him. Not even a vision of Chad, which he thought was odd because he knew that his visions of Chad were not real anyway.

For hours he waited for someone to come, anyone. It was not until late in the evening that he came to the most horrible of realizations; they must all be dead. They either drowned or burned in the fire on the ships, or both. He could think of no other explanation. Once again, he was the last of his kind. He was the sole inhabitant of the Amotekun City.

He sat down in the forest and cried. He screamed into the air, hearing his voice travel through the thick of the trees. He did not understand. Nothing made any sense to him. If there was such a thing as purpose, what was the purpose of all of this? What was the purpose of his finding his people, and then seeing them all get killed? What was the purpose of his being the only one left alive? Why had he not died with the rest of them? Why did the Keepers even bother...?

The Keepers. This was all because of them. They were the

ones who had called out to him, and they were the ones who had sent him on his meaningless journey. They had to be responsible for everything.

His sadness turned to anger. His anger wanted nothing more than to confront these Keepers. He made his way to the wide hole in the ground with the thick black vines leading into it and climbed down, proceeding across the vines until he found the opening. He went in the same way he had the first time, shape-shifting himself into a leopard and making his way down the tunnel lit with life-vines. It had to be real; he had not known that they were called life-vines until he met Amanzi.

As soon as he entered the room, he shifted back to human form and screamed at the top of his lungs, "Hello! Hello! Are you there? I know you are! Are you done with your little game? Did you have fun playing around with us? Did you have fun playing around with *me*? The game is over now. There is no one left but me! Show yourself!"

Tau felt the familiar sensation of the room slightly rumbling beneath his feet. The life-vines dimed and a brilliant light came out of the leopard statue's eyes and head until eventually, the long liquid metal thing he knew as The Keepers was once again in front of him. It moved around the room, changing from one face to another, and then it spoke.

"Hello Tau, I/we am/are pleased to see your return."

"Pleased? What sort of joke have you been playing? Does it amuse you to play with the lives of mortals?"

"The Keeper(s) does/do not understand."

"Why are you playing with my life?"

"I/we do not play with the lives of mortals, Tau. I/we am/are the Keeper(s)."

"Whatever it was that I was supposed to do, I failed. Like I said before, you picked the wrong guy for the job."

"On the contrary, Tau, I/we chose wisely. No one else could have completed the task in the manner in which you performed.

And with so many obstacles before you, you completed those tasks with magnificent bravery."

"Well I don't understand, then. What was the purpose of the whole journey? What was my purpose? Was all of this so that I might learn something?" Tau shouted at the Keepers with clenched fists as he watched the liquid form move around the room. His whole body shook with fury and confusion.

"You have learned much, young Tau. You are a magnificent representation of your people."

"What people?" Tau cried out. "They are ALL dead!"

The Keepers where silent for a moment. Tau dropped to his knees. Again, he began to cry.

The room was quiet, except for Tau's weeping, and the hissing under water sound that The Keepers made. Finally they spoke again. "It seems that you misunderstand the situation, and the current state of your people."

"I saw the ship burning, I saw people jumping into the water. No one has come back."

"This is true, yet The Tribe of Leopards survives."

"What? How many? How many were saved from the boats?"

"All of them."

"All of them?"

"Yes, including the one that you call Amanzi."

"You mean she's alive?"

"She is safe with her kind."

"And what of my grandfather, Dwe, Kamaria, Hondo...."

"All of them have survived. Your task was only to get them as far as you did. You have completed that task."

Though he was still confused, his tears turned into tears of joy at that news. "Where are they, then?"

"I/we have made a pact with Mami Wata. Her people, the Mer Folk, were there when the ships were burned. Your people have all been preserved."

"Preserved?"

"In the manner in which they have preserved their savior, the one called Behan'zin. They have done the same for The Leopard Tribe."

"You mean, like in the crystal?"

"Yes. The Tribe of Leopards is too important to the future of this world for them to be allowed to be destroyed by Brood forces. They will remain protected deep beneath the sea until they are needed."

"For how long?"

"Until such time as they are needed. When they are awakened, it will be as if no time has passed for them, no matter how long they are preserved."

"Then what about me?"

"You have fulfilled your destiny. You may live out your life however you see fit."

"I've barely gotten to know them, and already they are gone from me. I don't even know what has happened back home."

"The Brood was not kind to your home village. It is not the same as when you left it. You may not be…happy with what you find."

"Then I want to stay with my Leopard Tribe. I am one of them. If you say that I can live my life as I see fit, then I choose to be with them."

"You were never meant to be with your people for the duration. You were meant to save them."

"But you said, as I see fit. Are you going back on your word?"

"One moment."

There was a long silence as the silver liquid morphed into a sphere that hovered in the middle of the room. Tau watched it anxiously as the numerous waves and ripples continued to move across the surface of the silver sphere. After a while, it began changing into faces and moving around the room again.

"I/we can comply with your wishes under one condition."

"And what is that?"

"There will be a new destiny set before you."

"Um, o...kaaaaaay," Tau reluctantly replied, uncertain as to what that meant for him.

"You will be preserved here with us, in a state similar to that of your kinfolk. We have selected one who is worthy to awaken you when the time comes."

"One who is worthy? Who is that?"

"The chosen one has yet to be born."

"Yet to be born? How long are we talking about?"

"Until we have determined it is time. Once awakened, your responsibly will be to awaken the rest of your people. Once again, the fate of the Leopard Tribe will be in your hands."

Tau thought for a moment, and then spoke. "I understand."

The silver liquid moved down to his feet. Tau felt uneasy as it began to cover him.

"Wait, stop!" he yelled.

The liquid paused. "You have changed your mind?"

"No, I... I... I didn't know you meant right NOW."

"I/We perceive time much differently than you. Your perception of NOW is quite different than ours."

Tau thought about it for a moment. He then realized that the present moment was as good a time as any. What else was he going to do? He had no one to say goodbye too. His village was too far away and the Keepers seemed to think that he would not be happy if he went back. He thought about going to see Amanzi, if nothing else, to say goodbye. But he did not have a clue how to get to her.

"I guess you are right," he said to the Keepers. "It may as well be now."

The silver liquid continued upward, covering his legs, his torso, and his arms. For a moment, it stopped at his neck.

"I/we sense apprehension from within you. This is a decision that you must make freely."

Tau had not expected this to happen so quickly. The Keeper's did not waste any time. Yes, he did have a certain amount of apprehension inside of him. Like many times in his life, he was not quite sure what was going to happen. For a second, he almost changed his mind. Then he looked across the room. Chad stood there, leaning against the wall. He gave Tau a smile and a confident nod.

"I'm okay," he said nervously. "I told you, I didn't realize that this was going to happen so soon."

"Then you wish to proceed with your preservation? The next step will be to cover you entirely, and then the preservation will be instantaneous."

Tau closed his eyes. "Yes, I'm ready," he said, and then he held his breath in anticipation of the silver liquid covering him entirely.

The Keepers gave one final response. "So be it."

Also available, in The Ancient Lands series:

The Ancient Lands: Warrior Quest

Follow us on twitter and Facebook for updates on our on-going Ancient Lands Projects
Facebook/theancientlands
www.twitter.com/theancientlands
pinterest/jasonmccammon

Like the book? Go online and write a comment or review and be sure to tell your friends! Ask questions about the book on FB.

Suggested places to write comments and reviews:
Amazon.com
Goodreads.com
Facebook.com